MAKING THE CUT

THE SONS OF TEMPLAR MC #1

ANNE MALCOM

The Sons of Templar MC #1
By Anne Malcom
Copyright 2015 Anne Malcom

Cover: TRC Designs
Editing: Mary Yakovets

To my Mum, for letting me be anything I wanted to be.

PROLOGUE

WHEN I WAS in high school, I was goofing around with some friends on a playground. Wine and vodka were involved. Thanks to liquid courage — or liquid stupidity — I walked along the top of a jungle gym. In heels. I fell and broke my arm so badly the bone stuck out of the skin, and no amount of alcohol could anesthetize that. I thought those five minutes before I passed out was the most horrific pain I would ever experience.

I was wrong.

Now I knew there was a kind of pain so terrible it almost made you want to die.

Almost.

I wanted to live, despite how enticing oblivion was. I fought hard against the blackness that beckoned me.

"Oh, Gwennie, I will miss you. It seems like such a shame to let you go to waste, but you had to disobey me, then you tried to run. Not very smart." He shook his finger at me as if he was scolding a child, clicking his tongue as he did so. "But you did, you saw what you shouldn't have — so now you have to go. But not before we've had some fun with you."

I couldn't believe the vile words coming out of his mouth, the violence that had emerged from the man I thought I knew. The man I thought I loved. He circled me, perusing me coldly. I didn't know where this *creature* had come from. It lurked underneath the chiseled jaw, the messy auburn hair and the bright green eyes. The sculpted muscles that I had found so enticing were being used to inflict pain on me; the tattoos I thought were sexy were mocking me every time they flew past my face for a punch.

The other men laughed. One of them kicked me viciously, and a sharp sting erupted in my side. My stomach started to feel weirdly full. The phrase 'internal bleeding' vaguely floated into my mind. I didn't make a sound, but silent tears streamed down my cheeks.

"Got nothing to say, Gwennie? Funny, I never could get you to shut that smart mouth. I should've smacked you around more often," he mused, peering at me the way a fox watched its prey.

"Fuck you, Jimmy," I whispered, my throat raw and dry.

He pulled out a long knife from his belt and crouched down beside me. His attractive face was marred with a sick smile.

"No, baby, *fuck you*. Which is exactly what me and the boys are going to do, and after everyone has had their turn, I'm going to fuck you with this knife."

He ran the long blade against my throat. I should have felt a sting, because warm blood trickled down my neck. But I felt nothing. The pain that had nearly crippled me seemed to be floating away — my body was weightless.

"I think I'll go first, one for the road eh, Gwennie?" His accent caressed my name in a sick taunt.

My heart was beating furiously as I watched him undo his belt. The other monsters settled in for the show. He viciously seized my head and thrust his tongue in my mouth. I bit down as hard as I could, feeling satisfaction at the grunt of pain that came from the asshole's throat.

"Bitch!" he yelled, punching me in the face.

My head cracked off the concrete, white spots danced across my vision.

He grasped my head again and spoke in a soft tone. "Try that again, I'll put this knife through your spine."

I met his emotionless gaze with determination, and spat in his face. He laughed, slowly wiping his cheek before sucking on his finger. He thrust my legs open, and I tried to struggle, but my movements were slow, groggy. I wanted to fight, I *had* to fight harder than this, but my body was betraying me.

"I'm going to enjoy this, much more than when you were willing, this is more interesting, no matter how good you were in the sack," he whispered in my ear.

I barely acknowledged him, as consciousness started to leave me. I was going to die. I couldn't fight it anymore. I prayed that I would drift away before he violated me.

"Go to hell," I croaked, my parting shot.

Suddenly, the doors crashed open. "Police, freeze!" multiple voices yelled.

I must be dreaming, this is too good to be true.

Gunfire filled the air. Jimmy jumped up, firing shots in every direction. I watched as one by one, my captors collapsed, bullets peppering their bodies. Jimmy, the cockroach, struggled with the officers cuffing him, escaping the bloodbath unharmed. My vision blurred at the edges. The darkness that threatened to engulf me was yanking me downwards.

No, I can't die now, I thought desperately.

"Ma'am, stay with me." An officer filled my vision, taking off his jacket to cover my nakedness. "You're safe now. Paramedics are on the way, I just need you to stay awake."

I tried, I really did. I tried to fight the force pulling my eyelids down, but it won and everything went black.

CHAPTER 1

"WHEN IS she going to wake up? It's been over a week!" demanded a desperate voice.

"When it comes to brain injuries we have no certainties, and your sister's body was badly beaten, she needs time to heal," a woman's voice responded calmly.

I tried to open my eyes, but they were glued shut — I couldn't move my body. I started to panic. Was I paralyzed? *Please, God, don't let me be paralyzed.*

I put all of my effort into trying to force my eyes open, they didn't fought actively against me, as if they weren't my own. I gave that up and tried to move my mouth, make some kind of sound to alert the people around me that I was awake. But I couldn't, my body didn't want to obey me.

My panic grew as I realized I was trapped in my own body, unable to control it. Panic was quickly replaced by darkness as I tumbled downwards once more.

A loud beeping disturbed my sleep — it wouldn't shut up. I thought I'd be in tune to New York sounds by now, though this didn't sound like street noise. It was too close, right in my ear. Inside my brain almost.

I was sure my alarm didn't sound like that and Amy was *never* up before me. A sterile smell wafted into my nostrils, which had me instantly suspicious, our apartment was never clean enough to smell sterile.

Then the memories hit, their weight settling over me — what I saw, what happened after. The pain, not something I'd ever forget.

I tried to unstick my eyes, my vision blurry at first. It took a few minutes for the room to come into focus. I looked down the bed, noticing one of my arms in a cast, the other hooked up to an IV and the beeping machine that woke me up. My gaze wandered to the corner of the room, where a man in an army uniform was curled up in an uncomfortable looking sleep.

"Ian?" I rasped, my voice sounding like I smoked a pack of Marlboros last night. Which of course I would never do, regardless of the fact Carrie Bradshaw did. Yellow teeth and premature wrinkles? No thanks.

Ian stirred and then leapt out of his chair, at my side in a second. "Ace? Holy shit, you're awake! Thank fuck for that!" He pushed a little red button beside the bed, eyes on me.

"Yes, but I think I might have to go back to sleep for a bit, Ian," I mumbled, suddenly feeling exhausted.

"No, Ace, just stay awake ..." Ian pleaded.

I didn't hear the end before I drifted back into the abyss.

———

I opened my eyes to light streaming through the room and immediately realized I had to use the bathroom. My eyes were less sticky and less blurry, my head still foggy. I gave myself a moment to get my bearings then sat up.

"Holy fuckstick," I whispered as pain radiated through my broken body, tears welled up in my eyes. I would *not* let them fall.

Gritting my teeth, I swung my legs to dangle over the side of the bed, reaching out to the little IV trolley beside my bed.

"Okay, good work, Gwen, now stand up," I muttered to myself. I took a deep breath and gingerly reached my feet down to touch the cold tile.

"Ace!" My brother's voice exclaimed with a hint of panic.

I glanced up to see Ian striding from the doorway towards me, arms extended. I lost my footing and stumbled towards the ground, strong arms caught me before I made impact.

"What the hell do you think you're doing? You could have hurt yourself even more!" Ian growled.

"Well, I was doing just fine until you distracted me!" I snapped.

My brother smiled down at me, eyes twinkling. "I'm sure you were, little sis, but how about we wait for you to get a bit better before we try for any escape attempts."

"I wasn't trying to escape," I cried.

"Sure, you weren't trying to escape when you were getting your appendix out either, you were just 'stretching your legs' right?" Ian teased.

"I was!" I argued.

"In the parking lot?"

"It was a nice night, I liked the fresh air," I declared, inwardly grinning. I hated hospitals. Always have. "I wasn't trying to escape this time. If you must know, I need to pee."

"Um, hate to break it to you, Sis, but you don't need to get out of bed for that." He pointed down to a bag attached to me. One filled with pale yellow liquid that could only be one thing.

"Okay, ew." I screwed up my nose, not that I was embarrassed in front of my brother, but that was bag of pee. Gross.

"Well, I want to brush my teeth anyway, I feel like I ate a urinal cake," I informed him.

"Okay, Ace, let's get you to the bathroom before I pass out from your urine breath."

Ian scooped me up, directing us to what I guessed was the bathroom. I winced and bit my lip trying to hide my reaction to the motion. Ian's expression hardened immediately into a look I'd never seen before on his handsome face, one that didn't belong there.

"I'm going to kill that motherfucker," he muttered under his breath, voice shaking with rage.

"Now, what would that do to your impeccable military record?" I joked, trying to keep our exchange light, I wasn't ready for reality to hit just yet.

He opened the door and gingerly set me down on the bathroom floor, his expression tortured. He looked me in the eyes and stroked my face, as if to make sure I was real. "Don't joke about this, Gwen. Seriously, if I had lost you..." He shivered. "Mum and Dad are going to be heartbroken, I'm only glad they didn't have to sit waiting for you to wake up. I wouldn't wish that shit on anyone."

"No! We are not telling Mum and Dad!" I tried to yell, but my husky voice was barely below a whisper.

I relaxed when I remembered they were away on some cruise and unreachable for three weeks.

Ian frowned. "We'll talk about this later, now do your business. I'll be outside the door, okay?" He kissed me on the head softly and walked out.

I spotted a brand new toothbrush amongst Barney's entire cosmetic and skin care range. I guessed a little fairy called Amy had been in here.

I flinched mid brush as I caught my reflection. Both my eyes were swollen, black bruises lingered underneath them. A bandage covered my head and a scabbed over cut on my lip was tender against the brush. I touched my bandaged cheek gently, it looked like there were stitches underneath the white fabric. A long, scabbed over gash decorated my neck like some kind of gruesome necklace. I didn't look down any further. I couldn't. I gripped the edge of the sink with my one good hand, close to collapsing. An angry sob ripped out of my chest. Memories flooded through me, the pain, the faces of those monsters, and the fear, the paralyzing fear of thinking I was going to be raped and murdered. And by the man I thought I loved.

"Gwen, are you okay? I'm coming in!" Ian yelled through the door.

He burst in, looking worried. Beyond worried. Like he was bracing for something horrible. Or more horrible.

His eyes softened seeing me slumped against the sink. He gently pulled me into his arms.

"I was so stupid, Ian, I was so stupid," I sobbed into his chest.

"This was not your fault, Ace. It was those sick bastards. None of this is your fault." He framed my head with his hands, eyes glistening with moisture.

I had never seen my brother cry. He and my dad were the strong ones, Mum and I cried at anything. We sobbed at sad news stories and those television adverts about animal cruelty. Dad and Ian had spent their whole lives surrounded by our 'delicate female sensibilities.' Although, that phrase was only uttered once and thanks to the reaction it got, was never said again.

That was why I wasn't letting them find out about this, it would destroy Mum — and if Ian reacted like this, I couldn't handle my parents going through it too. It was my bad decisions that put me here, and I somehow had to find the strength to get through this without them.

"Ian, I'm okay," I tried to reassure him. Reassure myself.

"No, sweetie, you aren't, but you will be," my brother promised, scooping me up and walking us to my bed.

"Ian, you can't tell Mum and Dad, I'm serious, please," I begged.

"Of course I have to tell them, Ace," he snapped. "It would kill them if you went through this without them."

"No, Ian, it will kill them to see me like this. Look at me." I gestured at my face and Ian flinched.

"I am looking at you, Gwen, have been for the past week and a half. The image of you in this hospital bed, it's burned into my brain. I won't forget it, not until the day I die."

Tears welled up in my eyes and I chided myself. I couldn't be that emotional girl anymore. I had to be strong.

"Don't you get it?" I whispered brokenly. "I can never take that away from you. I wish so badly that I could. I can at least save Mum and Dad from having this imprinted into their memories as well." I gestured to myself again, albeit awkwardly with my bulky cast.

Ian's face softened and he reached down and touched my cheek. "Ace, how is it that you manage to worry so much about everyone else while you're the one that's been through hell?"

"Just lucky I guess," I joked weakly.

We were interrupted by the arrival of doctors and nurses, who did all my checkups, asked me lots of questions about where I lived, what year it was and who the president is. Luckily, I got it all right as I was more likely to remember who the president of Dior was.

A no nonsense doctor named Bruce informed me that I had a broken wrist (no shit, Sherlock), a fractured skull (the reason for my week and a half long coma), four broken ribs, stitches for a cut on my cheek, 'superficial' bruising covering most of my body, as well as suffering from internal bleeding, which I almost died from.

I had gingerly looked at my tender stomach, a bandage covering what would turn into a surgical scar. Ian was shaking with anger while the doctor listed my injuries as if he was making a grocery list. Seeing my staunch brother so close to falling apart hurt more than the bruises covering my body.

After the doctor left, Ian sat on a chair with his head in his hands, silent for a long time before he looked at me, his face a mask.

"Gwen, the doctor said you weren't, but I have to hear it from you. Did he...?" He stopped. "Did he...?" Ian choked on the words.

"Rape me?" I finished for him.

Ian flinched, then nodded sharply.

"No, he didn't, he came pretty close, but the cops got there just in time," I told him carefully, eyes on his clenched fists. "Ian..." I started, trying to think of a way to calm him down.

He pushed out of the chair so hard it clattered to the ground noisily. He turned towards the wall, throwing his fist at it, stopping before his hand made contact. I'd never seen my brother so angry. After being in the Army for almost twelve years, he had iron clad control over his temper, no matter how much anyone tried to rattle him. But right now it seemed like he was going to turn green and burst out of his clothes.

My brother and I were really close, always had been. Being five years older than me, Ian was my protector and best friend since the moment I was born. He walked me to school on my very first day, taught me how to ride my bike and the day he left for the army when I was thirteen was one of the saddest days of my life.

We grew up in New Zealand, in a small town, nestled away from the harsh realities of the real world, somewhere we were safe and happy. Sure it was sheltered, and the closest thing we had to couture was camouflage, but I wouldn't have traded it for anything. We had an amazing childhood, loving parents, never wanted for anything and grew up in a beautiful country where we rode our bikes everywhere.

Even when Ian grew into a teenager, with multiple girl-friends and an unnatural talent for all sports, he never forgot me, never acted too 'cool' for me. For a ten-year-old girl who looked up to her brother, that was pretty damned special.

A couple of years after Ian left, I started to get a bit wild. Mum and Dad didn't know what to do with me. I drank a lot, got bad marks at school, threw some pretty wild (legendary) parties and smoked a bit of weed. Nothing too out of the ordinary for kids my age, but not what my parents expected of me.

One night, after a party, I stumbled drunk into my house with my boyfriend when my parents were away. I knew I shouldn't be doing it, planning on losing my virginity to a guy I didn't love, but thought I had to do it sometime. I felt like the odd woman out amongst my sexually active friends.

Trent started kissing me and pulling off my clothes as soon as we got in the front door. I kissed him back for a while until he grabbed at my dress, trying to pull it up.

"No," I slurred, "I don't think we should do this anymore."

"Come on, babe, don't be a tease, you know you want to," Trent whispered, grabbing at my dress and pushing me against a wall.

I started pushing at him. "No, Trent," I protested, but he wouldn't listen.

The lights flickered on, and I heard Ian's bellow.

"What the fuck?"

Trent was ripped off me, and Ian held him by his collar, driving his fist through his face. Trent slumped to the ground holding a bloody nose.

"Ian, shit did you break his nose? Oh, man, I don't want to clean that blood up," I groaned.

Ian turned to me, anger radiating off him. "You okay, Ace?" he asked, using the nickname he'd had for me since before I could remember.

"Ummm yeah?" I looked at him expectantly. I hadn't seen my brother in two years and this was not the situation I would have liked for his homecoming.

He turned back to Trent yanking him up. "If you lay a hand on my sister again or so much as look at her, I'll kill you. Got it, asshole?"

"What's your fucking problem, man? She's my girlfriend," Trent shot back, the idiot.

"I'd say by the way you were forcing yourself on her, she's not your girlfriend anymore, dickbrain, now get out of my sight before I fucking lose it," Ian yelled.

Trent quickly glanced over at me, blood still pouring from his nose.

I shrugged. "It's not me, it's you."

He gave my brother a weary look then bolted.

"Great date!" I proclaimed sarcastically to his escaping form. I turned back to Ian and threw myself into his arms. "It's soooo good to see you," I slurred. "I missed you heaps!"

Ian squeezed me, then pulled back, anger returning to his gaze. "Seriously, Gwen, what would you have done if I wasn't here? You're wasted, that dress is too fucking short and Mum and Dad are gone — if I hadn't stepped in..."

"Don't worry so much, Ian, it's all worked out now and you're home!" I sang at him, my happy drunk buzz still firmly in place.

"Yeah, I am, but I have no idea who I'm looking at right now, Gwen. Drinking, partying, wearing clothes like *that*," he spat out the words in disgust, gesturing at my dress. "Mum and Dad have been telling me your grades are suffering, and you're skipping school? I don't know what's going on with you, Gwen, but you need to sort your shit out before you ruin your fucking life with actions you can't take back."

That was the only time I'd seen him really angry, and after seeing myself through his eyes, I got my act together. Well, not completely. I still caused a bit of trouble, but I got my grades back on track and stopped my mother from going prematurely gray.

The next time Ian saw me, I was doing pretty damned well for myself. I ended up getting a degree in fashion merchandising at university, my love of all things fashion being a part of me since I was old enough to dress myself. At twenty-one I graduated, moved to New York, got a job as a buyer for a department store and made myself a life. Ian stayed in the Army, travelling around the world, coming to New York a couple of times to see me, then going back home to see Mum and Dad.

That got me to thinking, I had only seen Ian a couple of months ago, he was meant to be on tour for another twelve months.

"Ian, how did you get here? Aren't you meant to be in some undisclosed location, water boarding terrorists and beating infidels into submission?"

Ian turned from the wall, breathing heavily, my question taking a while to penetrate. He ran his hand through his lack of hair and sighed. "Yeah, but I got an emergency call from Amy, she somehow got a hold of my number. That girl could run a country," he joked tightly.

"Amy?" I asked.

Amy was my best friend and roommate. I met her on one of my first days in New York. I was out having a drink in some trendy bar alone, which was scary, but I didn't know anyone and was hoping to meet some awesome *Sex and the City* types and bond over cosmos. I cringed, thinking about my reasoning now that I was a savvy New Yorker, but back then I was a naïve country girl from New Zealand.

I had just taken my first sip of my cocktail when some greasy looking guy had sidled up to me and seriously couldn't take no for an answer. After I had tried to politely decline his advances for the third time, I began to feel a little scared, not knowing a soul in the bar.

Enter Amy.

"Oh my god, babe, sorry I'm so late." She breezed in, squeezing between the sleaze ball and me.

I gazed at the gorgeous stranger with wide eyes as she took a sip of my drink.

"Andrew wanted me to tell you he got held up at the prison. They were just about to let him out when some guy made a comment about the photo of you he had in his bunk." She put the drink down and raised an eyebrow at me. "Beat the shit out of him. Don't worry, they're still letting him out, just a little later." She delivered this without a glance at the man beside her, who was very pale and looked at me with wide eyes before darting away.

I regarded the woman standing beside me, impressed. Her outfit was straight off a runway, a white silk shirt tucked into a Balmain leather pencil skirt and black Manolo Blahnik heels. Her thick red hair was piled into a messy knot on top of her head. She had emerald green eyes, an angular face and amazing skin. She was petite, but curvy in the right places. I was jealous, I wondered if she would divulge her diet and exercise secret to me if I bought her a Cosmo.

"Um thanks for that." I blinked, trying to figure out what had just happened.

She smiled at me. "No problemo, girlfriend, this city is full of assholes. They would kick me out of the sisterhood if I didn't do something about him. Plus, I just got stood up, needed a drinking buddy. You've got good taste in cocktails, impeccable style, and a cute foreign accent. You could just be my new best friend."

And we had been, ever since.

"Yeah, she's been here almost as much as me, but she's 'out getting supplies,'" Ian explained with finger quotes, bringing me back to the present.

As if on cue, Amy thundered through the door, arms full of flowers and shopping bags, followed by two of my other friends, Ryan and his boyfriend Alex.

"Holy fuck! You're finally awake!" Amy screamed, dumping all the bags at her Jimmy Choo clad feet.

She was dressed impeccably, black leather pants, a slouchy tan tee with an oversized black blazer on top and multiple gold necklaces strung around her neck. Even in a hospital bed, I couldn't help but appreciate her outfit.

She stared at me for a moment, standing in the middle of the room. "Girlfriend, don't ever scare me like that again, I lost my mind for almost two weeks," she whispered, her voice breaking and tears beginning to stream down her cheeks, mascara coming with them.

"I'm okay now, Amy," I whispered back, trying to sound strong.

"Okay?" she repeated in a shrill tone, anger replacing sadness. "Okay? She thinks she's 'okay.'" She directed a look at my brother, using finger quotes.

"What those bastards did to you..." She shuddered. "You almost died, G, the doctors said you might not wake up, and even if you did there was a possibility of brain damage. You're bruised and battered everywhere, so I would say that's the opposite of okay. I am going to kill those animals!" she cried, starting to sound hysterical.

I flinched, thinking about another person I loved going through hell.

Ryan, another one of my best friends, approached my bedside with a tender look on his beautiful face.

Ryan had mocha-colored skin, a bald head, and bone structure to die for. He was a male model and never had a shortage of jobs, plus he always looked like he had just strutted off the runway. Today was no different, he wore a deep red cashmere turtleneck sweater and black pants tucked into some biker boots. His boyfriend, Alex, was the day to his night, tall with pale skin and seriously built with muscles everywhere. His dark black hair flopped over his face, like he spent hours styling it, but Alex wouldn't be caught dead with any "girlie shit" in his hair. He was a macho man, and Ryan was so high maintenance he gave me a run for my money, but they loved each other, so it worked.

"Amy, take it down a decibel, only dogs communicate at that level," Ryan hissed. "Gwen knows exactly what happened to her and doesn't need reminding. She sure as shit doesn't need to try and calm down your crazy ass either." He glared at her.

Ryan stroked some hair off my face and failed to hide his wince at my battered appearance. "Baby girl." His voice was soft and his eyes glistened, for just a moment.

"All right, girl, let's get you into some of these wonderful satin PJs we picked up from Barney's and get you out of that hideous gown," Amy chirped in, sounding a lot more like herself.

Alex, who hadn't said anything since he walked in, joined my posse and gave me a kiss on the head.

"Babe, I love you, over the fucking moon you're finally awake. How about I take your brother for a beer while you get pampered by the cashmere mafia?" he suggested.

I smiled at him, knowing he had clocked my brother's anger as soon as he walked in the room. I knew he was trying hard to restrain his own fury, which was hiding behind his forced smile.

"Thanks, Alex." I glanced at my brother, who was studying me with a frown on his face.

"I'll be fine, Ian, get away from this place for a bit," I told him firmly.

He looked conflicted, but sighed. "We'll see you soon," Ian promised, kissing me on the head, leaving with Alex.

Ryan and Amy started fussing with my pillows and arguing over which PJ set would be less scratchy on my skin. Watching them, I knew even though something terrible had happened to me and I was a long way from being healed, I was going to be fine because of the people I loved, the people who would do anything for me and would always be there, every step of the way.

⸻

ONE YEAR LATER

I took one last glance at my city in my rear vision mirror. The place I dreamed about while sitting in a small town at the edge of the world. The city where my life had changed so much. Where *I* had changed so much. I was a stronger person now.

It took me six months to fully heal after my attack. I had gone to some really dark places and even now I was still plagued with nightmares, but I was determined not to let my life be consumed by this, not to live with the label of 'victim.' I had to leave New York — I had to leave my memories behind and have a fresh start. And boy, was I starting over.

Amy tried talking me out of opening a boutique clothing store in Amber, California, but as soon as I saw it while passing through on a buying trip, I fell in love. It was the classic small American town, a main street with everything in one place, from the grocery store to the barber. A town where everybody knew everybody, and that gave me a strange sort of comfort, reminding me of home. It also had a beach, but it was relatively undiscovered on the tourist trail, people preferring Malibu and Santa Monica a few hours away.

I thought back to when Ian had persuaded me to tell my parents about my attack.

"I love you so much, kid, and I'll always be here for you and respect your decisions, but you need to tell Mum and Dad about what happened, you know you do, I know it will be hard, but you gotta do it."

Like always, I listened to my brother's advice and rang them. After a long and tearful (on both sides) conversation, Mum and Dad took the first flight over, helping me recover, both physically and mentally.

After finding my little town, I immediately rang them and told them about my desire to move there and open my own store. Hearing the passion and happiness in my voice, which had been absent for a while, my parents gave me the money to buy the store and move to Amber.

My family was wealthy, but my brother and I were always brought up to work hard for what we wanted and I was grateful for that. We got a portion of our trust funds when we turned eighteen, and I used mine to move to the States and get myself an apartment on the Upper East Side, my ultimate dream after watching *Gossip Girl* — shallow, but I was young and had my dreams.

After working my way up to Senior Buyer position, I earned decent money, not to mention I still had a hefty portion of my trust fund. Nevertheless, my parents were adamant they were going to help me out. I guessed since they had no control over my nightmares, my recovery, or my scars, they wanted to help me get something that might get me back to my old self.

Of course, after Amy found out about my plans, even though she was a Manhattanite through and through – her family was *a* lot wealthier than mine – she decided that she wasn't letting me go alone.

"You're not going to the other side of the country to fuck knows where and opening up a shop without your best girl helping you out," she had said once I told her about the space I had bought.

So here I was, taking the long drive across the country to my new home and my new life.

And hopefully, to find some sort of peace.

CHAPTER 2

WHEN I ARRIVED IN AMBER, I sucked in a sigh of relief, some part of my instinctively knowing I had made the right decision. I took a week to do the forty-four-hour drive. I had done all the necessities when on a road trip: listened to power ballads, singing along at the top of my lungs, stopping at random sights along the way, and enjoyed the solitude.

I drove past where my store would be, and a smile lit up my face. Nestled between a cute little coffee shop and a bookstore — it was perfect. The three loves of my life within a stone's throw of each other, coffee, fashion and books. It sent a thrill through me to see my little sign with the word '*Phoenix*' scrawled across the sign hanging above the door.

I continued to my and Amy's new home — she had decided that she would fly in the next day. She had told me she wasn't spending days driving the country when she could "drink champagne and read Vogue on her father's jet."

Amy had picked our house and, after a huge argument, I bought it, but only if she agreed to be in charge of decorating and the expenses that went with it. She had spent the last few weeks on the phone with decorators and closing her computer screen every time I walked past, which meant I was itching to see it.

I pulled up the driveway and took a moment to take in our beautiful new house. On the end of a sleepy little street, slightly separated from the rest of the houses, was a stunning restored Victorian. It was three stories high with dove gray weatherboards. A stone path led up some steps to the second story, which had a huge porch wrapping around it. Another path led to French doors that housed the bottom story basement. The third story had a huge balcony jutting over the porch, more French doors opening to that. That was my room. Amy's was at the back, her balcony jutting onto the back yard and pool. I had to toss up between this and a smaller house by the sea, this one had appealed to me more.

I jumped out of my car and gave an excited little squeal. I glanced around, glad I was alone. The last thing I wanted was my neighbors thinking I was a crazy person. They'd find out soon enough that Amy was. I decided to forego unpacking for now, dying to see the house.

My heels clicked on the stones of our walkway. Even the porch was amazing. A gorgeous porch swing that looked like it could double as a bed was on my left, wicker table and chairs to my right. When I got inside, I looked around and my breath left me. The walls were white, the floors a beautiful polished wood. A white table with a huge vase full of pink orchids sat in front of me. Slightly to the right was the staircase, ahead of me, were the doors to the dining room and the kitchen.

I continued into the house on unsteady feet, into the beautiful living room with cozy white couches and chairs, which were centered around a coffee table. Patterned throws and pillows added a touch of class and vibrancy. The coffee table was stunning, it looked like a giant silver serving platter with dark wooden legs. A fresh vase of flowers and some candles sat atop it. A white glass cabinet sat in the corner, a mish mash of photo frames, books and bowls inside. Framed artwork covered the walls in simple white frames — I knew by looking at them they were by some seriously famous artists.

I wandered around the rest of the house in a sort of dream, barely taking in the black marble kitchen or the magnificent dining room. I climbed the stairs and opened the door to my room.

Cue another gasp.

It was my dream room. A huge, four-poster vintage bed sat in the middle of the room, with a white frame and delicate designs spinning around the legs. I ran my hand along the carved wood. Two white side tables were on either side, with glass lamps sitting on top. I spied an old dressing table in the corner with an array of perfume bottles and antique hairbrushes artfully displayed on it.

I walked over and sat on the stool, running my fingers over the brushes and smiled at the family photo sitting in a silver frame beside them. It was one of my favorites, taken just before I left for New York and when Ian had been home.

We were in the garden of our childhood home, Mum and Dad had their arms around each other, Mum pressing a kiss to Dad's forehead. My parents were night and day. Mum had golden blonde hair, styled softly around her face. She had always been beautiful, even in her fifties she was stunning. She was trim and very petite, and my father looked like a mountain man compared to her. His dark scruffy hair was peppered with silver, smile lines at the corner of his face only made him more hand-some, in a rugged type of way. He towered over mum, and even though he was approaching sixty, he was in good shape.

A twenty-year-old me was tucked into my father's side, laughing at something, my head thrown back, my long brown hair flying behind me. Ian was beside my mother, his arm around her waist, grinning over at me. Him, with his military buzz cut and strong jaw was an imprint of my father, the same hazel eyes, dark hair and cheeky smile. Our family had always been close, I knew how lucky I was to come from such a great home.

I moved my gaze to observe my reflection in the restored mirror. My chocolate brown hair was piled on top of my head, wisps hanging down here and there. My hand touched the spot on my cheek, where a small scar hid underneath my makeup.

I decided I looked like the old me, with slightly tanned skin and a heart-shaped face. My eyes were my best feature, jade green and maybe a smidge too big for my face, making me look too innocent for my liking — although it did help when I was younger. Being only five foot five and naturally petite, I was wearing six-inch heels. My body is lean, but with a larger ass than I would like and smaller breasts than I want. I worked freaking hard to keep my figure trim, and if I even *looked* at a cupcake, I gained five pounds.

I snapped myself out of my self-perusal when I realized I hadn't even explored the most important part. The closet.

I clapped my hands with glee as I opened double doors into an amazing walk in wardrobe with white carpet and an amazing purple rug running to the end of the room. A chaise lounge was positioned in the middle of the room, and there were even glass cases for my handbags.

"Heck yes, Amy," I whispered.

My bathroom was just as impressive. White tiles ran along the floor and halfway up the walls met with soft blue paint. A chandelier – yes, a *chandelier* – dangled atop the claw-foot tub, which was in the middle of the room, a white footstool beside it.

I had two huge sinks and mirrors with cabinets underneath them, more than able to house all of my beauty products. To the left of the sinks was a shower big enough to sleep in. I retrieved my phone out of my bag and dialed.

"Amy, you have outdone yourself. I'm speechless, the house is everything I could have wanted and more, you're a genius!" I said as soon as she picked up.

"I know, I know, my taste is impeccable. I knew you'd like it," she stated modestly.

"*Like* is an understatement. You seriously need to undertake a career in interior design. Or mind reading, considering this is exactly what I wanted."

"I can't exactly pursue a career in the physic realm, considering I am opening a business on the edge of nowhere with my best friend," she told me dryly.

I laughed. "Okay, well I need to unpack, I just wanted to tell you how much I appreciate this. Can't wait till you get here, love you."

"You're welcome, girl, see you tomorrow!" she chirped, ringing off.

I made my way back to my car on cloud nine and started the Herculean task of unpacking. My Mercedes was full to the brim, even with a lot of my stuff being sent ahead. What could I say? Being a girl and a buyer, I had a lot of shit. I opened my trunk, inspecting the sheer volume of bags for a second before trying to gather as many as I could into my arms.

"Need some help?" a deep voice asked from behind me.

"Holy fuck!"

I dropped all of my bags, nearly jumping out of my Manolos. I turned, intending to glare at the owner of the deep voice that had scared the bejesus out of me but stopped short. In front of me was a picture of pure male perfection. I looked a little harder. Well, maybe not so pure.

Tall, like *really* tall. I only came up to his shoulders and I was in six-inch heels. Rippling muscles threatened to tear the sleeves of his t-shirt and tattoos covered every inch of his impressive arms. His face was chiseled like a Greek god's, with a square jaw and cheekbones to die for. Midnight black hair brushed his sharp jaw, he looked like Chris Hemsworth's identical twin — well, his dangerous black-haired identical twin. A familiar intensity wafted off him, an air of menace in the way he held himself. Uh oh, this one was trouble, like serious trouble, the kind I swore off a year ago.

The hunk brought his hands up like I was pointing a gun at him, a grin highlighting his too kissable mouth, very kissable in fact. How could a guy who looked like he could bench press a car while making Vin Diesel cry have lips like that?

I bet he could do some things with those lips, wait...shut up ovaries!

"Whoa, darlin', didn't mean to scare you, just saw you with an arm full of bags and those are dangerous looking shoes to be carrying that amount of stuff on," he explained gazing down at my (fabulous) shoes.

His gaze traveled up my jean clad legs to my top, which I now decided showed way too much of my modest chest. He finished at my eyes, and we stared at each other. His gaze was hungry and very male. I was mesmerized for a moment, and felt an ache between my thighs. I snapped myself out of it. Quickly. I didn't need a man in my life, definitely not a man like *this*.

"Well, thanks for your concern, but I'm very capable of unpacking my car by myself, and for your information, I could run a marathon in these shoes," I replied sharply.

A full on grin lit up Thor's evil twin's face, and he looked down at various bags strewn between us then back up at me.

"It'll be much faster if I help. I'm not the kind of man to leave a woman in need and I'm also a sucker for an accent."

His voice was rough and threatened to make me spontaneously combust. I really hoped he couldn't see my nipples through my shirt. The man was some kind of crazy sex wizard.

He stepped forward and I slammed back into my car. My heart pounded at my rib cage, anxiety replacing the lust I was

MAKING THE CUT   27

feeling moments ago. Noticing my reaction, he immediately stopped in his tracks, a frown marring his beautiful face.

"I'm not going to hurt you," he told me carefully, eyes connecting with mine.

I swallowed. "Thank you for the offer, but I don't need any help, and if you don't mind I have a lot to do." My voice shook as I dismissed him.

He continued to frown at me. I felt uncomfortable under his dark gaze. This guy was intense.

"Okay then, if you're sure. I'm Cade by the way. I'll be seeing you round," he promised.

Not if I see you first.

He paused for a moment, eyes still locked with mine before he turned, strutting – okay, maybe not strutting, but how can a man move his ass like that without strutting? I swore he was a wizard – over to a black SUV across the road before I could reply. It was only then I noticed the cut, one that was far too familiar. It had a different insignia on the back — a skeleton, riding a Harley, brandishing a sword. The top rocker read: "Sons of Templars MC."

I braced myself against my car once again, struggling to stay up. My breath was shallow as I tried to chase away the horrible memories I had of men wearing vests just like that one.

You're fine, Gwen, he didn't hurt you. No one's going to hurt you.

I took a second to pull myself together before I began to pick up my bags scattered along the ground. I squinted up to see that Cade, sitting in his truck and had witnessed my whole meltdown. I quickly peered down again until I heard his truck drive off.

⊏⊐

I was at my store the next day, trying to sort through all my merchandise, humming to myself, delightfully content. Apart from my little incident with Cade, yesterday was a great day. I managed to get all my unpacking done and spend a wonderful night in my beautiful new home. I smiled to myself, thinking of how settled in I felt already. Bob Dylan's voice filtered through the air, contributing to my feeling of zen. I looked up when the little bell over the door rang, Amy leaned against the frame with a huge smile painted on her face.

"Jesus fuck, Gwen, I think I may like it here. I just went to grab us coffees from next door," she said, gesturing with the two takeaway cups in her hands, "and there was the most fuckable looking men sitting having coffee. I swear I almost came. What I would do to be those coffee cups..." she trailed off, waggling her brows.

"I'm glad there's something in this town that is to your liking, Amy," I replied dryly.

She set the coffees down and hugged me, enveloping me in a cloud of Chanel No. 5.

"I'm glad to be here, Gwennie, anything to help you get back to your old self." Her eyes glistened.

"No, we are not having sad or depressing thoughts in my wonderful new store, or our wonderful new home for that matter," I instructed. "We are starting fresh and there will be no mention of the dickwad, evil prick, okay?"

"Sounds good to me, girl. Now let's get this place sorted, and then go home, get changed and go see if we can find somewhere to get a half decent cocktail," Amy replied.

I gave her a blinding smile. This was why she was my best friend.

"Don't you think we're a bit too dressed up?" I asked Amy, looking down at my outfit self-consciously. My printed Prada skirt was skin tight, and my white blouse showed *way* too much cleavage.

"Bite your tongue, Gwen Alexandra," Amy scolded. "There is no such thing as being overdressed. Ever. You are not changing who you are just because we're not on our little island anymore, now let's go." She swatted my bum, strutting past me to the door.

Her outfit made me look like a nun. Her little black Gucci dress was halter neck, displaying her ample assets, and had an open back which dipped almost to her butt. With red lipstick, red shoes and her red hair tumbling past her shoulders, she looked amazing. If I swung that way I would totally hit that. Alas, my taste veered towards sexy sociopaths.

We arrived at a restaurant called Valentines — it was out of town, on a hill where you could see a view of the twinkling lights below and the ocean beyond that. A friendly man working in the bookstore had recommended it to me.

The place was amazing, it had an open plan layout with a few booths scattered around and was on two different levels, decorated in black and white with splashes of red. Floor to ceiling windows gave an amazing view of the ocean. It was buzzing with people. Once we were seated by our young maître d', whose eyes popped out after seeing Amy, we ordered our cocktails, obviously.

"So, how do you like Amber, Ames? Everything you could have ever wanted?" I teased.

"Well, since we spent most of the day in your store getting it ready, I haven't really seen much of it. Scratch that, I took a walk down main street for about ten minutes so I guess I have seen it all," Amy answered with dripping sarcasm. "And I did see those orgasms on a stick in the coffee shop so I am not writing this place off completely."

I smiled and sipped my cocktail, assessing the people around the room. More than a few were trying to sneakily stare at us, which I could understand in a small town, newcomers stood out. Especially ones that looked, walked and talked like Amy.

"I think we have sparked some curiosity." I smiled at a few people, coming from a small town I knew a smile would go a long way to stop people thinking I was an uptight bitch.

"Of course we have, babe. A town this small and women that look like us?" Amy rolled her eyes, taking a huge gulp of her drink.

"I'm so glad you're so modest," I told her dryly.

She flipped her hair. "I can't help that I'm gorgeous." She winked at me. "I wonder who I call to order a night with those Greek gods from the café today?" she pondered.

"I do not care, nor do I even want to think about men ever again. I'll be quite happy living with you for the rest of my life." I smiled sweetly at Amy while picking at some breadsticks.

Amy slapped my hand away. "Um ... carbs, girl? No. Drink your calories instead. And as much as I love you, and I really do, you will not keep me warm at night. Or give me mind blowing orgasms, so I think I am going to have to find a man toy to replace my B.O.B." Amy patted my hand tenderly, as if she hadn't just slapped it. "Speaking of man candy, check this out. Seriously, have all the hot guys been hiding in backwater towns my entire life?" Her face lit up, her eyes narrowing in on the newcomers.

I rolled my eyes, a smile playing on my lips, ready to sling out some sarcastic remark, but the words got stuck in my throat when I turned my head. There, at the door, stood Cade, looking imposing and far too sexy to be legal.

Who was I kidding? He probably wouldn't know a law if it spanked him on his delightful ass. His casual stance exuded power. I battled against my stupid ovaries, which were tingling, threatening to explode actually. His buddies ranked similarly on the sex-god scale, meaning Joe Manganiello had some serious competition. I gave them a quick once over. Yep, all tall, built with rippling muscles and danger radiating off them. I started to have trouble breathing, feeling hot and sweaty as terrible images flashed through my mind.

"Gwennie, Gwennie, helloo? Earth to Gwen." Amy waved her hand in front of my face. "Have those beautiful men stolen your ability to speak?"

I didn't answer, my gaze was locked on the men, more specifically, Cade. I was pretty sure the universe hated me, because they were being shown to a table not far from ours. I tried to sink down in my seat, pulling my menu up over my face, praying he wouldn't notice me. I was nowhere near that lucky.

Fuck you, universe.

His stormy grey eyes caught mine, and a weird spark ignited between us.

Don't fall for it again, Gwen, you know how this ends.

I shook my head and tried to focus on steadying my breathing. Amy, who had been watching me the whole time like I was having some sort of seizure, finally caught on, noticing the cuts the men wore over their shirts.

"Oh shit," Amy muttered. "Gwennie, it's okay everything's fine, we'll just leave." She motioned to stand up.

"No!" I damned near leapt over the table to grab her arm. "I will not leave just because of *them*, I will not let what happened to me make me terrified to eat in a fucking restaurant and enjoy a cocktail with my girlfriend!" I hissed, adamant I would not play the victim. I'd done that enough the past year.

"All right, let's get another round." Amy motioned for the waiter.

I peeked past my hair to see if Cade was still looking at me, and I caught his eyes once more. "Fuck," I muttered, turning back to the table to down my drink.

"That's my girl," Amy cooed. "Cosmos make everything better."

▭

After a few – I may have lost count – more cocktails and a wonderful meal, I decided I was feeling much more confident. I had made it my mission not to gaze in *his* direction all night, ignoring the weird pull that tried to yank my eyes there.

Amy was telling me some stupid joke, so I was laughing when I felt it. The sizzle in the air, the hairs on my arms standing up in awareness.

I moved my gaze upwards to see Cade and his buddies standing at our table. I gaped at Amy in a panic, the numbness of the alcohol wearing off.

"Good evening, ladies." Cade's deep voice sent shivers down my spine. That feeling was quickly replaced by panic. Bikers were mere inches away from me.

Amy saw my reaction and tried to diffuse the situation. "Whatever you're selling boys we ain't buyin', so run along and tinker with your Harley's or whatever." Her upper middle class breeding gave her excellent experience in a patronizing tone.

I clenched my shaking hands together meeting Cade's eyes, giving him my best bitch stare.

"Well, well, we have a feisty one here," one of the men drawled. He was huge and tan with a bald head, reminding me a lot of "The Rock" but a bit more rough round the edges. "No need for the sass, darling, we just seen you're new in town and thought we would come and introduce ourselves, maybe we could buy you a drink, even that girly shit." The Rock gestured to our cosmos.

"We are quite all right, thank you. Getting acquainted with the town's friendly motorcycle gang isn't really on our to do list, and I don't drink hooch, Rambo, or whatever motor oil you think passes for alcohol." Amy smiled sweetly. "You have a nice night now." Acid dripped from her tone. She turned her head to me and remained picking at the remnants of her dinner, acting as if the four – albeit beautiful – brutes were not still standing right in front of our table, dripping testosterone all over the place.

During Amy and Dwayne's (I christened him this) conversation, Cade's eyes had been glued to me, registering my fidgety movements and panicked stare. A frown marred his attractive face. I could only stare back at him, feeling a strange mixture of attraction and fear.

"Gwen." He spoke my name roughly and my pesky body reacted, the shivers returning.

"How do you know my name?" I squeaked, sounding like a scared child.

He continued to stare like I was some puzzle he couldn't figure out. "Not much gets past me, sweetheart, especially something like you." His gaze pierced my skin. I wanted to squirm, the attraction between us palpable. I managed to regain my wits when my eyes caught the "Vice President" badge on his cut.

"You're a regular Sherlock Homes. If you would excuse us, I just lost my appetite," I replied acidly and somewhat unsteadily got to my feet. Amy followed suit. I reached into my purse, grabbing what I knew was far too much and threw it on the table.

"Enjoy your night, boys," I muttered, before flipping my hair and doing my best – I'd had maybe *one* too many cosmos – to strut towards the door.

We made it to the parking lot and Amy was decidedly silent, either figuring out what kind of emotional state I was in and how to deal with me, or contemplating how hot all those men were. I was hoping for the latter. Unluckily for me, she had about three less cosmos than I did.

"Well," Amy started carefully while fishing for her keys.

"That was an interesting end to the night. Bikers, who would have thought?"

"Yep, well this is America, there is probably some small time gang of 'Sons of Anarchy' wannabes in every podunk town," I replied, going for flippant.

Amy wasn't buying it, giving me a look across the car.

"I'm fine okay, Ames? I'm not going to have a fucking mental breakdown because some guys said three words to us, have some faith," I snapped.

"Okay, girl." She unlocked the door and paused. "They were pretty fine."

Now I was the one to give her a look.

"You know for bad ass low-lifes." She carried on. "I would totally do Dwayne Johnson."

My head snapped up. "Oh my god he seriously could be 'The Rock.'"

We both burst out laughing, the tension from the exchange with the bikers disappearing.

Not completely.

I'd have to conquer my demons first. And those suckers were around to stay.

I tossed and turned in bed, sleep eluding me. The meeting with the bikers, and one in particular, had brought up issues that were already simmering just below the surface. I grumbled, picking up my phone, 2:05 am, great. I knew I would never get to sleep, so I threw back my covers and wrapped my kick ass silk kimono around my nightie clad body.

I crept downstairs, as not to wake Amy, although I didn't know why I bothered, that girl slept like the dead. I should know after trying to wake her up early every year for New York Fashion Week.

I grabbed a soft afghan off the couch and poured myself a glass of wine, or happiness as I liked to think of it. I stepped out onto our porch, lighting the small lanterns that sat either side of the comfy porch chair. I sighed and snuggled myself into the chair, nestling my glass of wine at my chest, taking small sips while getting lost in a daydream. A daydream about a certain sexy biker.

I imagined what my reaction would have been if I had not been royally fucked up by the prick whom I did not speak of. I definitely would not have dismissed him as coldly as I did at the restaurant — I certainly would have taken him up on his offer to help me with my bags when we first met. I more than likely would have had him in my bed once he stepped his motorcycle boot inside.

I wasn't some kind of harlot — the attraction between us was insane, way beyond normal, the kind of lust at first sight that I read about in my romance novels.

I wondered what he would be like in bed, would he take me rough and hard? Or slow, savoring every minute? I pictured him running his hands down my body, covering me with his huge muscles, dominating me. I slipped my hand between my legs, my panties damp.

"A little late to be sitting out here on your own isn't it?" A deep voice shocked me out of my sensual dream.

"Jesus Christ!" I yanked my hand out of my underwear, sitting up and sending my wine glass flying.

"No, sweetheart, don't think anyone has mistaken me for that do-gooder before."

Cade moved onto my porch, hands in his pockets looking too good at this hour. What was I thinking? He was probably up to all sorts of dodgy shit, like casing the neighborhood.

"What the fuck are you doing on my porch at two in the morning?" I whispered angrily, hoping the commotion had not woken Amy — unless Cade was here to murder me, or kidnap me and sell me into white slavery, then I hoped Amy was awake and in the process of calling the authorities.

"I think the more appropriate question is, what is a woman doing out on an unprotected porch in the middle of the night, not even aware enough to know when someone is within ten feet of her?" Cade shot back angrily.

I flinched back in surprise. *Was that concern in his tone?* "What do you care?" I replied, recovering quickly. "Isn't this like a prime opportunity for someone like you, poor defenseless woman, out alone in the dark?"

"No, baby, I like my women willing and aware," he said, slowly advancing on me.

I stepped my bare foot back, trying to distance my ovaries from his body, not noticing the glass surrounding me. A sharp pain erupted in my left foot.

"Shit!" I cursed. I lifted my foot to see blood spurting out of it.

"Don't move, baby, you'll make it worse."

Cade strode forward, glass crunching under his boots, before I realized what he was doing, I was in his arms.

"What do you think you're doing?" I screeched while squirming and slapping at him. "Put me down this instant," I commanded, trying to sound firm.

"Quit moving." Cade opened the door, directing us into the kitchen. "Where's your first aid kit?"

I ignored him. "Get out of my house and put me down, or I am calling the police," I threatened, while trying to deny that the proximity of his body was turning me on.

I should be committed, this stranger turns up on my porch in the middle of the night and somehow I manage to get horny.

"Now, how are you going to call the police when I have you in my arms? Seems to me that's a very empty threat." Cade gave me a squeeze, his face far too close to mine.

For a second, I forgot everything but the attraction between us. I knew he felt it too because the humor on his face disappeared, replaced with a primal stare. He leaned in, nose brushing mine, preparing to kiss me.

"Fuck," he whispered, face inches away from mine. His warm tickled my nose. He pulled back and I let out a little moan of protest. I clamped my hand over my mouth and began to regain coherent thought.

"Babe. First aid kit. Tell me where it is," Cade ordered, voice hoarse.

"Cabinet above the sink," I replied automatically, my brain still foggy from the almost kiss.

"Right."

He set me down on our kitchen island, then lifted my feet up so I was fully up on the counter, his hand brushing my bare leg. I gazed into his gray eyes and then back to his hand, which was resting on my upper thigh. I then glimpsed down at my foot, which was leaking a fair bit of blood. Cade followed my eyes, his face turned hard, focus moving to the first aid kit.

I regarded him from behind, his faded jeans fitting him like a glove. I checked out his ass, it was pure male perfection. Then I got a look at his cut. It was like someone splashed ice water over me.

What the fuck is going on? How have I let him in my house? A stranger and a biker! A biker who I'm far too attracted to and am losing all sensible thought around.

I swung my legs down, jumping off the counter, preparing to grab the phone or maybe a weapon of some sort. I was not prepared for the blinding pain in my heel, the pressure I was putting on it pushing the glass further in.

"Ouch," I hissed.

"Whoa there, sweetheart."

Cade's hands circled my waist, lifting me back up into my previous position. I ignored the tingle where his hands met my skin.

"Probably not the best idea, trying to walk with glass embedded in your foot."

"Well, I think it's probably a worse idea having a *biker*, whom I don't know, in my house in the middle of the night, so I was going for the lesser of two evils," I hissed.

"Now, baby, I ain't evil, well not at the moment anyway." His eyes flared. "I'm not going to hurt you," he told me firmly and moved to the end of the counter to look at my foot, bending down to get a closer look.

His hand gently touched the injured area and I flinched away from his touch.

Gray eyes met mine.

"I told you I'm not going to hurt you. I'm gonna get you fixed up."

For some strange reason, maybe the wine, or more likely blood loss, I believed him, relaxing into his touch.

"That's it, baby." He watched me for a second then went back to inspecting my foot. "Yup, that's in there pretty good," he muttered while grabbing some tweezers and antibacterial wipes out of the kit. "This is going to hurt."

"I think I can handle it."

"It's in pretty deep and I'll have to use antibacterial spray, that stuff hurts like a bitch," he said while studying my first aid kit.

"Yes, I'm sure you've had your fair share of experience in disinfecting, with stab wounds and bullet holes." I scowled at the top of his head.

"Oh, yeah, baby, you can only imagine what I have to deal with. I just don't want to hurt you."

His rugged face was surprisingly tender, inspecting my face while cradling my foot in his two giant hands. You know what they say about big hands...*wait, Gwen, focus!*

"I've had worse," I snipped, failing to hide the slight shudder in my voice from the closeness of this male who was having such a disturbing effect on me. I focused on my foot, which hurt like a bitch, but I suffered through it and tried to take my mind off it by interrogating Cade.

"What in hell are you doing outside my house in the middle of the fricking night anyway?" I asked, crossing my arms, mentally congratulating myself for bringing up such a sensible topic.

"Just doing my part for the neighborhood watch, baby," he replied without looking up.

"Yeah and pigs might fly. Seriously, why are you skulking outside my house? For the second time in twenty-four hours." Even as I relayed this information, I realized I should have been peeing myself right now, this was like stalker behavior 101. "And don't call me baby," I commanded as an afterthought.

"My buddy lives across the road, well for one more night at least. I was picking something up tonight, happened to see you on the porch," he explained, sounding far too reasonable.

"I think my stalker theory is more believable."

He didn't reply, I stared intently at the top of his head, his midnight black hair falling around his face and to his shoulders. I didn't normally like any kind of long hair on a guy, but man, he worked it. His broad shoulders and muscles strained his shirt, thick veins almost pulsing out of his arms. The tattoos covering his arms captivated me for a moment. I thought about those arms wrapped around me, of feeling his electric touch all over my body, and the wetness between my legs came back.

What the fuck is wrong with me?

Until now, the thought of any man touching me was repulsive and scared the shit out of me. But it was like my body was finally waking up — with a vengeance.

The irony was not lost on me that it was yet another dangerous man wearing a leather cut who turned me on. I had a serious problem. *Why couldn't I be attracted to a nice accountant with a paunch and a bald spot, someone whose worst crime would be to fashion?*

During my mental turmoil, Cade had finished nursing me and had began stroking my ankle, the animal look back on his face. I realized I was sitting on a counter, in a slinky kimono with an even slinkier nightie underneath. Damn my addiction to seductive nightwear.

"Gwen," Cade growled, the primal tone of his voice sent shivers down my spine. He straightened, and I swung by legs back down as he moved to stand in front of me, stopping between my legs, his crotch dangerously close to mine. *Gulp.* He kept staring at me as his hand cupped my cheek.

"You are fucking beautiful," he whispered.

I stared back at him dumbly, unable to think of anything to say. *Work brain!*

"So goddamned beautiful I want to kill whoever put all that fear behind those eyes," he declared fiercely.

I jumped, his words waking me from my mental coma. *How could he say this? He doesn't know me, we haven't even had a proper conversation.*

"You need to leave. Like, now," I ordered coldly.

"Baby—"

"I told you, don't call me that," I snapped. "Now, I thank you for helping me with my foot, even though it was your fault I cut it in the first place. I would appreciate it if you would get out of my house and do not come by here again." I was rather proud at how even and authoritative my voice sounded.

"I'm sorry about your foot, baby, I really am, but I'm not sorry that it meant I got to touch your skin, or get close enough to know how fucking good you smell." Shivers ran down my spine yet again. He didn't miss my reaction — he tugged my head towards him, his mouth inches away from mine.

"And fuck if I am going to taste you, Gwen, every inch of you. But not tonight, you need to get some sleep and rest your foot. I will be round here again, not in your kitchen but in your bed." His voice was firm, he was obviously someone who was used to getting what he wanted.

I yanked my head away from his, fighting both fear and arousal. "I am not some biker groupie who will drop her panties at your say so. I have something that you're probably not familiar with women, you fuck, something called self-respect. So don't flatter yourself into thinking I'm attracted to you, and I don't get how you think it's appropriate to say something that vulgar to a woman you barely know, but trust me, it's *not*."

Cade gave an attractive chuckle. "We both know that isn't true. I can bet your panties are dripping right now, 'cause I can't be the only one feeling this." He gestured between us.

"I assure you any attraction you feel is one-sided," I lied. My nose was going to be as big as Pinocchio's at this rate. "Now please leave."

"This ain't one-sided and you know it," Cade murmured roughly. "You are going to be mine, on my bike, and in my bed."

Without another word, just another intense stare, he turned to leave.

"Don't hold your breath...oh no, wait, please do," I called sweetly to him.

He stopped, fixating on the alarm panel beside the door. "I want the door locked, and this armed after I leave."

"Don't tell me what to do, you..." I paused, trying to think of an effective insult.

"Just fucking do it," he snapped. "I won't leave the porch until I hear the door lock." He strolled out closing the door behind him, I heard his footsteps stop.

"Fuck's sake," I mumbled under my breath, hopping over to lock the door and arming the alarm. Only then did I hear his heavy footsteps walking down the porch steps.

What an infuriating arrogant asshole, I thought, trying as hard as I could not to feel any warmth over the fact he wouldn't leave until he knew I was secure inside the house.

CHAPTER 3

AFTER FINALLY GETTING to sleep after four, and only after taking care of the dull ache in between my legs while unwillingly thinking of Cade, I woke up and looked at my phone.

"Fuckstick," I muttered in my sleep zombie voice.

"Well hello, sleeping beauty," Amy chirped, leaning against my door. She looked fabulous in her white sundress with a huge turquoise necklace and matching wedges, two coffee mugs in her hand. "I thought I might have to organize a herd of elephants to storm through here to wake you from your slumber," she joked, coming to lay beside me in bed and handing me sweet, sweet coffee.

I groaned as the previous night's events washed over me. "I was supposed to go into the store today and sort things out for the opening next week." I started to stress, taking a huge gulp of the precious nectar in my cup, letting it soothe me.

"It's Sunday, girlfriend, the day of rest and hangovers," Amy said. "Let's just chill out today, go grab some brunch, or more definitely late lunch, explore the town a bit more and enjoy a carefree day." She jumped out of bed and waltzed towards my wardrobe. "You grab a shower and I'll sort you an outfit."

"Okay," I sighed, pulling the covers back to get out of bed, forgetting about my foot until the pain reminded me. "Shit," I cursed, hoping Amy wouldn't notice the bandage. No such luck.

"What did you do to your foot?"

"Ummm..." I tried to think of some convincing lie, even though I knew Amy would sniff it out a mile away, we never lied to each other.

"Ohhh, I smell something interesting."

Damn our unnaturally close bond.

"Spill," Amy demanded.

"Fuck it," I grumbled. I then proceeded to relay the events of last night, in detail. After I finished, Amy sat at the end of my bed, wide eyed.

"Well, fuck me," she breathed.

Wow, my best friend was actually lost for words. That was an absolute first. She always had some response to any situation, even when we bumped into Karl Lagerfeld in the Hamptons one summer. She managed to get us invited to dinner with him. It was *awesome.*

"Fuck me!" she yelled and I jumped, her tone bringing my thoughts back from the Hamptons.

"No thanks, you're not my type," I mumbled back.

"Yeah, sounds like your type is tall, dark, and delicious," she replied sarcastically. "This is amazing. I seriously can't believe you were enacting some kind of scene out of a fucking romance movie right downstairs while I was asleep." She smirked. "I mean...shit."

"There is nothing to smile about, Ames, last night was a huge fuck up and I'm going to make sure I never see him again," I said, wondering how the hell I was going to avoid the sexy biker in a town this small.

"Newsflash, babe, we are in Siberia, you can't exactly avoid him, he's like one- tenth of the population," she argued reading my mind.

"Maybe a slight exaggeration, Amy." I rolled my eyes, gingerly testing out my foot. The pain wasn't bad enough to stop me wearing heels. It would take amputation for that to happen.

"You get the point." She waved her hand. "Anyway, why would you want to avoid that delicious hunk of stud? I mean, this is brilliant, you have come out of the nunnery," she exclaimed, clapping her hands and disappearing into my closet.

I followed her and sank into the chair in the middle of my closet. "This is most certainly not brilliant," I groaned. "Don't you remember last night? Not to mention the last time I hooked up with a sexy biker? Didn't end so well."

Amy flinched and I regretted my harsh tone. "For starters, *Cade*," she moaned his name, "is like a zillion times hotter than He Who Shall Not Be Named, and you can't just automatically assume everyone who rides a motorcycle is a psychopath. Just like you wouldn't stop wearing Prada if they came out with one bad collection." She flipped through my racks, pulling out a Givenchy tee.

"Well, men who are in outlaw motorcycle groups certainly aren't involved in church circles or neighborhood watch," I replied.

"Honey," Amy said softly, looking up from my shoe selection. "You don't know this man or anything about his club, and from what you've told me, he seems decent. I'm the first one to want to protect you from ever getting hurt again, but don't let what happened to you turn you into someone who judges people before you even know them. That isn't you."

Her words cut me deep and I knew she was right. I shouldn't be so bitter. But I also knew bikers and their gangs were trouble. Amy didn't see what I saw, so she couldn't know.

"Let's just forget about last night for now and not let a man complicate my first proper day in my new town with my girl." I gave Amy a smile.

"Okay," she agreed. "But life would be no fun without men to shake things up now and then, and as much as I love my B.O.B, nothing compares to the real thing," she advised before throwing my no doubt fabulous outfit at me.

The late afternoon sunlight, beginning to disappear behind the hills, kissed the horizon as Amy and I enjoyed a cold margarita on the back porch. I relaxed into my chair and let my head fall back, feeling the most content I had in a long while.

"That was an awesome afternoon, just what I needed," I told Amy, keeping my eyes closed.

We had had a delightful lunch at a cute little café, then proceeded to walk up and down Main Street, perusing all the shops along the way and generally just enjoying the town's atmosphere. And to my delight, we did not once hear the telltale rumble of Harley pipes, nor see a broadly built man donning a leather cut, so all in all, a great day.

"Yeah, it was actually kind of great, wasn't it?" Amy replied. "This little hole in the road is actually kind of growing on me."

I laughed. "That's great to hear, since we might be here for a while, owning a home and business here."

"Oh, I almost forgot," Amy continued. "I got us invited to a party, well, the closest this town does to party anyway, a barbeque? Tomorrow night, hopefully there will be some man candy there."

"What?" I spluttered. "When did you find the time to get yourself invited to anything? I was with you most of the day!" I sat up, turning to look at her.

"Remember when I went to get us some coffees when you were burrowed away in that bookstore?" she asked and I nodded. "Well, I got talking to the chick behind the counter, awesome girl and massive babe, she invited me and you to her barbeque tomorrow, you know since we are new in town and in desperate need of some friends?"

"I guess it couldn't hurt to get to know the locals," I pondered, wondering what kind of people we would encounter at this barbeque, and feeling kind of excited since I was, well, before the incident, a social person.

"I wonder if any of those delicious cops we saw today will be there." Amy was referring to the three handsome lawmen we saw having lunch at the same spot as us today.

I had a bit of a soft spot for men in uniform after my rescue. I always felt safe around them. Maybe I could go for a more sensible option in a man. My mind wandered to the sandy blond-haired policeman with a strong jaw, who was tall and *very* muscular. But my attention kept going back to a scruffy, black haired biker, with even more muscles than the toned policeman.

Urrrghhh, get out my mind! I screamed mentally at him.

"Um earth to Gwennie?" Amy waved her hand in front of my face.

"Sorry, was away with the fairies, what did you say?"

"I said you have to make those brownies you're so famous for, that will make us some friends for sure. You might even get marriage proposals with those things," she joked.

She was talking about the special brownies I only made once in a while because of their ridiculously high calorie count and my ability to polish off a whole batch without blinking.

"Well, that means we'll have to be up nice and early so we can go into the store and get things ready for the opening Wednesday night," I ordered sternly.

Amy giggled, then saluted. "Yes, sir."

I smiled and sipped my margarita, enjoying the company and the fuzzy feeling created by the drink, thinking I might just be enjoying life again.

I woke up after enjoying a blissful, nightmare free sleep, for once. I rolled over to look at the time, 6:00am. We weren't planning on going into the store until eight, so I had plenty of time for a quick morning run. I needed it after how much I had been indulging over the past few days.

I quickly donned my running gear, some short spandex shorts with a pink band at the top and a pink muscle top with a shelf bra. I completed the look with some pink Nikes. I slipped out the door with my headphones playing and began my run, getting lost in the music and the burn in my legs.

Exercise had been hard to get back into after all my rehabilitation, but running became a major part in getting me back to myself, a time when I could just escape into my own mind, my blaring music stopping my thoughts from wandering into dark places. After running for a good thirty minutes, I stopped at a street corner to stretch and give myself a breather.

I gazed around at the nicely kept houses and wondered where the fuck I was. Maybe getting lost in my music while running in unfamiliar territory wasn't the best idea. Well, that's why God invented iPhones.

Music still blaring, I tapped into my map, realized where I was and began to run in the direction of home. Not paying attention, I slammed straight into a hard body, proceeding to fall flat on my ass. Confused, I squinted up to see the sexy cop from yesterday, looking down at me with his mouth moving, but due to my music, I had no idea what he was saying. I yanked my headphones out of my ears.

"What?" I kind of yelled, sounding more than a bit unlady-like, but I guessed that ship had sailed when I fell on my ass.

"I just asked if you were okay. Sorry, darlin', but I just didn't see you until you slammed straight into me. You fell pretty hard, you all right?" he asked with concern and extended a muscled arm towards me. I took it, and he hauled me up.

I checked him out, closer I could appreciate him in all his glory. He was sweating from his own run, wearing cut off sweats and a tight NYPD t-shirt that clung to chiseled abs. I peered into his blue eyes and almost swooned.

I wasn't not kidding, he was one beautiful man. A shadow of blonde stubble covered his sharp jaw — his face had a kind of all American handsome look, apart from a slightly crooked nose, which only made him more endearing. Sweat beaded down the thick column of his neck and I followed it with my eyes, down to his seriously muscly chest.

I shook myself out of it. *What was it with this town and the men? Is this where male models came to retire and get badass jobs?* The sexy lawman was also blatantly checking me out, it didn't help my top had ridden up showing a fair bit of midriff. I yanked it down.

"I'm fine, thank you. Sorry, I got a bit lost and wasn't paying attention, completely my fault," I explained, breathless. I tried to straighten my ponytail, knowing I was a sweaty mess. I wasn't one of those girls who looked unruffled and amazing after a workout, I was reasonably sure I looked like a panting dog.

"No, ma'am, I should always be on the lookout for beautiful women running towards me, you're obviously new in town and... Australian?" he guessed wrongly.

I barely suppressed a frustrated sigh, I was so sick of Americans assuming I was from Australia, a pet hate for all Kiwis. "No, I'm from New Zealand," I said rather tightly. "And I have been in the States for almost five years now, legally, I promise," I joked, putting my hands up in mock fear.

He laughed, it was a great laugh. He was the man I should've been attracted to. Not that I didn't feel attraction towards this man, you would have to be dead or gay to not want to jump his bones. But it wasn't the same kind of desperate intensity I felt with Cade. It was official, I was totally fucked up, more attracted to the criminal than the man who locked them up.

"Don't worry, I won't deport you, not in my nature to let gorgeous woman go by choice," he joked back, eyes twinkling.

Was he flirting with me?

"I'm Luke by the way, the deputy sheriff round here." He held out his hand and I wiped mine on my shorts before shaking it.

"Gwen," I replied. "I'm opening a store here, right on Main Street?"

"Oh yeah, think I've seen that, next to the coffee shop right?" he asked, arms folded casually, feet wide apart, in what must be the masculine male go to pose.

"Yep, that's me, we have our grand opening on Wednesday night, you are most welcome to come." I invited him partly because I needed the numbers, and because...well, it was obvious he was hot and I needed to get back into the game.

"Wouldn't miss it," he replied, looking me up and down again, making me feel self-conscious in my lack of proper attire.

"Well great, see you then," I said brightly, preparing to leave. Or more accurately, run away. "I better get going, I've got lots to do. It was lovely to meet you, Deputy. Feel free to bring friends on Wednesday." I thought of Amy, and knew she would kill me if I didn't get someone for her to drool over, or more likely jump into bed with.

"The pleasure was all mine, Gwen," he responded, sounding far too seductive for his own good. "And please, call me Luke."

"Okay, Luke, see ya," I chirped, putting my headphones back in my ears, running in what I hoped was the right direction, feeling his eyes on me the whole time. *Good thing my butt looks great in these shorts.*

Just as I rounded a corner, almost recovered from my meeting with Luke, a dull rumble drowned out my music.

"Are you fucking kidding me?" I exclaimed out loud.

An older woman getting her paper off the lawn in her robe frowned disapprovingly at me and my outburst. I smiled tightly at her, my attention focused on the six or so bikes that had rounded the corner and were riding towards me. It was six-thirty in the morning, shouldn't bikers be sleeping off hangovers or kicking skanks out of their beds? I willed myself to look straight ahead and not look for Cade.

Don't look, don't look.

I peeked out the corner of my eye as they rode past. *Damn it! I have no self-discipline.* A helmetless – what was it with American's not wearing motorbike helmets, that shit is whack – Cade shamelessly checked me out while controlling a Harley. I had to admit, it was kind of impressive. I blushed, feeling the eyes of five other bikers on me as they rode past. I quickened my pace, trying to get into the safety of my house before I bumped into Ryan Gosling – at this point I wouldn't be surprised.

I flattened myself against the door as soon as I got inside, puffing from my run and my encounters. *That's it. I'm buying a treadmill, or maybe a whole gym. No, I just won't ever leave the house again.*

"Morning!" Amy's voice belted out. "I made you breakfast."

"Thanks!" I make my way into the kitchen.

Amy was at the breakfast bar, munching on granola, fruit and yogurt, a bowl for me sat beside her.

"How was your run?" she asked, between mouthfuls.

"You wouldn't believe me if I told you," I grumbled, plonking myself down beside her.

She stopped eating, her spoon halfway to her mouth. "Spill."

And I did just that, yet again replaying the barely believable events of the morning. I finished with the description of Cade on his bike, and Amy stared at me wide eyed.

"It's seven in the morning and *that* has already happened?" She shook her head. "I'm going to stick to you like white on rice for the rest of the day, baby girl, get myself some run ins with sexy males." She was half serious.

I laughed, digging into my breakfast. "I don't even want to think what's in store for us at this barbeque. I guess it would too much to hope that it is a meeting of kick ass feminists, or wait, lesbians?" I asked Amy seriously.

"Now what would be the fun in that?"

━━━

I slid my brownie into the oven and turned back to see Amy, shamefully licking the bowl.

"Hey!" I snapped. "Leave some for me!" I advanced on her.

Amy picked a knife up off the counter and hissed. "You try and eat any of this and I will cut you."

I giggled. "You don't scare me, Abrams."

Amy pondered for a moment then lowered the knife. "Okay, but we have half each."

I whipped my finger through the remnants of the mixture and brought it to my mouth and groaned. I stepped away.

"That's all I need, it's all yours," I said while untying my pink polka dotted ruffled apron. "I need to get ready for this barbeque."

"Well, make sure you dress hot," Amy commanded to my

back as I climbed the stairs. "With your luck, the cast of *Magic Mike* will probably be there."

———

I stood in front of my mirror, admiring my white sleeveless sundress and decided I looked pretty good. It clinched in at the waist and flowed down to just above my knee, showing a fair amount of leg. The whole back was sheer down to my waist, forcing me to go braless — not that it mattered with my tiny knockers. My hair was tousled into waves, tumbling past my shoulders. I decided on light makeup with pale pink lipstick. I finished off my look with a couple of silver bangles and my usual sky high heels, pale pink wedges with crisscross straps snaking up my ankle.

Amy wolf whistled at me.

I smiled at her over my shoulder. "Right back at you. Looking good, Abrams."

Amy looked great, no surprises there. She had on high-waisted white short shorts with a sheer white shirt tucked into them, her lace bra was showing in a somewhat tasteful way. A black belt knotted around her waist and she was wearing killer black heels. Her red hair was up in a messy ponytail and she wore little makeup.

"I'm going to have to fight off the men...and the women," I said .

"Exactly as I planned, grasshopper," she laughed, rubbing her hands together.

———

Walking down the driveway towards the back of an old but well restored Victorian, butterflies tumbled around in my stomach. It was an unfamiliar feeling, I usually loved a party of any form, enjoyed meeting new people. But now, anxiety chewed at my gut.

"Are you sure we shouldn't knock at the front door?" I asked Amy uncertainly as I shifted my tray full of brownies slightly.

"No, Rosie said to come straight out back." She strutted around the corner confidently.

I had to jog a little to catch up with her. Rounding the corner, I decided I was definitely nervous. A lot of people were scattered around the vast backyard. Both male and female, mostly around my age, but a few older people were mixed in. Amy and I were very overdressed by the looks of it. Everyone was mostly in jean shorts or casual dresses.

Not that it mattered, this was me, and like Amy said, I wasn't changing for anyone. Most of the looks directed our way were curious but friendly, apart from a couple of death glares coming from some very scantily-clad girls I would normally call skanks. But I wasn't judging by appearances.

"Amy, you made it!" A stunning girl ran over to us with a smile on her face.

She hugged Amy like she was an old friend and turned to me.

This town bred beautiful people. With tanned skin, shoulder length brown hair styled into messy waves and stunning blue eyes, this girl was a knockout. She was petite, tiny actually, even in the kick ass blue platform wedges she was wearing — she was a good head shorter than me. She wore white and black leopard print shorts, a white tank with a chiffon overlay and chunky necklaces tumbling down her torso.

I immediately liked her, not just because of her outfit, but because of the straight up friendly smile she was directing at me.

"You must be Gwen." She focused on my hands and grinned. "And these must be the famous brownies Amy was telling me about."

Jesus, how long did Amy talk to this girl for?

"It's lovely to meet you, Rosie. You have an awesome place." I recovered quickly as she took the tray out of my hands.

"Oh and your accent is so cute, and I *love* your dress."

"Thanks," I smiled. "I love your outfit."

She gazed down. "What, this old thing?" she joked. "Now, come with me and I'll get you ladies some drinks and introduce you."

"Drinks, great, point me in the right direction." Amy smiled, rubbing her hands together.

We followed Rosie to a little gazebo that had a table full of food and drinks. People were milling around nodding and smiling as we walked past. Rosie introduced us to a few people, who I immediately forgot the names of.

We grabbed our drinks, and chatted with Rosie, who introduced us to her girlfriends, Ashley and Lucy. They both cemented my theory that every person in this town were immortal, disgustingly attractive vampires.

Ashley had strawberry blonde short curly hair, pale skin and a light dusting of freckles across her nose. She was wearing a 1950s style yellow polka dot dress with a full skirt. Lucy's black hair was dead straight. She had dark eyes, curves to die for and great skin. I was starting to feel very inadequate.

"So, Gwen, you're opening a clothing store?" Lucy asked excitedly.

"Yeah, I used to be a buyer back in New York, so I thought having my own store would be great, maybe not so great for my shopping addiction," I joked.

"Oh my god, this is so great, this town needs somewhere to shop. It's such a pain in the ass driving two hours to get a half decent outfit," Lucy said. "When do you open?"

"Well, our opening is Wednesday night and I would love for all of you to come," I invited the girls.

"That would be kick ass!" Rosie beamed at me. "I'll make

sure to let all the girls know, make it a bit of a girls night out, will there be drinks?"

Amy almost spat out her mouthful. "Of course!"

The women laughed. "But feel free to invite boyfriends and husbands," I continued. "I've invited some of the hunky local law enforcement as well —"

"The sex on a stick cops," Amy interrupted. "Got to have some man candy there, and I think Mr. Deputy is keen on our girl here." She pointed at me with her drink.

"Amy, he was just being friendly." I shot a glare at her.

The women exchanged glances. "Really...do tell, which one?" Ashley asked.

"Although our men and police don't seem to get on the best," Rosie added, rather cautiously.

Uh oh red flags.

"What do you mean?" I probed, lead settling in my stomach.

Rosie began to say something, but her answer was drowned out by the roar of motorbikes,

"Oh shit," Amy muttered and I followed her gaze.

Oh shit was right.

A whole goddamned motorcycle gang had just arrived at the barbeque. Men of all shapes and sizes rounded the corner, some wearing jeans low slung with tight t-shirts under their leather cuts. A couple had bandannas wrapped around their heads. I saw a couple of – cringe – wallet chains, and of course, the amount of ink on them was insane. Full sleeves, neck tattoos, you name it, these guys probably kept the one tattoo parlor here in business. There had to be about fifteen of them.

I spotted Cade, and by the looks of it he had spotted me a lot earlier. He was wearing sunglasses (fucking bad ass aviators by the way) so I couldn't gauge his expression, but he looked pissed off. I couldn't handle that right now, though. I was too busy trying to deal with the fact fifteen men who looked like they could snap me in half without batting an eyelid were swiftly approaching our little group. The men in front of me were too familiar. I began to have trouble breathing, my hands shaking, my vision blurring.

Do not faint.

A hand settled on my shoulder. "Are you okay, Gwen? You look really pale," Lucy asked, her face knitted in worry.

"She's fine, just low blood sugar," Amy lied smoothly. "Rosie, where's your bathroom, I need to primp, all these men approaching." She continued sounding casual, only I could hear the edge to her voice. I heard Rosie laugh through the roar in my ears. I didn't pay much notice; I was too busy focusing on keeping my breath even.

"Straight inside, through the kitchen at the end of the hall, you can't miss it."

Amy gently pulled me along, holding me up. "You're okay, Gwennie, everything is fine I'm here," she cooed quietly in my ear. "Keep walking, we're almost inside."

I focused on putting one foot in front of the other and struggled to keep from collapsing. We finally reached a bathroom and I fell to the floor as soon as Amy shut the door.

She sat down beside me, stroking my hair. "It's okay, babe, no one is here to hurt you, just breathe." She spoke calmly, having dealt with many of my panic attacks after my accident, when I could hardly stand being out in public.

I took long, slow breaths and after a couple of minutes, I returned to some kind of normal state. "I think I'm okay," I told her shakily.

Amy smiled at me, then stood up extending her hand. I grasped it, unsteadily getting to my feet.

I splashed water on my face, completely ruining my makeup, but who gave a shit?

"I'll go out make an excuse and we can leave okay, Gwennie?"

I grabbed her hand. "No," I said firmly. "Those girls are really lovely and I will not let some fucked up fear stop us from having a good time and making new friends. He *cannot* take that away from me." Tears welled in my eyes but I refused to let them fall.

Amy stared at me a beat then smiled, but it was tainted with sadness. "You are one strong bitch, Gwennie," she whispered proudly.

"No I'm not, I've got you." I smiled sadly back. "Now, help me fix myself up so we can go back out there."

After some quick emergency makeup procedures, Amy and I ventured out into the party. The bikers had dispersed, some drinking beers and lounging on chairs, others laughing with each other with arms wrapped around women. We spotted Rosie, with none other than Cade, who had his arm slung around her shoulder.

He had a beautiful woman and was pursuing me? Prick.

"Gwen, Amy!" Rosie yelled. I felt a disturbing amount of male eyes on me. More than a few leather clad men were checking Amy out, some old enough to be our fathers. *Ew.*

"Get your asses over here, girls," Rosie ordered.

Amy half dragged me over to the prick, who still had his arm around Rosie. Lucy was talking intently to yet another sexy biker, this one tall with a buzz cut, an awesome goatee, and covered in tats. He was attractive, but had a very dangerous vibe coming off him.

"Gwen, you have to give me the recipe for your brownies, the boys fucking *love* them," she gushed, and one of the guys turned around from the food table.

"Bitch, those brownies are the fucking shit! I think I'm going to marry you." He smiled cheekily, he was quite young, Hispanic and very attractive, kind of like a bright-eyed puppy or something. But a fucking scary puppy, like a pit bull.

I smiled at his compliment, but I wasn't sure how much I

appreciated being referred to as "bitch." I got a pointed look from Amy at the marriage comment, and I couldn't help but laugh a little.

The man boy approached me, I started to feel a little nervous but stood my ground. He held out his hand, still smiling, "I'm Lucky."

I shook his hand and replied. "Gwen, and this is Amy." I gestured to my best friend, who held out her hand, grinning.

"Wow, we hit the fucking jackpot, two knockouts like you ladies coming to town, and you can cook...damn," he exclaimed.

I couldn't help but laugh at this guy's obvious fun loving nature. Cade's intense stare burned into me me. I glanced at him to come face to face with pure fury. I refused to lower my eyes.

"Omigod, I'm so rude," Rosie interrupted the little stare-off Cade and I had going on. "You've obviously met Lucky, but this is Bull." She gestured to the scary looking man with Lucy, who perked up upon hearing his name, and gave us a chin lift.

"Yo," he grunted.

"And this is my brother, Cade." She gave him a squeeze. I was shocked for a second.

Brother? Wow, I was a little quick to judge.

Cade released Rosie. "We've met," he barked before grabbing my arm and dragging me towards the house.

"What the fuck, Cade?" I heard Rosie's voice behind us, but we seemed to be moving at lightening speed, because all of a sudden we were inside someone's bedroom. Cade locked the door behind him.

I was a bit shell shocked and out of it from my episode earlier, so I didn't really take the opportunity to struggle, but I finally found my tongue, "What the fuck...?"

Cade advanced on me and backed me into a wall. His arms came up on either side of me, boxing me in.

"What are you doing here?" he whispered menacingly, he seemed seriously pissed. Maybe someone stole his wallet chain.

"What do you mean?" I hissed, trying to push him, but it was like pushing a brick wall. I tried not to appreciate his abs.

Tried and failed.

"What do you think you're doing, just dragging me away like some kind of barbarian? Were you dropped on your head as a child?" I asked sarcastically, weirdly not feeling any fear at being alone in a strange house with a seriously angry biker.

"Answer my question, baby. What are you doing at my sister's house, dressed like a fucking wet dream?"

"Don't be so crude, I'm here because I was invited, not that it's any of your business," I snapped.

"Coming into my sister's home, my boys seeing you looking like that, wanting a piece of you. Half of them have already seen you in that sad fucking excuse for an outfit you were running in, and you think this is 'none of my business'?" he asked dangerously, face so close to mine our lips were almost touching. A vein in his neck pulsed, his jaw tight.

"Well, yes," I said, starting to get a bit confused. *I mean, yeah, he said he wanted me in his bed, but what does he care about me being at his sister's party? We hadn't even had a proper conversation, let alone kissed! This was way too weird.*

"Jesus!" he bellowed.

I jumped at his tone.

He looked at me, his face softening a bit. "You don't get it do you, Gwen?"

"No I don't, and quite frankly, I don't think there is anything to *get*, you don't even know me –" I didn't get to finish because his hand snatched the back of my head and before I knew it, his mouth was crushing down on mine.

I was so surprised I didn't even try to fight it. His tongue invaded my mouth, my body plastered to his. I kissed him back and moaned into his mouth. I had never had a kiss this good in my life — I felt like I could come from just his tongue in my mouth.

His hands moved down my body, leaving a trail of fire in their wake. The kiss deepened, he put his hands on my ass and lifted me up. I didn't hesitate to wrap my legs around his waist. I bit at his bottom lip — I had never felt this frantic, this turned on in my life. We were interrupted by a knock at the door, and the sound of the door handle rattling.

"Cade!" Rosie's slightly panicked voice yelled. "What are you doing with Gwen?"

"What the fuck do you think he's doing, Rosie?" Lucky joined in. "A woman who looked like that, I know what *I'd* be doing."

Cade's arms tightened around me. "Fuck off!" he yelled savagely.

"Gwennie?" Amy's voice chimed in. She sounded half worried, half amused.

"Fuckin' hell," Cade muttered, sounding livid.

I giggled at the absurdity of the situation, maybe feeling a little drunk from the kiss. "I'm fine, Ames," I called back, trying to sound normal. "Be out in a sec."

She laughed. "Okay, babe, take your time." Her heels clicked as she walked away.

I turned to Cade, feeling my brain regain control of my body instead of my vagina. "Put me down," I ordered.

"No fuckin' way."

"Yes, way." I struggled. "Seriously, put me down." I glared into his gray eyes, which were glittering.

"Baby, I've got you where I've wanted you since the first moment I laid eyes on you, and after that kiss, you think I'm going to let you go? Fuck no." His gaze was pure masculine desire.

I got even more turned on, if that was even possible. I ignored the feeling and tried to be sensible. "Cade, in case you haven't noticed, there's a shit ton of people right outside." As if on cue, laughing and catcalls trickled through the open windows. Obviously Lucky had told the men about what he'd heard. "If you think you're getting anything from me in the middle of a stranger's bedroom, with all of *that* going on outside, then you're bat shit crazy."

Cade raised his eyebrows.

"And if you think *this* is going to happen again, anywhere, anytime, then you are mistaken. This was..." I struggled to think of an appropriate description of what this was. *Mind-blowing? Extremely hot? A mini orgasm?* "A lapse in judgment," I finished lamely.

Cade stared at me with that angry look back on his face, his hands roaming up my bare leg, tracing the edge of my panties. I let out a little moan. His eyes darkened.

"Baby, this will most definitely be happening again, and there will be a lot less clothes involved and I will finally get to fuckin' taste you."

I quivered, he stroked me over the top of my underwear, stoking the fire he'd already ignited.

"But you're right, I ain't fucking you in my sister's house with all my boys outside picturing it, you got way too much class for that." He continued to stroke, but faster and harder, his mouth kissing at my ear. "I am going to make you come, because I want to be out at that party and look at you, knowing I made you lose control and be able to picture what you look like with your pussy pulsing around my finger," he said hoarsely, putting pressure on my magic spot.

That pushed me over the edge, I screamed, he silenced me with his mouth. I shattered into a thousand pieces, my climax so intense I felt like I might melt into a puddle on the floor.

When I was finished, he put his forehead against mine for a

beat then lowered me onto the floor. My legs were jelly, luckily his hold on my waist kept me upright. I glanced down to see him straining through his jeans. He followed my gaze, grabbing my hand and rubbing it against him.

"Yeah, Gwen, see what you do to me. My dick is as hard as a fuckin' rock." He tugged me back against his hard body, attacking my mouth with barely restrained ferocity. "Now, I'm going to have to stick around for a bit 'cause Rosie will get pissed if I up and leave as soon as I arrive, that bitch has been planning this barbeque for weeks. But as soon as fuckin' possible, I'm leaving, and you'll be on the back of my bike. Got it?" His eyes were locked with mine. It was a statement, not a question.

I blinked, anger starting to bubble up inside me at being ordered around, but I wasn't able to fully get riled up after that mind blowing orgasm. Cade was still looking at me expectantly, like he was waiting for some sort of verbal response. I currently wasn't able to make my brain form coherent words.

"Oh, and, baby? We're going to talk about why the fuck you damned near fainted at the sight of me and my boys earlier. I've seen raw fear before, and it was all over your face."

Okay, now I was angry.

"Are you fucking *kidding* me?" I spat at him. "You think you can just waltz into my life, expecting me to open my legs at your say so and share personal details on your command, when we have not so much as eaten a meal together, never mind you asking me on a real date?" My voice rose to an almost full blown yell. "If you think I will ever willingly be in the same room as someone as arrogant and bossy as you, then your are insane." I yanked myself out of his arms, righting my dress and stomping towards the door.

"Baby..." I heard from behind me

I whirled around and give my best death stare. "I am *not* your baby, nor will I ever be," I hissed, my voice laced with venom. I slammed the door behind me.

I strutted right back into the party, with my head held high, ignoring the few yells and whistles that filled the air. I spotted Amy grabbing something to eat, so I headed her way.

"Well, you look....ruffled," Amy giggled when I reached her.

I glared at her. "Don't even start. I will not talk about what happened and we are no longer speaking of Cade," I ordered, snatching a carrot stick off her plate.

Amy gave me a salute. "Aye aye, Captain." I guessed she was enjoying the drinks.

I rolled my eyes and followed her as we headed to a table where Lucy, Ashley, and some of the other women whose names I had forgotten were sitting.

I sat myself down with a sigh, Ashley looked my way with a sly smile. "Everything okay, Gwen?"

"Yes, fine thanks." I smiled at her genuinely, even if it was a bit strained.

"You and Cade...sort things out?" Lucy chimed in, curiously.

"We just had to get a few things straight," I said tightly, but smiled again, not wanting these women to think I was a bitch. "Now, I hope you ladies will all be at the store early on Wednesday for some pre drinks and first pick on some of the merchandise?" I tried to change the subject, luckily women and clothing were a match made in heaven.

⸺

After whatever that was with Cade, I began to relax and chat happily with my new friends, drinking soda – keeping my wits about me – enjoying good food and actually getting along with some of the bikers, who would stop by our table every now and then. I even managed to completely ignore Cade, whose gaze burned a hole through me throughout the afternoon. As night started to fall, everything started to get a bit rowdier. Amy, who was not on non-alcoholic drinks, was getting very flirty with said bikers, and they were lapping it up. When I saw her trying to get some very scary looking tattooed man to dance, I couldn't help but snicker.

I spotted some of the same skanky girls giving me and Amy very dirty looks. I leaned over to Ashley. "So who are the girls over there currently giving new meaning to the phrase 'If looks could kill'?" I asked jokingly, not wanting to offend her in case they were friends or relatives, in small towns like this you couldn't be too careful.

Ashley made a face. "Oh, those are the token club skanks," she said. "The boys kind of share them. Rosie didn't want them here, but since they're 'with' — I use that term very loosely — Asher and Brock, she had no choice."

"Oh..." I said, lost for words. I continued to gaze at the bottle blond who was glaring at me like she wanted to scratch my eyes out.

Ashley noticed. "Oh, don't mind Ginger." She waved her hand. "She's Cade's go to...well, used to be," she added quickly.

The women had not missed the stares Cade had been directing at me all night. I swallowed and surveyed the girl more closely. It was hard to see, with the night growing darker and faint lanterns bathing the yard in a soft glow. She had short, layered hair, eyes rimmed with black eyeliner, big silver hoops in her ears, a short jean skirt and a tight muscle top on. The "biker whore" look was finished with motorcycle boots. This opinion did not come from the fact I may have been a bit jealous. Which was ridiculous.

I caught Cade's stare and rolled my eyes, glaring at him. The bastard just smirked at me! *Right, time to go.* I scanned around for Amy, who was dancing with Rosie.

"Well, I guess I better go, got a big day tomorrow, it was so nice to meet you and I'll see you at the opening, right?" I said to Ashley while I stood.

She jumped up and gave me a big old hug. I returned it, surprised at the display but welcoming it. Despite the whole Cade disaster, I felt at home with these women.

She held me at arm's length. "It was so awesome to meet you, Gwen, you and Amy are the fucking shit!"

I laughed.

"And there is no way I'm missing your opening," she continued.

"Glad to hear," I replied. "And remember to come early." I winked at her over my shoulder as I walked away.

I approached Rosie and Amy. "Right, lady." I smacked Amy's behind, which resulted in a few whistles. "I'm going to head home, you want to come or stay a bit longer?"

Rosie jumped in my face. "Don't leave, Gwen! We're doing tequila shots!" she exclaimed, sounding more than a little hammered.

"As much as I love tequila shots, and trust me I do, I have to take a rain check, got to get the store ready for Wednesday," I explained sadly. "But next time?"

Rosie grinned drunkenly. "You got it! Girls' night!"

"Sounds like a plan, thank you for such an awesome time and for inviting us," I continued, genuinely glad I came, despite the male drama.

"No problem, you girls are the shit," Rosie yelled, mimicking Ashley's statement.

"Yes, we are!" Amy chimed in, slurring her words slightly. "But alas, I will also have to decline on the tequila, as I don't want the boss to think I'm hungover tomorrow." She winked at me, then gave Rosie a big old smacker on the lips, earning a lot more whistles than my butt slap. She wrapped her arms around my shoulders and we began to wade through people, saying our good-byes along the way.

I caught a glimpse of Cade, who was striding purposefully towards us, brows narrowed. "Oh shit," I muttered under my breath. I so didn't want to deal with macho man bullshit right now. I wanted to go home, take a bath and get ready for my opening.

Just before he reached me, his phone went off, he glanced down at the display and scowled. I watched him answer the call, bark a few responses back, and then end it. He then made some kind of signal, which made all the men wearing cuts stand up and walk towards their bikes. Cade turned around and gave me a meaningful glare before hopping on his bike and roaring off.

"That was weird," Amy proclaimed drunkenly.

"Yeah, it was," I muttered, almost to myself.

CHAPTER 4

I GAZED AROUND MY STORE, smiling to myself, delighted at the finished product and amazed at what Amy and I had managed to get done. It was perfect, everything I had imagined it would be. The walls were pure white, as were the floors. A free-standing mock brick wall ran down the front of the store with a rack attached, giving it a rustic look to juxtapose the stark white. To the right of the wall, was a table of brightly colored sweaters and a shelf reaching to the ceiling, full of accessories. Looking towards the counter, there were some more racks and an old wooden table covered with candles and some jewelry. The fitting rooms had white doors, and each room was carpeted with bright patterned carpet.

I loved my store, it was a mix between stylish minimalism and rustic country charm, which I hoped would be received well by the residents of Amber.

I had been so busy with the set up, my mind hadn't wandered to Cade...much. I was glad I hadn't heard from him or caught him skulking around my house in the middle of the night. Well, that was what I told myself.

Amy and I had set up a table full of snacks, nothing fancy or pretentious, just great wholesome food. I made a giant batch of my brownies, barely being able to restrain myself from eating half of them. And of course, we had our contractors set up a temporary – I was thinking of keeping it – bar, stocked with ingredients for a couple of cocktails, some champagne and good old beer.

Amy had decided she would be the bartender for the night. I had argued with her on that one, wanting to hire someone so she was free to mingle with the guests. We were going to encourage the women to have a try on, so we could hopefully make some money.

Amy had replied, "Gwen, I will be serving alcohol, not only does a couple of cocktails loosen people's wallets, but what better place to mingle with people than at the bar, where people will be guaranteed to return to?"

I couldn't fault her logic.

It was after six and I wondered where Amy was. I told her that we had invited Rosie and her posse to come at six-thirty, so she'd better be here. I had gotten ready early, so I could put the finishing touches on everything without worrying about primping. Amy had left about an hour ago, saying she had to go and "get hot for the biker/hot cop man candy that may or may not be there tonight." Her words not mine.

I took another quick look in the floor to ceiling mirror. I had on a bright red dress. It was skintight with capped sleeves and a plunging neckline, exposing a fair bit of my not so ample breasts, but it worked for me, having been designed for small busted women – thank you, Mrs Beckham. I had kick ass matching red shoes, they were high, and I mean *high*, with a tiny stiletto heel and a pointed toe. There were tiny straps around my ankles embellished with little gold studs, giving my look a bit of edge. I had a couple of gold bangles on my wrist, but otherwise wore no jewelry, the dress and shoes spoke for themselves.

I had my hair up in a loose bun, with small curls escaping around my face. My makeup was not too over the top, a small amount of eyeliner, but a big amount of my absolute favorite mascara that made my lashes look lush. I had a subtle red gloss on my lips, not wanting to go too overboard with the red thing. I had to admit, I looked pretty good and judging on how Amy's jaw had dropped when she saw me, I guessed she thought I looked okay as well.

I wondered if Luke would be here tonight. I deliberated to myself whether I could muster up the same sort of electric connection I felt with Cade and channel it into a more sensible direction.

The clanging of the bell shook me out of my thoughts and Amy strutted in. It was my turn for a jaw drop. I thought I looked okay, but she was...wow. She was dressed in pure white, donning a strapless, bustier style top, which molded to her body perfectly, showing off her more than ample chest in a tasteful way. She paired this with a skintight white pencil skirt, skimming her knees. She had on my white strappy stilettos, which came up past her ankle and made her legs look amazing. Her red hair was curled into soft waves and she had little makeup on, apart from some amazing red lipstick.

"Well?" She did a little turn.

"I think I may just turn lesbian for you. Lady, you look smoking," I said with a smirk on my face. "Nice shoes by the way."

"Thanks." She flicked her hair, strutting towards me, straightening clothes now and then. "I got them at the best little store, right across from my bedroom, and they didn't cost me a dime," she said with mock shock.

I laughed. "Probably similar to the store I got these bracelets from then." I held my arm up in front of her and jingled the borrowed jewelry.

"Good thing we both have such great taste," she exclaimed,

not batting an eyelash at me wearing her seriously pricey accessories.

We spent the rest of our time before the girls arrived making and drinking cocktails to loosen up a bit. Amy and I were sitting in my kick ass antique patterned couch, sipping our cosmos when the door jingled and Rosie and the girls walked in.

Rosie was wearing an amazing long sleeved, fitted little black dress with black and gold sandals. Lucy was wearing skintight black, high-waisted pants with a silver cropped top showing off her toned midsection, pairing it with silver sandals. Ashley had on another 1950s style dress with capped sleeves, a flower print that finished at her waist and had a powder blue full skirt. It was awesome.

"Holy shit!" Rosie yelled. "This place looks incredible!" She rushed towards me and engulfed me in a huge hug. She released me, looking me up and down and letting out a whistle. "Scratch that, *you* look amazing, way to make us mere mortals look like shit." She glanced at Amy, who was busy chatting to Lucy and Ashley and making them drinks.

"Wowza, and Amy is making white look far from virginal," she declared, impressed.

I laughed lightly. "You look killer, Rosie, where did you get that dress?"

Up close, the dress was embroidered with hundreds of little beads that sparkled in the light. I needed something like that in my wardrobe, not counting my hundreds of other little black dresses.

"Oh some thrift store." She waved her hand. "It was way longer, but I gave it the chop and voilà! New dress! Enough about that. My brother is going to *die* when he sees you looking like that, seriously, I wouldn't put it past him to carry you out, caveman style," she giggled.

I blinked, shocked at the casual way she was talking about

Cade in relation to me. As if we were a couple, not two people who barely knew each other, apart from making out at her party. And he was coming *here*? I definitely didn't remember inviting him, I wasn't insane.

I started with the obvious question. "Cade's coming?"

"Well, yeah," she said, like it was the obvious answer. "I told him about the opening today and he said him and the boys would definitely stop by, you're here, free booze and hot bitches? Just try and keep them away."

I barely restrained a snort, hard ass bikers at a clothing store opening? Yeah right. I began to ask her if she was actually serious when Amy and the girls came over, arms full of cocktails. Amy thrust a full glass into Rosie's waiting hand and replaced my empty one.

"Right, bitches," she interrupted. "I think it is time for a toast." She thought for a second. "To new friends, new beginnings and new clothes!"

The women laughed, we clinked our glasses and downed a mouthful of the delicious brew.

"So, Gwen," Lucy started after finishing her sip. "Are you selling that smoking dress somewhere in this lovely place, or am I going to have to rip it off your back? Because that is gor - geous."

"Of course we have it, just in different colors, right over here." I directed her to a rack full of dresses as Ashley and Rosie began to look through racks. Within the first five minutes, the three ladies had armfuls of clothes ready to try.

"Just to inform, you ladies," I called over the doors of the fitting rooms as they were getting changed. "In New Zealand we have a thing called 'mates rates', which I assure you all you will be getting."

"Rock on!" Rosie yelled from the middle stall and I laughed.

I had lost track of the amount of times I had genuinely laughed since being around these women, not just the fake ones I had forced back in New York. Amy must have been thinking something along the same lines, she glanced at me with a proud smile, and I saw a tiny glisten in her eyes. Before I was able to say something, Lucy came out of the fitting room, looking stunning in the black, shorter version of my dress and exclaimed, "I have to have this, seriously have to!"

"Yes, you so do," I agreed.

After almost an hour of trying on, the girls decided on multiple items, I informed them of their totals.

Rosie blinked at me. "No, Gwen, that's not right, that isn't even the price of two dresses let alone three."

"Opening night special." I shrugged.

"No, we'll pay full price," Lucy put in. "We have to support our new favorite store."

"And I have to support my new best customers," I said back with a smile, the girls started to argue, but Amy butted in.

"Ladies, take the fucking discount, you're awesome, and Gwen and I are just grateful to meet such kick ass chicks on coming here, this is our thank you. No arguing," she ordered.

It was then that the girls conceded, thanks to Amy's no nonsense tone.

"But next time we are paying full price," Rosie decided.

I just smiled back at her, not saying a thing. At that point, the bell chimed and some women from Rosie's party piled in. I greeted them warmly, hoping I remembered everyone's name. After that, people continuously trickled in, some I recognized, some I didn't. World travelled fast in this small town, which was something I had banked on.

Everyone was lovely, including the man who owned the bookstore next door, whom I met on Sunday. He brought his wife Bernie, who was in her late fifties but wore her age well, with short red hair and a slim body. People in this town were freaks of nature with their good looks and impeccable style.

"Gwen dear, it's so lovely to meet you. Evan told me all about the 'beautiful young kiwi girl' who loved books just as much as he did! I'm glad as he has had trouble finding an avid reader in me." She laughed. "I will definitely be coming to visit you on a regular basis, I think." Her gaze landed on a stunning pair of heels on the shelf behind me.

"I look forward to it," I told her before getting whisked away by Rosie to meet more people.

It was about 8:30pm, my little store was packed and I was over the moon, men and women of all ages had come to welcome Amy and me.

I was wrapping a purchase when the bell chimed for what felt like the hundredth time that night, and hot cop Luke sauntered in. He looked good, and so did his buddies, who were trailing in behind him. Those were some *fine* all-American specimens. He was wearing a blue button up shirt, tucked into faded jeans, a big old belt buckle and cowboy boots. I glanced over at Amy, whose eyes were so focused on the newcomers she didn't realize the champagne glass she was pouring was overflowing. I chuckled, turning my attention back to Lily, the young girl buying the dress. "You enjoy that dress honey, it looks great on you," I said sincerely.

My eyes went back to where Luke was currently making his way towards me, eyes twinkling, saying hello to people as he approached, shaking hands and whatnot. I smoothed my dress stepping out from behind the counter. He got a full look at me and his eyes darkened, I blushed slightly at his reaction.

"Gwen," he addressed me roughly, grabbing my waist and kissing my cheek. My skin tingled a little at his touch. I was definitely attracted to him, but I couldn't help but compare it to the fire I felt when Cade's hands trailed my body. I mentally shook my head, focusing on Luke before my thoughts wandered too much.

"Luke, glad you could make it." I beamed up at him.

"So am I, darlin', you look..." he paused, hands still at my waist, "Stunning, although that does not adequately describe how beautiful you are in that dress." His voice was charming and held an undertone of desire.

I laughed nervously, very aware that his hand was still at my waist. "Stop, you're making me blush."

"Good, your blush is beautiful," he murmured.

I was still smiling, albeit timidly, when the bell chimed yet again. I didn't pay much notice, still focusing on how to handle this intimate situation and how I felt about it.

"Can I get you a beer?" I asked, gesturing towards the bar, stepping away from him. I caught Amy's eye, she looked slightly panicked. I narrowed my eyes, usually she would be thrilled seeing me talking to a hot guy.

That's when I felt it. The intense energy, the air almost sizzling. I turned away from the bar and locked eyes with Cade, who was pushing his way towards me with his eyes focused on Luke's hand, which was still resting at my waist.

"Shit," I muttered, fully stepping out of Luke's touch. "Sorry, Luke, could you excuse me for just a second? I have something to deal with. Amy will get you a beer." I tried to sound breezy.

Luke followed my eyes and started to look a bit dangerous himself. "You know Fletcher?" he questioned tightly.

I opened my mouth to ask him who Fletcher was when Cade descended upon us, expression dark.

"Crawford," he spat out the name like it tasted bad, glaring at Luke. He directed his gaze at me, eyes travelling up and down my body, and I got instantly wet at the hunger in his stare. His eyes snapped to mine. "Babe, outside. Now."

I opened my mouth yet again to tell him to go fuck himself, but more politely as I was at my store opening in front of the town and I wanted to sound calm and dignified. Before I could get the words out, Luke stepped forward, almost in front of me. Fuck, this didn't look like it was going in any direction that was good. People started to give us sideways glances.

"I'm sorry, Fletcher, but Gwen and I were having a conversation, which you are interrupting," he grumbled, authority ringing in his tone.

"I can see that, Deputy," Cade drawled sarcastically. "And now your conversation is over." He seized my arm and basically dragged me out the door.

I tottered behind him, mostly because I didn't want to cause a scene, but a little bit because he looked *hot*. Cade was wearing a black shirt, rolled up at the sleeves so you could see his thick arms covered in tattoos. His shirt hung untucked over a pair of very well fitting jeans. So well fitting I think the designer was owed a huge thank you by all of womankind. His outfit was finished with motorcycle boots and his cut overtop. It was the biker version of formal, and I had to say, I dug it.

We flew past Rosie, who was barely suppressing laughter and I glared at her. This made her laugh flat out. We made it outside and Cade continued to drag me down the street into an alleyway, backing me up against a brick wall.

"What in the *fuck* do you think you're doing?" I screeched, very concerned about the damage the wall was doing to my fabulous dress.

Cade cut me off by putting his hands on either side of my face, drawing me in for a brutal kiss. I halfheartedly struggled, but melted into him when he pressed his hard body into mine. Those abs undid me every time. I was lost for breath when he pulled away, his eyes pierced through mine, dark with desire.

"That was me beginning to show you how I feel about that dress, babe. I'll show my full appreciation later, but for now I want to know what *the fuck* Crawford was doing with his hands on you." His voice raised to near a yell at the end.

"I'm assuming Crawford is Luke and you're doing the usual ridiculous macho man thing by calling him by his last name," I retorted.

Cade roughly drew me closer, but I didn't feel afraid of him, which was crazy. I mean, I was attacked by bikers and here I was literally in a dark alley with one and the only thing I was feeling was irritation and arousal — a lot of arousal.

"Don't get fucking smart with me, Gwen, answer the goddamned question," he growled.

"I wasn't aware there was a question, Cade. I'm afraid I am not fluent in cave man," I said sweetly, continuing to bait him. Surprisingly, he didn't find me funny. He pounded his fist against the brick beside my head. I flinched, that had to hurt.

"I came in to see you, to carry on our conversation from the other night, to fucking apologize for coming on so strong when I obviously have to handle you with care, baby, and trust me, I will from now on."

His stare made my insides flutter.

"I see you in that fucking dress, looking so good it should be illegal and laughing with that prick, his hands all over you. Gwen, it took everything I had not to pound my fist into his face. You are *mine*. I know you don't understand nor like it at the moment, but you will, because what is between us is real and I know you feel it and you're scared," Cade accused.

I let out a breath, floored, a bit because I had never heard the rough biker talk so much but mostly because of what he said. I didn't like some of it, like, really didn't like the "you are mine" part, reminding me too much of what Jimmy thought of me. But unlike Jimmy, I don't think he meant like a possession, I think he meant something else. But the other stuff he said was kind of sweet, and I didn't know what to do with the caring side of the rough round the edges man.

"Cade, this is too much to process at the moment." I

attempted to sound calm. "I don't understand what's going on, why you felt the need to make a scene at my store opening and drag me onto the street, then lay *that* on me." My voice rose, but I couldn't help it, I was pissed off. "I need to get back inside, but we obviously need to talk."

Yeah right, we needed to talk, talk about how for some reason he thought we were some kind of item after only a couple of encounters and one mind blowing orgasm.

"You're overthinking, baby." Cade stroked my face. "But you're right, we'll get back in, you have your night and at the end of it you're on the back of my bike. No escaping this time," he told me firmly.

"Okay," I huffed, surprising myself. "But have fun trying to get me on a bike in this dress."

Cade raised his eyebrows, obviously expecting a fight, then his eyes darkened, "Don't worry, Gwen, you'll get on my bike." He glanced at my legs. "That fucking dress." He plastered my body to his and kissed me fiercely once more. The kiss was intense, I felt like something had seriously changed.

Shit's just got real.

Cade stopped, resting his forehead against mine. "Go back now, baby, or I won't be able to stop myself," he grunted.

"Okay," I breathed as he stepped back, sporting a serious hard on. I tried to ignore that and got to straightening my dress, which had ridden up, like, a lot. I finished righting myself to find Cade watching me through hooded eyes.

"You better hope this thing finishes early, babe, I've got plans for you," he declared roughly, adjusting himself.

I shivered and before I could reply, Cade snatched my hand, walking us back towards the store. During the short walk, I panicked. *What had got into me? Why did I suddenly give in?* I told myself I was never going to be with a bad boy again, but this was different, this attraction was crazy. Maybe I just needed to get it out of my system.

Who was I kidding? He just wanted a high class fuck and would throw me aside once he got it. I needed to get laid and I could do much, *much* worse, so I'd just enjoy the ride. Excuse the pun.

We emerged back in my store, the bell unfortunately alerting everyone of our presence. I was so taking that thing down. I felt almost every set of eyes in the place on us, particularly a hard glare from Luke, who watched intently from the bar. Amy had a shit-eating grin on her face, as did Rosie and the girls.

Cade, still holding my hand, leaned in. "Seems like we're popular, babe."

I turned and glared at him, he smiled back. Man, what a smile. I didn't think he could be any hotter.

"I'll just chill with the boys." He glanced to a small group of bikers from last night, most of whom I recognized, including the scary Bull, and Lucky.

"Gwen!" Lucky yelled. "Fuck, I thought this thing would be boring as shit, but you got booze and your brownies and a first-class amount of tail. This is fucking aces." He took a pull of his beer, looking pretty happy.

"I'm glad you're enjoying yourself." I couldn't help but smile back at him, his mood infectious.

"Yo, Gwen," Bull grunted. My heart rate went up a bit, the big man looking far too scary for my liking. Cade somehow noticed my slight panic and squeezed my hand.

"Bull." I nodded and did an awkward little wave at the other attractive men. "Boys." I got a few chin lifts back. "Well, I better get back to mingling and whatnot," I stuttered.

Shit, did I seriously just say the word "whatnot" in front of some serious bad asses? Mortification commence. I started to turn away in embarrassment, but Cade still had hold of my hand. He jerked me back to him, kissing me quickly but fiercely.

"Later," he whispered.

I could do nothing but nod, knowing that everyone was well and truly watching. I was feeling thoroughly humiliated. I walked away on unsteady feet, smiling tightly at people I passed. Luckily, Luke had moved away from the bar, to... I didn't know where, but I was secretly hoping he didn't see that little PDA.

I made it to the bar where unfortunately, Rosie, Lucy, Ashley and Amy were all standing, wearing looks of astonishment and amusement, and Amy smiling at me with flat out pride.

"Girl," Lucy began when I reached them. "That was hot. I mean, first Luke comes in looking like he wants to eat you up, then Cade arrives, looking like he's going to straight up murder the deputy and then basically drags you out. I don't have to guess as to what you two were up to, thanks to that intense lip lock just then."

The girls all laughed, I blushed.

"Amy, cosmo. Now," I ordered.

"All right, all right, keep your panties on, oh wait, did Cade already take them off?" she teased.

I picked up a peanut off the bar and threw it at her. She gracefully dodged it, handing me a drink. "Now, now, no need to throw party snacks, Gwennie."

I ignored her, taking a long needed sip of my drink.

"Told you my brother would drag you off," Rosie told me knowingly. "Shit, half the male population would drag you off if they had the chance."

I rolled my eyes.

"Oh and by the way, since Amy was busy with the bar, and you were, well...otherwise engaged," she snorted, "I just dealt with a few people wanting to buy stuff, don't worry I know how to work a cash register," she reassured me.

I welcomed the change of subject then had an idea. "Rosie, you don't happen to need any work at the moment?" I ventured cautiously, not knowing the protocol in asking Cade's sister to work for me.

I needn't have worried, she squealed clapping her hands. "Yes! I'm just doing some hours at the coffee shop, but I'm about to die of boredom."

"I can't guarantee a lot of hours yet, I'm not sure how busy we'll be, but we definitely need a third person," I replied.

"You are definitely going to be busy," Rosie agreed. "We have needed something like this store since like forever, and don't worry, I don't need full time or anything, just whenever you need me. I work part time at the garage for the club, so there's always something to do there."

She worked for the club? That was news. Though it shouldn't be surprising, Cade was her brother. And the VP.

"Since you're going to be working here, you're going to have to wear all the clothes, so go pick out some more stuff," I ordered with a grin.

Rosie squealed again and jumped into my arms. "I seriously *love* you, Gwen, this is the fucking shit!" She proceeded to pull away, grabbing Lucy and Ashley. "You bitches need to help me choose."

They both shot me warm smiles before disappearing with Rosie.

I turned towards Amy, leaning on the bar. "Well, looks like we have another employee." I sipped my cosmo. "I hope you don't mind me just hiring her without asking you."

"Mind?" she scoffed. "Fuck no, I'm over the moon, that girl is awesome! Stop trying to change the subject anyway," she demanded, knowing me too well. "What was that with the two hotties? It was like they were fighting over their shiny new toy — *that's* a position I wouldn't mind being in," she said dreamily.

"Trust me, you wouldn't want to be in that position, ever."

"Whatever, so you've finally decided to give in to the sexy biker?" she asked.

"No, not really, but fighting him was getting old, and I figure he'll have sex with me and lose interest, win win. The last thing I want is a repeat of Jimmy."

Amy glared at me, ready to interrupt but I didn't let her.

"So I have no danger of getting hurt when he taps and gaps, since I definitely don't want more than that, and you said so yourself, I need to get laid," I finished, draining my drink.

Amy considered me a beat. "Sweetie, I think that one wants you for much longer than one night. And you can't be scared to venture into something new, even though I am the first to be cautious over any guy riding a Harley, but from what I've seen he's nowhere near the same as The Prick. By the way, Cade is seriously checking you out right now, maybe leaning on the bar wearing that dress isn't the best idea," she laughed.

I didn't bother to move but glanced over my shoulder in Cade's direction, who was indeed checking my butt out with a hungry look on his face.

I straightened, my stomach pooling with heat at the gaze. "Whatever, I need to get back to helping out customers and talking to townspeople." I turned, then looked back at Amy. "Oh and by the way, I don't need a ride, I'm leaving with Cade tonight."

She raised her eyebrows.

"Don't say a word," I ordered.

She poked her tongue out at me, then spun to help people at the bar.

The rest of the night was a blur and people started to leave around 10:30pm. I had made some seriously good sales, so I was pretty pleased with myself. I found, to my dismay, Luke hadn't left. He cornered me not long after my chat with Amy.

"Look, Gwen, I know this isn't the place, but Fletcher is bad news. I won't say anything else, but I'll stop by the store this week, we can have coffee." He decided instead of asking. What was with the alpha males in this town?

Cade's glare was heavy at my back, so I didn't protest. "Yeah sure, Luke, sorry about...whatever that was before." I was genuinely sorry, he seemed like a nice guy.

"No worries, sweetheart, see you later." To my horror, he leaned in and kissed my cheek before leaving with a meaningful glare directed at Cade and the men.

"Crap," I muttered under my breath. I really didn't want the town's first impression of me that I was some skank, playing two guys within days of getting here.

I let the last of the guests out, only Amy, Rosie, and the small group of bikers were left in the store. I started to clean up, with Rosie and Amy helping. I guessed bad ass bikers didn't clean, because they just sat on the couches by the fitting rooms and talked in hushed tones with serious looks on their faces. Cade shot intense glances in my direction every now and then.

Just as we had finished, I grabbed two big trash bags and started to carry them towards the door, intending to put them in the dumpster in the alley. Strong arms took the bags from me.

"I've got them, babe."

"Oh, so bad ass bikers can't help clean up, but they can do the lifting?" I shot at him.

He smirked back.

I turned to see Rosie and Amy chatting lightheartedly with the rest of the men. I walked over to the little group, standing next to Amy.

"Are you okay to get home?" I asked her with concern, knowing she'd had one too many cosmos to drive.

"Yeah, girl, Brock here is taking me and Rosie home." She gave her best seductive look to a very attractive man whom I hadn't noticed, probably because all of my attention had been on Cade. He had longish blonde hair falling in messy waves around his face. His crooked nose looked like it had been broken a few too many times, but he worked the shit out of it. He had tanned skin, was quite lean but still built, looking almost like a surfer, apart from all the tats covering his arms and creeping up his neck. And the air of danger that seemed to waft from all of these men.

"Thanks, Brock." I tried not to drool.

"No problem, Gwen." He smiled at me, looking even more attractive. "Kick ass brownies by the way."

"Glad you liked them." I couldn't help but flutter my eyelashes a little. He was seriously hot.

Arms went around my middle and pulled me back into a hard body. "Ready to go, baby?" Cade whispered in my ear.

"Sure am," I replied, trying to keep the tremor out of my voice, feeling extremely nervous about being alone with him.

Rosie kissed my cheek, with Cade's arms still around me.

"Thanks for the great night, girl, and the job! I'll call you tomorrow." She looked behind me. "Catch you, big bro, take care of this one," she ordered Cade before sauntering out.

Amy blew me a kiss, winked at Cade, then followed Rosie and the men out the door. They all gave me and Cade chin lifts as they left, Lucky beamed at me. "Catch you, Gwen," he called cheerfully.

"Bye, Lucky." I waved at him. I really liked that kid.

As they shut the door, I realized Cade and I were alone. He spun me to face him. "Get your shit, babe, I'll get the lights and make sure everything is locked up."

I frowned at him, pissed at him ordering me around in my

store, before I could shoot back a sarcastic statement, he spoke again.

"And I appreciate you giving Rosie a job, babe, she's always loved clothes and shit. Didn't like her job making coffees and helping round at a dirty garage," he said sincerely, surprising me.

"I didn't do it for you, I really like your sister."

He smiled, giving me a firm kiss. "Thanks all the same."

I sighed, got my purse and keys and walked towards the front door. After locking up, Cade led me to his bike, which parked across the street. He grabbed a helmet from a little compartment under the seat and handed it to me. I took it, grumbling about my hair getting messed up, but putting the thing on anyway. He then handed me a jacket.

"Gets fuckin' cold on the bike, even in the summer. That dress ain't going to protect you from much."

No it was not, I thought.

I took the jacket from him and slid it on, savoring the musky, manly scent that clung to it.

Cade hopped on the bike. I took him in for a second, man he looked good on that thing.

"Well, Gwen, hop on," he ordered.

I glanced from Cade to the bike, trying to figure out how I was going to do this gracefully.

Oh fuck it.

I yanked my dress up and threw my leg over the bike, resting my heels on the little footholds and leaned into Cade. He turned to me.

"That was fuckin' hot, baby." He lay another scorching kiss on my mouth before turning to the front, grasping my hands and pulling them around his body.

He started the bike, it vibrated under me, the tremors travelling through my entire body, and we roared off into the night.

CHAPTER 5

WE RODE WELL OUT of town, the houses beginning to become few and far between. I hadn't been out this way before, not that I could see much anyway in the inky darkness. I just enjoyed being pressed up to Cade's hard body and the feeling of being on a bike again. I had ridden on a bike before, with The Prick, and I loved the adrenaline rush and the feeling of freedom that came from it.

We started to slow down and Cade turned down a driveway. A small house with a few lights left on came into sight. From what I could see in the dim light, it looked like a reasonably sized, well maintained beach house. I knew we were by the sea, the smell of saltwater invaded my senses. A black SUV was parked at the garage, and a surprisingly well kept garden surrounded the front of the house.

The bike slowed to a stop behind the SUV and Cade swung off. He held a hand out to me — what a gentleman. I took it, climbing off the bike, quickly yanking down my dress, which had ridden up to my waist. His eyes darkened, even blacker than the night surrounding as.

Cade walked me to the door, unlocking it and I walked into the house. I was interested to see what his house looked like, but I didn't get the chance. As soon as the door shut behind us, Cade pressed me up against it, mouth on mine.

I was surprised but quickly gave in to the kiss. His hands roamed over my body and I moaned into his mouth. The urgency between us was frantic, I was desperate to get more from him. He yanked up my dress roughly, hands going to my ass. I wrapped my legs around him and he lifted me effortlessly. He carried me in what I guessed was the direction of his bedroom, but I was impatient, grinding on his hard body. He obviously couldn't wait either, because he put me down on my unsteady feet.

"Arms up, baby," he commanded roughly, eyes black.

I immediately complied, raising my arms above my head. My dress was ripped off me, leaving me in my lacy red underwear. His eyes devoured me and a low growl erupted from his throat.

He shrugged his cut off his shoulders and threw it down beside him, eyes on me the entire time. I put my hands to his shirt and began to unbutton it, drowning in his turbulent gaze. As I got to the last button, I pulled his shirt down his arms and ran my hands up his stomach.

"Holy shit," I couldn't help but mutter.

He was ripped, I mean, eight pack. I thought those were just an urban legend. I wrapped my arms around his neck and hauled him down to me, needing his mouth again. He growled once more, lowering me to the floor, his hard body covering mine. His mouth left mine and trailed kisses down my neck. Ripping the cup of my bra down, he sucked on my nipple, I moaned, feeling like I was going to come already. While he sucked on my nipple, his hands traveled into my soaking panties and stroked me. I let out a little scream, I had never felt so responsive to anyone before.

Cade lifted his head. "Christ, baby, you're so wet." Then his head went lower. Way lower.

He continued to work his fingers on my clit, fucking my mouth with his tongue. That pushed me over the edge, waves of pleasure engulfed me. I slowly came down, feeling shaky, Cade staring at me.

"Watching you come, baby, the most beautiful thing I've ever seen." His words were low, barely audible.

"Cade, fuck me," I whispered, and his eyes went wild.

He pulled his jeans down, I heard the rustle of a condom, then, I shit you not, he *ripped* my panties off. I didn't realize that happened in real life.

"God, baby, this is all I have wanted to do since I laid eyes on you." He didn't say another word, he just plunged inside me.

I screamed into his mouth, pain and pleasure combining into an intense but amazing sensation.

Cade stopped, looking worried, but also pained. "Baby, you okay? Did I hurt you?" The cords in his neck were pulsing from his restraint.

"Don't stop," I managed to moan.

He immediately listened, pounding into me, filling me completely. He took me urgently and hard. It was the most amazing sex I had ever had. I felt another orgasm building as he continued to plunge into me. I screamed out his name as my insides clenched and pleasure washed over me once more. Cade grunted as I milked his release from him.

I was delirious with pleasure, it took a while for me to surface. Cade was settled on top of me, bracing himself on his elbows so he wasn't squashing me. His intense stare burned through me. He didn't say a word, just picked me up and strolled into his bedroom, laying me down on the bed.

"Don't move," he commanded

I watched him leave the room and go into what I guessed was the bathroom to take care of the condom. I realized I was still wearing my shoes but nothing else. I felt a bit self-conscious about being this exposed. I was mostly comfortable with my body, but I still felt uneasy about my small breasts during sex. I sat up to take off my shoes just as Cade entered the room, looking beyond sexy in the dim light. He stood naked in front of me, frowning.

"Babe, what did I say about moving?"

"I was just taking my shoes off," I began to argue.

He gently pushed me down on the bed, kissing me senseless, then whispered. "Let me."

He travelled down my body leaving a trail of fire where he kissed me, leaving out the most important part until he got to my feet. He slowly undid each shoe then slid them off, lifting up my leg and kissing the bottoms of my feet. He travelled back up my body, stopping between my legs looking up at me with savage look on his face.

"Gonna eat you till you come, babe, then I'm gonna fuck you, make you come again."

I was unable to say anything as he settled between my legs and blew my fucking mind. The things he could do with that tongue. As I recovered from another world-shaking orgasm, Cade whispered in my ear. "You taste so sweet, Gwen, like honey."

He reached beside his bed, where he tagged another condom, sliding it on and pushing into me, getting to work on orgasm number four.

———

I woke up feeling dazed, registering Cade's arms tightly around me. I was tucked into his shoulder, my leg thrown over his thighs. The dull morning light shone through the windows, the curtains hadn't been drawn.

I peeked at Cade, who was still sleeping. God, he was attractive, his inky black hair mussed over his face, stubble covering his chin. I gazed down at his body, which was even more jaw dropping in the light of day. His arms were seriously big, not body-builder big, like Navy Seal big — muscles built to be used, not paraded around in a gym. Tattoos covered his arms and chest. I moved my head up to study them more closely, but Cade's arm tightened around me.

"Morning, baby," he grumbled, voice rough from sleep.

He hauled me up his body, devouring my mouth. I wasn't usually a fan of this kind of thing in the morning, not before mutual teeth brushing anyway, but I got lost in his kiss.

His hands roamed over my naked body, I felt his hard on pressing my stomach.

I smiled getting an idea. My mouth left his, traveling down his body, licking his abs – could you blame me – then grabbing him in my hand. I licked the small bead of wetness on the tip. I was a little bit nervous, he was big, but I was confident in my ability.

"Baby," he groaned when I took him in my mouth, sliding my tongue along and following my mouth with my hand. I moaned, getting turned on over the amount of power I had over this man.

"Jesus, Gwen," he growled.

I slid my tongue along the underside of his shaft and brought my hand down my stomach, rubbing my clit as I took Cade further into my mouth. I felt his hand on my head and he thrust up, fucking my mouth.

"Gwen, unless you want to take all of me right now, you better stop," he grunted.

I rubbed myself frantically, the start of an orgasm pulsing through me. Cade groaned as he spurted into my mouth. I whimpered and swallowed it all, my orgasm breaking me apart. I sat up and Cade hooked under my arms, pulling me up his body.

"Fuck, baby, you are the hottest little piece I've ever had, your mouth is goddamned magic," he told me, voice rough.

"Glad I could be of service." I winked at him dreamily.

Resting on top of his body, I took a proper look around his bedroom.

Definitely a man's room, clothes were strewn about. There was a huge dresser in the corner, with deodorant and spare change atop it, a Harley poster behind it. He had an en suite to the side, and his bedside table was cluttered but tidy. I glanced at the clock beside the bed.

"Fuck!" I yelled. I tried to scramble off Cade, but his arms held me like a vice.

"Jesus, Gwen, you trying to give me a heart attack? What?" he asked, sounding slightly irritated and amused at the same time.

"I slept in, that's what. I was meant to be at the store like an hour ago!" I kept scrambling, but Cade's arms were solid. I blew the hair out of my face and glared at him. "Cade, let me up," I ordered sternly.

"Calm down, babe, it's not the end of the world, so you're a bit late. You own the place, no big," he said nonchalantly, hands trying to distract me by squeezing my ass.

"You may not think it's a big deal, but it's my first proper day of being open, being late is not responsible. Crap, where's my phone? I bet Amy's been calling me." I pulled at his arms. "Seriously, Cade, let me up now! I have to go."

I started to panic, I hated not being organized, it had been a kind of obsession since my attack. I liked to be in control, set my plans out.

Cade frowned, then released me.

I huffed. "About time." I started to get off the bed, but arms yanked me back, I squealed, Cade silenced me with a kiss.

"Needed your mouth before you left this bed."

"Well, if you remember correctly, you had my mouth not five minutes ago," I replied smartly, scouring the floor for my underwear.

"I remember, babe, be sure about that," he grumbled.

I flicked my head back to him, seeing him lying on the bed, hands behind his head, looking pretty relaxed.

"Can you give me a ride back to my house?" I asked. "Or give me a number for a taxi?" I added, not wanting to expect him to run around after me, this was just sex after all.

"I'll take you, babe," he clipped, watching me.

"Thanks," I replied, still looking for my clothes, then remembering they would most likely be in the hall, after last night.

I blushed thinking about that, and was very aware of Cade's eyes on my naked body. I didn't like that. The morning light was streaming through the windows, making it all too easy to see my scars. I didn't want him to notice them and ask questions, so I quickly swiped a t-shirt off the floor and threw it on. I turned back to Cade. "I'm borrowing this."

His eyes grew dark and he looked at me with fierce intensity. "Yeah, babe," he replied.

Weird.

I turned. "I'm going to get my dress...man I have to do the walk of shame!" I whined while walking out the door, Cade's manly chuckle followed me.

I stepped into the hall towards what I thought was the direction of the front door. I'd been a bit too busy last night to remember the layout.

I peered at pictures scattered on the walls, one of Cade and the men I saw at Rosie's, all grinning at the camera, outside a garage. Another was of Cade and Rosie, with an older, hard looking woman with dark hair, blonde streaks and familiar gray eyes. She was a biker babe and was beautiful, but it looked like she had seen a lot in her life.

I turned my gaze away, focusing on the mission at hand, which was not taking a trip down Cade's memory lane. This was just a one night stand after all.

"Aha!" I whispered, finding my dress and the tattered remains of my underwear.

I quickly whipped off Cade's tee, savoring the musky scent and trying to think of a way I could sneak it out without him noticing. Alas, my Prada was not big enough to hide it.

I pulled my dress on and shoved my ruined panties in my purse, which was lying beside the pile of clothes. I quickly checked my phone. Six missed calls, three from Amy, three from random numbers, a couple of voicemails and a text.

Amy: Hey, girl, I'm guessing you are in the midst of a sexfest (woo fucking hoo!) so don't worry, I have opened the store, and Rosie is with me. No rush, we have things sorted. Glad those cobwebs have been cleared.

Kisses xxx

I laughed out loud at Amy, silently thanking the gods that my friend was not as slutty as I was. At least not last night. I was going to rush, though. My store was my dream and I wasn't going to let a man distract me from putting a hundred percent into it.

I still had my phone open on Amy's text when Cade's voice whispered in my ear. "See, baby, no rush."

I jumped, hating people sneaking up on me. I whirled my head around, directing my second glare of the day at Cade. It didn't help I had not consumed one ounce of caffeine, luckily my orgasm would be enough to sustain me.

"Don't do that, you scared the bejesus out of me," I said tightly. "And don't read my texts over my shoulder, that's rude."

He ignored me, wrapping his arms around me, running them

up my body, caressing my breasts. I couldn't help but moan, just a little.

"I think we better keep working on getting those cobwebs out, babe, don't think I was thorough enough," Cade told me gruffly.

I so didn't find that funny. I pulled away from him – with extreme effort – and crossed my arms. "I need you to take me home now, please."

Cade frowned. "That keen to get away, are we?"

"No, I just have work to do, a job? Do you know what that is?" I said with a slight bite, wondering if he even had a job, one that didn't include committing felonies.

Cade's frown deepened. "Yeah, Gwen, I do," he clipped. "Get your shit and we'll go."

Uh-oh, maybe I was being a bitch. I thought about apologizing but was just too stubborn for that. "I'm ready," I said, trying to avoid his angry stare.

He picked up his jeans and pulled them on *commando* before slipping on the tee I was just wearing. There was something very intimate about that.

"Right, let's go." He all but pushed me towards the front door.

I quickly took in what I could see of the rest of his house. We were walking towards the foyer, with a coat rack piled full of jackets and a couple of pairs of boots below it. As we approached the door, I glanced to my left to see an open plan living room/kitchen area jutting off the foyer.

It was sparse, with a couch that had seen better days sitting in the middle, an old afghan thrown haphazardly over the back. In front of it was a cluttered coffee table, littered with beer bottles and what looked like motorcycle parts. A huge TV took up a lot of space in the room, it looked top of the range. Boys and their toys. I mentally shook my head. To the right of the living room was a big kitchen with a breakfast bar sitting in front and stools in

front of that. I craned my head to get a better look, and hadn't
realized I had all but stopped walking, that was until I felt Cade's
heavy glare.

"Babe," he clipped staring at me, a hint of amusement
dancing in his eyes.

"What?" I asked slightly irritated with him for interrupting
my nosing.

"You want to get to your store or you want to get the floor
plan of my house?"

I screwed my face up at him. "My store, thank you," I
muttered and continued to walk towards the door, where he
stood.

Someone pounded on the door, loudly. I jumped, the obviously strong fist banging on the door brought back some nasty
memories. Cade glanced at me, looking puzzled before he
opened it.

The man on the other side of it did nothing to help my
already fragile nerves. He was big, not as tall or as built as Cade
but still imposing, built like a pit bull and looking about as nice —
this guy was scary.

Bald head, maybe in his early fifties, he had a black goatee
covering his chin. A tattoo crawled up his neck, words I couldn't
make out. He was wearing jeans with a black thermal and a cut
over top. My eyes zeroed in on the "President" patch on his cut. I
looked back to his face and into his eyes, which were currently
focused on me.

One look at this guy and I knew. I didn't know with Jimmy.
Well, not until it was too late because he hid it under his good
looks, his charm and his intoxicating presence. But after being
around the people Jimmy associated with, and after my attack, I
knew. I knew bad when I saw it. It's not something in a person's
eyes, it's a *lack* of something. Humility, compassion, I didn't know
for sure. I didn't know how to describe it. But when you'd looked

evil straight in the face, you don't forget the shape of it. I knew I was looking at a version of what nearly got me killed over a year ago.

He was now glaring at me, pointedly looking me up and down, in a way that made me need a shower. I glared right back even though I was scared shitless on the inside. The "Prez" gave me one last leer then dismissed me, focusing on Cade.

"We got a problem at the garage. Your skills are needed. Now," he ordered, without a good morning, hello, nothing.

Cade's frown, already deep at seeing the wordless exchange between me and his "President," turned into a glower.

"I'll drop Gwen off and be there in twenty," he declared with an edge to his voice.

"No, you come now. Get one of the prospects to come up and take your bitch home." The "President" gave me a sneer, looking at Cade as if he expected him to jump to attention.

What an asshole. I knew that bikers referred to women as "bitches" and I didn't like it, but most of the time it was offhand, came natural. This guy meant it to degrade me, dismiss me. Especially by the glance he flicked my way, like I was some whore.

I guessed, though I couldn't be sure, this might be a usual occurrence for Cade — as another thing I knew about bikers, was they liked to fuck, often, and with different girls, most of whom were disposable.

The air got thick and Cade's glare went thunderous.

"Steg. I got Gwen. Ain't one of the prospects coming to get her. Told you I'll be twenty fuckin' minutes," he ground out.

Steg glared right back at Cade, then me, looking like he was ready to blow his top. "And *I said* we need you. Now." His face was red, he obviously didn't like being talked back to.

"Yeah, well, since you need me, you're going to have to wait," Cade declared with barely contained anger. "I'll be there in twenty."

I bit back a smile as Cade seized my hand, pushed past red-faced Steg and directed me towards his truck. I wondered why we weren't taking the bike, then I glanced down at my dress, reasoning that it wouldn't travel well in daylight. I wondered if Cade had thought of that, if so, that was pretty darned considerate.

"Get in," he ordered, opening the door for me.

He slammed my door shut once I was in, rounded the truck, hopped in, started it and roared down the driveway. We drove in silence for a bit, a very loaded silence. Cade's anger took up all the room in the cab.

I fidgeted, trying to think of something to say. I knew mentioning, whatever just happened was not the best idea, but I struggled to think of another topic of conversation. I doubt he wanted to discuss Karl Lagerfeld's latest collection.

"What the fuck was that, Gwen?" Cade yelled, breaking the silence.

"What was what?" I asked back, with false confusion.

"You know what. Whatever the fuck passed between you and Steg just before. You don't even know him and you looked at him like he just ran over your puppy. Granted, he is not a good man, but fuck that was the first time you laid eyes on the fucker." His eyes turned back to the road, waiting for an answer.

"I have no idea what you're talking about," I said defiantly.

"For fuck's sake, Gwen, stop fucking lying!" he bellowed, hands tightening on the steering wheel.

I sighed, letting my ignorant act fall. "I know what bad looks like, Cade. And I know what he is, and it's bad that lies behind his eyes," I whispered, my eyes on the road.

Cade's gaze was heavy on me. "How do you know what bad looks like, Gwen?" he asked, his voice low and gentle.

I ignored him and looked out my window, wishing I hadn't said anything, but I couldn't help it, Cade was already consuming me. It was like I didn't have control when I was with him. He seemed to be able to make me say anything, *do* anything. I needed to get that control back.

"Gwen," he said my name firmly, demanding attention.

I turned my head to stare at him. "I just do." I didn't elaborate.

"That ain't an answer, baby." His eyes were locked on mine. I wondered how long he could drive like that.

I held his eyes. "It's all you're getting, *baby*," I mimicked his tone, sarcastically.

His eyes went back to the road. "For now," he muttered under his breath.

We finally got to my house, the rest of the ride had been silent. As he pulled into my driveway, I got all my stuff together, ready to jump out of the truck, dash to my door and lock any and all men out for the rest of eternity. But bad ass alpha bikers had the sixth sense — he grabbed my arm, firmly, but not enough to hurt.

"Not so fast, baby." He moved his hands to frame my face, pulling me forward and kissing me so intensely I momentarily lost all coherent thought. He drew back, not too far, hands still on either side of my head. "Got shit to do, I don't know how long it's going to take, but I when I'm done we're gonna talk. About how you know 'bout all kinds of bad and why you go as white as a fuckin' ghost when men wearing cuts get within five feet of you."

His icy grey gaze looked determined. Shit.

Rage started to boil up within me. *How in the fuck does he think after sleeping with me once he has the right to order me to tell him anything?* I opened my mouth to tell him to go and fuck himself but paused. I had been fighting him, cursing at him since this whole thing began and look where it got me, screwed in more ways than one. And only in one way I liked. Did I not read enough romances to know that the badass alpha males liked the sassy women who threw attitude? They liked the challenge. I decided to play this a little differently.

I leaned into Cade, who was still holding my head, and touched my lips lightly to his. "I've got to go, honey." I watched as he gazed at me in surprise. "Do whatever you got to do, I'll see you later," I finished sweetly.

I hopped out of the truck, walking towards my door without looking back. Only when I got inside did I hear him leave.

After taking a lightening quick shower and getting ready faster than I thought I could, I made it to town just before lunch. I stopped by the local deli to grab me, Amy, and Rosie some sandwiches. One of the many things I loved about America was their sandwiches. Americans did not fuck around with their sandwiches.

Arms full, I braced myself as I entered my store, expecting a full inquisition the moment I got my Gucci clad foot inside. But luckily both girls were busy with customers.

"Hi, everyone," I chirped, smiling at the customers, recognizing some of them from last night.

I strolled towards the counter, intending to dump our lunch on it, when a perfectly groomed woman stopped in front of me. She had chocolate brown hair, which was styled in a complicated but totally awesome updo. Her makeup was outlandish and almost over the top, but somehow she made it tasteful. She was wearing head to toe pink. Don't ask me how, but she made it work. Looking to be in her early thirties, she was curvy and gorgeous.

"Girl, I heard you were in a tug of war with the two hottest men in this town, both on opposites sides of the law." She raised a perfectly shaped eyebrow at me before continuing. "Not that I am judging. I would *so* go there, either way. I would have paid to see the face-off between those two boys. It looks like Cade's pretty much staked his claim on you, considering you were on the back of his bike last night and you're rolling in here at this time." Her southern twang was so slick it was a miracle I could understand her.

I blinked, unsure of who this woman was, how she knew all of this and how to respond to everything she just said. She didn't sound bitchy, just overly nosey, but friendly. "Um..." was all I managed before she got started again.

She put her well-manicured hand over her chest. "Now where are my manners? I'm Laura Maye. I own the bar down the street, and after looking in your store, probably your best customer." She gestured with the shopping bags I hadn't noticed before, which were a dusty pink with white ribbon handles and stamped with the word "Phoenix." My bags were the shit.

"Got to run anyway, doll, I'm late for a facial. I'll be back real soon, though. Want to hear all about last night." She blew me a kiss, strutting out the door, yelling over her shoulder. "Bye, Amy girl, nice to meet you, see yah, Rosie!"

The girls both waved back. I stood frozen for a second, in one of those, did that just happen moments. This town was weird. But in a good way.

I continued to the counter, dropping the bags of food, turning to see both Amy and Rosie looking at me with smirks on their faces. I resisted the urge to flip them the bird, seeing as they were both with customers.

"Lunch," I announced.

I turned on my heel and stomped into my office before I could get any teasing questions. I ignored the muted laughter behind me.

Another thing I loved about my store was the back office, it was small, but awesome. I had it painted a dusty pink, my white desk in the middle of the room. A couple of Vogues were stacked on one side, and a tray of candles at the front of my laptop. Behind the desk was a light yellow upholstered swivel chair. To the left of my desk was a pale yellow printed couch, and on the back wall was a huge framed photo of my hometown back in New Zealand. It was taken when Ian had dragged me along with him to go hunting one winter when he was home. I did this under huge protest. The sight of blood made me squeamish, seeing the animal carcasses that Dad and Ian brought home on a semi-regular basis was enough for me. I had said as much to Ian, but he laid the guilt trip on me.

"Sis, I'm not home for long, who knows when I'll be back next."

I grumbled about it, but I went. I still to this day don't know why he wanted to spend his short leave hunting animals when his job was to hunt humans. Despite my complaints, I actually enjoyed it, not the killing animals part, but the hiking in the hills, amongst the beautiful scenery with my brother who I missed dearly.

I took the picture when we got to the top of the mountain. With the view of the whole valley we lived in, and then some. Our hometown in the winter was magical. Snow capped the hills, temperatures that dropped to well below freezing, causing the bare trees to turn white with frost. It had been early morning, the sun had just risen, a soft pink dancing on the horizon, and the street lights of the town still twinkling. It was amazing, our small town nestled among the rough hills, the whole valley dressed in winter white. I loved that picture.

I sat behind my desk and cranked up my laptop, sipping the coffee that was slowly contributing to normal brain function, after half of it had been screwed out of me last night. My phone rang from the depths of my handbag, I managed to answer just before it went to voicemail.

"Hello," I greeted nervously, hoping it wasn't Cade. I hadn't given him my number or anything, but he was a super badass with super badass powers. Or more likely he got it off his sister.

"Sweetie!" my mum screamed.

I relaxed into my chair, smiling. It had been a while since I had heard from either of my parents, I missed them.

"I've been thinking about you, things have just been so busy I haven't had the time to ring! How was the opening? You getting settled in okay? Making any new friends?" My mum shot multiple questions at me at once, I was used to it.

"The opening was great, I'm emailing you pictures of the store now." I started typing on my laptop. "We're settling in fine, Amy did a freaking great job of the house, but I'm sure you've already seen it all."

"Yes, yes, Amy sent me pictures *ages* ago, I had the final say in most design decisions," Mum told me matter of factly.

I rolled my eyes. "Of course you did, Mother. And yes, we are making some awesome new friends. Amy got us invited to a party the other night. It was heaps of fun and I met some lovely people, one of whom I hired to work in the store. Looks like we are going to need her, things are busy already. I think a clothing store was exactly what the female residents of Amber needed."

I glanced up to see Amy leaning against the door jamb, munching on a sandwich. '*Mum*,' I mouthed at her.

"Hi, Lacey!" Amy shouted, mouth full.

"Amy says hi, Mum," I said sarcastically.

"I heard her, honey. I'm so happy she's there with you, you have such a great friend in her," Mum murmured softly.

"I know, Mum. How's Dad?" I asked after my father, because, like Ian, he took my attack pretty hard. He felt like he should've

MAKING THE CUT 103

protected me or something, no matter that he was on the other side of the world and it was my stupid decisions that nearly got me killed, but they were both macho men who blamed themselves.

"He's doing good, sweetie," Mum answered, voice still soft. "He's off on some trip, down in Stewart Island, thank god, he was driving me insane."

"Mum! He's retired, which he deserves, he's worked very hard through his life," I snapped.

"I know," my mum snapped back. "But he doesn't know how to be retired, he just annoys me and now he isn't working, all he wants is sex."

"La la la la!" I shouted, cutting her off. "I do not need to hear about that, ew."

"You are such a prude, Gwen, you're a grown woman, you should be happy your father and I have a healthy sex life," my mother chided me.

"Whatever, Mum. I do not need to know details. Capice?"

"All right, all right," she conceded, for about a millisecond. "How about you, sweetie? Any men in your new town?" She sounded almost hopeful.

"Nope." I lied. "None at all, this town has no men. Well, not under the age of fifty anyway."

Amy, who was still leaning at the door, shamelessly listening, narrowed her eyes.

"Don't listen to her, Lacey!" she shouted, trying to wrestle the phone from me.

"What is Amy saying? Gwenevere, are you lying to your mother?" Mum asked sharply.

"No, Mum, sorry, really busy, got to go. Love you," I called, still trying to fight off Amy.

"Don't you dare..." mother's angry but amused tone ordered before I ended the call.

I glared at Amy, who was now leaning casually at my desk, taking another bite out of her sandwich, as if nothing happened.

"What the fuck was that, Abrams?" I screeched.

"What?" Amy shrugged. "You should tell your mother about your two sexy suitors and about your no doubt wild night last night." She smirked.

"That's the last thing I'm going to do, my mother does not need to know about my sex life and especially not about Cade. She would die," I exclaimed dramatically.

"I doubt that," she replied dryly. Then, with a smile on her face, she waggled her brows. "Now, tell me all about your wild night of passion between you and sexy Cade." She looked like an excited child. "I am sooooo glad you finally got laid, was about time. How hot was it? On a scale of one to Channing?"

"Hot," I answered. "Like, I lost count of the amount of orgasms I had, hot." I decided to give her a little. I usually told her everything about my sex life, but for some reason I wanted to keep last night to myself. Between Cade and I.

"Holy shit, really? How big was his cock? Is he rough and hard or gentle and slow?" she demanded.

"I am telling you no more." I decided, and her face fell. "I will say, my favorite La Perla underwear was ripped, *ripped* off me."

At this, she fell back on the couch, dramatically fanning her face.

"Enough about me anyway," I continued. "Anything happen between you and Brock?"

Amy sat up abruptly, frowning. "No. Why would it? He's an asshole."

I sat back in my chair, not expecting Amy's defensive reaction. "Wow." I held my hands up in mock surrender. "I was just asking, he's hot and seemed nice and you were giving him the look," I teased.

"He is not that hot, nor is he nice, nor was I giving him the look," she snapped.

"Were so," I shot at her.

"Were not."

"Whatever! How's the morning been?" I asked letting her off the hook, but something definitely went on there, something I would find out later.

"Ohmigod, it's been crazy, girl! Word spread. Like, fast. People have been coming in from out of town to shop, we got ourselves some big spenders. Just because people live in a hick town does not mean the woman ain't got style. "

"Better get to work then."

The store wouldn't be the real work. It was making myself not think of Cade and whatever he'd awoken inside me.

CHAPTER 6

AMY WAS RIGHT, word spread, like, crazy fast. Amy, Rosie, and I were run off our feet for the rest of the week with women coming in, some for complete wardrobe overhauls. I was going to have to do a new order soon, a big one.

Working out on the floor really helped me figure out what the populace of women wanted, but I had heaps to do, so I would need to hire more staff. And luckily, with the way things seemed to be going, I would more than be able to afford it.

I also spent the week trying to evade Rosie's multiple questions about me and Cade. She seemed itching for us to get together, no matter I hadn't heard from him since the Thursday morning he left because he had, "shit to do."

It was now Tuesday, the following week. I definitely expected to see him, keen as he seemed. And even though this should have been what I wanted, I found it hard to keep my mind off him. I had been non-stop with the store, but Cade was constantly in my head, and I was kind of hurt, he declared me as "his" one minute then no communication the next.

I did get a distraction with Luke coming in every morning

and delivering me a coffee, which had become a bit of a ritual when he discovered I had a substance abuse problem when it came to caffeine. We didn't talk much, given I was usually always busy, but it was nice. I really liked him, and he was definitely hot, but not like Cade. I told myself I would give him a chance. The next time he asked me for dinner I wouldn't blow him off saying I was too tired, I would say yes.

━━

I was at the counter, Rosie had gone to get lunch, and I had given Amy the afternoon off, since we were quiet. I was flipping through some look books, circling stuff I thought I might order for the store, when the bell over the door chimed.

I looked up, smile on my face ready to greet a customer, and my eyes met Luke's. As he sauntered up to the counter, I mentally congratulated myself for deciding to go out with him. He looked good. His blond hair was tousled and swept over his face, and he was clean shaven. I'd never seen him with so much as a shadow of stubble.

He was wearing his uniform, and fuck did he wear the shit out of that thing. He pushed his aviators to the top of his head as he approached the counter and rested his hand on his gun belt, out of habit, I thought. But man, did that make him look even hotter.

"Gwen," he greeted me, his rough voice caressing my name.

"Luke," I breathed, glad about my outfit choice.

I was wearing short, white tailored shorts with a dusty pink silk shirt tucked in. My hair was up in a messy ponytail and I had multiple gold necklaces wrapped around my neck. I had on my third favorite pair of heels, they were pink with a criss cross of straps rounding my ankles. I felt good, confident.

His eyes assessed me, a small smile on his lips. "Thought we could go outside the store and grab some of your drug of choice and perhaps some lunch?" he asked, eyes twinkling.

I started to tell him I couldn't until Rosie got back when I heard the chime of the bell. Rosie bustled in, hands full, looking down to make sure she wasn't spilling anything.

"Hey, girl. I got us lemon cake as well, because Dylan makes the most kick ass lemon cake. Seriously, it's almost better than sex," she yelled, making her way towards us. She looked up and froze when she saw Luke, red crept up her cheeks. "Um, hey, Luke," she muttered sounding embarrassed.

Weird, she didn't usually get embarrassed, about anything.

"Hey, Rosie." Luke gave her a chin lift. "You're right, that cake is the shit, can't say it's better than sex, though," he teased and Rosie's blush deepened. She scooted past him, handing me my coffee, eyes looking anywhere but Luke.

"Thanks, babe."

"No problem!" she replied with false brightness and the gears started to turn in my head.

Shit, did she have a crush on Luke? She was never here when he came in the mornings, so this was the first time I'd seen them together. My spidey senses were picking something up, the way she avoided making direct eye contact with him and was as red as a beetroot. I bet she was struggling with this crush, considering the mutual hatred Luke and Cade had for each other.

"See you've got coffee, babe," Luke's voice interrupted my thought process.

"Um yeah." I met his eyes, deciding there was no way I'd even think about starting something with him, especially if Rosie liked him.

And if I was honest with myself, I didn't like him, I would just be using him to try and quell the hurt of Cade using me and then forgetting about me, although that's exactly what I said I wanted. God, I hated being a girl sometimes.

"Babe?" Luke asked through the fog in my mind.

Damn, that was twice in a row I had retreated into my mental trance while I was supposed to be participating in a conversation.

"Sorry, what?" I replied, sipping my coffee, trying to sound alert.

Luke chuckled. "I asked if you wanted to go for a walk instead."

I looked to Rosie, who was sipping her coffee and trying not to frown, whether it was because of Cade or because of what she obviously felt for Luke, I wasn't sure.

"Sure." I turned to Rosie. "You going to be okay on your own for a while?"

"Yeah, fine. Take your time!" she replied with more of that false brightness.

"We won't be long," I assured her, grabbing my shades and coffee.

Luke put his hand to the small of my back, opening the door, he kept it there, directing me towards the beach.

"So how's your day going?" he inquired conversationally.

"Good!" I exclaimed. "Today is the first day since we opened we haven't been run off our feet."

Luke looked at me sideways while we keep walking. "That's good to hear, sweetheart."

"So how's business with you? Crime running rampant on the streets of our little town?" I joked. My words did not have their intended comedic effect, Luke's face turned hard.

"Been quiet since the boys been out of town," he said, still watching me closely.

"The boys?" I parroted, my voice high.

"Yeah, the Sons have been off on some ride, no doubt causing trouble in another county." His tone was bitter.

Guess that explained why I hadn't heard the roar of Harley

pipes down the mean streets of our town, and why I hadn't seen Cade.

"Um, so I'm guessing there's no love lost between you and the club?" I asked softly, trying to tread carefully.

Luke gave me a look, then gestured for me to sit on one of the tables outside the deli. We hadn't really addressed what had happened the night of the opening, I was sure Luke didn't miss what went on with Cade and I.

"That's a bit of an understatement, Gwen," he replied, voice tight. "They're a gang, not a club, whatever they say different is a lie. They are criminals, and they've brought trouble and death to this town. I'm doing everything I can to stop that, to put them where they belong, which is behind bars."

I blinked. Shocked at not only his statement but the raw emotion in his voice.

"Death?" I asked, a sick feeling curled up in the pit of my stomach.

"Yep, every now and then one of the Sons is killed in some shady way or another, or someone connected to them. They never used to hurt women, though." He looked away as if he was remembering someone.

I struggled with nausea. "They hurt women?"

Luke nodded sharply and was silent for a moment. "Her name was Laurie, sweetest girl you'd ever meet, I grew up with her. She fell for one of the boys and fell hard. Didn't matter what he was into, what her parents thought. Trust me, they were not impressed to say the least, but they also loved their daughter, wanted her to be happy." His gaze was intense and full of anguish. "Guess the boys had something going with a rival gang, drugs, pussy, I don't know what it was about. Anyway, the gang decided enough was enough and they needed to teach the boys a lesson. Grabbed Laurie one day, said they would kill her if the boys didn't back down."

I gulped, knowing the story didn't have a happy ending. Luke continued, eyes on mine.

"They didn't give a shit, even fuckin' Bull. He was supposed to love that girl, didn't leave the goddamned clubhouse. The next day Laurie was dropped off in front of the clubhouse. Raped, savagely beaten, stabbed. Her fucking *face* tattooed. She died in hospital the next day." His voice was flat, almost devoid of emotion, but his jaw was hard.

I couldn't believe what I was hearing. "How long ago did this happen?" I asked with a shaky voice.

Luke still had that faraway look in his eyes. "Just under a year ago."

A year?

Tears ran down my face, I was unable to control them. This story sounded too similar to what happened to me — shit, it almost happened at the same time. Was this some kind of sick karmic joke?

Luke seemed to shake himself out of his trance when he saw my tears. He gently pulled me into his arms. "Fuck, Gwen, you okay? I'm sorry, I didn't mean to be that harsh."

The words didn't register and I continued crying, my breath hitching. This was meant to be my quiet little town, I was meant to heal here, not have my wounds ripped open again. How cruel could fate be? To thrust me into a situation which posed so many similarities to one that almost killed me. How stupid could I be? To jump straight into bed with someone who came from a world that almost killed me.

I was so out of it I didn't hear the approaching bikes, didn't notice Luke's hands tightening on my shoulders. I was so angry with myself for breaking down, I had been holding this all in since I first encountered Cade, this was the last straw.

"What the fuck?" Cade's voice rumbled from behind me.

Speak of the Devil and he shall appear.

I blinked the tears out of my eyes, glancing up to see Cade standing in front of us, arms crossed, stance threatening. When he got a good look at my face, his anger turned palpable. He was flanked by Lucky and Bull, both wearing blank expressions under their sunglasses.

"Crawford. Take your hands off my woman, then explain to me why *the fuck* she is in that state," Cade commanded, his voice full of restrained fury.

"Watch your mouth, you forget who you're talking to, Fletcher," Luke clipped. "As far as I know, Gwen is not your woman."

Still, he took his hands off me.

"Not forgetting anything, Crawford. I know I am currently talking to a prick who not only had his hands on my woman, but made her fucking cry. And trust me, she's fucking *mine*," Cade promised, shades on me.

I stood on shaky feet. Cade took a step towards me, stopping when I retreated.

"Baby…" His was voice gentle, as if it was just the two of us.

"Stay away from me," I whispered brokenly.

Luke stood in front of me protectively. "You heard her, Fletcher, beat it."

Cade scowled at Luke, then dismissed him, focusing on me. "Whatever he said to you…"

I couldn't deal with this. Any of it. I turned away and ran, ignoring the male shouts behind me. I ran in the direction of the beach, not knowing where else to go. I reached the sand, pausing to take off my shoes. I walked until the water was kissing my ankles. I stood, looking blankly at the horizon, a million thoughts running through my head.

I must have been there for a while, because my feet and ankles were numb when I blinked my demons away. But at least I could feel, at least I was alive. Unlike Laurie. I didn't know her, but she could have been me so easily. Still could be if I didn't sort myself out.

I slowly walked out of the water, choosing not to react when I saw Cade leaning against his bike with his arms crossed, watching me. I turned my back to him, sinking down into the sand, watching the waves, trying to beat away the demons still knocking at the corner of my mind.

"*She was beaten, savagely, raped, stabbed. Face fucking tattooed.*"

Jumbled words from Luke's short but heartbreaking story rushed through my mind. Beaten. Stabbed. Raped. Sweet girl. Clueless girl. Like me, she just fell in love with the wrong guy. Yeah, that guy didn't kill her, but she would still be alive if it wasn't for gangs and their fucking politics.

I didn't react when Cade sat behind me, his powerful thighs coming around either side of mine. Strong arms pulled me to his chest. I sat rigidly, trying to work up the strength to fight him off. Problem was, all of my strength was going towards not having a mental fucking breakdown. It was focusing on what an idiot I was for letting another man, so much like the one that almost killed me, into my bed, under my skin.

"Babe," he murmured in my ear, voice soft.

I ignored him and continued looking blankly at the sea.

"Crawford had no fucking right to talk to you like that, badmouth the fucking club." He still sounded soft, he was angry, but he was checking that anger for me.

I went as hard as stone. "God forbid he badmouth the fucking precious club," I hissed. "Never mind the girl that was *murdered.*"

At my words, Cade tensed. "You don't know anything about Laurie, Gwen."

"Yeah, I do. I know she fell in love with a man, a dangerous man, who at the time seemed exciting, made her feel alive. And no matter how dark things got, the love was still there to make it seem light, so she could ignore the signs, the big fucking flashing red signs that should have made her run the other way. But she didn't and that got her dead. Raped. Beaten. Dead." My voice cracked at the end.

Cade flinched at my words, his arms tightening around me. Then I was in the air, turned so I was straddling him, his hands at my face.

"Need your eyes, Gwen," he muttered, staring at me so hard I was sure he was staring into my soul. That he was examining the broken pieces of it.

"Bull loved Laurie. Fuck, never seen a love like it. They were the last two people you'd ever think to be together. Him, a huge fucker with tattoos. She was tiny, smaller than you, babe, with blonde hair that shone like the sun. Smile, Christ, she had a great smile, made everyone happy just by being around her. They didn't seem like they'd fit, but you saw them together, you knew, they fit perfect for each other, made sense."

"Cade..." I interrupted, not wanting to hear anymore, but his eyes turned hard.

"I'm speaking now, babe, shut it. Wait till you hear the whole fucking story before you say one more word." His voice was tight. "We had shit going with another club, not gonna elaborate. But that shit got bad, brothers both sides felt the hits. But no women, fuck, women never see that kind of shit. Until that day. Laurie went for a walk, a walk in the town she lived, place she felt safe, happy. They snatched her right off the street, broad daylight, fuckin' witnesses." Cade's eyes turned feral, he was devastated and furious.

Of its own volition, my hand reached up to stroke his cheek.

"Soon as we found out, had to lock Bull down. He was ripping things apart, in a rage like I never seen, he couldn't check it, couldn't rein it in, couldn't help Laurie like that. We had boys out looking for her, even got the fuckin' pigs involved, 'cause we knew what they'd do to her. Didn't help. We got the call, telling us to back down or they'd kill Laurie. We knew they'd kill her either way, these weren't the kind of guys to just drop her off, unharmed. Minute they got what they wanted they'd put a bullet in her brain. We were in an impossible position."

I felt the pain in his voice. I immediately knew Luke was wrong, those men did care about this girl, but Luke's mind was so clouded by hate, that he couldn't see the love.

"Cade – "

"I'm speakin', babe." He sighed, looking to the ocean then back at me. "We gave in to those boys, there would have been blood, a shit storm we couldn't weather, the town couldn't weather. We knew either way, Laurie got dead. So we tried to find her, ripped apart the fucking countryside looking for her. We couldn't, they dropped her off the next day. Left her alive, barely, they did that on purpose. It was the worst day of my goddamned life, seeing that girl like that, seeing my brother, unravel. Life went right out from behind his eyes." He blinked. "He's empty now. The only way he got through any of it was 'cause of the club, because we had his back, pulled him through." Emotion saturated his voice.

I stared into his eyes, lost for words, fresh tears streaming down my cheeks. Cade's thumbs wiped them away. Seeing the grief, the raw pain in his eyes, something in me clicked. This wasn't Jimmy, wasn't even close. Jimmy's boys didn't give a shit about me, didn't blink as they beat me, as they watched Jimmy beat me. I saw the love that Cade had, love for his brother, love for that girl. The pain he obviously felt, still felt.

I was so conflicted, he was obviously different, and the men in the club were different. But that didn't mean the club was, it caused her death, no matter what way you looked at it, no matter how much it broke their hearts. I had no words, no kind whispers to make anything better, so I touched my mouth to his. That's when my actions stopped. He gripped the back of my head, thrusting his tongue into my mouth, his kiss unraveling me, draining me.

He fell back on the sand and I fell on top of him. His hands travelled down my back, resting on my bottom, kneading it. Delightful shivers ran down my spine as I ground up against him, needing to feel closer.

Then I realized where we were on a beach, in public, in broad daylight.

Shit!

I sat up quickly and Cade frowned, trying to pull me back down and after being unsuccessful, he sat up.

"Babe, like your mouth, like you on top of me, especially after all that. What the fuck?" he growled.

"We're in public, Cade," I declared, righting my shirt and darting my eyes around the beach. Thankfully there wasn't anyone in the immediate vicinity.

"So?" He stared at me, annoyed.

"So? I thought that might be enough of a deterrent. We could get done for indecent exposure!" I blew the hair out of my face to see him smile.

"Baby, was kissing you. Wasn't fuckin' you, and sure as shit wasn't going to expose any of you, that's for my eyes only. Although you are exposing more than enough in those shorts." His gaze narrowed, dropping to my legs.

"These shorts are the shit," I snapped, sensitive to people criticizing my fashion choices.

"Yeah they are, your legs look amazing in those things, all I can do is imagine them wrapped around my back, and that will be what every other man will be thinking when he looks at you." He raised his eyebrows. "Not too keen on men thinking about my woman like that."

His woman. It hit me. He considered me his, considered us

together, as he had done pretty much since the first moment we met. That was intense, too intense. Given all the information I had learned about him and the club, I wasn't sure that was what I wanted. We had slept together once, okay more than once technically, but we had spent only one night together. A handful of amazing make out sessions, multiple orgasms, and limited conversation did not a relationship make.

I couldn't deny this man was under my skin, there was something between us, something I couldn't describe, but something that seemed to turn this relationship up to warp speed. With a regular guy, this would freak me out — with someone who represented a past I was trying to escape, it made me want to run for the hills.

"Gwen?" Cade asked softly, interrupting my inner monologue.

"I can't do this," I whispered, watching as his face hardened.

"Yes, you can, Gwen. Don't let that prick deputy get into your head," he said fiercely, holding me tight.

"This has nothing to do with Luke, I just can't do *this*." I gestured between us. "There's things you don't know about me–"

"Well then, tell me," he interrupted roughly.

I shook my head, lifting myself off him, expecting him to hold me in place. Surprisingly, he let me go, helping me get to my feet, then grabbed my hips softly. His gray eyes pierced mine.

"I know you feel this, Gwen, this thing between us, it's not fucking normal, but don't run away because you're scared."

His gaze, the electricity sizzling between us made my resolve waver.

"I need time to think about this, can you give me that?" I conceded.

He sighed, bringing my forehead to his. "Yeah, baby."

I had a feeling even if I had a hundred years, I wouldn't be able to figure it out.

I was curled up on our porch reading a book, or trying to read, when it was yanked out of my hands.

"Hey! I was reading that." I scowled at Amy, who was standing above me, one hand on my book, one on her hip.

"Oh really? Is that why you haven't turned a page in the last half hour?"

"It's a very engrossing page. I find that reading it a couple of times brings about a richer understanding of the complexities of the characters," I countered.

Amy raised a brow.

I sighed. "Fine! I keep staring at the same sentence because I can't stop thinking about Cade. Happy?" I pouted at her.

She perused me for a moment, then gripped my arms and heaved me up to stand in front of her. "No, I am not happy. I am supremely disappointed at the revelations of the other day's events. While I completely agree with your decision, I am sad because I've never seen you like that with a guy, especially one that rivals Chris Hemsworth on the hotness scale. But you know what they say, the best way to get over a guy is to get under another. So let's go!" She herded me into the house.

"Where are we going? Last time I checked there weren't any men hiding in my closet that I could get under." Well, as long as you didn't count my vibrator.

"Ha ha, Gwen. You're not going to attract any men wearing a football shirt and sweat pants, so you have to change into my black Gucci dress."

"It's a *rugby* top not football, and if I was back at home, my appreciation for the All Blacks would have the men lining up to talk to me," I argued as she shoved me into her closet, which was equally as impressive as mine.

"Yeah, well, I wouldn't like to know what kind of men they

would be, but here in *America*, a hot-blooded male responds to tits, ass, and leg. You've got those in abundance." Her gaze flickered to my chest. "Maybe not the first one, but the other two make up for that."

I scowled at her as she threw me her dress, but took it, pulling off my shirt.

———

It had been three days since my conversation with Cade on the beach. I had kept myself busy, but he kept invading my thoughts. No matter how much my rational self pointed me firmly away from him, other parts of my body, like my vagina and my heart nudged me in his direction. I almost drove out there last night, only stopping myself when I was actually in my car.

It didn't help I'd heard the rumble of Harley's multiple times in the past few days and had actually seen him drive past me when I was walking out of the coffee shop. Our eyes had locked for a quick second, even from a distance my thighs had quivered. It took all I had not to chase him down. Luckily, I was carrying precious cups of coffee, which were otherwise known as my sanity, so I could not relinquish them, even to chase a sexy herd of bikers down the street.

That was not normal behavior. So maybe Amy was right, maybe I did need to look at distracting myself with someone else, or at least consume huge amounts of alcohol. I wasn't going near Luke, knowing that Rosie was into him. It would be totally against girl code, and even if she didn't like him, my feelings for him were purely platonic, no matter how hot he was. He had called me to apologize for that day and I had assured him it wasn't his fault. He had said nothing about Cade, thankfully, but did turn up this morning at the store with my coffee and light-hearted banter.

Like nothing had happened.

I wished I could act like that too.

━━━

A desperation for normalcy found me at Laura Maye's bar, with Amy at my side. I had expected some country themed saloon after meeting Laura Maye, but I was pleasantly surprised. The place reminded me of a trendy place in New York. The bar ran down the middle of the room, it had a shiny chrome top with green leather stools along it. Floor to ceiling windows exposed the ocean's breathtaking view, with classy booths running along the windows.

"You girls finally made it! And don't you both look fine, the men in here are going to be fighting over each other to get to the pair of you." Laura Maye appeared from behind the bar, kissing us on the cheeks like old friends.

I couldn't help but smile at this woman's warm and friendly nature. "It's so nice to see you again, Laura Maye, your bar is amazing. I can't believe we haven't been here sooner."

She winked at me, directing Amy and me to a table with an amazing view right beside a group of handsome looking men in suits. "I 'spect you've been busy, Miss Gwen, but I don't see you with any man tonight, so why not get to know these gentlemen? Just in town for the weekend, on business." She winked at us again. "I'll get you ladies some cocktails, coupla my specialties, you'll like them, and they've got a kick." She sauntered off, her heels clicking on the hardwood floor.

"That woman is something else," I exclaimed, settling into my seat, looking over at Amy.

"I know, don't you love it? I think she's the only person in the world who can actually make head to toe leopard print work. I respect her for that alone."

I giggled, agreeing with her. I noticed the men from next door glancing over at us. They were pretty attractive, and in their Armani suits, completely opposite to the biker who was dangerous to my emotional health.

"Here we are, ladies, compliments of the gentlemen at the next table over." A waitress set two delicious looking cocktails in front of us with a knowing smile.

Amy raised an eyebrow at me, bringing her glass up to mine. "I'll drink to that."

I clinked mine to hers with a smirk.

It was forced, but I was trying to pretend it wasn't.

"No way! You like the All Blacks?" I directed a cocky smirk at my best friend, who was getting very close with Travis, a handsome advertising executive.

"I was going to wear an All Blacks top out tonight, but my *friend* here assured me it would not be very attractive." I pointed with my cocktail glass, lucky not to spill any. Laura Maye was right, these were potent.

Jeff, the guy to my right, slung his arm over the back of my seat. "Trust me, sweetheart, you in an All Blacks top would be smoking," he flirted, eying me up and down. "Not that I don't appreciate the dress."

I smiled at him and sipped my drink, feeling delightfully buzzed and enjoying some harmless flirting with a hot guy. That's as far as this was going. Just flirting. As much as I was enjoying myself, I couldn't picture myself actually doing something with this guy. I kept picturing a brooding dark-haired man in leather. Fuck it. Maybe I just needed more cocktails. I drained my drink.

"Can I get you another drink, Gwen?" Jeff asked, leaning in so I could feel his breath at my ear.

"Yes, please," I replied softly back, giving him my best sexy gaze, which may have been hampered by previous cocktails.

"You won't be buying her anymore drinks," an angry voice declared from above me.

I turned my head in surprise to see not only Cade glaring at Jeff like he was going to strangle him with his tie, but also Brock, who was glowering at Amy. This could not mean good things.

"I wasn't aware Gwen had a boyfriend," Jeff said smoothly, not indicating he was the least bit intimidated by a huge pissed off biker and his equally huge pissed off friend.

"I don't," I said at the same time Cade growled, "She sure as fuck does."

"For fuck's sake. Gwen, come with me," Cade commanded through clenched teeth.

I grabbed my purse, deciding that talking to him would be the best way to avoid these two nice men getting beaten up in Laura's lovely bar.

"I'll be back in a minute," I told Jeff, who looked uncertain to let me go.

"No, she won't," Cade barked, grabbing my arm as I stood up.

Brock and Amy seemed to be having the same kind of problem as us, but Amy looked like she would cling to the seat if Brock attempted to move her. I let out a little giggle as Cade pulled me away, disappointed I wouldn't get to watch that drama unfold.

"What the fuck, Gwen?" Cade snapped in my face as soon he pulled me into a bathroom and locked the door.

I struggled not to sway at all of the sudden motions. Why did bathrooms have the magical power of making you realize how drunk you actually were?

Cade's eyes ran up and down my body and the intensity of his gaze made me instantly wet. He obviously didn't want me to answer his question, because he had me up against the wall before I knew what hit me.

His mouth was on mine, his hand fisting my hair, the kiss wild, frantic. His hands were everywhere, his grasp on my hair rough and his kiss was merciless. Without thinking, I wrapped my legs around his hips as he lifted me, hands on my ass. I moaned when he pulled up my dress, grinding his erection into the thin lace of my underwear. My hands reached between us, fumbling at his belt.

Cade pulled his mouth from mine, breathing heavily, eyes blazing. "Gwen, you're mine," he told me savagely, pushing my underwear aside, thrusting inside me.

I almost screamed, but he silenced me with a kiss, wildly pounding me against the wall. He was rough, urgent as he plunged into me and I loved it. I bit his lip, yanked at his hair and he growled, fucking me harder. I felt an orgasm rip through me like wildfire, milking a release out of Cade.

We stayed connected, both panting, damp from our exertion. Cade slowly lowered me down, gently pulling out of me. I felt stickiness against my thighs, realizing we didn't use a condom. Cade reached over for some toilet paper, gently cleaning himself from me.

"Fuck, I am so sorry, baby, I didn't mean to get so carried away." His hand smoothed my hair and he looked almost worried. It was quite a novel expression on his gruff stubbled face.

"It's okay, I'm on the pill and I'm clean," I replied breezily, the alcohol giving me no reason to worry.

Cade's gaze locked with mine. "That's good to hear, baby, and I'm clean too, I promise you. I've never fucked anyone bare, no matter what." He shook his head. "But with you, it was fucking amazing."

"Yeah, it was," I agreed smiling at him, enjoying my little

holiday from common sense that these lovely cocktails were treating me to.

"Can I take you home now, baby? I think we need to get you into bed." His eyes were hooded.

I smirked. "Yes, I think we do."

⌐══⌐

I woke up feeling warm, too warm and like my throat was made of sand paper. I reached blindly for precious liquid, hoping drunk me had been looking out for hungover me. The body behind me reached away and came back handing me a bottle.

"Had a feeling you would need this," a half asleep voice grumbled.

I didn't reply, opening the cap and downing the entire bottle, silently thanking the Lord for this small favor.

"Better," I murmured to no one in particular before snuggling back into a hard chest. The chest vibrated underneath me, and a hand reached to stroke my hair.

"You need an aspirin, baby?" Cade asked when he finished laughing.

I took stock of my body, I was feeling slightly nauseous, that could have been because I just necked an entire bottle of water too quickly. "No, thank you," I replied politely, not moving my head off the muscled chest, enjoying the feeling of his hand in my hair.

"Okay, well let me know if you change your mind, I didn't realize how drunk you were until I got you on my bike last night. I was shit scared you'd fall off the entire ride home." His voice was rough from sleep, and seriously sexy.

I scoffed. "I wasn't that drunk, I managed to hold on, I'm here, aren't I?"

"Babe, you passed out face down on my bed, fully clothed.

Not that I didn't enjoy discovering what underwear you wore underneath your dress, I just prefer you conscious," Cade remarked dryly as I realized I was wearing his tee and my panties.

Then I groaned. "We had sex in the bathroom of Laura Maye's bar last night," I declared, mortified. "Oh my god, I can't believe I did that." I faced planted into Cade's chest, hoping to stay there until my embarrassment wore off, in other words, forever.

Cade wasn't having that, he pulled me up so I was laying on top of him and we were face to face. His gray eyes were serious.

"Don't be embarrassed, Gwen, that was hot as fuck. But I owe you an apology, for taking advantage of you. I just couldn't stop myself, I haven't been able to get you off my mind for three days, then seeing that guy all over you, and you in that dress...I lost all self control."

"You didn't take advantage of me, I knew exactly what I was doing. I just wasn't completely aware of my public surroundings."

Who was I kidding? The public surroundings made it even hotter.

Cade looked relieved, then framed my face with his hands, face still serious. "I meant what I said last night, I've never fucked anyone bare, I'm clean."

I nodded. "So am I."

Cade's gaze turned hooded. "But fucking you, with nothing in between us, gonna want to do that more often, baby. And by that, I mean every fucking day." His hands delved into my panties, I moaned when he got to my sweet spot.

"We are going to have words about you and that asshole who was all over you...after," he declared, pushing a finger inside me.

My eyes rolled to the back of my head. "Mmmhmm, after."

I emerged from the bathroom after some seriously amazing love-making, to curl back up with Cade. He pulled me close to his chest, kissing my head. I didn't take him for a cuddler, but I dug it.

"Time to talk, baby," his voice was soft, with an edge.

I groaned, feeling like a chastised schoolgirl, but met his gaze.

"I was never intending on anything with Jeff, I couldn't bring myself to move past harmless flirting. I was only out because I was trying to get my mind off you and to stop myself from driving out here and being in the exact position I'm in now," I blurted out in one breath.

"First off, babe, no such thing as harmless flirting, not with you. You don't flirt with anyone, got it?" He spoke roughly, his gaze intent on mine. Nor did he wait for a response. "Secondly, why were you trying to stop yourself from being here? It's a pretty fucking great position if you ask me."

I blushed. "Yes, those positions were pretty great." I stopped, trying to find the right words to explain, without divulging my dirty past. "It was just too much for me, your world, I didn't think I could handle it." I glimpsed down at his chest, tracing his tattoos with my fingertip.

He grabbed my chin, drawing my eyes to meet his. "And now? You can handle it." It was more of a statement than a question.

"Yes, I think I can handle it," I said softly.

Whatever it was between us was too strong to fight, and I didn't want to fight it. So far I liked the way Cade made me feel protected and safe. Also extremely sexy and most importantly, happy. I might be making a huge mistake by going near this world again, but I was willing to take the risk. I wanted to trust my instincts and dive into something scary but exciting

"I know you can handle it," he stated with certainty.

I decided to believe him. For now.

CHAPTER 7

"BABY."

Cade was on top of me, making love to me, tender, slow.

I moaned, throwing my head into the pillow as he rubbed me in circles while pushing in slowly. I was close.

"Baby," Cade repeated. "Look at me."

I immediately lifted my head, locking eyes with him. I lost my breath at his expression, it was intense, full of blatant lust and awe.

"Fuck, I missed you on the road, couldn't stop thinking about you."

He thrust inside me again and I unraveled, screaming loudly, keeping my eyes focused on his. I watched, through my own pleasure, as he came. It was amazing to watch such a staunch, strong man lose control.

Afterwards he rested on his elbows, not giving me his full weight. He kissed my nose, moving as if to pull out, I wrapped my legs around his hips not wanting to lose him.

"No don't leave yet," I whispered.

He gazed at me softly, staying a beat before pushing up and

walking to the bathroom. He returned with a washcloth, gently cleaning me.

I was falling deeper for him. Things were moving past pure physical attraction.

And it was dangerous.

Maybe deadly.

———

We had two days together after the night at the bar before he had to leave again for a week. We spent every possible moment together in those two days, and most of our time was spent in bed. I had missed him a lot, and he had missed me, obviously. He called me every night he was away, not that he was much of a talker, but just to 'check in.' It was nice knowing he thought about me while he was gone and made the effort to let me know.

When he got home, he picked me up from the store on his bike, taking me straight to his place. We were all over each other as soon as we got in the door, much like last time, but this time, he fucked me against the door. It was ah-ma-zing. He then carried me to his room, slowly took off my clothes, then made love to me. That brought me to now. Lying on his rumpled bed, naked, staring at the ceiling, feeling content. Cade settled in beside me, pulling me to his side. I instantly snuggled into the crook of his shoulder, stroking his tats.

"Gwen."

"Hmmm," I half answered, distracted by his tattoos and his body.

"We gotta talk."

Still distracted, I muttered, "Okay."

"You're going to tell me what happened to you," he spoke gruffly as if he expected something horrible. Which was right, horrible was just the beginning.

I turned to stone. I knew he felt it because he started to stroke my back gently.

"What happened to put that fear behind your eyes? What makes you flat out panic when the boys get too close? What made you say what you said on the beach that day? What gave you the scars?" He lightly traced the scar on my cheek, the evidence of a ring tearing open my face, then my stomach, where the doctors had opened me up because I was bleeding internally.

They curled up in my belly, the poison memories that would taint what we had. I couldn't have my happiness for a second without this eating at me, so much so that Cade noticed and he wasn't going to give up until he knew the ugly truth. Then he probably wouldn't want me. Because I was broken, scarred, *dirty*.

His jaw was hard, but his gaze was tender. I knew he felt anger, without even knowing what actually happened, he was already pissed off.

"Cade," I whispered brokenly. "You don't want to know."

"Gwen, I do," he said firmly. "I need to know so I can start fixing you." His gray eyes locked on me, determined.

The blow hit my stomach.

Fix me?

He knew I was broken. If he knew that, there was no hope for me anyway, he wouldn't let this go. I took a deep breath, preparing. I looked at his face, at his strong jaw, covered in dark stubble. I struggled to meet his gaze, but I had to, one last time before it was full of pity and disgust. I watched him for a long moment before I began.

"I moved to New York when I was twenty-one. Always knew I wanted to, since I was little, I'd tell people I was going to live in New York. Manhattan to be exact. People in my small town in New Zealand didn't really know what to say to that, they would mostly shrug it off, no one really left. Maybe to move a couple of hours away, but few really saw the *world*. So they dismissed me. I was determined."

Cade smirked, a half smile breaking the hard expression on his face. "Bet you were, baby."

I rolled my eyes, trying to hide my nerves. "Anyway, after seeing the wrong side of the tracks for a year, I nearly lost my dream, but luckily I had someone to set me straight. I got my shit together, got a degree and moved to New York. Never been happier, had my apartment, had a job. Had my city." I smiled at the memory of how young I was, how carefree. "I met Amy, we were friends instantly, I made heaps of other new friends, there were some guys, no one special."

I took a deep breath and didn't meet Cade's eyes.

"Then I met Jimmy. He was different than all my glossy Manhattanite friends. He was a biker, wore a cut, rode a Harley and was gorgeous. I was infatuated, the novelty of being with a 'bad boy,' a real one, so different than my new friends and my old ones, his dangerous but exciting world enticed me, sucked me in."

Cade watched me intently jaw hard, super alert since I mentioned Jimmy wore a cut. I soldiered on.

"I got immersed in his world, I spent too much time with him, not enough with my friends. I wasn't stupid, I knew he was into shady stuff, but he never let me see too much, I didn't really want to know so I never asked — naïve, I know."

I shook my head, angry with my past self.

"Anyway, one night I went to visit him at his apartment, which I never did, because he lived in a seriously dangerous part of town. He didn't like me coming there, but I had a surprise for him for his birthday, I was excited. So when I walked up his stairs I wasn't prepared to see Jimmy blow someone's head off, to feel their blood on my cheek."

"Jesus, fuck, baby," Cade muttered holding me tight.

I continued, ignoring him, lost in my memory. I was so scared that night, I had just seen a man die, watched the man I loved kill someone.

"His name was Carlos." I paused. "The man Jimmy murdered, his name was Carlos. He had three children and a wife. He was just a regular guy who made a couple of stupid choices, which led to him owing the club money. Money, which he couldn't pay back. So Jimmy murdered him." My voice was small and weak.

Cade's hand circled my back. I looked at him, tears glistening in my eyes.

"His wife's name is Rosa, she loved him with all her heart. His children are five, seven, and fifteen."

"You were close with him, baby?" Cade asked softly, eyes never leaving mine.

I was surprised at his question. "No. Didn't know him," I replied.

This was Cade's turn to look surprised. His expression was intense, unreadable.

"I found out who he was, after. I wanted to know. Needed to. I saw a man's life end in front of my eyes, I wanted to know who he left behind. I talk to Rosa at least once a month." I didn't mention that I also give her monthly payments to help her keep her children fed and clothed.

"Anyway, after I saw that, I ran, I didn't think. I don't know how he didn't catch me, I don't think he realized I was really there until I was halfway down the stairs. I heard him yell to me, I kept going. I managed to get to my car, somehow."

It was a miracle I had a car. No one in Manhattan had a car, but I did, since I had always had one and didn't like the feeling of not having one in an unfamiliar country.

"I don't know why I didn't drive to a police station." I shrugged. "I was in shock I think, flight instinct firmly in place. I made it to my apartment and started to pack a bag. Don't know why I did that either, my plan was to leave, get on a plane and get the fuck out. I didn't think at that point I was a witness to murder, I was too freaked.

"As I was packing, I heard banging at the door, hard, loud. I knew it was Jimmy's boys, I had met them before, knew they were bad straight off. Seen it in their eyes, but I was blind, blind to Jimmy. I was in love," I scoffed. "Or thought I was. Anyway, they kicked the door down, came at me and punched me. I'd never been punched before, it hurt."

Cade's arms were now vices and anger radiated from him. He was shaking with it, I thought his jaw might shatter, it was clenched so hard.

I kept talking.

"I blacked out or they knocked me out, I'm not sure which. I woke up, in a warehouse, naked, tied up. That's when I saw Jimmy, *really* saw him, the evil. Saw past his charm and good looks that he wore like a mask. He beat me and they watched, the big men with their cuts, their evil smiles, sometimes throwing in a kick. They did it for hours, always stopping before I passed out. Then Jimmy decided they would rape me, him first for old times' sake."

I rolled my eyes, engrossed in my very own horror story I didn't notice Cade had stilled.

"By this time, he had fractured my skull, dislocated my shoulder, broken my wrist and ribs. And his buddies had kicked me so hard I was bleeding internally. I was dying. But he still decided that wasn't enough. I was also to be gang raped. Luckily, by then I had been missing for over twenty-four hours, my neighbors heard the break in, saw me getting carried off, the police lucked out, someone caught the plates on the van I was taken in. They found me just in time."

I was so lost in the story, I still didn't notice Cade, lying like a stone, arms around me.

"What I also didn't know was police had been looking for Jimmy, for a long time. He was a very wanted man, one of the top ten most wanted in America, to be exact. I didn't know I was sleeping with a murderer, a rapist, a sadist. I thought I loved him. I know now I didn't, that it wasn't real." Tears welled up in my eyes and I didn't let them fall. "I spent one month in the hospital, six more recovering, doing rehab. I tried to go back to work, tried to stay in my city, but I couldn't. And one day, I found Amber, and it just made sense. This place, it was me, I could heal here, forget."

I took a deep breath, needing to get it all out.

"That's why I reacted the way I did when I first saw you, when I saw the guys from the club. They brought up some memories I had associated with bikers. I know now that you're different, but it is still a world that represents everything I went through."

I finally got out of my trance and looked up at Cade, realizing something was wrong. He was beyond angry, there was no word to describe the sheer rage that was written all over his face.

I laid my hand on his chest and pushed up a bit, "Honey..." I whispered softly.

"Gwen, get off me," he hissed.

The sick feeling settled in the pit of my gut again, a blow connected with my stomach like I had been physically punched. I didn't say a word, just crawled off him, defeated. He knifed up, walking to the wall, punching it viciously. I jumped as he put his fist through the plasterboard, dust flying everywhere.

"Fuck!" he bellowed before putting both hands to his head and looking down at the floor.

I watched him cautiously, unsure of what to do. I knew he wouldn't hurt me, but I had never seen anyone this angry. Not even Ian, and he saw me bruised and battered and almost dead. I guess maybe he checked it, saw I couldn't deal. Cade most definitely hadn't checked it.

I sat on the edge of the bed, feeling exposed. I threw on his tee, unsure if this was the right move, but I knew if he told me to leave I'd take this, as a reminder. He sensed my movement, his eyes roamed to me. Something registered, his expression changed and he slowly approached the bed, crouching in front of me. Anger saturated his expression before it softened.

"Baby, I'm not going to hurt you." He tread carefully, thinking his reaction had set me off.

"I know," I whispered, eyes locked to his.

His head jerked with surprise. He gently pushed me back on the bed to cover my body with his. He stroked my face tenderly, like I was made of glass.

"This swine, Jimmy, he got a last name?" Cade asked carefully, his quiet tone still shaking with anger.

"Yup," I said slowly. "O'Fallhan," I told him on a slight whisper.

Something flashed through Cade's eyes, something too quick to catch, recognition?

"You know him?" I asked softly.

"No," he said stroking my head. "What prison is he in?"

"Ummm, Attica," I answered, having memorized all but his prisoner number, needing to know where he was, where he would be for the rest of his miserable life.

"Why?" I added, getting a bad feeling about the questions.

"No reason, babe, just need to know that fucker is locked up, or else I would hunt him down and kill him. Still might." His voice was even, too even, like he didn't trust himself to raise it.

Cade's reaction rattled me, he was obviously really angry for me. More importantly, it showed how much he cared about me.

"No, Cade, he doesn't deserve to die." I stroked his cheek.

Cade directed a dangerous look at me.

"A man like that, being locked up for the rest of his life is exactly what he deserves. Death is too easy for him." I watched as the look on Cade's face turned to a sad sort of pride.

"You are the strongest woman I've ever met."

Cade's mouth descended on mine and he kept me distracted, helping to keep the demons at bay.

For now.

———

I was lying on top of Cade, sated from yet another round of love making, tracing my fingertip over the skin on his left pec. I had never really had the time to inspect his tats up close. And man, they were kick ass. He was covered, but not in stupid, poorly done scribbles, he was a work of art. He had a huge tat, spanning his chest, two doves, one on each side, pulling a script which read "Keep the Faith." Then above his left pec was an intertwined set of scales with "Peace" on one side, "Order" on the other.

His full sleeve started at the top of his neck, with a huge angel sprawling from his shoulder, spanning his back and arm. His forearm became so thick with tats, I was engrossed discovering them all, I actually lifted his arm to get a better look. I forgot for a second that he was an actual living, breathing man.

"Like what you see, baby?" he growled.

I peeked up through my eyelashes at him. "Your tats are the shit," I whispered back, and his eyes got that funny intense look they had when I was wearing his tee.

"You hungry?"

"What?" I was thrown at the abrupt change in subject.

"Food? You know the stuff we eat to survive?" he asked deadpan.

I burst out laughing and didn't stop for a while. I knew Cade was starting to get pissed off when he hauled me up his body and growled, "Babe."

"Sorry, Cade, I think that's the first time you have actually attempted something resembling a joke," I wheezed, wiping a tear from underneath my eye dramatically. "I decided to savor it."

I smirked and he just stared at me. He then picked me up, walking us to the kitchen before unceremoniously plopping me down on his kitchen counter.

"Cade!" I jumped off the counter as he pulled bacon and eggs out of the refrigerator.

"What, woman?"

"I don't have any clothes on," I said stating the obvious.

"Not planning on walking out the door anytime soon, babe."

Cade set a fry pan on the stove before walking back up to me and setting me back on the counter. He stayed there, standing between my legs, hands either side of my body.

"Besides, I like the view. And I like knowing, if I feel like it, I can fuck you, no barriers to worry about."

He gave me a quick bite on the breast to make his point, then cupped me between my legs. My eyes rolled back into my head, that area highly sensitive.

"Yeah, but I am sitting naked on your kitchen counter, it's not very hygienic," I breathed out.

Cade smirked. "I don't give a fuck, babe, in fact I may never wash that counter again. Now stay," he ordered before turning back to the stove.

My temper made its appearance. "Did you just order me like a dog?"

Cade eyed me. "Nope. Dogs listen a fuck of lot more than you."

I huffed, wide eyed and decided to ignore him. I looked around his kitchen, it was quite big, for a bachelor pad. All the appliances were stainless steel, not brand new, but nothing crappy either. His countertops were white, his cupboards brown. It ran into a sort of dining area at the back of the house, where a cluttered wooden dining table sat in front of a set of French doors that looked like they led out to a patio area.

Without being able to stop myself, my gaze went back to Cade, putting bread in the toaster. Unlike me, he wasn't naked. He had put on his jeans, commando, top button undone. He had his back to me, and I got the chance to marvel at the huge tattoo covering his whole back. It was similar to his patch, the grim reaper riding a bike under a road of skulls, with script reading "Sons of Templar" at the bottom. The background was flames, and they were so vivid they looked almost real. Even though I wasn't a big fan of skulls and crossbones, I had to say it was awesome.

I realized we had been sitting in silence for quite a while, not uncomfortable, I guessed with the amount of words we had shared throughout the day, silence might be good.

"How old are you?" I asked, curious. He was definitely older than my twenty-five years, but I couldn't quite figure out how much.

He glanced at me from the stove. "I'm thirty-two."

My eyes popped out. "Seriously? Wow, you're an old man."

He turned off the heat. "You didn't seem to mind an old man fucking you ten minutes ago."

"No, well as long as you don't put your hip out," I continued, teasing. "Don't you want to know how old I am?" I asked after he didn't reply.

Cade glanced at me. "Already know how old you are, Gwen."

That was a surprise. "What, did you do a background check on me or something?" I joked, my brows narrowed when he just looked back at me. "Did you seriously do a background check on me?" I asked in a sharp tone.

"Babe, as soon as I saw you outside your house, knew I had to have you. I had one of the boys look you up, so I knew what I was working with. I hardly call looking up your Facebook page a background check," he replied, amusement dancing in his eyes.

I opened my mouth then closed it again, unable to think of a response to this. Cade turned back to our food. A phone ringing made me jump.

"That's yours, babe. Ignore it. I only just got you without interruptions, I don't need drama from your crazy best friend." Cade turned back, expecting me to obey.

But I didn't, of course. After scowling at his back for the comment about Amy, I leapt off the counter and ran in the direction of the ringing. I wouldn't normally, but that was Ian's tone. I hadn't heard from him in months, due to him being in fuck knows where doing fuck knows what. I worried about him all the time and wasn't going to miss a chance to talk to him. I skidded into the foyer where I found my bag and searched through it as my phone kept ringing.

"I'm coming I'm coming," I chanted hoping it wouldn't ring off. I grabbed it then put it to my ear. "Hello!" I shouted breathless.

"Ace!" Ian yelled. The connection was slightly fuzzy, but man, it was good to hear his voice.

"Ian! Thank God, I was getting worried. Hold on one second."

I quickly put the phone down and grabbed Cade's tee, which was thankfully at the front door. I felt weird talking to my brother while I was standing there naked.

"I'm back. Ian, I've missed you so much. Where are you? When are you coming home? Are you okay?" I shot at him, thinking I might have inherited my mother's trait when it came to phone conversations.

Ian read my mind. "Jesus, Ace, you're as bad as Mum." I heard the laugh in my brother's voice and smiled.

"Can't tell you the answer to the first two, but yes, I'm fine," he reassured me, sounding healthy enough.

I breathed into the phone, letting out the worry I didn't even know I was carrying. "I'm so glad to hear that, Ian, it's so hard not hearing from you for months at a time, I get so worried!" My voice rose a bit at the end. "I think you should retire, get an office job, something where you don't have the possibility of getting riddled with bullets," I ordered voice shaking, I guessed I was a bit raw from the day's events.

"Bloody hell, Gwen, cool it, I'm as tough as an ox, you know that."

I sniffled, letting out a little laugh.

"Anyway, how are you is the more important question?" he asked with concern. "You settling into your new town all right? Managing everything okay?"

"Yeah, Ian, everything's fine. Great actually," I told him with a smile in my voice. "This town is perfect. I wish you could see it. Kind of reminds me of home. I just know you'd love it."

"Well, baby sis, was going to surprise you, but fuck it. I've got leave coming up, just for a few days, and we're currently closer to the U S of A than NZ, so I'll be coming to stay with you for a couple of nights."

I squealed, yes a full on girl squeal. Loud. I jumped to my feet and bounced up and down like a little kid.

"Ohmigod!" I shouted, smiling wide at Cade who appeared in the doorway, arms crossed.

"Jesus, babe, lucky I don't have neighbors," he grumbled, scowling at my phone, no doubt pissed off I didn't obey his orders. I scowled back, shushing him with my finger.

Ian, who was laughing at my reaction, stopped abruptly,

"Who's that, Ace?" he asked, voice hard.

He was protective of me, with good reason. I blanched thinking of how the hell I was going to handle his reaction to

Cade. And there was definitely going to be a reaction. After seeing his sister almost die at the hands of one biker, I didn't think he'd be too impressed I was with another one.

"Who?" I asked innocently.

"The fuckin' man in the background." My brother's voice had turned hard.

"There's no one, just the TV." I hated lying to Ian, hated the scorching look Cade was directing at me.

"You're lying, sis, but I got to go," he said, sounding pissed. "I'll be there in a couple of weeks, call you when I get to the States. Take care of yourself, love you."

"See you then, Ian. Love you." I rang off and was immediately confronted by one unhappy biker.

"What the fuck was that, babe? Who is Ian? And why in fuck's name did you lie?" he asked, voice menacing.

I stared at him, and couldn't help but smile, rushing into his arms. He caught me, not expecting it, he went back on one foot.

"Ian's coming for a visit in two weeks!" I sang. Ignoring the grumpy look on his face, I kissed him.

"Want to tell me who Ian is, babe?" he clipped, still unhappy.

I stared at him confused and realized I hadn't told him about Ian. I forgot that we hardly knew each other because it felt so right between us. I hopped down, but Cade kept his hands firmly around my waist, face close to mine. I smiled up at him, giddy with excitement, even in the face of his mood.

"Ian's my big brother!" I watched as his face changed, but he still seemed pissed, so I elaborated.

"Ian's in the Army, not like run of the mill, but Navy Seal type shit. Or the NZ equivalent." I waved my hand. "Anyway, I don't know exactly what he does, I know it's dangerous, I know I never hear from him, hardly ever see him and I miss him like crazy. Worry about him every day."

Cade's face softened.

"Can't tell you how good it was to hear his voice, I haven't seen him in a year. He managed to get to New York while I was in hospital." Tears welled in my eyes, I shook my head, forcing myself to think happy thoughts. "Anyway, that doesn't matter, I get to see him next week!" I chanted, whipping out of Cade's arms and darting into the kitchen.

I plonked myself on the counter, where I saw two plates of food. I sat in front of the smaller one, obviously meant for me. I reached down for my toast when Cade's arm snatched my wrist and he turned the stool around to get in my space.

"Real happy for you, Gwen, don't get me wrong, glad you get to see your brother, since you obviously love him and have been worried. But you haven't answered my question." His face was close to mine.

"What question?" I asked, genuinely confused.

"Why did you lie to him? He obviously heard my voice, why didn't you tell him you had a man?" Cade sounded seriously ticked.

I bit my lip, unsure of how to approach this. Cade reached in and grabbed my lip.

"Don't try and distract me, baby."

"I wasn't!" I protested, but he kept glaring at me. I rolled my eyes feeling mildly irritated at this intense man. "Well, we are new and I don't really know what *we* are. Plus, I didn't really want to tell my big brother, who saw me lying in a hospital bed half dead at the hands of my biker ex, that I was currently involved with another biker," I explained, trying to be gentle.

The look on Cade's face said I hadn't been.

"I ain't him, babe, nothing like him. I would never fucking hurt you. I would take a bullet rather than hurt you," he growled. "As to what we are, you fucking know, you fucking know you're *mine*, my Old Lady."

I sat back, winded. I didn't know he thought of me as his Old

Lady, that was serious. He didn't feel the love at this moment, though.

"And I'm getting fuckin' sick of you pigeonholing me into your biker stereotype," he finished, snatching his plate then storming through the kitchen and out the French doors.

"Shit," I mumbled under my breath. I played that wrong.

I sat forward and started eating my bacon and egg sandwich. I sensed Cade needed some time alone, and I was starving. I would think about the calories later, or never. I had more than worked them off with Cade earlier.

I polished off the last bite of my delicious sandwich, slid off my stool and washed my plate. I decided to clean the kitchen, partly because it needed it, partly because I was putting off talking to Cade. I finished, then made my way out to the back-yard. When I stepped outside, I couldn't help but gasp, the view was amazing.

The ocean yawned in front of us, a small pathway led to the sand. There was tile beneath my feet, a huge barbeque to the left of me, a big old picnic table and fire pit in front of me. Some really awesome outdoor chairs were to my left, where Cade was sitting with his feet up. He didn't glance my way. I gingerly walked over to his chair, standing for a second, then hopped on top of him, straddling him. I was very aware I wasn't wearing any underwear and my bare female parts were rubbing against his delicious, denim clad male parts. I tried not to let it distract me as I met his eyes.

"Bout fuckin' time, baby," he grunted, pulling me down to him, claiming my mouth in a rough kiss. I was slightly surprised but not complaining.

"Sorry, I um, didn't really handle things the best before—"

"No you fuckin' didn't," Cade interrupted.

"Let me finish," I snapped.

Cade smirked, only he could get me pissed off mid apology.

"I was just excited to hear from my brother, and he's pretty protective of me, was even before everything with Jimmy. We're close, thick as thieves since we were kids. Since he's older than me, he's always tried to look out for me. Somehow he blames himself for my attack." I shook my head. "Ridiculous, but I know it affected him, deep, seeing me in that hospital bed. And I just know what his reaction is going to be to you when he meets you. It just sucks because I want the men in my life to get along." I pouted.

"Men in your life?" Cade repeated, voice rough.

"Well, yeah..." I said, trailing off.

He smiled, like flat out beamed, and it was beautiful, but I didn't get to enjoy it before he claimed my mouth for a passionate kiss. He pulled back, resting his head on mine.

"Get why your brother's going to react, babe. Seeing you, lying broken in the hospital at the hands of some sick fucker. That will mark a man. Mark his soul." His voice was hard, but I saw strong emotion in my man's eyes.

"So I'll cut him some slack, first time he meets me," he conceded.

"Thanks," I muttered, sarcastically.

Cade pulled me back into the recliner chair, and we watched the sun set. Who would've thought, I'd watching the romantic sunset with my rough biker.

There was no place in the world I'd rather be.

CHAPTER 8

WORD TRAVELED FAST in small towns, everyone seemed to know about Cade and I, now we were official. I had constant visitors to the store subtly asking me about my new relationship, and they all seemed happy for me. Amy was the happiest, she had literally clapped her hands the first time she saw Cade and I together. Needless to say my man had gotten the all-important best friend's approval.

It was Friday and I was happy, deliriously happy. The past three days with Cade were amazing – we had a lot of sex, mindblowing sex. The store was great, I'd just hired a young girl, Lily, to come in part time, while she studied. She was twenty and stunning. Her blonde hair was parted straight down the middle, going to about her mid back. She had blue-grey eyes, a slender figure and great style. I hired her on the spot. She was shy, but lovely.

It was just her and me, as we were closing in an hour and Rosie and Amy wanted to get ready for the party at the clubhouse. Apparently there was always some kind of party on a Friday. I let them go early because Cade was picking me up and taking me straight there. I was nervous, but had dressed accordingly, planning on going to the party straight from the store.

I was wearing tight – I mean made for me – tight black skinny jeans, with red sky high spiked heeled sandals. I was also wearing a silk, red camisole that came into a v between my breasts and had super thin straps that crossed over at my back where the top dipped, *way* low. My hair was up, curled with a few strands hanging down. I had just finished redoing my makeup — I decided to go for smoky, kohl rimmed eyes and minimal other makeup, because every classy girl knew, you either did up your eyes or your lips, never both. I kept my jewelry minimal, with some diamond studs and some silver bracelets. I was hoping my outfit was appropriate, I hadn't been to a biker party before, Jimmy never let me, so I didn't know what to expect.

I came out of the back room, with my freshly done makeup.

"Whoa, Gwen, you look hot!" Lily exclaimed.

"Thanks, girl, but do I look 'biker babe' enough?" I asked, contemplating my reflection in the mirror.

She looked me up and down. "You are your own version of a biker babe and you work it."

I smiled at her as the door over the bell chimed. Ginger, from Rosie's barbeque strutted in looking like Queen Slut. Nasty, but I was discovering I had a jealous side, and she did indeed look quite the slut.

She had an inch of black roots contrasting her bottle blonde hair – that girl needed a hairdresser, stat. She was wearing heavy eyeliner and lipstick, proving my makeup theory. She had on a tight leather vest, with nothing underneath, her more than ample cleavage threatening to bust out. Her midriff was showing and she was wearing a low slung frayed denim skirt that I would have considered a tacky belt. On her feet were strappy black stilettos covered in little rhinestones. I repeat, *rhinestones*.

I formed a hopefully genuine smile and directed it at Ginger.

"Hi there, how are you?" I chirped, trying to sound friendly. I also tried not to throw one of my display candles at her poorly-dyed head.

Ginger stopped just short of the counter, cocking her hip out and putting her hand on it. Uh oh, total bitch stance. I eyed the candle.

"Well, I'm not that fucking great. 'Cause some snooty, upper class bitch thinks she can just roll into *my* town and take *my* man," she spat, narrowing her heavily made up eyes at me.

I kept a somewhat lessened smile on my face, turning to Lily, who was looking a little pale in the face of a possible smack down. "Lily, honey, why don't you go home? We're almost done for the day."

She looked relieved, but snuck a glance at Ginger. "Um, are you sure you're going to be okay on your own?"

"I'll be fine, girl, see you tomorrow." I tried to sound bright, but I was really pissed.

The only reason this bee-atch should be in my store was for the makeover she surely needed.

Lily gave me a worried glance and directed a scowl in Ginger's direction before she hurried to the back.

I turned back to Ginger, who was currently tapping her tacky heel at me. "You need to leave," I ordered firmly, crossing my arms.

"Fuck that, bitch, I come to tell you to stay away from my man, and stay the fuck away from the club," she snarled, leaning forward.

I couldn't help it, I let out a little laugh. This did not help Ginger's temper. "Are you serious?" I wheezed. "You are actually coming into my place of business, swearing at me, insulting me, when you haven't even actually met me, to tell me to stay away from your man? Like we are in some bad romance movie?" I rolled my eyes, taking a step towards her.

She stood strong, looking like she'd actually want a bitch fight. Who was I kidding? They were probably her cardio, the reason she stayed so skinny was thanks to slut showdowns.

"Unless I was mistaken, it was Cade in *my* bed last night, not yours. And I have never, not once heard him mention your name. So if you'd excuse me, I have a business to run." I looked her up and down. "Unless you need help with something?" My tone and my gaze implied she definitely needed help, in more ways than one.

She went a little pale during my speech, but now was sporting a smug grin. "He might want a little taste of some high class pussy, but he'll come back to me. He always does, and if I'm not mistaken, he was in *my* bed last Saturday night and it was *me* who sucked his cock so good he swore he never had better."

She scowled as my stomach dropped, but I didn't let the look on my face falter.

"I see you were not taught basic manners, nor were you taught that that kind of crude language is tacky on a woman. Now I will repeat my earlier statement, please get the heck out of my store." I narrowed my eyes at her, daring her to challenge me.

Queen Bitch Slut gave me one last scowl before she turned on her tacky heels. Once she was out of sight, I supported myself on the counter and took a deep breath.

Cade had said he was on a ride last weekend, and I didn't think he'd lie. I trusted Ginger as far as I could throw her. She was lying to get at me. All I needed to do was ask Cade, which I would do. I took one more breath, used my yoga breathing, calmed down a bit and started tidying the shop.

I kept busy with odd jobs until closing time came around and the bell announced Cade's arrival. I was bent down at the sweater table, refolding some stuff.

"Hi, honey, won't be a sec," I called over my shoulder.

Two hands settled on my hips, Cade's hard length pressed into my behind.

"Fuck, babe, it should be illegal for you to wear this kind of shit, I don't like what the boys will be thinking about when they see this." His hand traveled down the bare skin of my back.

"Cade, someone could walk in," I protested weakly, already turned on.

He pulled me closer and his lips circled my neck, soon I wouldn't care if the whole town came in and watched.

"Door's locked, Gwen, need to fuck you before we leave." His voice was hoarse with desire.

I felt a delicious dip in my stomach and got instantly wet.

"Here?" I whispered, looking over my shoulder. We were hidden from the window, only just. My eyes locked on Cade's, which were molten.

"Here," he declared gruffly.

He roughly kissed me before reaching his arms around my body and cupping my breasts, tugging on my nipples so I felt a mixture of pleasure and pain. I moaned.

"No bra? Not sure I like the fact your nipples could poke through this top for everyone to see," he growled.

I couldn't reply, I just reached for my jeans and unbuttoned them. One of Cade's hands left my breast, slipping into my underwear.

"Fuckin' sopping. My baby's always ready for me." He rubbed me, knowing how close I was already.

"Cade," I pleaded.

"What, Gwen?" he asked as he continued rubbing, my breath hitching.

"Need you inside me," I managed to grind out.

"No, you're going to come on my hand, then I'm going to fuck you, then you gonna come on my dick."

His hand worked faster, I all but collapsed on the table, his callused hands bringing me to orgasm. Cade's arm pushed me down, keeping my ass in the air while he rolled my jeans to my ankles. I heard his belt buckle undo, then he was inside me, hard, rough, exquisite. I screamed, sensitive from my orgasm, relishing the feeling of him filling me in this intense position. He pounded me hard, his mouth at my neck.

"Cade," I moaned.

He didn't reply, just plunged deeper, took me harder. I gripped the table as he slammed into me, biting at my neck. I lost control yet again, my muscles clenched around him. Pleasure and pain took over my body as he bit harder into my neck while he climaxed.

We stayed like that for a couple of seconds, both recovering. Cade gave me light kiss on my shoulder then pulled out, I straightened and tugged up my jeans.

"I'm just going to go and clean up," I told him quietly, my voice weak from the sex, and maybe Ginger's words lingering in my brain.

Cade must have sensed something because he clutched my chin.

"Everything okay, Gwen?" His eyes searched mine.

I looked back at him and forced a smile. "Yeah, fine," I said brightly, turning towards the bathroom.

"No bitch is okay when she says 'fine,'" he muttered.

After cleaning up and fixing my hair and makeup, I came out to see Cade leaning against the door, a paper bag in his hands.

"Ready to go?" I asked, shutting off the computer.

"Got something for you today." Cade handed me the paper bag.

I stared at his outstretched hand, taken back. We had only just got together and he was giving me presents? I was liking this man more and more. I quickly took the bag out of his hands. I reached in to reveal the most awesome leather jacket I had ever seen. It was black and the softest leather I'd ever felt. Being a buyer, I knew it was good quality. It was light but had a thick lining, cropped, biker style, with awesome gold zips.

I beamed at Cade. "This is kick ass!" I nearly yelled, and he smirked. I slid it on. Perfect fit. "Thanks, Cade, I love it," I told him, reaching up to kiss him.

He really smiled this time, and I savored it, smiles from Cade were rare.

"Glad to hear that, you need something to keep you warm on the bike, and you look fuckin' hot in it," he replied. "Now let's go, I'm gonna show you how we party."

My smile faltered a bit, I tried to hide it. I was a little nervous about going to the clubhouse with all the big biker men there. I had encountered the guys a couple of times, they were always polite, albeit a bit gruff. I knew they wouldn't hurt me, they were Cade's brothers, and from what I could tell, decent men. Cade, like always, noticed. He pulled me to him, touching our foreheads.

"I'll be with you the whole time, babe, you won't leave my side."

We arrived at the clubhouse — it was out of town, in the industrial area. It was fully fenced, with big gates, had a sign outside with "Lucas Lincoln Mechanics" and had a flag with the patch on it. The gates opened as we rolled up, revealing the party to be in full swing, and it was only about 5:30pm.

There was a mechanic area and office up the front, but towards the back there was a big house with a huge deck opening onto a grassed barbeque area to the left. There were people and bikes everywhere. People on the deck were sitting down sipping beers, more people were scattered around the lawn. Most of them were gruff looking bikers, some with arms around a woman or multiple women. The women ranged from young to old, some dressed similar to me, others wearing outfits similar to Ginger.

I spotted Amy in the parking lot, having a very intense looking conversation with Brock. Amy's head turned in our direction, she said something to Brock, then attempted to walk back to the party. He grabbed her arm and she sent him a death glare jerking her hand away and storming off.

"What was that?" I wondered aloud as Cade parked the bike.

Cade and I had slept together every night and we had done this at his house, which meant I hadn't seen much of Amy. When he came into the store with the boys, there had been some weird looks passing between Brock and Amy, even though she swore they were nothing.

"None of our business, babe," he replied.

"Of course it's my business, she's my best friend. There's something going on there, no matter what she says." I spoke more to myself than him.

I hopped off the bike and scowled at him for his reluctance to help me figure out the mystery, turning on my heel to walk towards the party. His hands circled my body, yanking me back into his hard chest.

"Not so fast, baby, can't have my Old Lady walking in on her own looking like that," he whispered in my ear.

I rolled my eyes, not saying a word as he slung his arm around my shoulder and walked us towards the party. There were a lot more bikers here than at Rosie's, some a bit older, probably early forties and fifties, they still looked pretty good, some pretty scary. I spotted Steg, sitting at the head of one of the tables with an attractive older lady in his lap. He was glaring at us, or more precisely, me. I tried to ignore it, leaning into Cade.

"Are all these guys in your club?" I asked, nervous.

He drew me closer to his body. "Nah, a lot of them are from some other charters, here to do some business."

I watched as he gave some guys chin lifts, I then looked around, interested. I had seen little of his life with the club. Cade would either come and get me from home late, or a couple of times he had picked me up from work and we would have dinner together. We hadn't been able to spend a day together yet, I was busy working non stop and he also had been working. I found out he was a mechanic, but I knew he had some other businesses on the side, connected to the club.

"Want a drink, babe?" he asked as we made our way through the throng of people.

"Yeah, I'll have a beer," I replied, not paying attention. I was too busy checking out the people we passed, some of the women giving me curious looks, others flat out glaring. I noticed Cade had stopped walking and was gaping at me.

"Beer?" he questioned.

"Well, yeah," I replied, seriously. "I was drinking beer long before I discovered cosmos." I winked.

He shook his head, grinning. I would have to show him later just how well I could drink beer. Better than some of the men here, I reckoned. I was a Southern girl after all. I spotted Amy and Rosie at the table up ahead and waved at them once they saw me.

"I'll just go see the girls, you go do whatever, say hello to your boys and bring me back a beer."

I went onto my toes, intending on giving him a quick kiss. He gripped onto me tight and thrust his tongue into my mouth, full on making out with me. Cat calls and shouts made a blush creep up my cheeks.

"Did we really need the PDA?" I murmured.

"Just reminding the boys of what's mine," he replied with a grin.

"Whatever." I walked off towards the girls without another word.

He'd assured me he wouldn't leave my side, and I knew he'd stick to his word, but I didn't want his brothers' first impressions of me to be that I already had him whipped. As if you could have a man like Cade whipped. I wouldn't mind him whipping me though, we could totally make one of the rooms in his house into a red room of pain. What was I thinking about again?

I approached the girls and was delighted to see Lucy and Ashley at the table as well, sipping beers. I had been spending a lot of time with Rosie's friends since we'd met them, they were always hanging out at the store when we weren't working. We had everyone around for dinner last night. It was funny, these well-groomed and stylish women were the last people I would have expected to be at a biker party, but these were their child-hood friends. Not to mention the men were freaking hot.

"Girlllll!" Lucy shouted as I got to the table. "You are looking *fine*. Red is for sure your colour!" I was guessing they were going well on the beers.

"Thanks," I replied sitting beside Amy, who gave me a smile, but it looked forced. I frowned at her in a "what's wrong" look, but she just shook her head. Weird. I turned my attention to the girls.

"You ladies look smoking if I don't say so myself."

And they did. Lucy's midnight hair was curled, loose around her face. Her lips were painted blood red and she was wearing faded jeans that fit her like a glove and a black halter with a neck-line that plunged almost to her bellybutton. Somehow she made it look sexy, but not slutty.

Ashley was wearing a white sundress, skimming down to her knees. It was clinched in at the waist and had a wide band before it spread out into a full skirt. A jaunty pink printed scarf was tied around her neck. She looked like she had walked right off the set of *Mad Men.*

Rosie's style was ever changing, she almost dressed as a different character every day. Today it was biker babe. Wearing a ripped Harley tee, tucked into short denim cutoffs with a fringed leather vest over top, she looked edgy and cool. I loved her designer motorcycle boots. Balenciaga, if I wasn't mistaken.

Amy had gone all out. No wonder a lot of the men were currently giving her hungry looks, apart from Brock, who was sitting at the table across from ours, scowling. Her red hair was piled into a messy ponytail, she had on the shortest leather shorts, ever, paired with a red bustier style top tucked into her shorts. Her heels were red booties with leather laces.

"So, Gwen..." Lucy started, mischief in her tone.

"So, Lucy...?" I replied smirking.

"Things look like they're going good with Cade, you two make one hot couple."

I snuck a glance at Rosie, knowing she was happy for us, but still feeling weird.

"Gwennie, I could not be happier for you and my big bro, finally he has got an awesome chick instead of some skank!"

My stomach dipped at her words, thinking about my conversation with Ginger.

"Speaking of skanks," Ashley muttered and I followed her gaze.

My stomach well and truly dropped seeing Ginger talking to Cade within a group of men and stroking his arm.

"Bitch!" Amy snarled from beside me, shooting to her feet.

I grabbed her hand and she glared down at me.

"What?" she accused. "Aren't you going to do something? She's practically humping Cade." She pointed as Ginger sidled up to Cade. He scowled at her and shrugged her off, but she stayed close.

"What do you suggest I do, Amy? Walk over there and rip her tacky earrings out?" I asked sarcastically.

"That would be my suggestion," Rosie put in, giving Ginger a death stare.

"Mine too," Ashley chirped.

Amy raised an eyebrow at me smugly. "See?"

I towed her back down beside me, taking a swig of her beer.

"That's what she's trying to get me to do." I moved my eyes around the table, "She's a shit-stirring bitch just trying to start a fight. I'm not even going to bother to acknowledge her existence," I stated, deciding not to tell them about my encounter at the store, knowing there would be no stopping Amy from going into bitch smack down. She may have been an Upper East Side princess, but she wouldn't hesitate to give a skank a bashing, especially for me. She really warmed to Cade, seemingly impressed at how he treated me and how happy I had been lately.

"Whoa, Gwen." Rosie gaped at me in astonishment. "You are like, super restrained, I don't know any of Cade's exes who wouldn't be up there ripping Ginger's throat out."

"That's probably why they're his exes," I said, taking another pull of Amy's beer.

I was slightly pissed that my boyfriend hadn't gotten mine like he promised. Maybe I was more pissed about the him "talking to a slut" part. "Now can we stop wasting breath on Queen Bitch and talk about something else?"

"Gladly." Lucy started talking about one of the men from another charter who she was crushing on.

Not long after that, I got a tap on my shoulder and turned to see Lucky smiling down at me with a beer.

"Hey, Princess, Cade got caught up, asked me to give you this." He handed me the beer and sat down beside me.

"Thanks, Lucky." I smiled at him. "What's new?"

He rolled his eyes, then gave me a sad look. "Bitches,

Princess, they're driving me crazy, don't know what they're thinking half the time, drives me insane," he grumbled. "Sorry," he added looking sheepish.

I laughed. "It's okay." I took a swig of my beer. "Tell me all about it."

Lucky didn't need much convincing, he launched right into the stories of his women troubles, talking easily to me. I started to like him more and more as the conversation went on. He obviously had respect for women, he just dated too many at the same time.

During our chat, more men came to shoot the shit and introduce themselves. Most were friendly, albeit scary. Some were flirty and very attractive, giving Amy lots of attention, which she was lapping up. I started to feel a little intimidated by the men. As the night went on, they were getting rowdier, but I pushed through it, drinking more beer. Lucky stayed by my side for ages, something about him kept me feeling calm.

I was starting to get a bit pissed Cade hadn't showed up, primarily because of the way Ginger was with him. I scanned the yard and couldn't find either of them. Great. My eyes did fall on Bull, though, sitting apart from the group, in front of a fire drum. I saw his eyes in the flickering light, and something in them alarmed me. I got up purposefully. Lucky stood too.

"All good, Princess?" he asked, the concern in his eyes registered. Cade had told him, the prick.

"Yeah, Lucky, I'm fine, just got to do something," I replied.

He followed my gaze. "Wouldn't if I were you, Princess, he doesn't like company so much lately."

"I'll be fine," I responded before turning into the party and making my way over to Bull.

After multiple glares from some of the women and winks from the men, I made it over. I sat beside Bull on the bench and he didn't even look up.

"Don't want company, Gwen," he muttered, staring down at the beer in his hands.

"Too bad," I shot back and he glared up at me, hoping to scare me away.

I didn't move, he shrugged and returned to contemplating the fire. I followed his gaze, watching the flames, sitting in silence for a bit. I had also seen Bull a lot during the past week, him and Cade seemed to be attached at the hip. Every time I saw him, I became more concerned.

"Haven't told anyone this," I started, speaking softly. "Not even Amy, my brother, no one. I would appreciate it, if after I tell you, we keep it between you and me." I hoped he wouldn't go running to Cade. Bull continued to ignore me, and I decided to take it as agreement.

"I tried to kill myself six months ago," I stated, voice flat.

Bull's body stiffened, but he stayed silent.

I was telling the truth, only me, the doctors that treated me, and one other person knew about it.

"I was going through some shit—" I started.

"Know about that," Bull clipped.

"Cade's been sharing I see." I was annoyed but kept on speaking. "Anyway, I wasn't dealing with things well, wasn't eating, going through intense rehab. I hardly slept, nightmares, flashbacks, whatever." I shook my head. "Memories of the night, their faces. Sometimes I would wake up screaming, screaming so loud the neighbors would call the cops — they were convinced someone was getting murdered. Eventually, they stopped calling." I swallowed. "I saw what I was doing to my friends, family. I wasn't coping, I was a burden on everyone I loved. Caused them pain, I could see it in their eyes, and I couldn't stand it. I couldn't stand the feeling I had under my skin either, the feeling of dirt, scum. I couldn't get it out no matter how hard I tried, couldn't get clean. I decided one day I couldn't lived trapped in my nightmares, I refused to." I took a breath, Bull was staring at me intensely.

"So I made a plan. I had a date, a date when I was going to finally put myself out of my misery and put my family out of it too. Yeah they would grieve, but at least they wouldn't have to watch me rot from the inside out. They wouldn't have to experience me fading away, worry about me all the time. The date came closer and adrenaline started running through my veins, I got a bit perkier, knowing the end was near. Not happy. I would never be happy."

I felt a lump start in my throat, but I had to keep going, Bull had to hear this.

"It was a Monday and I didn't want anyone to find me, find my body. I didn't want to do that to the people I loved. So when everyone was at work, I was going to call the ambulance, once I knew it was too late. I was just about to swallow a whole bottle of sleeping pills when my friend turned up. Lucky for me I had a friend who had been watching me, knew the signs. He had a gut instinct he said." I looked Bull in the eyes, putting my hand over his. He flinched but didn't pull away.

"He saved my life," I whispered. "I wasn't grateful at the time, I was angry, so angry. Why couldn't he let me make my choice, have control, get peace? Why couldn't I have some power when everything else was taken away from me?" I gazed back into the fire.

"Didn't get it then, I didn't think life was worth living. I didn't understand how cruel that choice would have been on the people who cared. I didn't understand how much they cared. I had been too wrapped up in my own sorrow. I started to realize, though, I saw the love I had around me, I started to see again." I regarded him fiercely. "I know the look, Bull, know the dead behind someone's eyes when they have given up, planning something, going to check out."

He narrowed his empty eyes.

"I know it 'cause I used to see it in the mirror every day." My eyes glistened. "I can't even imagine your pain. To feel what you carry around, what you've lost. But I know what she felt." Bull's grip on my hand tightened. "I know what she went through. I went through the same, but the man I loved was the one killing me, beating me. She knew the man she loved would be doing everything in his power to get her back."

Bull flinched.

"She would have died feeling that love, Bull. My heart weeps for you, truly." I stared into his lifeless eyes. "Don't give up, don't let those fuckers take two lives instead of one. You got love around you, I haven't been here long, but I can see it. Don't give up." I gave his hand a squeeze and stood. "If you're going through Hell, just keep on going. You'll make it out eventually," I whispered, leaning in and kissing his cheek, before I walked back to the party.

I'd said my piece, whether it was my place or not. A hand grabbed my arm roughly. I panicked for a second before my gaze locked with Cade's.

"What the fuck, babe? I've been searching for you everywhere and you're off in some dark corner will Bull?" he hissed, eyes dark with rage.

I smelled alcohol on his breath and wondered if he was drunk. Did he and Ginger share a bottle of Jack?

I ignored his hurtful words. "Don't let him out of your or the boys' sight," I ordered sharply.

Cade's eyes snapped to attention.

"Why?" he barked.

"Just don't. And make sure he isn't armed," I continued and understanding flickered in Cade's eyes.

"Fuck!" he bit out, completely sober.

I nodded in the direction of the fire. "Go sort out your brother, I'll go home with one of the girls."

"No, you'll stay here, in my room, I'll show you there now. Wait for me," he ordered. "Can't be without you tonight, baby."

I smiled a sad smile and began to nod, that was until I saw lipstick on the side of his neck. I wasn't wearing lipstick. I didn't want to make a scene, distract him from helping his brother, but I sure as shit wasn't sleeping in the bed he most likely fucked Ginger in either. I'd probably catch Chlamydia.

I pulled on his arm. "Just have to say a quick goodbye to the girls, won't be a sec." I quickly pecked his cheek and scampered off, knowing he was hot on my heels. I reached the table where Amy was currently chatting up Dwayne.

"Well, there you are! Cade's been looking for you everywhere, he is not a happy chappy!" Amy chanted.

"You drive?" I asked quickly.

Amy caught my tone and nodded. "Couldn't drive now, though. I'm three sheets to the wind, girlfriend," she sang.

"Give me your keys," I commanded holding out my hand.

She grabbed them out of her purse and threw them to me.

I saw Cade approaching out of the corner of my eye and I gave Amy a hug while whispering in her ear, "I'm taking your car, don't say anything in front of Cade, just goodbye, text me if you need to be picked up."

She frowned at me as I released her, but she nodded.

"See you, girl," I said loudly, then turned to the rest who were looking well and truly hammered, I blew them kisses. "Bye, ladies!"

"Bye, Gwen!" they all yelled over my shoulder as Cade dragged me into the clubhouse.

We marched into the entryway, then through into a huge bar/living room where more partygoers were drinking and getting a bit friendly on the couches. I blushed and glanced away.

I caught a glimpse of double doors with ornate carvings on them and the word "Church" above the doors.

Cade's hand around my waist directed me out of the room and into a long hallway with various doors off it, some very distinct moans coming from behind the closed doors. I screwed my nose up, thinking I was going to have to hear people going at it while planning my escape in Cade's room. But we went up some stairs and the sounds quieted. He unlocked a door at the top of the stairs and led me into his room. It was more like a mini apartment. Again, like his house, it wasn't tidy, an unmade bed lay before us. My stomach clenched at what probably went on between those sheets not long before. He expected me to sleep in those soiled sheets? Prick.

Tears welled up in my eyes and I quickly blinked them away, stepping out of Cade's grasp to survey the room. There was a dresser with the club's emblem framed above it, a small fridge and cabinets to one side. What looked like doors to a balcony were on the left of the bed and an en suite to the right.

Cade leaned against the closed door, watching me circle the room, a carefully blank look on his face. Suddenly, without warning, he shoved off the door and was on me in two strides. I was plastered against his hard body and his mouth attacked mine, his hands everywhere. I couldn't help my body's initial reaction, but my mind caught up, eventually. I stiffened, trying my hardest not to pull away and kick the asshole in the balls.

Cade sensed my anger and drew back, gray eyes intense. "Babe?"

I mentally shook myself, knowing I had to act normal. I wouldn't put it past him to lock me in here if he knew I wanted to leave.

I stroked his cheek. "Go to Bull, Cade," I whispered. "He needs you."

Cade frowned, knowing something wasn't right, but I could feel his concern for his brother.

"Okay, Gwen, but I want you naked in my bed when I get back," he commanded. "And after I fuck you, you're going to tell me how you knew about Bull."

I barely restrained an eye roll, him ordering me about came too naturally.

"Okay, Cade."

He stayed rooted on the spot, not taking his concentrated gaze off me.

"Go," I urged, pushing him away from me.

He nodded sharply, walking towards the door. When he made it, he turned, hand on the doorknob.

"Lock this behind me, baby. The party might get a little out of control, and with the boys from other charters here, I don't want someone stumbling in here by mistake."

He waited for my nod before leaving.

I heard him pause outside, so I walked over to the door, clicking the lock in place. Only then did I hear his footsteps leave. I slowly sank down onto the floor, hands in my face, feeling like shit. Firstly, telling Bull about my suicide attempt was hard. No one knew. Except Alex. Somehow, that strong macho man saw what was coming and stopped me from ending my life. I was forever grateful for that. He still called me almost every day to make sure I was coping. The only way he wouldn't tell anyone was if I agreed to therapy, and I did, even had Skype sessions since I had been here.

And secondly, even though I was trying hard to deny it to myself, I really liked Cade, felt it down to my core. And it hurt like hell that he just went and fucked some slut with me outside, drinking with his brothers and his sister. My breath hitched a little as I cried through my silent pity party.

"Pull yourself together, Gwen."

I pushed off the floor, took a deep breath and grabbed my purse, which Cade had thrown on the bed. I slowly unlocked the door and peeked out. I could still hear the dull rumble of music and voices, but upstairs seemed quiet. I slipped out, making my way down the stairs, trying not to listen too hard at the goings on behind slightly open doors.

I made it through the hallway, now the tricky part, how the heck was I going to make it through the huge party area full of people? The room was relatively dark, I guessed people were using it to get lucky in lieu of beds, so I crept past unnoticed. I slipped out the front door and into the shadows, away from the party, to Amy's car, which was thankfully parked out of the way.

I sighed a huge sigh of relief once I was in. But shit. The compound gates. How was I meant to get out? Did I have to have some code word or secret handshake?

"Darn it!" I whispered angrily, smacking my hands on the steering wheel.

Out of the corner of my eye, I saw the headlights of a couple of motorcycles heading towards the gate. Luck was on my side. I quickly pulled the car out and followed the bikes out of the now open gate and into the night.

Faces. Blood. So much blood.

A man's head exploding in my face, I felt pieces of brains on my cheek.

Pain. So much of it.

Jimmy's face, yanking my legs apart, laying atop my broken body. There is no one here to save me.

The knife was against my neck, leering eyes watched the life seep from me. I screamed, screamed for help until my throat was raw.

Suddenly, someone was shaking me and light flashed in my face. I blinked, disorientated for a second. Cade's worried and angry face filled my vision.

"Gwen. What the fuck?" he demanded.

I was still confused. *I'm in my bed.* It was still dark outside. *Wait, how did he get in here?* I glanced down and saw a gun in his hands. This was a lot to take in.

"Why do you have a gun?" I asked, one of the many questions I had, but half asleep, that was what I deigned most important.

Cade's expression turned stormy. "Well, after finding an empty bed and Amy's car gone, I came here to hear you screaming bloody fucking murder. Wasn't coming in unarmed. What the fuck was that, Gwen?" he bit out.

I sat up in bed and he sat on the side, arms crossed. "Nothing," I mumbled, embarrassed. "Just a nightmare."

"Didn't sound like any fuckin' nightmare," he growled, his face softened and stroked my face. "Baby," he whispered, concern on his rugged face.

I ignored this. "What are you doing here?" I snapped, now that I was a bit more awake my sass came back, so did my anger.

Cade glared at me. Obviously I wasn't the only angry one.

"Well, like I said, Gwen, got kind of fucking worried coming back to an empty bed, with no explanation as to where you were. Especially after all the shit with Bull."

I forgot my anger a second and laid my hand on his arm. "Is Bull okay?" I asked with concern.

Cade's eyes hardened even more. He was obviously upset about his brother but didn't want to show weakness. "No," he clipped. "We've got him on watch until we can sort something. He's alive, though. Thanks to you."

I crossed my arms over my chest, partly to hide my skimpy nightie. I watched as Cade's hungry eyes zeroed in.

"I'm glad to hear that he's still breathing at least," I whispered sadly. I lingered in my sadness for a moment, then snapped my head up. "You need to leave," I spat at Cade, remembering myself.

Cade scowled and stood up, undressing. "Like fuck I'm going anywhere. I had a hard fuckin' night and the only good thing about it was knowing I'd get to slide into you at the end of it. I'm staying here and you're telling me why you left," he told me, like it was his choice to make.

I hauled the covers back, my anger back with a vengeance. I tried to ignore Cade's gaze on my body. I stood toe to toe with him, glaring up at him.

"So you were planning on fucking me after you'd already had your dick in some skank?" I hissed, watching Cade's eyes widen. "Classy, Cade. How dare you think you can come waltzing into my life, claim me as your 'Old lady,'" I inserted air quotes here, "make me stupidly believe I *feel* something for you and then fuck around right under my nose?" I poked him in the chest. "I am no idiot and I'm not going to let some biker asshole hurt me in any way, shape, or form, ever again!"

Cade seized my hand at his chest roughly and grabbed my hip with his other hand.

"You better watch how you are fucking talking to me," he snarled menacingly. His anger pulsed around me.

"Why? You going to smack me around now?" I hissed at him, trying to struggle out of his hold.

"You know I wouldn't, Gwen, even if it might smack some goddamned sense into you."

His arms were like a vice around me.

"Stop struggling, Gwen, and what the fuck? I haven't had my dick in anyplace but your sweet pussy tonight. Although, I'm feeling this pussy might be a hell of a lot more trouble than it's worth."

His words cut through me, I struggled not to double over, but I kept my brave face.

"Don't insult me by denying it, asshole. Ginger came to see me tonight, filled me in on where your cock's been." I watched Cade's face harden even more. "And I saw the lipstick on your neck with my own eyes."

He let me go to stride around the room, fists clenched.

"Fuck!" he yelled.

I flinched, slightly afraid. He noted this but didn't tone it down.

"Didn't put my dick anywhere near that toxic pussy, Gwen," he stated quietly, looking me in the eyes.

I gulped, suddenly unsure, but still knowing how easy it was for men to lie. I was confused, but I wasn't going to give in.

"Where were you for the whole night then, Cade?" I asked, praying for some sort of explanation.

Cade was still glaring at me, eyes wild. "Club business, Gwen, none of yours."

I snorted. "None of my business?" My voice was bordering on shrill. "So is it my business when you fuck someone else?"

"She came onto me, pushed that bitch off. Wouldn't touch that trash when I knew what a sweet piece I had in my bed."

His gray eyes were piercing into me, I couldn't help but wonder if he was telling the truth. I didn't like that I had a small inkling of doubt curling in my stomach.

"Yeah, Gwen. See you're getting it now," he spoke slowly. "You're so fucking quick to judge me, any excuse to question what we have. Take the easy way out. Fuck this, I don't want to have to deal with your shit, no pussy, no matter how sweet, is worth this."

I felt a sick feeling in the pit of my stomach at his harsh words. Shit, I may have really fucked this up. Cade walked up to me and roughly put a hand on my neck.

"Congrats, Gwen. You got what you wanted. I'm gone."

He kissed me hard and firm, then without a second look, strode out, slamming the door behind him.

I sank onto my bed, thoughts racing through my brain. My nightmare, the first one since Cade had been in my life. Cade's concerned face, outweighing his anger as he woke me. Crap, I had been such I bitch. He was right, I was quick to judge, but fuck, he knew what I went through. He was gone the whole night, then expected me to believe him without further explanation.

I let out a frustrated little scream, then promptly burst into tears. I should have been glad, his world, the MC, the "club business," the jealous skanks.

Death.

That was all I wanted to stay away from. But my feelings for Cade ran deep. Like that dreaded L word. I couldn't explain it. I'd known him for what? Three weeks? And we'd been fighting for half of that time. But I guessed romance novels and every cliché about men and women were right.

Love doesn't make sense.

Now I'd lost it, before I even knew I had it. But this wasn't entirely my fault. Cade acted like an asshole.

This was too much to deal with. I turned to hug my pillow, crying myself to sleep.

CHAPTER 9

I LAY on the sun lounger in my backyard, welcoming the comforting rays of heat against my skin. My "relaxing" playlist sounded in my ears, up as loud as I could get it to scare away any unwelcome thoughts. My hands closed around a cold margarita, my body welcoming the chill in the scorching weather.

It was Sunday. I spent the whole of Saturday working at the store, trying to act normal, and failing, if the girls' treatment of me was anything to go by. No one mentioned Cade, so I guessed he had filled Rosie in. I stayed late on Saturday night, catching up on paperwork, as I had received a text from Amy saying she wouldn't be home as she was in the middle of a "fuckfest," which made happy, that girl needed to get laid.

I couldn't sleep in an empty house that night, and without any word from Cade, my mood was definitely down. I tossed and turned all night, dozed off about four, then woke late. After cleaning the entire house, I looked out at the beautiful weather and decided not to let my black mood ruin a sunny day.

So I mixed up a batch of margaritas, put on my bikini and decided to get a tan and get drunk. I wasn't planning on doing it alone, but Amy wasn't answering my texts or phone calls so I guessed she was still busy, that guy had stamina.

So here I was, drinking on my own, trying to focus on the fact I was alive and healthy, not a sad, single, most likely alcohol dependent spinster. The ring tone of my phone interrupted my song and I looked at the display and gave a small smile.

"Alex!" I greeted one of my best friends with false brightness, not wanting him to be concerned about my mental state.

"Gwen," he rumbled, a classic man greeting. "What's wrong?"

No nonsense, this guy knew me too well. Unfortunately, I hadn't gotten around to telling him about Cade. Okay, I purposefully didn't tell him. Alex was almost as protective over me as my brother, especially after my suicide attempt. Knowing I was involved with yet another biker would not help settle his mind.

"Nothing," I chirped. "Just had a late night last night, didn't get much sleep." I went for half-truth, I hated lying to my friend.

"Doesn't sound like nothing," he persisted.

"Promise, it's just lack of sleep. Now seriously let's not talk about me, I'm sick of it," I joked. "How are you? How's Ryan? How's my city?"

Alex's deep chuckle sounded down the phone. "All good, babe. Ryan is missing his two partners in crime though," he sighed. "He's driving me crazy, can't even handle a couple of weeks without you two. I think a visit will be in order in the not too distant future. Not only to see you, but to save my sanity."

I let out a little squeal and clapped my hands. "You *so* have to come. I've been missing you two as well. Ryan will love our little place, and I'm sure we can find something for you to do, kill some animals or something," I suggested.

"Animal hunting is more Ian's territory, babe," Alex replied, making me suddenly remember Ian's imminent visit. Not that I forgot completely, it was just pushed to the back of my mind.

"Ohmigod, Alex!" I shouted.

"Jesus, Gwen, don't pop my eardrums."

I ignored this since people seemed to say that to me a lot and continued. "Ian's coming to stay next week! Can you believe it? I haven't seen him in so long, I've been so worried about him. Now he's coming to stay and gets to see my new life," I babbled, the only silver lining in mine and Cade's breakup being I wouldn't have to deal with Ian's reaction.

"That's great, Gwen." Alex didn't sound too excited.

"Great? Are you kidding me? It's fucking awesome!"

"Are you going to tell him?" Alex asked.

I immediately knew what he was talking about and my mood plummeted.

"There is no reason to upset him, Alex." I tried not to sound angry but I was kind of pissed. We had talked about this. I didn't want to put anyone through the trauma of what I almost did.

"He would want to know, Gwen," Alex pushed.

"No, Alex, he wouldn't. I couldn't put him through knowing that I was ready to check out because I couldn't handle living anymore." I took a breath, Alex was silent down the phone, so I continued. "He already has to live with the image of me in that hospital bed, he still somehow blames himself, knowing that I wanted to kill myself is not something I'm going to put on him, Alex. Christ, I hate that you have to have it on your shoulders."

"Not a burden, Gwen," Alex said quietly. "Not when I know you're living, laughing again."

I smiled down the phone.

"Not a burden," he repeated.

"Please just accept that I won't tell Ian?"

He paused. "Okay, Gwen, it's your choice."

I breathed a sigh of relief at his response, then quickly changed the subject. We chatted for a couple of minutes more, then said our goodbyes, with Alex promising he and Ryan would be down as soon as they could.

I blasted my music back up and continued to suck down my margarita. After an hour or so, I decided the combination of hot sun and a heavy hand with tequila was not a good idea. I was tipsy, well on my way to smashed, and getting smashed on my own was not healthy in the least. So I got up, planning on getting some food and gulping down some water to sober myself up.

Headphones still in my ears, I looked up to see a figure standing on the back porch. I screamed, my glass went flying, smashing against the tile. *Shit we're not going to have any glasses left if people keep sneaking up on me.* My vision focused, Amy was wearing a barely there bikini, her mouth was moving as she walked towards me.

"I can't hear you!" I yelled while I pulled my headphones out.

She approached me, carefully stepping past the broken glass. "I said, watch the fricking margarita glasses! Those are our most important kitchen item!" she declared, hugging me.

I glared back at her. "And where have you been, you dirty slut?" I accused, only slurring my words slightly, and waiting for the graphic details of her "fuckfest." That girl left nothing out when filling me in on her sex life. She got a weird look on her face that I couldn't decipher in my almost inebriated state.

"Let me get you another drink and I'll fill you in."

I watched as she drained her full glass, raising an eyebrow.

"What?" she asked defensively. "I have to catch up, you're three sheets to the wind already, you alcoholic!"

I gasped in mock offense. "I am not an alcoholic! Me and alcohol just enjoy a very close relationship."

She laughed and turned to the house to get us more drinks. A brilliant thought entered my mind.

"Amy!" I yelled at her.

"What?"

"I've just had a brilliant idea!"

She waited a beat and then gestured impatiently "Which is...?"

"Let's have a pool party!" I said. "Girls only," I quickly added.

"Call Rosie and the girls when you get inside and tell them to come around, we can order pizza or something. I don't really care about food, as long as we have enough booze."

Amy grinned at me. "I like the way you think, girlfriend."

I smiled back then added, "Oh and bring out a broom as well."

"What did your last slave die of?"

"Disobedience," I deadpanned.

I heard her laughter all the way back into the house.

Hours later, our girls only pool party was in full swing, and I was definitely smashed. The sun had set, but the temperature was still scorching, and I was currently lying on an inflatable lilo in the pool watching all my crazy new girlfriends dancing to some pop song under the dim outside lights.

I smiled at them all, Amy, Rosie, Lucy, Ashley, and a couple of their friends who I had met Friday night. We'd even managed to rope Lily in, convincing her to just *try* a margarita. Considering the way she was dancing, she liked them. I watched them a minute more then lay back and watched the stars swirling above me.

Wait. I don't think stars are meant to swirl. Maybe being this drunk in a pool isn't the best idea.

I paddled down to the shallow end and slid into the chilly water before climbing out.

"Gwen!" Rosie screamed over the music. "Come and dance!" By the look of the way Rosie was moving her body, tequila was definitely winning tonight.

"Just a second!" I yelled back, raising my empty glass. "Need a refill."

Amy caught my statement. "Might have to make a new batch, I finished the last of it." She thought for a second. "Wait." Her face was serious, so I stopped and faced her.

"What?" I asked, almost concerned.

"We don't have any margarita mix left!" she cried, and the girls' faces all dropped.

I giggled. They all looked like Amy told them she was amputating her left arm.

"No biggie, girls, we'll just go and get some more," Lucy chimed in. "I'm sober so I'll go to the liquor store."

Amy threw her arms around Lucy before pulling back and holding her shoulders. "I love you," she declared dramatically.

I watched Lucy laugh and grab her keys. "Won't be long, girls."

"I'll come too," I called to Lucy while pulling on my denim cutoffs. I didn't bother with a top, the weather was still fricking hot, and why did I need one anyway?

I grabbed my purse, slipping my feet into some sandals before following her, slightly unsteadily, to her car. We chatted about all sorts on the way to the store before the inevitable came up, the subject I had managed to avoid all night.

"So what's going on with you and Cade?" Lucy asked carefully.

I sighed, looking out the window before turning back to her. "Nothing."

She raised an eyebrow.

"We broke up." A drunken giggle spurted out of me. "Although we were barely together."

Lucy didn't look convinced. "I've known Cade all my life. He has had a lot of girls..."

I snorted, massive understatement.

"But the way he looked at you, the way he treated you. You were different. No way would he let you guys break up after this little time together."

"Well, he did." I tried not to sound bitchy. "Let's not talk about it, okay?"

She glanced at me worriedly a second then nodded her head. "Okay, sweetie."

We pulled into the liquor store, there were a couple of cars outside, it looked almost busy for a Sunday.

I hopped out, tottering towards the store with Lucy by my side. Once we entered, I was made aware of my state of undress by the florescent lights and two college age boys at the counter leering at me. Whoops.

I glanced over at Lucy, who was wearing a white crochet, see through sundress over her bikini. She obviously didn't care, so neither should I, I deduced drunkenly. I gave the boys a jaunty wink over my shoulder, and their eyes nearly popped out of their heads. Lucy smacked me playfully.

"Tease."

She then blew one a kiss.

"Right back at you, sister."

She looked innocently at me. "They are kind of hot."

I rolled my eyes, men, or more adequately *boys,* were the last thing I needed. "How about you go and get some more precious liquor and I will go and get some chips?" I asked, feeling a sudden hankering for nachos.

"Meet back here in ten."

I sauntered through the aisles grabbing various foodstuffs I decided I needed until my arms were overflowing with treats. I made my way back to meet Lucy, feeling slightly lost. I turned the corner towards the counter, spotting Lucy, stopping dead when I realized who she was speaking to.

Cade stood with his back to me, wearing his usual perfect fit jeans, wife beater and his cut. His muscled, tattooed arms looked good enough to lick, I wonder what they tasted like. No, wait, I was getting side tracked, stupid alcohol. He was with Bull and Brock, both of whom spotted me just before I was about to hide behind a display of cereal.

Shit.

They looked me up and down and Brock grinned. What he was grinning about, I had no clue and I had no time to ponder it. I began walking again, with no other choice now that they had spotted me. Lucy caught my eyes over Cade's shoulder. Cade must have noticed this and he turned around.

Crap, I couldn't handle this, especially in my drunken state, I would probably forget why I was mad at him and try to lick his bicep. I was about to drop my loot and run from the store when one of the college boys stopped me in my tracks. I swayed and the boy grasped my shoulders, steadying me.

"Whoa, do you need help, honey?" he drawled, checking me out shamelessly.

I returned the favor, he wasn't bad looking, if you liked that Abercrombie and Finch look. Shiny blonde hair styled carefully, a pink Ralph Lauren polo shirt which showed off his lean but muscly arms. His eyes were blue, contrasting with his suspiciously too tan skin. I felt like he spent longer on his hair than I did. Not my type at all.

"Um," I tried to think of a polite way to turn him down.

"We're off to a party, if you want to come?" he interrupted me. "A sexy woman like you would be more than welcome. We could have some fun you and me."

I screwed my nose up, not worrying about being polite anymore, this guy was obviously a douche. I opened my mouth to tell him to get lost when a strong hand pulled on college boy's shoulder, yanking him away from me. The motion made me drop all my food. I stared down at the floor, upset at the prospect of picking it all up.

"Get your fucking hands off her," Cade growled.

My head snapped back up to see Cade holding the boy by the collar of his polo shirt, a face like thunder.

College boy looked like he was about to pee his pants. A broken laugh erupted from me, I couldn't help it.

Cade's gaze cut to me a second before turning back to the boy, who was currently struggling to get out of his grip, glancing at Bull and Brock who were at Cade's back, arms crossed.

"Sss-sorry, mman," he stuttered. "I didn't realize she was your girl, my mistake."

Cade let him go and he literally ran out the door.

I glared at Cade, not knowing where to start with this ridiculous performance. He dumped me, what did he care that some college kid was hitting on me? Hell, I could fuck a whole heap of frat boys if I wanted. Not that I ever would. But I had the right as a single, independent, sexually free woman. That would take far too long to explain to a Neanderthal like him, and I wanted to get back to the party and forget this ever happened.

"Well, thanks, Cade, you made me drop all my precious snacks," I whined, glancing out the doors to see a Range Rover speeding off. I raised my hand in that direction. "And ruined my chances with my Abercrombie," I finished.

He didn't need to know I never would have gone near the future stockbroker.

I watched as Bull and Brock tried to suppress grins and Lucy's eyes nearly popped out of her head. Cade's thunderous glare intensified. I ignored this, bending down to begin picking up my food. I swayed a little and would've fallen on my butt if it wasn't for Cade roughly pulling me up, frowning deeply, his eyes locked on my bikini-clad boobs.

"You're drunk," he stated.

"Good spotting," I responded. "You should be a detective."

He ignored that remark, shrugging off his cut. Before I realized what he was doing, he slid it through my arms.

"What are you doing?" I protested and tried to pull away, unsuccessfully.

"Brock," he barked, ignoring me. "Pick up this shit, pay for it and take it back to Gwen's."

Brock nodded, picking up my stuff in one scoop before heading to the counter, where Bull had all but dragged Lucy.

"I'm sorry, all of that testosterone must have blocked your ears, what are you doing? I don't think I'm too eager to be patched into your little club." I tried to take off his cut, but Cade's hands grasped mine.

"I'm covering you up. Jesus, Gwen, what the fuck do you think you're doing walking around in public wearing next to nothing? I can see your fucking nipples through that scrap of fabric. Don't get me wrong, I love seeing them hard and pert, but I sure as shit don't want any other man having that view of your body." He was talking low, but it seemed like a yell.

I was speechless for a second, which Cade took advantage of by dragging me out of the store and towards an SUV. I regained some form of coherent thought as he actually lifted me into the truck.

I tried to open the door to get the heck out of this situation, but Cade had some kind of super speed and was in the truck and had the door locked before I could even touch the handle. Well, either he had super speed or alcohol had seriously slowed my reflexes. I was going for the super speed. I glared at him and he ignored me, backing the truck out of the parking lot.

"Cade," I said quietly.

"What, baby?" he replied, seemingly concentrating on leaving the lot.

"What the fuck?" I yelled, which made the asshole turn towards me.

"Jesus, Gwen, I value my eardrums," he told me calmly.

"Why does everyone keep saying that to me? I do not appreciate getting dragged out of a liquor store by some asshole who just dumped me two days before without a second thought. So excuse me for being a bit *pissed the fuck off!*" I screamed at him.

He gazed at me a beat then turned his eyes back to the road.

"Didn't dump you, Gwen," he spoke quietly.

I rolled my eyes. "Oh so do the words 'no pussy is worth this' actually mean let's get married and have children?" I asked smartly, and loudly.

"Fuck you've got a smart mouth, babe," Cade bit out. "Gonna fuck that smart mouth tonight."

I felt my anger rise to another level. *Was he serious?*

"Are you high? You will be doing nothing of the sort. I don't know how you usually treat the women you fuck, but you cannot just hurt me and expect me to come running whenever you need your dick sucked. Find another fuck toy."

Cade glanced at me, a mixture of tenderness and arousal on his face. I tried my hardest not to get turned on, but my body betrayed me yet again as wetness crept between my legs.

Fuck you, ovaries.

"I'm sorry I hurt you, baby," Cade apologized, sounding sincere, and — regretful?

He stopped the truck, and I only now took notice of where we were. I had been focused on not scratching Cade's eyes out and tequila made it hard to concentrate on too many things at once. The view took my breath away. We were up at some kind of lookout, the ocean was below us and the twinkling lights from the town to the left. If I hadn't been so pissed I would have thought this was a lovely romantic spot. But alas, I was raging.

"What are we doing here?" I ground out, crossing my arms.

"Needed to get a couple of things straight with you before we went back to your place," Cade replied, watching me intently.

I felt uncomfortable under his gaze, the kind of uncomfortable that made me squirm, in a good way.

"I don't like that you said 'we.' There is no 'we,' Cade. You will be taking me back to my house this instant, I have a party to get back to."

Cade raised his eyebrows. "No invite for me then?" he asked playfully.

"No. I make it a point not to invite ex-boyfriends to my home, especially when the one in question has dumped me the day before." I scowled at him. "Besides, it's girls only, no cocks allowed. Literally and figuratively, so you're out on both counts."

He suppressed a grin, the bastard. I turned away from him to stare at the ocean. Silence dawned on the cab before he broke it.

"Gwen, I've said I'm sorry and I'm sick of this shit."

I started to reply, but Cade unbuckled my seatbelt and hauled me across to straddle his lap. I didn't even bother to struggle this time. I just gave him my best Medusa stare. It didn't seem to have its desired effect because he stroked my hair tenderly and his other hand rested lightly on my ribs, brushing my breasts.

"I was pissed off that night, Gwen. Pissed off that fucking Steg had me on business that meant I would be away from you, knowing that you would be uncomfortable around all the boys. And knowing what you looked like, even after I claimed you, those boys are only human and you are fucking beautiful."

He paused, running his thumb along my lip. It took all of my willpower not to open my mouth to him.

"I got pissed when I saw you and Bull talking together, even though I trust that brother with my life. I got even more fucking pissed learning my best friend was planning to put a bullet in his brain and I hadn't even noticed." I watched the emotion dance in his eyes but said nothing. "And I was fucking pissed when after dealing with that, I had to go out and find you after I specifically told you to stay put."

I opened my mouth to protest that little statement, but he kept talking.

"Not used to a woman defying me, Gwen. Don't like it. But at the same time it makes my dick hard as fuck."

His gaze turned hooded, eyes darkening with desire. I felt the evidence of this pressing into my shorts and struggled to suppress a moan.

"And I was fucking scared shitless walking into your house and hearing that scream, baby. That scream, it was goddamned terrifying. Knowing what haunts you, knowing I can't do anything to help it, pissed me off the most." His face was haunted, and his eyes searched mine. "And that whore playing with your mind, trying to fuck things with us. Icing on the fucking cake. Got no excuse, Gwen, couldn't deal, so I left. I hurt you in the process and I didn't mean to. All this has been stewing in my mind, I've been trying to find a way to apologize. But shit, baby, we are not broken up."

I didn't know what to say after all of that. I was still a tiny bit pissed, but man, he didn't say a lot most of the time, but when he decided to talk, he made it count. His finger, still at my mouth, trailed down my chin and unbuttoned his cut to open my almost bare breasts against him. He hissed, and I felt him grow even harder beneath me. I couldn't help but let out a little moan.

"Haven't fucked you in two days, feels like forever since I've slid into that tight pussy."

His rough hands caressed my breasts and I threw my head back, pleasure already overwhelming me. I ground my hips against his, hearing his guttural groan. Cade's hand pulled my head to look at him.

"Look at me, Gwen."

I locked eyes with him and he yanked me into a mind-shattering kiss. I lost all coherent thought apart from the feel of his body, his tongue, his scent.

I reached around to untie my bikini, taking it off but leaving his cut. My body was lifted and Cade took a nipple in his mouth.

"Cade," I breathed as he tweaked my other nipple roughly. I almost screamed. "Need you," I whispered brokenly, trying to undo my shorts.

It was kind of awkward in this cramped space.

Dammit, why did I have to wear shorts?

I didn't want my body leaving his to take them off. Cade solved this dilemma by reaching down to my shorts and ripping them off. I repeat *ripping them off*. Ripping some flimsy lace is one thing, but denim shorts? Whoa.

I didn't think much after that, his fingers entered me, stroking me as he unbuttoned his jeans and replaced his fingers with his cock. This time I screamed, riding him fast and hard, overwhelmed by pleasure. Cade pulled my head down to his, thrusting slowly from beneath me, keeping his mouth inches from mine.

I looked into his eyes as the pressure built, almost floored by the amount of emotion, reverence in his gaze. My orgasm took over and I heard Cade's grunt as I clenched around him, milking his release. I collapsed against him, his strong arms circling around me. We were silent a while, Cade still inside me.

"Baby, the vision of fucking you wearing my cut, something I won't forget till the day I die." Cade bit my neck.

I giggled a little and started to get up, but his arms stopped me.

He rested his forehead against mine. "No way I can ever

repay you for saving Bull's life, baby." His gaze was serious. "The club, me, are in debt to you. Saving a brother's life, babe. Shit."

I stroked his cheek. "I don't need any repayment, honey, just knowing that Bull is getting the help he needs is enough. And knowing my old man won't be losing his brother," I said, emotion seeping into my voice.

Cade smiled. "So I'm your old man again?" he teased.

"I guess." I smiled back.

Cade's face turned serious again. "Care about you, Gwen. A fuck of a lot, more than I have anyone," he said fiercely.

My heart fluttered. "I care about you too, Cade," I whispered, touching my lips to his.

I felt him inside me as he deepened the kiss, slowly beginning to make love to me again, his mouth never leaving mine.

⊏⊐

We eventually made it back to my house and I spotted more than a few bikes as we pull up.

"Looks like cocks have crashed the party, babe," Cade stated as he got out.

I couldn't help but be glad, it would be nice to be surrounded by my friends and Cade's brothers. Cade opened the door for me, lifting me out and directing me towards the house, I stopped him.

"Honey we'll just go straight out back, everyone is still out by the pool by the sounds of it." I tried to pull him to the side of the house, but he wasn't budging. Instead, his hand gripped me firmly around the waist and again he steered me towards the front door.

"We'll go out there once you go and change," he said firmly while opening the door.

I gazed up at him in disbelief. "I'm in a bikini not fricking lingerie, and it's a *pool party*, what if I want to go for a swim?" I protested.

Cade all but pushed me up the stairs. "You're still half drunk, baby, and you're going to be drinking more, swimming is not the best idea."

"Seriously?" I was gob smacked. This was out of control. What did he expect me to wear to the beach? A zoot suit?

"Seriously, babe. And it might be my brothers out there, but Christ, that thing covers fuck all and after everything that went on tonight, I'd rather they not see my woman's nipples."

We made it to my room and I stopped to glare at him, not wanting to get pissed so soon after we had made up.

"Cade, you worry too much, there will be plenty of other girls in bikinis for your brothers to ogle at." I patted his arm reassuringly, trying to get around him to go downstairs.

"Please, baby?" he asked, and damn if I couldn't say no to that sexy man.

I huffed. "Okay." I slowly took off his cut and handed it to him silently.

He slid it back on, eyes on me, devouring me with a look. I turned my back to him, walking towards my wardrobe, untying my top and dropping it to the ground. I stopped to peek over my shoulder at Cade, who was standing in place watching me intently. I gave him a wink then slid my bottoms off and sashayed into my closet.

He groaned. "Baby you're killing me."

I laughed and quickly changed into a pale yellow strapless sundress, falling above my knees. I let my hair tumble around my face, taking a quick look in the mirror.

Shouldn't have done that, what a mess. My skin was pink from being in the sun, my face was definitely flushed from getting thoroughly fucked and my eyes seemed a bit vacant. Even though my escapade with Cade had sobered me up considerably. I guessed that was a testament to how much tequila I had consumed.

I walked out of my closet to see Cade holding the picture of me and my family on my dresser, looking at it intently. He looked so strange in my room. Friday night had been the first night he come here, we had spent every night at his house, primarily because we could be as loud as we wanted. He was so masculine, and my room was so girly, but somehow he fit. He glanced up at me, taking in my outfit.

"Better?" I gave him a twirl, making sure my dress flew up enough so he could see I wasn't wearing any underwear.

He hissed. "Still too fuckin' gorgeous."

I laughed. "Whatever, I'm a mess."

Cade set the photo down, pulling me into his arms and kissing me fiercely.

"You are stunning," he stated. "So much it's taking every ounce of willpower I have not to throw you down on that bed and bury myself inside you for the rest of the night."

He grabbed my hand to drag me down to the party before I could let him.

⸺

It was after midnight and we were all sitting around our huge outdoor table, drinking and laughing. I was sitting on Cade's knee, his strong arms around me, feeling deliriously happy. A few people had gone home, so our group consisted of Rosie, Amy, Lily – surprisingly – Lucy, Brock, Bull, Dwayne (I still didn't know his real name so I kept calling him Dwayne which him and the boys found hilarious), Lucky, Cade, and me. There was something weird passing between Amy and Brock. I still hadn't gotten it out of her who she was with all weekend, I was guessing Brock, but her lips were sealed. Which was weird, because you usually couldn't shut her up. I was definitely going to grill her tomorrow.

Bull seemed better, he was still quiet, sucking on his beer, mostly observing. Lucy seemed to be the only one who could talk to him, so she did her best. I was still worried about him, but at least he was around friends, and Cade had told me that he was staying with Lucky.

I was glad about this, I loved Lucky, he was always happy, a genuinely caring guy. Funny, because he looked like a hard ass, but I deduced he was a big softie. When I told him this, he had groaned.

"Don't ruin my carefully crafted reputation, bitch. I will cut you."

I had burst out laughing, which only made him sulk more. I looked around the table at my new friends and smiled, feeling a happiness that had nothing to do with the amount of tequila that was currently in my system, which was a lot. The last people I thought I would be hanging out with, joking with, hell, sleeping with, were bikers. Funny how the world worked.

I tried not to think too deeply about life and fate and all that shit. I instead focused on my man's hard body underneath me and hands which were absentmindedly stroking my leg while he was discussing something with Brock. He left a trail of fire where he touched me, my body reacting as if we hadn't just had sex, twice, only a couple of hours ago. I squirmed against him, placing one of my hands on his rock hard thigh and squeezing it.

Cade stood abruptly, taking me with him, gathering me in his arms.

I let out a little squeal.

"My woman is ready for bed," Cade declared to the group at large before turning on his heel without another word.

I gave everyone a lame little wave.

"Night, everybody! Thanks for coming!" I shouted. I

smacked Cade's shoulder. "Cade. That was rude, we didn't even say goodbye properly," I scolded, giving him my best drunken glare.

He climbed the stairs with me in his arms with little effort.

"Babe, you squirming against me, feeling your heat and knowing you're smashed. You're lucky I lasted that long," he growled, striding into my room and throwing me roughly onto the bed. His eyes were hungry and dark as he surveyed me.

"Gonna fuck you hard, baby. Looking forward to drunk sex with you."

I didn't say another word, well nothing intelligible after that.

CHAPTER 10

I WOKE SLOWLY with a slight headache, thanks to my old friend tequila — nothing I wasn't used to, and I had definitely had worse. Cade's body was behind me, his arm holding me tightly to him. He was possessive, even in his sleep.

I was happy because I didn't have to rush off and open the store. We were closed on Mondays. And Cade had mentioned he didn't have to go into the garage until late afternoon, so I had the morning with him. Something I hadn't had as I was always rushing off early to get to the store.

I slowly tried to free myself from his grip, so I could get up and make us some breakfast that we could eat in bed. I moved carefully, trying not to wake Cade. I didn't know why I tried, he was some big badass who was aware of shit even in his sleep. His arm tightened across my stomach and his stubble scratched at my neck.

"Where you going, baby?" Cade asked, voice gravelly.

I relaxed into his body, grinding my booty into his hard erection as he kissed my neck.

"Was going to make us breakfast, but now you're awake I

would rather do something else," I mumbled, as Cade's hand moved up to roughly cup my breast.

"If it involves me fucking you, or my dick in your mouth I am all for it. Anything else, fuck no."

I moaned as his erection pressed into me and his fingers roughly tweaked my nipples. Cade pushed me onto my back then raised himself on top of me, hands running down the sides of my body, then cupping in between my legs. My eyes rolled to the back of my head, headache long forgotten about, all I needed was Cade, best hangover cure ever.

"Fuck me, Cade," I demanded, peering at his handsome face.

He bit my lip, not saying another word, just roughly pushed into me. I cried out in pleasure as he gained momentum, pounding me hard.

"You are mine," he grunted, not stopping.

I didn't reply, I was too lost in pleasure. He grabbed my face roughly.

"Gwen, you are mine. Say it."

I breathed out, struggling to get any words together.

"I am yours," I managed to whisper.

That's all he needed to hear and no more words were spoken.

We were finished, Cade was still on top of me, still inside me. I was taking a while to come down from my high, relishing in having Cade back in my bed. Even two nights without him was hard. Uh-oh, this was not good, I seriously liked this guy, but luckily by the way he was looking at me, I think he kind of liked me too.

"Didn't like being away from you, Gwen." Cade was obviously able to read minds as part of his bad ass repertoire.

"Specially didn't like being away from this." His eyes moved down to where we were still connected.

"So you just want me for my body," I joked.

His eyes turned serious. "I want you for a fuck load more than that, baby."

Butterflies flew in my stomach at his words, and a happy glow came over me.

He stroked my face, pushing inside me even further. I let out a soft moan.

"Again?" I whispered disbelievingly, we had had a lot of sex over the last twelve hours.

"Again," he said before he turned me on my stomach and proceeded to rock my world.

After our second batch of love making, I went to the bathroom to clean myself up and to make sure I don't look like Medusa. I cringed when I saw my reflection. My face was slightly red, burnt from the sun and flushed from sex, my hair was a massive rat's nest.

Cade must like me if he still wanted to have sex with me when I looked like this. I smiled to myself, splashing some water on my face before entering my room. Cade was sitting up, sheets to his waist, perfect body on display, he was scowling with his phone at his ear.

"I don't fuckin' care, Steg, we scheduled the meet for this afternoon and that's when it's going to happen," he bit into the phone, looking seriously pissed. He paused, obviously listening to his President's reply.

"Yeah well, they should've thought of that before they peddled their product on our turf. I'm not standing for that." Cade glanced at me and his frown deepened. He listened a bit more. "We will address that issue at church. But this afternoon we are going to make sure those bastards know where we stand and make sure they won't do it again. We need to send a message. Not talking about this anymore." He hung up without a goodbye.

I glanced at the bedside table where his gun was resting. I wasn't too happy to have a weapon in the house, much less so close to where I slept, but I hadn't said anything the nights I had spent with Cade because we were at his house. When I did question why he had a handgun, he had just raised an eyebrow at me and declared he had a permit and it was for protection. He didn't elaborate.

We hadn't yet talked about his role in the club. I bit my lip, realizing I needed to know it all. I wasn't having another relationship where I was kept in the dark up until I watched a man die in front of me. Cade noticed the look on my face at hearing his conversation and watched me carefully.

"Gwen, come here," he ordered.

I ignored him, crossing my arms and leaning against the doorframe.

"Who are the 'bastards' you're sending a message to?" I asked quietly.

"Come here, baby," Cade repeated, not answering my question.

"I'm guessing this message might be made with the help of that." I pointed my head towards his gun.

"Fuckin' hell," Cade breathed, throwing the covers back and prowling up to me, boxing me in against the doorframe. "You never do what I say," he stated roughly.

"You never answer my questions," I shot back. "Cade, it has to be full disclosure with me, I can't be one of those women who doesn't question where her man has been, why he carries a weapon. I've *been* one of those women. Didn't work out so hot."

Cade's eyes darkened and I felt his fury. I knew he hated

what happened to me, I didn't like to throw it in his face, but he needed to understand.

"Shit, baby. You're not going to like what I have to say, the club ain't boy scouts."

"I figured that," I replied. "Full disclosure, Cade."

He stared at me a beat then pushed away from the door, running his hand through his hair. I tried not to get distracted by his naked body and I managed.

Barely.

He pulled me to him, directing both of us back onto the bed. He then positioned me atop of him, so I was straddling him and he sat up, hands circling my body.

"This might make you reconsider things between us," Cade told me seriously, expression grave.

"It would take a lot to make me want to walk away from you," I whispered and his eyes flared.

He sighed then started talking. "The MC was founded by my grandfather and a couple of his buddies when they got back from Vietnam," he began.

I was already surprised. I didn't know much about club politics, but knowing he was the grandson of one of the club's founding members made him pretty important.

"Think they were lost after the war, didn't come from the best families, they were brothers. Maybe not in blood, but in every other way that mattered. The war changed them, they came back, didn't know where they fit back into the normal world. They definitely weren't cut out for nine to five jobs. So they formed the Sons, with the garage for a start, they then moved into other areas — they also ran and sold guns."

Cade watched me closely, his arms were tight around me, as though he was preparing for me to try to run from the room. I stayed put. I was shocked. I didn't expect the club to be law abiding citizens, but running guns? That shit was serious. And dangerous.

"They made alliances with some heavy hitters, made a lot of money and made a name for themselves. My father took over when my grandfather died of cancer. They were liked around town though, people respected my father, they felt protected by the club. You see, even though they were breaking the law, anything that happened in Amber was under their watch. They didn't stand for drugs, the town was kept safe from shit spilling over from the big cities."

He was trying to convince me that even though they were criminals, they still cared about their town.

"My father was good friends with the sheriff, Bill. Crawford's father."

I raised my eyebrows. Well, shit. Both boys followed in their father's footsteps. And a sheriff, friends with a member of an outlaw motorcycle gang?

"Bill knew the club was up to shit, but turned a blind eye, as long as shit didn't spill into his town, there was an uneasy understanding. So the club grew, more brothers joined, got charters around the country. I watched the club grow, all I wanted to do was get patched in, soon as I could. Then shit went down with the Spiders, a rival gang who didn't like the Sons controlling a big portion of weapon sales on the West Coast."

Whoa, that sounded serious. I thought about the damage those guns did, killing people, widowing women like Rosa. My jaw hardened.

Cade noticed, his body stiffening but he carried on. "Things came to a head when I was fifteen, a year off being able to prospect with the club. The Spiders attacked the club when they were on a run, hell of a firefight, my father was killed, among others."

Cade spoke clinically, his voice emotionless. I saw that it still hurt him though, those wounds hadn't healed.

I stroked his face softly. "I'm so sorry, Cade," I whispered.

"Long time ago, Gwen. I'm good with it," he lied. "Anyway, with my father dead and me being too young to take over the club, Steg stepped up. He was my father's best friend. Ruthless bastard, but I respected him, hell, I looked up to all the brothers. He was power hungry though, shit, still is. Some of the brothers were hesitant about keeping in the gun business after losing friends."

He looked at me, I nodded to keep him going.

"Others wanted revenge. I admit, I was a fucked up teenager full of anger, I wanted to kill every one of those motherfuckers. Steg's a real smooth talker, he kept everyone in the business, the money was too sweet anyway. He took me and Rosie in, looked after us, as well as he could."

I was surprised at this, there was obviously something going on between them now, Cade didn't seem to be feeling the love for his father's best friend.

"What about your mother?" I asked carefully, remembering the woman in the photo.

Cade laughed coldly. "She took off when Rosie was two, wasn't cut out for being a mother. Held her down too much, at least that's what she told me."

"Shit," I whispered, feeling sad for Cade, not being able to imagine not having a loving devoted mother.

"Don't pity me, babe," Cade growled, face hard. "She was a crappy mother, did us a favor by leaving. Rosie suffered not having a woman around, but Dad did his best. She still comes to town every now and then. My mother. Stays for a couple of weeks then takes off." He looked at me. "We're not talking about my family history, though. You want to know about the club. What we do."

I gulped, I did want to know about his family, but I needed to know about the club first. I needed to know if I could handle being around to learn about his family.

"Do you still run guns?" I asked, voice small.

Cade's face was stony. "Yeah, babe, we do."

My stomach dropped and dread crept up my throat. Could I deal with that?

Cade took my face in his hands, his eyes searching mine. "Trying to get away from the guns, babe, few of the brothers like the money but not too keen on the risk, especially after Laurie."

I flinched at the mention of Laurie. "That was because of the guns?" I asked, wondering if I would get the honest answer.

Cade seemed to be contemplating what to say before reaching a decision. "Mostly, yes. Spiders have always hated us, but things picked up when we tried to cut in on some of their customers."

So many thoughts were running through my mind, I didn't know where to begin to process this.

"We're going to go legit, Gwen," Cade promised. "Been trying to get the club to do it for years, most of the reason behind the boys sticking with the guns is the money, so I've been acquiring legitimate businesses owned by the club to get us some of the same income. Garage does well in its own right."

I was intrigued. "What other businesses does the club own?"

"Valentines, for one."

Wow that was a surprise, a classy joint like that being owned by bikers, it made me smile.

Cade's expression lightened a bit. "Yeah, that was Lucky's idea, fucking goldmine that place."

"What else?" My mind was ticking over, wondering about the sincerity to his words.

"Couple of bars and a strip club next town over."

I narrowed my eyes. "Strip club?"

"Yeah, babe." His face was blank as if telling your girlfriend you owned a strip club was as normal as telling her you liked Vin Diesel movies.

"Just a strip club? Or does it specialize in happy endings?" My voice was dangerous.

"Don't peddle pussy, babe, strictly stripping." Cade's voice had an edge, like he was almost finding my reaction amusing.

"How involved are you in the running of this club?" I asked, trying not to sound like a crazy jealous girlfriend. But I was feeling like taking a drive to this strip club and burning it to the ground.

Or at least checking it out.

Cade smirked, definitely finding this part of the conversation amusing.

"I check in every now and then, take care of the books and most of the security side of things." His eyes were twinkling.

I didn't say anything else, chewing all of this information over. So not only was my boyfriend selling weapons, he also "checked in" on a strip club. And looking like him, I bet he got a fair share of attention.

But I was focusing on the wrong bit of information. Owning a strip club wasn't against the law, but selling guns on the black market sure as fuck was, those guns weren't used for good deeds.

"Babe." Cade's voice brought me out of my head and I saw an almost worried look in his eyes. Strange, he always seemed so under control, but he seemed rattled.

"Give me a second."

I didn't move off him, I doubted he would've let me anyway, his arms were tight around me, bordering on painful, relaying some emotions he wouldn't verbalize. He was scared of losing me.

I thought about the reality of what he did, aside from it potentially landing him in prison for a long time, it also put him in a huge amount of danger. I was already worried sick about Ian, now my mind would be constantly wondering if my boyfriend was going to be arrested or shot. He said he wanted to get out of the business, he sounded like he meant it and the look of disgust while he was explaining it convinced me.

But how long would that take? And I was sure not all of his brothers would be happy with that idea. Plus, you couldn't just inform dangerous people, 'Sorry, we don't want to sell you guns anymore, don't worry we won't tell anyone about your illegal activities, as long as you keep us off your Christmas card list.' I bit my lip. *Shit!* I really knew how to pick them.

Cade's fingers softly brushed my mouth.

"Hard for me to concentrate on not claiming that mouth when you do that, baby," Cade murmured.

I felt down to my bones that this was special. What we had, it was not something you threw away easily. We seemed to be moving at warp speed, which felt insane and right at the same time.

"You're serious about getting rid of the guns?" I whispered.

"Never been more serious about anything in my life." His hand circled my neck. "Well, until recently," he added.

My heart leapt at the statement, but I needed to know. "How long will it take?"

Cade paused before answering. "Don't know, babe, been working my angle for a while now, making progress. But this shit moves slow, it's hard to get these men to see some different way of life when this is all they know."

"Ballpark," I demanded.

Cade sighed. "A year, at the most. Things are already in motion."

I contemplated this. Would Cade and I be together in a year? My heart told me yes, my head didn't know what to think.

"Planning on you being in my life for a while, Gwen. You will be around when the club turns legit," he said firmly. "If you decide this doesn't change anything, I want you, like I've never wanted anything in my life. I want to make sure every fucker in the world knows you're my Old Lady, that no other asshole will touch you. I don't want this shit with the club to taint you, to jeopardize us."

"Old Lady?" I repeated quietly, knowing the meaning behind that term, the commitment it represented. He had said it before, but we never talked about it.

Cade brushed my hair back, his eyes never leaving mine. "Yeah, Gwen."

Wow, I thought it took a lot for biker men to commit, and Cade was slotting me in long term like it was just natural. I wanted to be in there, but I didn't know if I could accept what the club was doing. The club was a part of him, and he wouldn't leave it if I couldn't deal.

Could I handle this?

I could hardly handle a couple of days without Cade.

Could I stand living in this this town, no doubt seeing him everywhere if I couldn't get right with this?

I was probably going to regret this decision, you'd think I'd know better with my past. But I didn't.

"Those guns you sell, they kill people, innocent people," I whispered.

Cade's eyes were hard on me. "Don't pull the trigger, babe, people get killed with or without guns."

"Guns make it a heck of a lot easier when ending someone's life only takes a second," I argued softly.

Cade ran his hand through his hair, clearly frustrated. He roughly lifted me off him, jumping off the bed to pace the room. He turned back to me.

"Don't think it doesn't weigh on me, Gwen, what those guns do to people, whose hands I put them into. I think about it all the goddamned time. Fuck!" His voice ended on a yell, it was hard to watch, seeing this kind of emotion on my usually staunch man.

I didn't say a word, conflicted emotions were stewing in the pit of my stomach.

"I may be involved in this shit now, baby, but I swear I'm going to get out. The club will never be squeaky clean, and I'm never going to put on a suit and chain myself to an office from nine to five. That's not me. The club is in my blood, riding bikes, it's in my blood." His voice radiated passion, his expression fierce, eyes not leaving mine.

"The club may be in muddy waters now, but I'm going to make sure the way I earn a living, the way I provide for my family doesn't involve me being shot at, or facing a long stay in the state penitentiary."

I sat at the edge of the bed, taking all of this in. And shit, was this a lot to take in on a Monday morning after we had just made up and I was still nursing a hangover.

Cade knelt before me, hand at my neck. "Like I said, babe, this has been brewing for a while, but the moment I saw you, hands full of bags, all class, down to your fucking shoes. I knew."

I looked at him intently. "Knew what?"

"That I had to get out of the guns, get out of that life, get away from the bitterness that I tasted on my tongue. So I could have sweet."

Shit. What do you say to that? My forehead pressed against Cade's.

"A year," I whispered, that's what I would wait.

Cade's eyes flared in surprise, and his whole body seemed to relax.

"I can't be in the dark about what you do in your life, Cade. I know there are Old Ladies that know nothing and like it that way. I also know it's an all or nothing kind of gig."

I had so many other things I wanted to say. What happened if he went to prison? What if he got killed? What kind of accessory did that make me? Knowing what the club did and doing nothing about it. A year was a long time to have to deal.

But the way Cade was looking at me now, what I felt when he touched me, when he spoke beautiful words in his gruff tone, I had to at least try, or I would be wondering for the rest of my life.

Cade sighed. "I know, Gwen. I won't tell you anything that would even get you close to danger. You get the bare minimum. I don't like the thought of one ounce of that shit tainting you. But I won't lie to you," he promised, and I knew he meant it.

"Okay," I said quietly.

I was sure about my decision to stay with Cade, but scared about the life I had just agreed to. Cade pulled me into his lap, kissing me so intensely that I felt like I was being branded down to my soul.

"Babe, what you know, what I feel for you, you're in deep. You're mine, no one touches you, no one puts you in any kind of danger now." He kept a firm grip on the back of my neck before repeating. "Mine."

Even in this somewhat intense moment, the feminist in me felt kind of pissed the way he kept referring to me as "his", like some kind of kid who had a new toy. I opened my mouth to tell him to tone down the macho man bullshit, but another angry female beat me to it.

"Fuck you!" Amy yelled. "Get out of my house this instant before I call the police and inform them some *biker asshole* is trying to rob me," she screeched dramatically.

I scrambled out of Cade's lap to run to the door so I could witness what sounded like a lover's spat, which I had seen a lot of throughout my years with Amy. They were always entertaining. It must've been Brock she had out there, I was desperate to get the lowdown on that situation.

I reached the door, attempting to open it, but Cade blocked

my exit and the front row ticket to the show. I scowled up at him. Damned macho super speed. He regarded me like I was a naughty child, shaking his head. I poked my tongue out at him to reaffirm this belief.

"Calm the fuck down, babe." I heard Brock's calm voice, almost entertained at Amy. "You don't threaten to call the pigs on me, ever. Do it again and I'll put you over my knee." He sounded threatening and sexy all at the same time.

Since Cade wouldn't let the door budge, I stood there, trying to struggle with him. Deducing I wouldn't get anywhere, I settled for eavesdropping.

"Ugh, I can't believe I ever even considered letting such a Neanderthal, cocky, criminal, asshole into my bed. I won't be making that mistake again. Now get. The. Fuck. Out." Amy's voice was pure ice.

There was a beat of silence, and I could almost feel the male fury.

"I can't believe I bothered sticking my dick in some uppity snooty bitch. Don't worry, sweetheart, won't be coming near you again," Brock yelled before stomping down the stairs and slamming the door behind him.

Whoa.

I looked wide eyed at Cade. No guy had ever talked to Amy like that before, it looked like she had met her match, and lost. I bet she was feeling pretty upset right now. I moved Cade's hand gently off the door before reaching up on my toes and kissing his cheek.

"I have to go to her, honey," I told him softly.

Cade seized my hips, plastering my body against his and laid a hot and heavy one on me.

"Yeah, babe, got to go and sort a few things with Brock. I'll be back soon to take my lady to breakfast."

I looked at him, puzzled. "What do you have to sort with Brock?"

"I'll tell you when I get back, go to your friend." He kissed my nose before turning to get dressed.

I got distracted by his muscled tatted body, full on perving at him. Cade caught me staring and gazed over his shoulder with a raised eyebrow.

"Babe, Amy?"

"Right," I whispered and turned back to the door, pulling my robe off the back then opening it. Cade's chuckle followed me as I closed it behind me.

I spotted Amy across the landing, standing in her nightgown, staring at the stairs, looking dazed. This must be bad, Amy wasn't a girl to look "dazed." I made it to her and put my hand on her shoulder.

"Sweetheart, you okay?" I asked softly.

Her head snapped to me. "Yes, I'm fine, Brock's just an asshole." She tried to sound blasé, but I knew my friend too well.

"You have been avoiding this subject around me for too long, Amy."

I directed her to the sitting room that we had between our bedrooms and sat her down on the sofa.

"I know that's partly my fault for being so wrapped up in my own shit that I haven't had the presence of mind to properly grill you," I continued, voice firm. She was avoiding this subject no more. "But you have my full attention and you aren't leaving this room until I get some answers. Now spill."

I watched her bite her lip, a suspicious wetness glimmering in her eyes before she let out a groan. "I'm in love with someone," she declared.

My mouth dropped open and I closed it, then opened it again, but I decided I had no words, so I just managed to look like a fish out of water.

My shock was understandable. Amy didn't *do* love. She had fun with men, none lasting longer than a month or two. She wasn't one of those girls who pretended they didn't care about men then secretly stalked them; she generally got bored easily and wasn't interested in settling down. I suspected it had something to do with her parents and their relationship, but that was something she never talked about. After struggling with words for a while, I managed to choke out a question.

"Who? Brock?" I wondered if she was experiencing the same relationship on speed that I was.

An expression of panic crossed Amy's face, but it was gone before I could question it.

"Of course not. It's someone back in New York, you don't know him," she said quickly. "He's one of my brother's friends, travels all the time. You never met him. His name's... Tom."

"I need more information."

I was struggling with the thought that I had been so blind I hadn't even realized my best friend was in love with someone. That made me an A class jerk.

Amy looked uncomfortable, but I gave her a look and she started to explain. "Well, when my brother first introduced us, I just felt it, I can't explain it. There was an electricity between us."

I nodded, knowing exactly what she meant.

"I knew he felt it too, he tried to keep away from me, but it didn't work. We were like magnets. But he's in the Air Force, hardly ever in the country. And when I say hardly ever, I mean a couple of times a year. So he told me it would never work."

She looked pained at this, I stroked her hair.

"Oh, Ames," I sighed, knowing to a degree what she would be feeling.

"Yeah, I told him I'd wait, till he finished his tour. Whatever it took. But he wouldn't hear of it. Didn't want me stopping from living life. So he broke it off. I was majorly pissed at him, tried to forget him. Didn't work so well. Especially when I saw him with my brother when he was home on leave. That killed." Her voice shook, betraying the depth of her emotion.

"I can't believe you never told me any of this, Amy," I scolded, feeling a little pissed, at her for not telling me, but mostly at myself for not noticing.

Amy looked genuinely regretful. "I'm sorry, Gwennie. I wanted to tell you, but I could hardly get my head around it myself. I couldn't deal, then you got hurt and no way was I letting some stupid problem of mine take up any of your headspace. I wanted you focusing on getting better."

Fuck. Another thing that bastard had fucked up. I wasn't there for my friend when she needed me. That hurt. Tears threatened at the corners of my eyes, I looked to see a couple running down Amy's cheeks.

"And Brock?" I was curious as to where he fit into this equation.

Amy's expression turned from heartbroken to pissed in a millisecond, it was almost funny. She let out a frustrated groan.

"Brock is a prick."

I raised my eyebrow. She rolled her eyes, knowing I saw straight through her.

"Okay, I'm attracted to him. A lot. But he is so infuriating, we disagree about everything, he will never back down on anything. And he is such an alpha male it makes me sick."

"But you like him," I deduced.

Amy looked conflicted. "No." She fiddled with the lace on her nightgown. "Maybe. Yes. Shit! I don't know, Gwen. I still have feelings for Tom, it's not something I can just turn off. But Brock is under my skin and I can't understand how I can even like him, Tom is so different."

"We can't choose who invades our head space," I explained.

"If that was the case, I'd be married to some moderately attractive banker with a boring life and a BMW."

Amy snorted. "Yeah right, Gwen, you would go insane in like, a minute."

"Would not," I argued.

Amy rolled her eyes at me. "Whatever, you can't tell me you prefer anyone over Cade, he is smoking, and the way he looks at you makes *me* blush." Her eyes went dreamy and she fanned herself jokingly.

"We are not talking about me at the moment. There has been far too much of that lately. You are going to finish telling me what's going on with you and Brock."

Amy sagged back onto the couch, covering her eyes with her hands.

"Well, nothing's going on now. We've been dancing around each other ever since we met, the attraction unbelievable. I tried to stay away from him, then running into him the other day at Laura Maye's bar we kind of argued then made up then argued again. Then after the club party we spent the whole weekend in bed." She looked sheepish. "But I set things straight yesterday, planning on keeping away from him. Then last night I was smashed and horny, so he stayed. And this morning he started getting all intense talking about me being his 'Old Lady' whatever the fuck that entails."

My eyes widened at this statement, maybe the men in the Sons did move fast.

She caught my expression. "I know, right? It's like we screw a couple of times and bam, commitment. Fucked up. I would rather wear head to toe Versace for a week straight than be his 'Old Lady,'" she scoffed.

"You said this to him?"

"A version of it."

I couldn't imagine Brock would've liked hearing that too much, if he was anything like Cade.

"Did you mention anything about Tom?" I asked, deciding not to educate her on what a big deal the "Old Lady" label was.

Amy looked at me like I'd grown another head. "Are you crazy? Fuck no. Why would I tell some guy who I kind of have some weird intense feelings for that I am still hung up on another guy, who may or may not come back to this country alive? I just don't know how to process this. How can I love one man and not be able to stop thinking about another? Even if most of the time I feel like poking him in the eye with a mascara wand." The poor girl looked seriously troubled.

"I don't know, Ames," I sighed. "I wish I'd been able to be there for you throughout the Tom situation, but I can be here now. And I can tell you for a fact, the men around here are intense and seriously hot. And they have a way of getting into your head and your heart. But this is a conversation that is way too complicated to have without my old friend, coffee. Let's consume some of this heavenly drink and mull it over," I instructed, squeezing her knee. "You have my support, whatever you decide, don't let fear stop you from exploring this thing with Brock."

"When did you get to be such an expert?" Amy asked as we walked towards the kitchen and closer to the coffee that I needed to inject into my bloodstream.

"Didn't say I was an expert, just making it up as I go along," I confessed.

"Well that makes me feel shit loads better."

"If this all turns to shit we could always run away together and buy a house in the Caribbean?" I suggested over my shoulder.

"Yeah, I might just take you up on that."

After dissecting every piece of information I could get out of Amy, I showered and dressed to get ready for Cade picking me up and taking me out for brunch.

Not that he would ever say the word "brunch," I didn't think his body would physically be able to produce the word. He managed to sneak out at some point during my discussion with Amy. That man had some serious stealth skills.

I put the finishing touches on my outfit, my mind ticking over everything that Amy had told me. How could I be so wrapped in my own life that I didn't realize my best friend was going through some serious inner turmoil? And not realizing she was in love with someone? Shit, I was officially the world's worst best friend.

I was so poisoned by Jimmy that I isolated myself, only seeing Amy a couple of times a week, and when I did see her, she spent most of her time trying to convince me to stay away from Jimmy. I was lucky that she had stuck by me, even after I had ignored her advice. I fiddled with my earring, trying to think if Amy had ever mentioned Tom before, I was pretty sure she hadn't. I was curious and she hadn't even told me his last name so I couldn't Facebook stalk him.

"Cute dress, Gwennie, from the store?" Amy's voice shook me from my thoughts.

I turned to see her lounging on my bed. Maybe everyone had crazy stealth skills? Or it was more likely I retreated into my mind so much I had no awareness of the world around me.

"Yeah it only came in on Saturday, almost sold out already," I told her, focusing on the conversation at hand.

"No wonder, good advertising, you going out in that. Every woman in this town will be wanting one," she told me looking me up and down.

I laughed, checking my appearance in my mirror one last

time. My dress was a white and blue print, similar to a Greek tile design. It had capped sleeves, a plunging neckline and a slightly flared skirt finishing well above my knees. I paired it with white strappy sandals and a blue bag.

God, I loved owning a clothing store.

"Oh, before I forget, can you please handle the store on Friday when I go and pick Ian up from the airport?" I asked, dropping some lip-gloss in my Fendi.

Amy's face paled slightly. "Ian?"

"Yeah, Ian, my brother? He's coming to stay for a couple of days, remember?"

Amy stood, still looking off. "You never told me he was coming," she accused.

I frowned. "Didn't I? Sorry, I thought I did, my brain is all over the place at the moment." I paused, not being able to place the expression on her face, what was with the reaction?

"He's staying here?" she asked strangely.

"Yeah, of course, it's not like we don't have the room. I want to make the most of the time he's here, we should have dinner tonight and plan some activities."

Amy narrowed her eyebrows at me.

"Are you okay? You never make that expression, you always say it gives you premature wrinkles," I teased.

"Yeah, fine. And it does," she answered, changing her expression. She got up off the bed and walked towards the door. "I'm going for a run, will see you later," she announced.

My eyes widened and my spidey senses kicked in. A run? Amy didn't run. She watched what she ate specifically so she didn't have to endure "torture disguised as exercise."

I didn't have time to think anymore on this as I heard Cade's bike pull up. I rushed downstairs, calling out a goodbye to Amy, promising myself to get to the bottom of her behavior tonight.

As I stepped outside, I drank in the sight of Cade, sitting on his bike, sunglass clad and looking too sexy for his own good. He was wearing all black, as usual, the tee under his cut tight enough I could see the outline of his muscles underneath. His hair was delightfully messy as usual, falling to his chin. It seemed he was checking me out also, but was doing it with furrowed brows.

"We might have to take my car, Cade," I called out. "This dress won't travel well on a bike." I gestured down my body, grabbing my keys out of my purse, waiting for him to get off his bike. He pushed off his bike, striding towards me and snatched my keys out of my hand.

"Hey!" I protested. "Didn't anyone teach you it's rude to snatch?"

"Go inside and get changed," he ordered, voice gruff.

I stared at him a moment, then pushed my sunglasses onto my head. "Excuse me?" I asked menacingly, in the tone that every man should recognize from a woman. That was the, "if you don't reconsider what you just said shit is going to go down" kind of tone. Cade obviously wasn't familiar with this tone.

"I'm not fond of repeating myself, babe. Now go and get changed into something that doesn't show half your fuckin' tits and which covers a hell of a lot more leg."

I narrowed my eyes at him. He did *not* just say that.

"Okay, well instead of going to brunch, I think we should find the nearest museum and tell them we have the find of the century," I snapped.

Cade pushed his own sunglasses to his head, revealing angry eyes. "What the fuck are you talking about, Gwen?"

"All cavemen were supposed to be extinct," I said evenly. "Until now." I waved my hand at him. "I'm sure scientists would *love* to study this specimen, unchanged through thousands of years of evolution."

"I'm not finding that smart mouth funny right now, Gwen.

Change, now." He sounded like he was about to lose his temper and he wasn't the only one.

My temper had risen to epic proportions, I was surprised steam wasn't coming out of my ears. I was physically unable to form a response for a moment. Cade was scowling at me, arms crossed in his "I'm a badass everyone must obey or else" stance.

"A little thing happened in the not so distant past, Cade. Something called feminism, which means that women have the right to do a lot of things, like vote, get equal pay, oh, and *wear whatever the fuck they want.* There is no way I'm letting anyone tell me what to wear, ever. If you wanted a timid 'Old Lady' who would don a full-length fucking burka at your request, you've got the wrong one." I was breathing heavily at the end of my little speech, my glare dared Cade to argue.

Cade glared back before yanking me towards him, plastering our bodies together, his hands firmly at my ass.

"This is mine, Gwen." He exclaimed, squeezing my behind. His other hand roughly cupped my breast. "These are mine."

I tried to pull away, very aware I was getting fondled in broad daylight. Cade's grip was firm, I hoped none of my neighbors were watching.

My breath hitched as his hand left my breast, sliding down my body and slipped under the skirt of my dress, lightly brushing over the top of my panties.

"This is most definitely fuckin' mine," his gravelly voice declared.

I opened my mouth to remind him that we were in public and could be scarring the young children who lived across the street, but his hand left my panties and cupped my face.

"Don't get me wrong, baby, you look fuckin' gorgeous in that dress. It makes me want to rip it off you and bury myself deep inside your sweet pussy." The hardness on my stomach was proof of that.

My stomach dipped with desire, I couldn't help but lick my lips.

"Problem is, I know every other male that sees you looking like that will be thinking the exact same thing," Cade continued. "Hate thinking some bastard will have his eyes on parts of my woman that should be for me only."

I rolled my eyes. "You need to tone it down on that ownership thing, Cade. No other man is going to touch me, but you. I'm going to wear what I want, you just have to deal with it."

"Fuck, I know, Gwen. I just haven't felt so goddamned protective about a woman, ever. You drive me crazy. Wear what you like, but next time make sure it is motorcycle appropriate. Ain't letting your fashion choices affect me riding with my woman pressed up against me."

Cade gave me a fierce kiss before opening the passenger door for me. Guess he was driving. Stupid macho man. I sighed dramatically and got in the car, deciding to pick my battles.

CHAPTER 11

THE REST of the week passed in a blur. Cade and I spent every night together, but he was busy sorting out stuff with the rival club and shipments so he didn't get in until late. He didn't tell me much, just the bare minimum, like he promised.

I still had doubts in the back of my mind about whether I had made the right decision, sticking with him when I knew he was breaking the law. But every night he slid into bed with me, giving me mind blowing orgasms and a connection I couldn't yet fathom, I knew I couldn't give it up.

I also saw Luke a couple of times, he popped into the store with coffee and lunch. He was a good man and I enjoyed his company, but I had told him firmly that I was with Cade. At this, his jaw had gotten hard, but he had no further comment. I hoped he got that we were only ever going to be friends. I took to trying to open his eyes to Rosie, whom he looked at more as a kid than a woman, she obviously had a major crush on him and he was too blind to see it.

I didn't tell Cade about seeing Luke, I didn't want to lie to him, but I also knew what his over protective reaction would be. I didn't want that spoiling how happy we were, especially with Ian's visit this weekend. I was seriously getting worried about my brother's reaction to Cade.

This came to a head the night before Ian was due to arrive, and Cade and I were in bed. I was tucked into his shoulder after he had just thoroughly fucked me. He was absentmindedly stroking my back, looking up at the ceiling.

"I've been thinking," I started carefully.

Cade glanced at me. "Whoa, babe, that's dangerous."

I rolled my eyes and continued cautiously. "Maybe you should stay at your place while Ian's here."

Cade stopped stroking. "Ain't no fuckin' way that's happening, Gwen."

Damn, I knew this wasn't going to go well.

"I just don't think it's a good idea, me and you sleeping together with Ian staying downstairs. It's already going to be hard for him to accept us being together, let alone you staying in my bed."

Cade's anger turned palpable. "Him accepting that you are with another biker lowlife?"

I propped myself up on my elbow, looking down at my seriously pissed off boyfriend.

"That's not what I meant, Cade. Ian would be hard on any man he met after Jimmy. He will never stop blaming himself for failing to protect me."

I hated bringing up Jimmy to Cade, it affected him in a way I couldn't understand.

"I get that, babe, but I'm still not staying at my place," he said firmly.

"Can't you just do this for me?" I pleaded.

"Fuck, Gwen, your brother knows you're not a virgin and this is your house."

"I know, Cade, but it will still be uncomfortable for him. I've been looking forward to his visit for so long, the last time we saw each other was in the worst possible circumstances, I just want as little drama as possible." I stared at Cade with wide eyes.

"Puppy dog eyes don't work on me, Gwen," Cade clipped.

"What does work on you then, Cade?" I purred.

I raked my nails down his chest, straddling him and he automatically gripped my hips. I rubbed myself against him, feeling slightly raw but still good at the same time.

Cade growled and his hands stopped me from moving. "Don't use that pussy to try to convince me, Gwen. I'm not changing my mind."

I glared at him a moment, then let out a frustrated scream. "You are infuriating!" I huffed, leaping off him and turning my back.

Cade ignored my obvious annoyance and pulled my back into his body.

"Ain't sleeping alone in bed when I know I could have this sweet body pressed up against me," Cade informed me roughly, holding me tight.

I ignored him, body stiff.

"Well, you're not getting anything from me, Mister. These legs are now closed. I may not be able to stop you from sleeping in my bed, but I can stop you getting inside me."

Cade let out a low chuckle. "Now that I would like to see, Gwen, you can't get enough of my cock. You got the greediest pussy I've ever had."

I let out a frustrated gasp, but didn't even bother replying, knowing my silence would probably piss Cade off more. It only amused him. He rubbed his stubble against my neck and kissed my collarbone.

"Night, baby," he whispered gruffly.

I squeezed my eyes shut, but couldn't help myself from burrowing closer into his body.

―――

I stood excitedly at the airport's arrivals entrance, unable to stop myself from fidgeting as I watched travelers greeting various loved ones. I craned my head, looking for my brother. Impatience quickly took the place of my excitement and I thought back to this morning when I was up at the crack of dawn, unable to sleep and Cade for once didn't wake.

That was good, because he loved his morning nookie and no matter what I said the night before, I knew I wouldn't be able to resist his sex wizard powers. I decided to leave for the airport early before he could wake up and demand to come with me. That was something I wasn't standing for, I needed some drama free time with my brother before I laid my relationship upon him. Cade was pissed if his text was anything to go by.

Cade: You will have a red ass tonight.

I smirked re-reading the text, which I had ignored. I kind of wanted to get a red ass tonight. I glanced up from my phone to see Ian's large form standing out from the crowd. I shoved my phone in my bag and ran towards him, weaving through the crowd to leap on my big brother.

"Ian!" I screamed, throwing my arms around his neck.

My brother's body vibrated as he chuckled, arms circling around me in a tight hug.

He pulled me back, holding me at arm's length, scrutinizing me. It was as if he was looking for outward signs of me falling apart.

"You look good, Ace. Great actually."

He smiled and pulled me into another bear hug before I had

MAKING THE CUT   215

time to return the favor and make sure he wasn't riddled with bullet holes. Tears ran down my cheeks as Ian released me.

"I'm so glad you're safe," I hiccupped, giving him a quick once over, making sure I wasn't missing any injuries.

He looked the same, big and muscled and imposing in his military uniform, his cap hiding his close-shaved head. I frowned, spotting a faded scar on his eyebrow. Ian, guessing what I was about to say before I opened my mouth, ruffled my hair and slung an arm around me.

"Don't start, Ace, few knocks is all part of the job." He directed me towards the exit, not at all confused by being in a strange place.

I frowned up at him. "When are you going to change jobs to something which has a little less knocks?"

"Don't start on me, Gwen, I only just got off the plane, you sound just like Mum. I'll stop when I decide its time, no sooner," he replied tightly.

I opened my mouth.

"No arguments," he ordered.

I huffed, but conceded, I wanted to enjoy this time. As we walked into the parking lot, Ian spotted my car and held out his hand.

"Keys."

I rolled my eyes and rustled through my bag. "You know your penis isn't going to fall off if you let your sister drive her own damned car," I shot sarcastically, handing him my keys.

"I value my life, Ace, and I didn't come back from a war zone just to die in a car wreck caused by my baby sister's heavy foot," he joked, popping the trunk and throwing his duffle in.

I scowled at him as he opened the door for me.

"So I got a *few* speeding tickets back home. Those cops were out to get me. I'll have you know I haven't gotten a single one since I moved here," I informed him smugly, failing to mention that was because the police here hadn't known me since I was a baby and were very susceptible to subtle flirting.

Ian raised an eyebrow. "The only reason you didn't lose your license, Schumacher, is because the cops actually liked you. And I wonder how many doe eyes you have blinded Yank police with to get out of said tickets?" he pondered, seeing right through me.

I poked my tongue out at him. Having my sibling back turned me into a child in less than twenty minutes, apparently.

The two-hour ride home was filled with conversation. Well, more me babbling on about the store, Rosie and my love of Amber with Ian letting out a grunt every now and then, sly smile on his face. I deliberately left Cade out of my conversation, trying to avoid that land mine for as long as possible. I halted my babble as we drove into Amber, pointing at various places.

"There's my store!" I shouted. "You want to go in and meet Rosie and see Amy?"

Ian got a strange look on his face. "Nah, Gwen, we can do that later. How about you show me how to get to your place so I can dump my shit and you can cook me a feed."

"Charming, Ian, you haven't seen your sister in months and already you're ordering her around," I complained with fake shock.

"There's got to be some benefit to having a sibling as crazy as you are," he deadpanned.

As we pulled up to our house, Ian let out a low whistle.

"Not too shabby, Gwen."

"Wait till you see the inside. Amy has outdone herself."

I jumped out of the car excitedly, waiting while Ian grabbed his duffle from out of the trunk.

"Hurry up, Ian," I whined like an impatient child.

"You don't have to wait for me, Ace. I'm sure I'll figure out how to make it through the front door by myself."

Sarcasm was a family trait. I was about to shoot something equally smart back when the roar of a motorbike sounded down the street.

Oh shit.

How was it that Cade even knew we were back? Him and his bad ass magical powers would be the death of me.

Ian's jaw turned hard, he regarded me with concern as Cade's bike came into view, he obviously expected me to have some sort of reaction. Boy, was he in for a surprise. Cade pulled up behind my car and Ian dropped his duffle, pushing me behind him.

"Get inside the house, Ace," he ordered, looking ready for a fight as Cade swung off the bike.

I touched his arm. "It's okay, Ian, I um... know him," I said quickly as Cade approached.

Ian raised an eyebrow, still looking on his guard as Cade came to a stop in front of us. Both of the men looked at me, crap.

"So, Ian, this is my boyfriend Cade." I tried to sound breezy, make it not a big deal. But Ian's expression moved from disbelief to flat out fury very quickly.

Cade held out his hand, looking almost uncomfortable, I would have found it funny if it wasn't me.

"Good to meet you, Ian. I've heard a lot about you," he said roughly.

Ian was staring at Cade like he was some piece of dirt on his shoe. I did not like the way this meeting was going down. My phone ringing made me jump and I reached into my bag and answered it, grateful for the reprieve.

"Sorry, I can't talk at the moment, I'm currently involved in a macho man showdown, whoever this is I will call you back later." I was about to hang up when a sickeningly familiar voice spoke in my ear.

"Oh, Gwennie girl, moved on from me so quickly? Tut tut, I will have to punish you for that lassie, if you're still alive after what I've got planned for you."

My stomach dropped and I felt my body start to sway, threatening collapse.

This can't be happening.

I let out a choked sound, but was unable to speak.

Ian and Cade watched my reaction, instantly on high alert.

"Baby?" Cade automatically stepped towards me and Ian stepped in front of him, hand on my arm.

"Who is it, Ace?"

I gazed blankly at both of them while Jimmy continued speaking.

"Nothing to say to me, my sweet Gwennie? No apologies for putting me in prison, you stupid little cunt!" His voice rose and I flinched, feeling weak and helpless just like I did when he almost killed me.

Cade had managed to round Ian, because his hand was at my waist, his eyes bore into mine.

"Give me the phone, Gwen," he barked.

I ignored him, finding some strength from his touch. "You deserve to rot in prison, Jimmy," I whispered, venom seeping into my tone.

"Don't worry, Gwen, I won't make any mistakes next time we meet, and I most definitely will be fucking you this time, I'll make sure you are bleeding from the inside out..."

I didn't hear anymore because the phone was ripped from my hands. Cade pressed it to his own ear for a second and listened, body turning to stone. I watched his expression turn to a look of pure fury, which I had never seen before.

Ian clutched my shoulders. "Gwen, who is that?" Concern saturated his voice.

I couldn't reply, my eyes were locked on Cade, who was staring at me, phone to his ear.

"Listen to me, you sick fuck. You will never touch a fucking hair on my woman's head ever again. You haven't broken her, not even fucking close. You haven't tainted her because she is a goddamned miracle. She will *neve*r know any violence at the hand of a man for the rest of her life, I'll make sure of that. I'll also make sure I hunt you down and feed you your own dick before I put a bullet in your fucking brain." Cade hung up the phone and threw it against the driveway, smashing it. I regarded the scene blankly, unable to process anything.

"What the fuck?" Ian spat at Cade.

Cade ignored him, striding towards me, tugging me away from Ian and lifting me into his arms. He carried me inside like a bride, I would have found that funny, maybe, if I wasn't feeling numb. Cade sat on the couch in the living room cradling me in his arms, Ian hot on his heels.

"That was him wasn't it?" my brother bit out, shaking with fury. "That fucker is meant to be in prison!" Ian yelled, making me flinch.

"Ian, check yourself or get the fuck out of here," Cade ordered, glaring at my brother before directing a soft gaze at me.

"You're okay, Gwen, you're here with me and I won't let anything touch you. You're safe," Cade told me firmly, arms tight around me. I realized I was shaking.

"Get her a shot, tequila," Cade ordered my brother, who glared at him a moment, but disappeared to do as he asked.

"Gwen, talk to me."

I couldn't reply, my mind was still replaying images I had buried deep, images that Jimmy's words had thrust to the surface. Cade lifted me up and placed me on the couch, kneeling in front of me with his hands at my face.

"Look in my eyes, baby, get out of your head. You're safe, always will be." His words were a promise, eyes blazing.

Ian entered the room, shot glass in hand, which he quickly handed to Cade. Cade held it between us.

"Drink," he ordered, his firm tone rousing me slightly.

My shaking hand wrapped around the glass and I threw it back, feeling the burn of the alcohol warm my insides.

"Good girl."

I stared into his steely grey eyes, finding my strength. Cade's previous words sounded in my ears, fighting away the demons. I smiled at him weakly.

"So meeting my brother went well," I remarked dryly.

Cade looked at me intensely, then pulled me in for a rough kiss, despite our audience.

"You sit with Ian for a bit, baby. I've got to make some calls, okay?"

I nodded slowly and Cade watched me a beat then stood.

"You want to tell me what the fuck is going on?" Ian asked Cade, face hard. "How the fuck can that prick call her? He's in prison."

My thoughts exactly. *Shit, was he out?* My body started shaking again.

"Cool it and sit with Gwen while I find out what the fuck is going on."

Ian looked seriously pissed at being ordered around, but one look at me had him joining me on the sofa. He drew me into his shoulder.

"I promise you'll be okay, Ace, no one will hurt you."

I didn't say anything, I just rested my head on his shoulder, trying to listen to Cade, but only hearing a few raised curses.

"This is bullshit," I whispered quietly to myself.

How the fuck can this fucker almost kill me once, hurt not only me but everyone I love and then once I am healed come and rip me open and ruin the first time I see my brother?

Fuck that. I was not going to be a weak broken woman anymore.

"This is bullshit!" I yelled suddenly, struggling out of Ian's arms to stand and pace the room.

"Ace..." he started, standing to approach me.

I threw up my hands pushing him away to continue my pacing. "Seriously, what the fuck, Ian? This cannot happen all over again. I won't let it! That piece of shit is not going to ruin your visit, and he certainly isn't getting to me anymore. I am happy. Happy!" I glared at him, my expression contradicting my words, but I didn't care, I kept ranting. "The prick is in some jail in New York, eating filthy prison food, getting infections from homemade tattoo guns and most likely taking regular ass rapings from a man named 'Big Earl.' I am here, running a successful business, living in a beautiful town surrounded by friends. I have a sexy as shit man who cares about me and a brother who has my back no matter what," I declared fiercely.

Ian directed a sad smile at me. "Gwenevere..." he said quietly using my full name.

I held up my hand. "I'm not finished," I snapped before stomping up to him, clutching his shoulders to make him listen. "Don't you see? I will not have you directing those looks full of pity at me anymore, and I sure as shit don't want you to have to handle me like I'll break at any moment. You don't need to. I'm okay, it's taken a while and it's taken that crazy fuck's phone call to make me fully realize it, but I'm *okay*." I smiled into my brother's eyes, hoping he got me.

I sensed movement out of the corner of my eye and turned to see Cade, face unreadable, leaning against the doorframe, arms crossed watching me. I moved my gaze and it landed, surprisingly, on Luke, who was in his uniform, looking openly concerned but with a hint of a smile. How did he get here so fast?

"How long have you guys been standing there?" I wanted to know how embarrassed I should be.

Luke's face broke out into an all-out smirk. "Big Earl?" Amusement danced in his eyes.

A lot embarrassed as it turned out.

I shrugged. "Hey, I don't know too many prison nicknames, my knowledge goes as far as *Shawshank*," I joked, trying to keep the jovial mood.

Luke's face softened and he entered the room, engulfing me in his arms.

"I'm so sorry, sweetheart," he whispered in my ear.

I opened my mouth to reply when Luke was suddenly standing a good distance away and Cade stood in front of him, anger palpable.

"Hands off, Crawford," he ground out, barely controlling a growl. "You are here in a professional context only, keep your fucking distance."

Luke glared back at Cade and I rolled my eyes, which Ian caught, giving me an amused expression.

"Not another macho man stare off, please! I can hardly breathe with the amount testosterone in here. Cade, do not talk to Luke like that, he is my friend," I scolded Cade and he turned to me, death stare directed in my direction now. Whatever. I ignored this and sent a soft glance in Luke's direction.

"Please, Luke, sit down. Thank you for coming, can I get you anything?" My mother taught me there was never an excuse for bad manners, even if my crazy ex-boyfriend had just called me from prison, threatening to rape me.

Luke, instead of sitting, turned to my brother and held out his hand. "You must be Ian, it's great to finally meet you. Gwen's been looking forward to your visit. Sorry it had to start out like this."

Ian looked surprised but took Luke's hand giving it a firm shake. Cade also looked surprised, and pissed. He obviously figured out me and Luke had been talking.

"Nice to meet you too, glad to see Gwen has a friend on the right side of the law," Ian said, directing a pointed look at Cade.

I scowled at him, obviously my brother was still not happy with my boyfriend. Great.

Cade grabbed my hand and sat me down on the couch. He didn't join me, just stood beside the arm of the chair, hand lightly on the back of my neck.

"Now the pleasantries are over, can we please cut to how the fuck this bastard got Gwen's number, or how the fuck he got a phone in the first place?" Cade barked in Luke's direction.

Luke looked from Cade to me, obviously deciding not to engage in any hostilities. He sighed and sat across from me, scrolling through his phone. My brother stayed standing, eyes on me, or more specifically, Cade's hand on me. I poked my tongue out at him. He needed to lighten up on the whole protective brother thing.

"Okay, so I just got off the phone with New York lockup. According to the Warden, O'Fallan paid one of the guards to smuggle him in a cellphone, which he had one of his men program your number into." Luke tried to sound detached and all business, but his jaw was hard.

How did they do this so quickly?

"How did they even get my number?" I asked. I Decided to ignore the super-efficient and scarily quick response from Amber PD. "My cellphone number isn't anywhere. I made sure only a few people had it, specifically to avoid something like this happening."

Luke ran a hand through his hair, looking frustrated. "I don't know, Gwen, that's all the info I could get for now. Either one of these guys is a master hack or someone has given up your number." He said the last part gently, but that still didn't mask his true meaning.

My stomach dropped as three pairs of male eyes focused on me.

"That's not possible, only the people I love have my phone number and they sure as shit wouldn't give me up," I told them all firmly.

"You sure about that, sis?" my brother asked quietly.

I glared at him. "Well, no, Ian, I guess Ryan could have given me up. You know the guy who slept beside me for two weeks after I got out of hospital so I wouldn't be alone? Or maybe Alex, who followed me around the whole of New York whenever I went out, so I would feel safe? Or fuck, maybe Amy, my best friend who uprooted her whole life to move out here with me?" I paused, breathing heavily, about to list all of my new friends who I trusted just about as much, but a firm squeeze on the back of my neck stopped me.

I glanced up to Cade, his expression was still unreadable.

"Give your brother a break, baby. We just need to explore every option. Don't worry, we'll sort this, you'll never be getting a phone call like that again."

His voice was firm, sure. I trusted him. I trusted all the men in this room. Ian looked slightly taken aback at Cade backing him up and I fought a smile.

Luke cleared his throat, standing. "Okay, Gwen, I better be going, just wanted to come and fill you in face to face, make sure you were okay." He slipped his phone away.

I stood, feeling Cade's arms at my waist. "Don't you need a statement from me or something?" I asked Luke, surprised.

He locked eyes with Cade for a split second before his gaze came back to me.

"No sweetheart, we can see the phone records as proof of the call and we have Cade's statement. I'll call you when we have something new." He gave me a smile, shook my brother's hand yet again and nodded stiffly to Cade. The room was silent for a moment after he left.

"So, Ian, what's new with you?" I asked with only a hint of sarcasm.

———

I laid a plate of food in front of my brother, along with a beer.

"Thanks, sis." He rubbed his hands together. "Looking forward to this, there ain't exactly five-star restaurants where I'm stationed."

I grabbed my own plate and sat across from him. "Well, I don't think I'm a world renowned chef either, Ian," I replied, amused.

"Pretty darned close." He took a bite and groaned. "Come on, what do you marinate this steak in?"

I tapped my finger to my nose. "I'll never tell," I teased before adding, "Oh and I made peanut butter cup torte for dessert."

My brother's eyes lit up. "No shit?" he all but yelled, mouth full.

"Eww, yes, you ape, did Mum teach you nothing? Don't talk with your mouth full, I would rather not wear your dinner." I gingerly picked up a piece of steak that had flown from his mouth onto my shirt and threw it back at him.

Ian just chuckled and continued to devour his dinner. I focused on my plate and smiled, happy that the mood had lightened.

After Luke left earlier today, Cade also split, saying he had "shit to do." That was probably a good idea, after a more than rocky introduction and that phone call, Ian and I had needed some time to talk.

Although we hadn't actually talked about anything important all day, I showed him to his room, made him some lunch then showed him round Amber. He was very impressed and agreed that it reminded me of home.

I showed him around my store, which he didn't say too much about, he was an alpha male, girly clothing shops didn't exactly excite him. Weirdly, only Rosie and Lily were there, and they both had no idea where Amy was. Making up with Brock, I hoped.

After that, we had laid by the pool drinking beers, and Ian told me some funny stories about the boys from his unit. I knew a couple of them, and one of them, Keltan, was my brother's best friend from back home. He was like a second brother to me, so I was always happy to hear about him too. We seemed to have let the events of this morning be temporarily forgotten so we could spend some quality time together.

Which brought us to now, having my kick ass steak – if I did say so myself – and joking together, like we always had. Still no word from Cade or Amy, which had me slightly concerned, but I'd hear from them both at some point, hopefully.

"So, Gwen. You and this Cade guy, what the fuck?" Ian's tone brought me out of my thoughts.

I sighed, I had known this was coming. "I knew you wouldn't give him a chance. Please try not to judge him based on appearances. I did that when I first met him and I regret it. I really like him, Ian."

I tried to give him my puppy dog eyes to soften him up, but he just scowled back.

"Jesus, Gwen, another biker? These guys are dangerous, I don't want you getting caught up in this again," he barked angrily.

I let out a frustrated noise, sounding like a petulant child.

"You don't even know him, Ian. Please just reserve judgment until you know him a little better. He does actually care about me."

Ian gave me a look. "Yeah, I can see that, that's what I'm worried about," he muttered.

I rolled my eyes. "Seriously? You're angry because my boyfriend *likes* me?"

Ian put down his knife and fork, rubbing the back of his neck with his hand. "It's just intense, Ace, the way he looks at you. Christ, you haven't even known each other for two months."

I kept looking at him, doing what I used to do when we were young and I wanted something. Staring at him looking sad, refusing to speak until he gave in. Ian, knowing my game, growled and picked his knife and fork again.

"Fuck it. I'll try my best to be civil to the guy," he conceded before focusing on his food.

I beamed and began to talk about something else when the door slammed and Amy stormed in glaring at me, not even glancing at Ian. She pointed her finger at me angrily.

"You!" she yelled before approaching the table and standing in front of me.

What now?

"I can't believe the Prick Who Shall Not Be Named called you and I had to find out from freaking *Lucy*! I mean, I love the girl, but I don't want to find this shit out second hand. You should have called me the moment you got off the phone with that maggot so I could call him back and reach down the phone and castrate the fucker," she finished, voiced raised to a near screech at the end.

I gave her a second, knowing that she was just upset for me and a teensy bit of a drama queen.

"Hello, Amy, how's it going? Want to say hello to Ian who

just got here from some unknown war zone?" I asked sarcastically narrowing my eyes.

Amy blanched a little, as if she didn't realize Ian was even here, she glanced across to him and smiled tightly.

"Sorry, Ian, I didn't mean to be rude was just a little preoccupied with the whole 'Gwen getting a phone call from a murderous psychopath' situation."

I was about to reply, when Ian pushed back from his chair, staring at Amy with a weird look on his face. He advanced on her in two strides and engulfed her in his arms. She looked surprised for a second, then melted into his embrace.

Ian released her, looking her up and down, eyes twinkling. "You look great, Ames," he said softly.

She returned the favor, her gaze scanning him until her eyes rested on the scar I spotted today. She nodded her head towards it. "Just another one to add to the collection," she remarked dryly.

Before I could think too much of this strange display, they both seemed to snap out of whatever it was and sat down, Ian back to where he was, Amy beside me. She took a pull of my beer and grabbed my fork, which was halfway to my mouth, eating my last piece of steak.

I glared at her. "That was my last piece, you bitch."

Amy said nothing, just smirked. Her face suddenly got serious. "So what happened with this phone call, Gwennie? How did it even happen in the first place?"

I told her about what Luke told us, leaving out the part about one of my friends possibly giving out my phone number because that was just bullshit.

Amy was fuming. "Right, I'm calling my father and he can talk to one of his buddies about sorting out the guards at that prison," she snapped, betraying her upper class breeding.

"Can we not worry about it right now?" I pleaded, standing to take our plates and serve dessert.

"How about we talk about where you've been all day, Abrams?" I shouted over my shoulder as I got the torte and some plates out. "Having some make-up sex with Brock maybe?" I gave her a wink, walking back to the table. Her face blanched, a panicked look on her face was quickly replaced with a glare.

"Who's Brock?" Ian clipped, jaw hard.

I set the plates down with a smirk. "Oh, just some guy that won't take Amy's shit but is so totally under her skin."

Amy scowled at me, quickly glancing at Ian, who was staring at her with a blank look on his face.

"He's no one. No one special, and I certainly won't be talking to him again. Subject closed," she exclaimed grumpily before dumping a huge piece of torte on her plate.

I raised an eyebrow, she usually avoided refined sugars and carbs like the plague. She scowled at me yet again. "It's my cheat day," she declared defensively.

I held my hands up, serving myself a piece, choosing to ignore the weird atmosphere and instead enjoy the deliciousness of peanut butter and chocolate.

I heard the roar of a Harley and smiled. I hadn't heard from Cade since he left, and I was glad he was ignoring my request not to sleep with me while Ian was here. I needed him tonight.

Hearing the Harley too, Ian gave me a look, not as excited as mine.

Amy caught this and she pointed her fork at my brother dangerously. "Look here, Mr Soldier, don't you dare try any of your macho man bullshit and be a dick to Cade. He can handle it, I have no doubt about that, but we don't need the drama. He cares about your sister and makes her happy, that's all you need to know," she said firmly, holding a stare with Ian until he nodded stiffly, grabbing his plate and getting up.

"Thanks for the amazing grub, sis, but I'm knackered." He

heaped more cake onto his plate before shrugging his shoulders at me. "If I get hungry in the night."

I let out a giggle as he kissed me on the cheek. He nodded at Amy and walked down the hall to the guest bedroom.

I quickly turned to Amy as I heard the front door open and close.

"What the hell was that?" I inquired.

Amy looked at me innocently. "What?"

I glared at her disbelievingly. "You know what. You and Ian, what the hell is going on? You guys were acting weird."

"No, we weren't."

"Yes, you were."

"Were not."

I let out a frustrated groan, yanking her plate away.

"Hey, what the fuck?" Amy asked angrily as I swiped the serving plate away and stood out of her reach.

"You don't get any more until you tell me what's going on," I declared, holding both plates up in the air. I was vaguely aware of Cade's eyes on me as he entered the room, grabbing a beer.

Amy scowled at me, then at Cade. "Your girlfriend is evil," she stated, pushing past me and snatching a piece of cake before running upstairs.

"That will go straight to your ass," I yelled to her back.

"Fuck you!"

I laughed, turning towards Cade, who was leaning against the breakfast bar with a raised eyebrow. "Dare I even ask?"

I dumped the plates on the counter and began tidying up. "Nope, just girl stuff." My mind was still stewing over the weirdness between the two people I loved.

Cade remained silent and stayed where he was, which was weird. He always had to have his hands on me.

"Where have you been today?" I inquired softly, not wanting

to sound like a whiny bitch, but also needing him to tell me more about where he'd been disappearing off to.

"Club business," he clipped, taking a chug of his beer.

I didn't answer, waiting for him to elaborate or tell me what was going on. There was just silence, apart from the sound of me cleaning the dishes. The silence lasted a while, until I drained the sink and turned to look at my broody man. Our gazes locked and we just stood there for a moment staring at each other.

It never got old checking Cade out. He had a rough growth of stubble shadowing his face and along with his long black hair, he looked wild and sexy. His muscles nearly burst out of his black tee shirt he wore under his cut, his veins pulsing underneath his tattoos.

I licked my lips, feeling a tingling between my legs as my gaze neared his eyes. His look was intense, hungry, roving over my body. I was only wearing my yoga pants and a racer back singlet, but the way he looked at me, you would have thought I was wearing my sexiest LBD.

Without a word, he stalked towards me and seized me, covering his mouth with mine. The kiss burned out of control, Cade lifted me up and I wrapped my legs around his waist. His mouth never left mine as he carried me up the stairs. I was thrown on my bed and Cade jerked my pants off, lifting me to get my underwear off at the same time.

"Cade," I groaned, my voice rough with arousal.

His dark gaze stilled me. "No talking," he commanded. He unzipped his jeans, just to free himself, leaving the rest of his clothes on.

He leaned down, lightly kissing my inner thigh before reaching up to take off my tank. I was fully naked and Cade covered me, fully clothed. There was something terribly erotic about that. He roughly tweaked my hard nipple, I cried out as his other hand worked between my legs.

"Quiet," he instructed gruffly.

He covered my mouth with his own before roughly thrusting into me. I moaned loudly into his mouth, raking my fingers down his cut as he pounded into me mercilessly. My orgasm ripped through me, melting me into little pieces. I arched my back, unable to take the intensity as Cade continued his thrusting. I felt him shoot his release into me, which sparked me to melt all over again. I took a while to come back down to earth, opening my eyes to Cade staring down at me with an intensity that was scary.

"I love you," I murmured into those grey eyes.

Shit. Where did that come from?

Man, I couldn't keep my mouth shut, I hadn't even properly admitted it to myself until today and here I was blurting it out.

Fuck.

I realized I had closed my eyes, embarrassed and pissed off at myself. I gingerly opened them, afraid to see Cade's face. He hadn't moved and was still staring at me with that intense gaze that seared my soul.

Crap.

"Um, sorry, that so shouldn't have come out...I was just high on an orgasm, you know?" I sounded like a total dweeb, who said "high on an orgasm"? "Well, no, I –"

"Shut up," Cade interrupted me, which was a good thing, who knew what I would've said next. I bit my lip, waiting for him to say something.

"Say it again," he demanded.

"What?" I asked shyly.

"Fucking say it again, Gwen." His voice was hard, almost emotionless, but one hand reached to softly frame my face.

"I love you," I all but whispered. "I've loved you since you scared the shit out of me outside my house, even though I couldn't admit it to myself until now."

His eyes flared, but he said nothing. After a beat, he plastered my mouth to his in a passionate kiss, setting me on fire all over again. He drew back, eyes still hard, but full of emotion.

"Needed to hear that, baby." He kissed my forehead and pushed off me, buttoning his pants back up. "Got to go. Got some club business that can't wait. Fucking Spiders causing some shit, need to lock it down before that shit spreads." His voice was grim, but focused.

My heart dropped.

I tell him I love him and he gives me a quick kiss and is going to bail? Well isn't that a kick in the vagina.

I couldn't deal with this naked while he stood above me fully clothed. I moved to get up, to cover myself, but Cade's arm landed on my chest, stopping me.

"No, Gwen, this is exactly what I want to picture in my mind for the rest of my night. My girl, freshly fucked, orgasm all over her face, my cum running out of her. Naked, looking like a fucking goddess."

He gave me a rough closed mouth kiss before standing again, giving me a long look then he was gone.

CHAPTER 12

"NEEDED TO HEAR THAT. That's what he said? Are you sure you heard right, like maybe your ears weren't working right after minding blowing sex?" Amy asked, sipping her coffee, looking at me hopefully.

I stared back at her, feeling sick. "Nope, that's definitely what he said. Then he left. Crap, I am such an idiot," I whined, putting my head in my hands.

Amy patted my back soothingly. "That man loves you. Anyone can see that, he's just being all bad ass biker and doesn't want to say it because he's afraid if he does his balls will automatically belong to you."

I raised my eyebrows at Amy. "Really? I think he just doesn't love me and has now run off to set up a club in Mexico and I shall never see him again," I exclaimed sadly, downing the rest of my coffee, getting up to get more. I needed a shot of whiskey in it.

Amy waved her hand. "Don't think like that. Men are idiots, just give him time."

I made it to the coffee pot and let out a frustrated scream. "Fuck! No coffee, great."

I seriously thought I might cry. On the best of mornings, coffee was the only thing that got me functional for the day, on this day I needed it hooked up to an IV.

"Chill. Last time I checked they were still making it." Amy said calmly. "I'll get dressed and go and get us some." She got up, still in her nightie.

"No, don't worry I'll go, I'm dressed," I said.

I couldn't sleep last night so I had gotten up super early and gone for a run, which was the reason I was up and dressed so early on a Saturday.

"I'll go to the café and get us something for breakfast too. I'm sure my brother will need some sustenance if he ever awakes from his coma," I joked.

Amy sat back down, sipping her coffee and reading the *New York Times* on her iPad. "Good, I couldn't be fucked anyway."

After getting not only coffee for me, Amy, and Ian, I also bought half the café's pastries and muffins, not knowing what Ian would feel like. Okay, maybe partially so I could eat my feelings.

Just as I was pulling into my driveway, my phone rang. Glancing down, I saw it was Cade. Shit, I had no idea how to deal with that, so I decided to do the mature adult thing and ignore the phone call.

I managed to get all of our coffees and treats in one hand, thanks to my waitressing days, just in time for Cade to call. Again. *Crap.* I had to answer or he'd go all protective man crazy and presume I had been kidnapped and was being held for ransom. I juggled my packages and answered the phone while walking towards the door.

"Hey, can I call you back? I'm kind of trying not to drop this precious liquid they call coffee," I joked, trying to make the mood light, like he hadn't just broken my heart last night.

"I'm just about at your place now, am stopping by with the boys..." Cade started, but that's all I heard because when I opened the door, I was assaulted with the sight of Amy and my brother making out.

I repeat, *making out.*

He was wearing only boxers, no shirt. Amy was still in her nightie, which Ian had hitched up to almost her waist. I gasped, dropping my coffee, momentarily forgetting its life-giving qualities.

"Oh my god," I said quietly not realizing I was talking into the phone, and not to myself.

Amy and Ian, startled by me dropping the coffee, both gaped at me.

"Baby? Are you okay?" Cade's voice sounded in my ear, but I was too busy processing the scene in front of my eyes to answer.

"Oh my God. My eyes!" I shouted dramatically.

Ian gave me a cheeky smile while Amy rushed towards me, looking very guilty.

"Gwen! What the fuck is going on?" Cade yelled. I hung up, not wanting to deal with that as well.

I turned, deciding to walk back outside, maybe hoping I had opened the door into a parallel universe, and if I walked back in, everything would be normal. I was such an idiot, how could I not realize? Amy saying she was in love but making up some vague guy. The way they were acting around each other.

Shit I am a moron.

Third graders could've figured it out. The door opened again as I paced the front lawn. Amy ran down the porch, looking more than ruffled, her nightie haphazardly pulled down.

"Gwen, stop, listen to me. I'm sorry I didn't tell you it's just —"

I turned to her, suddenly angry, directing my anger at her, when I was really pissed at myself for not noticing sooner.

"It's just what, Abrams? You've been screwing my brother and lying to me about it?" I shouted at her. I strode over to her, shoving her in the chest. "We never lie to each other. Ever. Jesus, how could you not tell me?"

"Gwen. Stop, we can explain." My brother emerged out of the house, dressed at least.

I held out my hand to him. "Stay out of this, Ian, this is a chick thing. You don't have a vagina, so you don't understand."

After stumbling a bit from my push, Amy was standing straight looking pissed at me now. She shoved me back, hard.

"Don't push me!" she shouted as I stumbled, almost falling on my ass.

I got in more of a rage and hardly noticed the rumbling of Harley's' racing down the street. I just glared at Amy and tackled her to the ground sitting on top of her, struggling with her arms.

"It's my *brother*, Amy. Do you not think I would've been happy for you two, you stupid idiot?" I yelled in her face, as she wrestled me, rolling us both over to a mass of arms and legs. She pinched me as I got back on top of her.

"Ouch! You bitch." I was about to pull her hair when strong arms dragged me up. I fought them, watching Ian help Amy to her feet.

"Chill, babe, Jesus," Cade whispered in my ear.

I ignored him, instead I focused on my brother and Amy, standing beside each other not touching.

"Why didn't you tell me?" I repeated, this time quieter.

Amy regarded me sadly. "Shit, I don't know, Gwen. First it was because I didn't even want to admit how I felt, let alone admit it to you. Then things got complicated, you got hurt and there was never a right time."

She looked up at me sheepishly, her gaze wandering behind me and her face paled. I turned, awkwardly, as Cade's arms were still around me. Brock was standing with Bull, Lucky, Dwayne, and some other guy I couldn't remember the name of. They all had amused smirks on their faces, which made me cringe, knowing what kind of show they had just witnessed. Well, apart from Brock, his jaw was hard. He was glancing between Ian and Amy.

Oh shit.

Ian caught on to who was staring at who and his jaw went hard also. He not so discreetly stood in front of Amy, not only staking some sort of fucked up claim, but covering her barely clad body with his own. Uh oh. Time for damage control.

"This is not the time to discuss any of this, okay? Go back inside and put some clothes on, Amy, the neighbor's boys will be snapping photos of you with their phones."

Amy looked down as if only just realizing the twins were dangerously close to popping out.

"Ace, we'll talk inside okay? Just calm yourself first, we don't want anymore brawls in the living room," Ian muttered dryly before directing Amy inside, his hand on the small of her back.

"I'm still mad at both of you, in fact I'm not speaking to you as of now," I yelled at their backs before slowly turning to the bevy of bikers standing on the curb. I blushed as they all watched me expectantly. Brock was glaring at where Amy disappeared back in the house, looking like he was about to explode.

"Wow, Princess, looks like we know who to come to if someone needs a lesson given to them." Lucky smirked in my direction before bursting out into laughter. The other men smiled openly, even the side of Bull's mouth was twitching.

A blush crept up my cheeks. Shit, they would all think I was insane now.

"Sorry you had to see that, guys, I guess I just lost my temper." I shrugged, no other explanation crossing my mind.

"Fuck, don't say sorry. That was the hottest thing I've seen in ages." Dwayne gave me a wink and I screwed my nose up at him.

"Enough," Cade commanded and the men immediately

looked more serious, although amusement still danced in their eyes.

"Back to the club, will meet you there in five," he continued gruffly.

The men nodded and climbed on their bikes. Brock was the only one who didn't, still standing stiffly, glaring at the house.

"Brock," Cade barked.

Brock moved his gaze slowly, then nodded. "Fuck this shit," he grumbled, climbing on his bike, roaring away with the others.

I peeked up at Cade gingerly, who released his hold on me and grabbed me by the shoulders.

"What the fuck was that, Gwen?" he all but roared, shaking my shoulders roughly.

"Well, I just found out Amy had been lying to me and I kind of overreacted," I explained, pissed at his reaction, he needed to calm down. It's not like I intended to give him and the guys front row tickets to the "Gwen and Amy Smack Down."

"Not that, you on the phone before. You didn't answer me and it sounded like you were in trouble, you know how fucking worried I was? I call, you answer. I ask what's going on, you fucking answer!"

He let go of my shoulders and started pacing, his hand running through his hair. He stopped, striding back to me.

"We are dealing with some dangerous shit right now, baby. Shit with the Spiders ain't good. After trying to deal with that shit last night, I hear your voice on that phone call, fear the worst." He grasped my neck roughly, staring into my eyes. "Don't do it again. I don't relish having that fear ever again."

I nodded and Cade roughly kissed me before slinging his arm around my neck and directing me to his bike.

"Let's go to the club for a bit, babe. The boys are in the mood for a barbeque breakfast, and I'm in the mood to have your pussy for breakfast." He nuzzled my neck and my stomach did a dip.

Cade swung on his bike and handed me his helmet.

"Maybe I should stay, sort this out with those two," I said, pointing back at the house.

Cade gave me a look. "I think you guys all need some time to stew this over, 'specially you. I don't want you engaging in another fight that makes every male in a five mile radius go hard as stone."

"Ewww, you're talking about my brother too." I scrunched my nose up in disgust.

"Your brother is a hot-blooded male, and his focus was on Amy not you. I'm not talking about this, get on the bike, babe," Cade ordered.

I gestured down at myself. "I look like shit."

I hadn't changed after my run and I was wearing tight black leggings, a baggy white singlet which showed the sides of my hot pink crop top and some stomach. My hair was falling around my face as I had lost my hair tie somehow in the struggle with Amy, and I was sure my face was all red.

Cade's face turned stormy, he reached across and yanked me until I was straddling his lap. How the bike didn't topple over, I didn't know.

"You are fucking stunning, did you not see my boys having to adjust themselves looking at you? Much as I wish every man didn't have that reaction looking at you, it's inevitable. You could be in a garbage bag, you'd still look fucking irresistible. Don't say shit like that again."

He squeezed my ass and I couldn't help but grind against his jeans, the thin fabric of my leggings rubbing against him. I leaned in and kissed him, biting him roughly on the lip.

"Jesus, Gwen, you know how hard it is not to screw you right here? Fuck the neighbors." His voice was rough with desire.

I smiled and hopped behind him, putting on my helmet and wrapping my arms around my man.

⊏⊐

We arrived at the clubhouse to see the guys all outside, some drinking beers with women in their laps, others laying down on bench seats looking asleep.

As we got off Cade's bike I turned to him. "Beers? It's nine in the morning."

"It's been a rough night," he replied.

I shrugged. I guessed I couldn't judge, there had been a couple of times in Uni I had woken up and started my day with a beer. Maybe more than a couple.

I'd just graduated to mimosas now.

Cade drew me to his side as we approached the group. I spotted Steg staring at us thoughtfully, there was no hostility in his gaze this time. The woman standing behind him with her hands on his shoulders was glaring at me, eyes narrowed.

"Who's she?" I whispered to Cade.

"That's Evie, Steg's Old Lady. They've been together for years, she helped raised Rosie. She's the closest thing to a mother Rosie had," he said, giving the guys chin lifts.

I contemplated this a second, looking at the woman. She was older, but attractive. Her black hair was long down her back and side swept bangs did little to hide heavy makeup. She was curvy, wearing a tight lace blouse with a black bra showing. A silver hooped belt was slung around her waist over top of tight jeans. Multiple silver necklaces adorned her neck. It was the ultimate biker chick look. She was still glaring at me when we got to the courtyard. I held her gaze not wanting to look timid or weak.

Cade squeezed my shoulders. "Don't worry about her, babe, she's just protective over the club. She gives you any shit though, you come to me."

I didn't reply, as the men all shouted a chorus of hellos, grunts, and chin lifts.

"Well, hello there, Tyson, seems I missed quite a show, let me know when you're next rearing for a fight, I would pay to see that," Buck, one of the older members who I had become friendly with yelled at me.

I gave him a wink back. "You'll be first to know, Buck." I laughed good naturedly as some of the men give me a few more jibes.

Cade sat us down at a table where Lucky was plowing through his breakfast.

I poked him in his muscled arm. "I wonder who had the big mouth and told the guys about my little incident that happened like *ten minutes ago,* asshole."

Lucky grinned at me, mouth full. Gross, what was it with men?

Cade pulled me closer to his side. "If I hear anyone talking about my woman in any way that is more than PG, I will rip their balls off," he said forcefully to the group, glare in his voice. I let out a slight giggle as he kissed my nose.

"Hungry, baby?"

"No, but I would murder for a coffee," I replied with seriousness, thinking back to the precious java I dropped earlier.

Lucky, who had finished his mouthful, shouted, "Ooh she's threatening murder now, someone get her a coffee, quick." He smirked at Cade, who leaned over and punched him in the shoulder.

"Not another word," he told him evenly.

Lucky saluted him with a smile, rubbing his arm getting back to his breakfast.

"Coffee." Cade smiled at me.

One of the Sweetbutts – Lucky explained to me that the hangers on, girls who fucked different members of the club, were called this – stopped and placed her hand lightly on my shoulder before quickly pulling it away, glancing at Cade.

"I'll get your coffee, Gwen, how do you take it?" she asked, taking me by surprise.

"Um, no, it's okay I can—" I started to reply, but Cade interrupted me.

"Black, two sugars, I'll have one too," he told her, barely looking up.

She nodded at him and turned to get our coffees.

I spun to Cade. "I have legs, Cade. I'm quite capable of getting my own coffee," I informed him snippily.

"That ain't the point, babe, it's a respect thing. You're my Old Lady, they need to know their place, which is below you. Libby was doing what she should, showing you respect."

I eyed at him disbelievingly but his face was serious. "That's ridiculous."

Cade's gaze turned hard. "That's how the club works, babe, get used to it." His tone communicated that the subject was closed.

I pursed my lips, itching to argue, clearly I had a lot to learn.

Libby came back with our coffees, placing them in front of us, obviously knowing how Cade took his.

I smiled at her. "Thank you, Libby," I said sincerely. If I had to let them run around after me, at least I could be nice.

"That's okay, Gwen." She smiled nervously and walked away.

I leaned into Cade, who was in the process of piling his plate. "So do many of the men have Old Ladies?" I asked genuinely interested.

"Nope," Cade replied. "Me, Steg, and Ranger." He nodded towards an attractive man in his mid-forties who I hadn't met yet. He was sitting at another table, one arm around a very pretty woman, probably early thirties with long blonde hair. Their position was similar to the way Cade and I were sitting. The blonde caught me looking and grinned, I gave her a friendly smile back.

"I'll introduce you later. Ranger and Lizzie have been off on some school trip with their kids or some shit, that's why you haven't seen them round," he explained through mouthfuls.

Well, at least my man didn't talk with his mouth open.

"How come there are so few?" I questioned, looking around at the men, at least fifteen of them were milling around, three was not a very high number of men with women.

Cade regarded at me intensely. "Takes a special kind of woman to be able to handle this life. Also takes a special kind of woman to make us want to settle down. Got more than enough bitches willing to offer up their pussy, none of them Old Lady material."

A crude explanation, but still kind of sweet. I leaned in and kissed Cade on the cheek. An intense gaze passed between us, and I wondered if he was thinking about what I said last night. He couldn't verbalize an "I love you" but at least I knew he cared about me a lot. I tried to convince myself that was enough.

"I'm going to use the ladies room," I informed him, standing.

"I'll take you."

"It's okay, Cade, I think I can manage on my own." I gave him a look before turning to walk into the clubhouse.

After using the facilities – they even had a specific ladies room – I checked my reflection to make sure I didn't look like a total disaster. Surprisingly I didn't. I just looked...happy. Even though I wasn't covered in makeup or clad in my designer clothes, I felt confident. Cade did that to me. I turned to walk out, coming face to face with Evie.

"Shit!" I jumped, hand on my chest.

She directed a scathing look at me.

"You scared me," I told her, choosing to ignore the glare.

"You should be scared, darlin', you don't belong here, doubt you'll be able to handle this life. Sooner you figure that out the better." She stepped closer, trying to intimidate me. I refused to move, refused to let her make me feel inferior.

I leaned into her. "With all due respect, you don't have a goddamned idea what I can and can't handle. I'm here to stay, so you can give up on your scare tactic bullshit. You're not getting rid of me that easy," I replied, voice hard and confident.

She arched a well-manicured eyebrow, looking me up and down. "Well shit, the little princess has a backbone." She sounded almost impressed. "Evie." She held out her hand. I took it.

"Gwen."

"Well, Gwen, you're not what I expected, but you do anything to fuck with the club, I'll rip your head off," she told me conversationally.

"I'll keep that in mind," I replied dryly.

She smirked at me. "Let's get a drink, I've got mimosas in the kitchen, that's if the Sweetbutts haven't been sneaking any. Which they wouldn't, if they knew what was good for them."

She seized my arm and pulled me towards the kitchen. I guessed Queen Biker approved of me, and it would be rude to say no to a mimosa. We entered the kitchen, and to my surprise, Steg was leaning against the counter. My stomach dropped, I so did not like this man, but I had to make an effort and I couldn't be disrespectful.

I smiled at him, head held high. He gave me a chin lift, "Gwen," he murmured, voice rough.

Evie sidled up to him, stroking his chest. "Baby, what you doin' in the kitchen? One of the Sweetbutts could've got you whatever you needed," she purred.

Steg rubbed her ass, eyes on me, I struggled not to squirm under his gaze.

"Nah, sunshine, was after a word with Gwen. Knew you'd

bring her in here for your stash." He gave Evie a look and without a word, she nodded.

"See yah outside, sweetheart." She kissed him, then strutted out the door.

I gulped, feeling mighty uncomfortable being alone with this man, but still not wanting to show it. Steg gazed at me a second, then gestured to a small table with some chairs.

"Sit, Gwen. This won't take long."

It didn't escape me that this was not a question. I sat down, palms sweating. I couldn't shake the first impression that I had of this guy. Steg sat across from me, hands clasped in front of him, smiling big at me.

"So I just thought we could have a chat, since we weren't properly introduced when we last crossed paths." He leaned back in his chair, reminding me of some sort of sleazy businessman.

I didn't know what to say so I just nodded, he took this as a cue to continue.

"I'll admit, Gwen, first impression, I thought you were just Cade's latest piece. Thought he might've wanted a taste of some high class pussy. But by the looks of it, my VP has it bad for that pussy." His tone was official, which totally contradicted the crudeness of his words.

I gritted my teeth. "If what you mean is Cade and I are serious about each other, we are."

He smiled again, like some sort of predator. I would say it was more a show of teeth than a smile, but whatever.

"Yeah, that's what I'm trying to say. I just wanted to get a few things straight." He leaned back in now, eyes focused on mine. "Firstly, I wanted to thank you for what you did for Bull, you tipping Cade off saved a brother's life. The club owes you for that."

I inspected my hands, feeling uncomfortable. "It was nothing, I don't expect anything in return," I murmured.

"No, but that's the way our world works, you saved a member. That's a big deal, accept it."

I smiled tightly and nodded.

"Secondly, I get that a woman like you might not be entirely comfortable with our way of life, which means this will rub off on Cade, put some ideas in his head. That is not happening. I'm not having some piece of ass fucking with my club, so you got any problems with what you see or hear, you don't say a word, you fucking pack that tight ass back to the city."

Steg's tone brokered no argument, it was not cruel exactly, but firm. But the way he was ordering me around, trying to delve into my relationship pissed me right off, my anger outweighed my intimidation of this man. I stood, my chair squeaking as I pushed it back.

"I don't think you have any right to command me how to act within my relationship, especially since you don't know me worth a damn. Cade loves this club, I would never fuck with that. He makes his own choices and I'm sure as shit not going to be some whiny girlfriend who nags him twenty-four seven. If you tried to get to know me before spouting out this crap, you might have figured that out."

Steg arched an eyebrow and gave me a dangerous look. "Since you're new to the club and what you did for Bull, I'll give you a pass for that little outburst."

He stood and slowly stepped towards me, getting close enough that I felt his breath on my face. I refused to step back, jutting my chin and meeting those cold expressionless eyes.

"You are an Old Lady, which means you are off limits to the boys and we give you some form of respect." He paused. "But you ever talk to the fucking President of this charter like that again, you'll wish you didn't."

He didn't say another word, just tagged a beer and walked out. I let out the breath I didn't realize I was holding. Fuck, well he just decided to wave his dick around. It was starting to dawn on me how different life in the club was going to be, it was like a whole new set of rules, where women were obviously expected to serve food and suck dick. Cade cared for me, obviously. But the burn from the unreturned "I love you" was still scorching the back of my throat.

"Gwen, what the fuck?" Cade's voice shook me out of yet another mental battle. He was in front of me and hauled my body flush with his. He looked pissed. "Saw Steg and Evie walk out, what did they say to you?" He sounded ready to explode, and I knew he'd go out and rip into them both if I mentioned either of my little talks.

I stroked his face, smiling hopefully convincingly. "Nothing, Cade, they were just properly introducing themselves since the whole time I've been with you we haven't officially met." This was the truth, just not the grizzly details. Cade wasn't buying it.

"Bullshit," he growled. "Evie's a tough bitch, she's more likely to scratch your eyes out than roll out the welcome wagon. And Steg is too far up his own ass to talk to someone without an ulterior motive. What the fuck did they say, Gwen?"

I gave him a peck on the lips, which he barely responded to, he just kept frowning at me. "It was nothing, Cade, seriously."

He didn't look convinced so I kissed him again, this time running my tongue across the seam of his lips.

"Didn't you promise you were going to have a different kind of breakfast than the one you just ate?" I whispered, nibbling his ear.

He was still frowning, but I felt his hard on pressing into me. Without warning, he threw me over his shoulder. I let out a surprised gasp and he swatted me hard on the backside.

"Know you're not telling me the full story, Gwen. I'll leave it for now, I'd much rather bury my face inside you than talk about either of those snakes anyway."

Without another word, he carried me to his room.

━━━

All the lights were on as Cade and I approached my house, it was late and I was shattered. After Cade and I spent a couple of hours in his room at the compound, we spent the rest of the day there. Cade and the boys had "church" for a while, which gave me a chance to hang out with Lizzie, who was super cool, and Evie who still scared me just a little.

Surprisingly, I had an awesome day, leaving out the conversation with the hard ass President of a motorcycle club and the one from his equally hard ass Old Lady. I got along with all the guys really well, and despite their appearances, they treated me with nothing but respect, which maybe had to do with Cade glaring at anyone who talked to me.

Although they were friendly, there seemed like there was a bit of tension in the air, someone was always watching the cameras on the gate. Cade was on his phone a lot and Steg was locked away in "church" for most of the day. It worried me, knowing Cade had said there was conflict with another club. I knew better than to ask Cade for any more information, he was intent on telling me as little as possible. I was still determined to ask him later, using a couple of tactics that I had up my sleeve, or down my shirt.

I hopped off the bike and started towards the door when Cade pulled me back.

"You okay with them now, baby?" he asked, nodding towards the house.

My heart melted a little with his concern, maybe he didn't love me, but my biker was still pretty sweet to me.

"Yeah, I'm good actually. I just reacted a little crazy this morning, I've got so much going through my head it just threw me. I'm actually really happy for them, but where does that leave Brock? I know Amy cares about him, and he's obviously into her."

If his behavior today was anything to go by, he definitely cared for Amy and he was pissed at the turn of events. He spent the entire day drinking and barking at anyone that dared talk to him.

Cade let out a sigh and looked up, as if asking for divine intervention. "Babe, I hate dealing with this chick shit. I know Amy has Brock tied up in knots, and I can't have my brother unfocused. She needs to sort her shit."

I nodded, feeling protective over both my brother and my best friend, not wanting either of them to get hurt. But I also didn't want this fucking this up for Cade and his brother.

"This is a tangled web. You regret hitching your horse to my wagon now?" I asked, half joking.

Cade grabbed my neck, eyes serious. "I thank the gods every day I wake up next to you, baby, this shit will sort itself out. Nothing would make me regret putting you on the back of my bike," he declared fiercely before kissing the bejesus out of me. "Now let's get this over with." Cade walked me to the door.

Amy and Ian were sitting in the kitchen, suspiciously far apart. I felt the tension in the air. They both looked up as we walked in.

"Gwen!" Amy came running over, hugging me tightly after I stepped away from Cade.

"I am so sorry you had to find out like you did, Gwennie, we should have told you a while ago, but things were fucked up," she blurted in a rush, looking upset.

"I'm sorry too, Amy. I should have never pushed you this morning, that was a bitch move. I was just taken by surprise, but I'm happy, if you two are happy?" I glanced between Amy and Ian, who were not even peeking at each other.

I gave them a look. "Things changed? You looked pretty into

each other this morning," I teased, but neither of them cracked a smile.

Ian stood. "Look, sis, we've just got some things to sort out, which is between the two of us before you say anything." My brother knew me too well, I had just been about to interrupt to play couple's therapist.

"I've got something to tell you, all of you if you want to sit," he continued.

My curiosity peaked. "Okay, let's go sit out by the pool, it's a nice night and I hate discussing anything at the table, it brings back bad memories of the conversations Mum and Dad had with me in high school."

Ian laughed, remembering the many interventions my parents staged during my wild child phase, some of which he experienced via speakerphone while he was on tour.

"Oh and drinks, I need a glass of wine," I added.

I had switched to water after one mimosa today and now I felt like I needed some relaxation in the form of vino.

"Got it, babe." My wonderful man was way ahead of me, pouring a glass of wine for both me and Amy.

"Did I mention I love him?" Amy said seriously.

I gave her a playful shove. "Back off, sister, you're already making out with my brother, stay away from my man."

She laughed. "Right, I don't want to have to have another boxing match in the front yard." She tried to make the mood light, but her glance was darting to Ian, who was watching her unsmiling. His brooding was interrupted by Cade.

"Beer?" He held out a bottle towards Ian. I held my breath, this was the alpha version of an olive branch. I watched as Ian paused, then begrudgingly took the beer.

Yes!

Amy and I exchanged a no look high five, we were best

friends after all, and she was watching the exchange thinking the same thing as me.

Ian scowled at us. "Girls, outside, now." It was disturbing how much my brother ordered us around like Cade did to me.

We sat down outside and I gazed over at my brother expectantly.

"Well?"

"Jesus, Gwen, you've barely got your ass in the chair. Same as when you were little, no patience."

I rolled my eyes. "I can't help that I'm a naturally curious person, Ian. It's what you love most about me." I ignored his snort. "Now spill."

He took a tug of his beer before looking between Amy and me. "My next tour of duty ends at the start of next year," he began. My heart started pounding, hoping this was going where I thought it was going. I nodded frantically for him to go on.

"After thinking about it, and all the shit that's been going on, I've decided it will be my last tour. I'm getting too old for this shit anyway."

I let out a squeal and leaped out of my chair to hug my big brother. "This is so freaking awesome, Ian!" I exclaimed, giving him a kiss on the cheek while he chuckled. "Seriously, soon I'll be able to stop checking every news site in the morning to see what new horrors are going on in the world and worrying which one you are experiencing." I looked him in the eyes with a tear running down my cheek.

"Come on, Ace, no tears, you know I hate it when you cry. Plus, you should be happy about this, it's what you and Mum have been nagging me about for years."

"I am happy, you dork! I'm just emotional. Oh my god, I have to tell Mum, she will be so happy. I'll call her right now." I jumped up, turning to run into the house to get my cell when Ian stopped me.

He glanced at his watch. "Ace, it's four-thirty in the morning back home right now."

I waved my hand, "Mum won't care, she's an early riser."

Ian gave me a look. "I'll call her, Gwen. Just wait a second. Jesus."

"Okay, okay," I conceded, watching my brother stare over at Amy, who hadn't said a word since the announcement.

"Ames?" he said softly, eyes so full of love it almost made me cry.

She scowled at him, eyes red and angry, her glare marring her face.

"Fuck you, Ian," she shot back, venom lacing her voice. She shoved her chair back and stormed inside.

I was not expecting her to react like that. Ian obviously wasn't either. He drained his beer and pushed back his chair with so much force it toppled over, then he followed Amy back into the house.

"Well, shit," I exclaimed after the door had slammed. I glanced over at Cade, who was reclined back in the chair, legs straight, crossed over each other. He even sat like a fricking alpha male. I skipped over to him, jumping on his lap, so I was straddling him.

"How cool is that? Ian coming home. Aside from Amy's reaction, this is awesome!" I kissed Cade excitedly.

"Great news, babe. Happy my girl is going to have one less worry on her hands." He deepened our kiss and all other thoughts left my mind.

<hr />

"Thanks for letting me leave early, Gwen, you rock!" Rosie said as she checked her cleavage in the store mirror.

"It's nothing, I'm not going to twat block you if the guy is as hot as you say he is."

Rosie turned, a serious look on her face. "Oh he is, you could cast him in marble and create a piece of art out of this man." She got a dreamy look on her face and I laughed.

"Go!" I ordered. "And have wild sex with this guy."

She ran up and kissed my cheek.

"Don't worry I intend to and don't tell my brother I'm on a date. Now, *he's* the ultimate twat blocker. I couldn't lose my virginity until I was nineteen, 'cause he had the guys beat up anyone who freaking kissed me," she ranted angrily before replacing her scowl with a smile. "Got to go, my Greek god is waiting!" she sang before all but skipping out the door, which was no mean feat in six-inch heels.

I smiled, wondering if she was serial dating to get Luke out of her mind, then I scolded myself. *I mustn't meddle.* Oh, who was I kidding? Of course I was going to, but first I'd see how her date went.

I busied myself with tidying the store. It had been a long busy day and it was still an hour till close, I wanted to get out of here ASAP. Dwayne was sitting outside on his bike, like he had been for the past three hours, I bet he was bored shitless.

It had been a crazy week. Ian had left two days ago, which sucked. I hated saying goodbye, but it was so good knowing I wouldn't be doing it for much longer. The last days of his stay had been relatively uneventful, Amy was still refusing to talk to him after some fight they had which she wouldn't tell me about. Her reluctance to tell me anything when I was dying to know what was going on was getting annoying. We were best friends, she was morally obligated to tell me everything. Ian was the same, telling me it was between him and Amy no one else.

Apart from that tension, we enjoyed hanging out, almost like old times. He was even making an effort with Cade, who wasn't around much, but they still got along when they were together. I was happy, whether it was for my sake or not, I was glad.

Things between them got even less tense on Ian's last night. We were about to go to Valentines to dinner, with Amy even agreeing (grudgingly) to come. Cade had announced he "had to have a word" with Ian and instructed us to go and drink cocktails before dinner.

This had made me immensely curious and slightly pissed at being ordered around, but Cade had given me one of his no nonsense stares. Amy and I had spent two cosmos discussing what they could have been talking about before they arrived, Cade (gasp) smiling, which was a rare occurrence for my hard ass biker.

I had grilled him later that night asking what they were talking about, but he refused to tell me, only saying, "It was guy shit, babe, nothing for you to worry about."

No matter how much I tried to persuade him, he said no more. Which had me sulking because I was even more curious.

The next morning, I had gotten up to see Ian leaving Amy's room. He gave me a cheeky grin and a shrug when I looked at him questioningly. All I knew was that Amy had emerged looking grim and refusing to come to the airport. Ian instructed me to wait in the car while they said their goodbyes. He refused to tell me what was going on during the car ride to the airport. No one was telling me anything.

I turned into a blubbering mess saying goodbye to him.

"No more crying, Ace. Won't be much longer and you'll be wishing you could drop me off at the airport," he joked and my tears stopped and a huge grin erupted on my face.

"You're moving to the States?" I squealed.

"Nothing's set in stone just yet, but some of the boys and I are planning on opening a security business in L.A," he explained, grinning too.

I jumped up and down, slightly dramatic. "L.A. is only two hours away, this is awesome!"

"All right, Ace, calm the theatrics, people are staring. Oh, and you've done okay with Cade, he's not a total asshole. I'll be worrying about you a lot less knowing you're with him," he ground this out as if it was physically painful to admit and I smirked at him.

He gave me a kiss on the cheek. "Got a flight to catch, see you in no time, Gwen. Love you." He turned to the boarding gate with his duffle thrown over his shoulder.

"Love you too! Be careful, don't get shot," I ordered him, a few people gave me sideways glances. Ian turned and gave me a salute before disappearing around the corner.

▭

As soon as I had arrived home from the airport, red eyed from shedding a couple of tears on the way home, Cade had been waiting on his bike. The men were all with him. He explained the situation with the Spiders had gotten worse and he was going to have a man on me at all times. I argued this, finding it hard to swallow that I would have someone following me all the time, it was creepy.

"Don't fucking argue about this, Gwen. You don't have any say. You think I'm going to even let there be a slight chance of you being in danger? I'm not having anything ugly ever touch you again. When I'm not with you, you have one of the boys with you. No more discussion."

I had caved, obviously. It worried me a lot that Cade was

putting a guy on me. I wasn't worried for myself, I knew the boys would take care of me, but that meant Cade was in a lot of danger, I didn't like that at all. He needed to speed up this process of getting the club clean.

I hardly saw him the next few days, he'd crawl into bed with me late in the night. He would make love to me then fall asleep with his arms tight around me, not releasing me until the morning, when he made love to me again before leaving. It was not a fun situation. I missed him and worried about him.

———

The cling of the bell brought me back to the present. I smiled as a pretty young girl walked in.

"Hi, sweetie, how's it going?" I called to her from the counter.

She didn't reply, her face blank as she approached me, setting a gift bag in front of me.

"This is from Rico," she said before turning to leave.

"Wait!" I called to her, rounding the counter, grabbing the bag.

"I think you have the wrong person, I have no idea who Rico is." I held the bag out to her.

"You Gwen?" she asked and I nodded. "It's for you." She turned and walked out.

"That's weird," I said to myself.

But never one to not open a present, I took the wrapped box and set it on the counter. I ripped open the box and screamed.

CHAPTER 13

BLACK TARANTULAS SCAMPERED out of the box and crawled up my arms, I continued screaming as I swatted them off and tried to get as far away from the box as possible at the same time. The door crashed open and Dwayne entered the store, gun drawn. He took one look at me and his eyes flared.

"Get them off!" I screamed, as they crawled through my hair.

He was at my side in seconds, hands in my hair and at my arms getting the last of those creatures off me before stomping on them.

"Outside. Now," he barked.

He didn't have to tell me twice. I darted out the door, pulling at my clothes with him following close behind.

He looked me over quickly. "You okay?"

"Um..." I stuttered, unable to process what just happened. I couldn't stop running my hands up my arms, I could still feel them *on me*.

"Cade? Get down here, now. The Spiders paid a visit to Gwen's store, sent a message." Dwayne talked into his phone, eying me up and down like I might faint at any moment. Luckily

I was a girl from the country and had a brother who liked to gross me out. I was staying conscious.

"Gwen, are you okay, sweetheart?" Evan from next door approached me looking worried. "We heard you scream, what happened?"

"Um...I had some unwelcome visitors," I told him, restraining a hysterical laugh, only half paying attention. My mind was on other things, like the reality of another dangerous gang setting their sights on me. Again.

"Gwen!" Luke ran towards me, gun drawn. I noticed a couple of people had approached, obviously hearing the commotion. I didn't realize my scream had been that loud

How was it that Luke was always around when something shitty happened to me? I was glad, but I couldn't be the only person in this town who got in these situations. Okay, maybe I might be the only person in this town who got a box of eight-legged devils delivered to them, but surely he had speeding tickets to write or drug rings to bust.

I watched Luke take me in, then glare at Dwayne, who had just got off the phone.

"What happened?" His face was a mask of concern. His eyes darted around looking for threats, they settled on Dwayne again for a second before he put his gun away.

"Well, I got a delivery," I began, feeling aware of the amount of people around. "Um, and it contained insects of the eight-legged variety. Not at all like the delivery of shoes I was expecting," I answered, giggling at the ridiculousness of it all.

Luke hissed. "The Spiders." He returned his glare to Dwayne, who ignored him. He started running his arms up my own, eyes searching.

I tried to pull them away, but he caught my wrist. "What are you doing?" I asked angrily, in any other situation I wouldn't mind being felt up by a hot guy, if I wasn't madly in love with another hot guy that was.

Luke stepped closer, looking like he was going to get between us.

Dwayne didn't glance up. "Looking for bites," he grunted.

My stomach dropped. I didn't think of that. Were tarantulas poisonous? Did my first aid kit have anti venom? I didn't think so.

"Bites," Luke repeated quietly.

The roar of Harley's, and what looked like the whole club, approaching drowned out any further conversation. Cade all but threw his bike on the sidewalk, sprinting over to our little huddle. His eyes darkened seeing Luke, but his concern for me obviously trumped a macho man showdown.

Cade pushed both Dwayne and Luke out of the way and grabbed me, inspecting me as if he was expecting stab wounds. He seemed satisfied with my lack of bleeding because he drew me into his shoulder.

"What the fuck happened?" he barked at Dwayne as the rest of the club approached.

Dwayne's jaw got tight. "Heard Gwen scream, went in and she was covered in fucking tarantulas."

I heard some of the men curse behind me and felt the air turn electric.

"Was just looking for bites when you arrived," Dwayne continued, and I heard a sharp indrawn breath from Cade. He roughly pulled me to arm's length, running his hands up my arms as Dwayne had been doing before.

"You feel a sting anywhere, baby?" His eyes didn't leave my body and his voice was laced with barely restrained fury.

I shook myself out of my mental fog and took stock of my body. I felt like I was about to throw up and I could still feel them in my hair, but no pain.

"No, no sting," I answered quietly, shivering. "Are you sure you got them all, Dwayne?" I ran my hands through my hair quickly, hoping not to encounter any creepy crawlies.

"You're good, babe," he grunted.

Luke appeared in front of me, eyeing the bikers with distaste. I noticed that a couple more cops had joined the party, standing slightly back, hands on their weapons.

"Gwen, do you want to come down to the station? Make a statement?" Luke asked firmly, eyes on me. I opened my mouth to answer, but Cade beat me to it.

"That's not happening, she's on the back of my bike. I'll take her somewhere to keep her safe." Cade's arms settled around me, and I felt safe already.

"She will be safer at a *police station* than anywhere else in this town," Luke bit out, not looking at Cade. "Gwen?" he questioned expectantly.

I suddenly felt a lot of eyes on me. The men were waiting for me to answer and reality hit me, what I said would determine if my loyalty lay with the club, if I trusted them to deal with the problem.

I cleared my throat uncertainly. "Thank you for your concern, Luke, but I'm okay. I just need to get away from here," I said quietly, feeling Cade's body relax a fraction.

Luke's gaze turned thunderous. "Gwen, you can't be serious. Do you realize a dangerous gang just made a serious threat against you? You are in danger, we can protect you," his voice raised and I could tell he was finding it hard to keep control.

"We are more than capable of protecting Gwen," Cade answered for me in a low voice.

Luke raised a furious eyebrow "Just like you protected Laurie?" His voice was filled with venom.

I gasped at the cruelty in his voice and his callousness for bringing up Laurie. I felt the anger of every member humming in the air, and everything happened at once.

Bull, who had been standing back, rushed forward, gaze murderous, reaching for Luke. Cade pushed me out of the way before grabbing onto Bull, along with Brock and Dwayne. They were barely able to keep him restrained, his eyes lost every inch of humanity the second Luke had uttered Laurie's name.

Steg stepped forward calmly, standing toe to toe with Luke, who had his weapon out, as did the other officers who had approached. "No need for the weapon, Deputy," his voice was soft, but dangerous.

Luke glared at Steg. "Your boy was about to assault an officer," he stated coldly.

"No assault here, but if you mention that girl one more time there will be, and your little boys playing dress-up will be able to do fuck all to help you." Steg's stare was filled with promise, and I was unable to take my eyes away.

Holy shit, this was intense. Lucky appeared beside me and he loosely draped his arm around my shoulders. His usually carefree face was distorted in anger.

"Did you just threaten an officer, *Steg*?" Luke spat out his name like it tasted bad.

Steg regarded him like he was shit on his shoe. "Nope, I just made a promise to a jumped up asshole. Now, there's no crime here. Gwen has refused to make a statement so I suggest you fuck off, *Deputy*, before I have a word to the sheriff about your conduct."

Luke glowered at Steg with a look of pure hate before holstering his weapon and gesturing for the others to do the same. He then directed a hard look at me.

"I hope you know what you've gotten yourself into, Gwen," he told me softly, looking disappointed, before he turned and strode away.

Steg let a moment pass before barking out orders. "Lucky, take Gwen back to the club, get the prospects to gather up the women and the kids and anyone else they could use against us. We're on lockdown."

Lucky nodded and began to walk me towards his bike.

Wait, lockdown? What about my store?

This was all happening very quickly, and I didn't like how I was being passed around like a sack of potatoes. I needed to talk to Cade. He needed to tell me what the fuck was going on.

"I've got Gwen." Cade moved away from Bull, who was breathing raggedly and still being held by Brock and Dwayne.

Lucky stopped walking and turned us around just in time to see Cade and Steg in a heated stare off. I barely restrained a snort, why did so many alpha stare downs happen when I was around?

"Not having Gwen on the back of someone else's bike," Cade declared firmly, eyes locked on me.

Steg regarded him calmly, like he had Luke. "Need you here, need to canvas the store, see if we missed anything and get rid of our eight-legged friends. Then we got to find these fuckers and end them. Need your head on straight, so rein it in."

Cade was as stiff as a rock when Brock clapped him on the shoulder.

"Come on, brother, let's get these bastards, then they won't be able to get near Gwen again." He gave me a wink.

Cade looked as if he was having an internal battle before his face turned suddenly blank. "Fine," he clipped out, glaring at Steg.

"Rosco." He gestured to a prospect who I didn't really know.

"Yeah, Cade." He addressed him respectfully.

"You follow Lucky and Gwen, don't let them out of your sight. You make sure no one follows and that we have enough boys at the club. You clear?" he ordered, authority in his tone, which kind of turned me on, despite the situation. And despite the fact I was a little pissed, he clearly hadn't disclosed how serious things had gotten.

Rosco nodded. "Yes, sir."

Cade strode over to me, eyes narrowing at Lucky's arms on my shoulders. I ducked out of them and into Cade's, he squeezed me so tight I lost my breath.

"Don't worry, Cade, I'm fine. You go and do whatever you need to do." I was surprised at how strong my voice sounded. I wasn't going to betray my true feelings, or interrogate him on the street. It could wait until it was just the two of us.

He stared at me with his face still blank. "Fuck, Gwen, I'm so sorry you got caught up in this shit. Nothing else is going to touch you, I promise. I'm going to kill every last one of those mother-fuckers," he declared roughly.

I gulped, hoping this wasn't the promise it sounded like. He kissed me hard before nodding to Lucky, who gently directed me towards his bike. He handed me a helmet silently without the usual joke I had come to expect.

I got on his bike, putting my arms lightly around his waist before stealing a glance at Cade, who was talking with Steg, arms crossed. He gave me a glimpse before disappearing into my store.

⌐⊐

"This is bullshit!" Amy exclaimed for about the third time, pacing around the room. "I mean, I get that the guys need to do some-thing about the sick fuck that sent the spiders." She visibly shiv-ered. "I still don't know how you could've dealt with that, G, I fucking *hate* spiders, those little fuckers have no reason to be on this earth." She shook her head, trying to find her way back to her point. "But why am I here? I'm not an 'Old Lady,' thank fuck." She glanced at me. "Sorry, I didn't mean it like that."

I waved my hand. "Don't worry, I'm starting to wonder what

I've gotten myself into," I said truthfully, the events of today starting to hit home.

How stupid was I? Getting myself into another situation that involved a ruthless gang. I didn't know if I could deal with going back to constantly looking over my shoulder in fear. I wanted my normal, carefree life back.

But I loved Cade.

Crap. What a twisted web I had managed to get myself into. Pardon the pun.

Amy raised an eyebrow at my comment, but it didn't stop her rant.

"I know I'm your best friend, but I'm not involved in the club and I'm certainly not valuable to this club. I am so busting out of this *place.*" She scrunched her nose in distaste as she cast her eyes around the huge common room littered with beer bottles and the occasional condom wrapper.

I didn't disagree with her there, this wasn't the best environment, but we didn't have much choice, there were armed guards at the gate and a couple of prospects and members standing watch outside. We didn't have much of chance of escaping, not that I really wanted to at the moment. This rough place was where I felt safest at right now.

Fucked up as it was, I trusted these men, knew they would protect me with their lives if necessary. That was one thing I had learned about the club, they were fiercely loyal and once you were in, everyone had your back. The men really were brothers and they had deep love for one another, even with the problems Steg and Cade seemed to have.

We were currently alone, some of the men had called various friends of the club and ordered them to get here and others had gone to pick some of the women up. Amy and I were first to arrive. I had a sneaky feeling Brock had something to do with the prospect who dropped by our house and practically "threw her on the back of his bike" – Amy's words.

"Just relax for a second, Abrams, you're going to ruin the soles of those Choo's with all that pacing," I said.

She immediately stopped, frowning down at her heels and slumping down next to me on a barstool.

I stood. "We're in front of a bar, let's see if I can rustle up something drinkable to make this experience a little more enjoyable." I jumped over the bar and inspected what I had to work with.

"Cosmos?" Amy asked hopefully, head in her hands.

"No such luck, but we do have tequila," I said holding up the bottle.

"Margaritas?" she asked, a smile creeping onto her face.

I gave her a look. "We are in a biker clubhouse, Amy, I doubt the big rough alpha males have margarita mix."

Her face fell.

"We're just going to have to strap on our balls and drink it straight," I declared solemnly pouring us some glasses.

At that point, the door burst open and in walked Rosie, Lucy, and Ashley. They were closely followed by Evie, Lizzie, and to my surprise, more than a few Sweetbutts, arms laden with groceries. Rosie's eyes lit up when she saw us, and even more when she spotted the bottle in my hand.

"Tequila! I love you girls, Jose is one of my best friends in lockdowns, and I brought margarita mix." She held up a paper bag.

Amy leapt off her bar stool and hugged her. "I love you," she told her sincerely.

I gave everyone smiles as they approached, Rosie detangled herself from Amy and hugged me across the bar.

"Holy shit, Gwen, I heard what happened. Are you okay?" Her face was scrunched with worry.

"I'm fine now and will be even better with the help of tequila," I reassured her, telling myself not to twitch at the memory of insects crawling up my arms.

"You are one strong bitch." She winked at me. "I'll dump the groceries and dig around for our drink mix so we can get this party started." She strolled towards the kitchen where the Sweetbutts had disappeared.

Lizzie walked up to me and gave my hand a light squeeze, eyes kind. "How you going Gwen?" she asked softly.

"I'm okay thanks, Liz," I smiled at her, introducing her to Amy before noticing two little humans hiding behind her legs. I rounded the bar and crouched down in front of them.

"Why, who have we got here?" I asked playfully, sneaking a grin at the two kids who were peeking at me shyly.

A boy and a girl, both with jet black hair and both gorgeous. The girl was about five, with shoulder-length ringlets and a cheeky smile. The boy was a bit older, standing more confidently at his mother's side.

"I'm Jack." The boy held out his hand to shake, I held back a laugh at the child's manly demeanor.

I tried to fight visions of little children with Cade's steely grey eyes. Not the time to get clucky. I gave his hand a shake. "Well, it's a pleasure to meet you, Jack, what's your sister's name?"

He stepped around his mother to stand in front of me. "You sound weird, are you from another planet or something?" he asked seriously and I couldn't hold back my laugh this time.

Lizzie joined me before her face turned stern. "Jack," she scolded, "that wasn't polite."

He gazed up at his mother, confused.

I straightened and ruffled his hair. "I sound different because I'm from a country way on the other side of the world called New Zealand," I explained.

"That's weird," he said before running off to play with a couple of other kids I hadn't noticed arrive.

"Sorry about that," Lizzie said while scooping up the little beauty beside her.

"Don't even apologize, he's hilarious."

She rolled her eyes. "Yeah, sometimes I want to scream at the little shit, he's too much like his father, it's scary."

I laughed, happy to see the obvious love in her eyes. I lightly pulled on her little girl's curl. "What's your name then?"

"This is Lily," Lizzie replied when the little girl burrowed her face in her shoulder. "She's a bit shy."

I chatted with Lizzie for a bit until she had to go and put Lily down for a nap. I was about to turn and sit back with Amy, who had already downed two shots when Evie approached and hugged me. I gingerly hugged her back, surprised at the hard woman's show of tenderness. She released me and stroked my face, reminding me of something my mother would do.

"You all good, honey?" she asked and I nodded. "Good, don't worry, the men will take care of those animals, finally. That's the last time they go near our women."

Her voice was filled with anger, but her eyes seemed to water. She must've been thinking about Laurie, this incident bringing horrible memories to the surface. I gave her hands a squeeze and she smiled at me.

"Enough talking, let's get down to business. I'll get the Sweet-butts on cleaning this dump up and making food. I'll find places for everyone to sleep, you want to be in charge of the most important thing?"

"What's that?" I asked.

"Booze," she replied.

"Only if that includes me drinking some."

The rest of the day passed in a blur of activity and cocktails. I was surprised at the number of people, although Cade said there wasn't many Old Ladies, that didn't mean there wasn't a heck of a lot of women involved with the club. There was also a good amount of children, most of whom belonged to club members, results of divorce or one night stands.

Everyone was banding together, helping out with food and getting along really well. It was interesting seeing the people behind the men, people connected to the club in some way or another, people who could potentially be in danger. They didn't seem too worried about the possible threat. The atmosphere was light, with only a couple of worried faces. I asked Lizzie if lockdown was a regular occurrence. She assured me it wasn't, telling me that danger from the club rarely touched its extended family. I wanted to believe her, but with what happened today I was finding it hard and was feeling very conflicted.

Tequila helped me with that, by the time my head hit the pillow, I was feeling pleasantly buzzed. But no amount of alcohol could stop me worrying about Cade, who I hadn't heard from all day. I lay staring at the ceiling until I heard heavy footsteps ascending the stairs and the door opening quietly. I sat up and watched Cade as he closed the door behind him.

"What are you still doing awake, baby? It's late." Cade's voice was soft as he sat on the bed stroking my face.

"Couldn't sleep," I replied. "I was worried about my man."

A tender expression crossed his face, one that he only ever gave me, his hard and gruff exterior reserved for the rest of the world.

"I'm right here, baby, whole and unharmed." He stood, beginning to take off his clothes, resting his cut on the back of a chair. I regarded it in the dim moonlight, feeling mixed emotions for the piece of leather.

"How long is this going to go on for?" I asked quietly, still staring at the chair.

I felt a pause in Cade's movement for a second before he continued undressing. He entered the bed, resting his body on top of mine.

"It will be over soon, baby, I promise." His voice was intense, rough. "You don't know how sorry I am that you got caught up in this shit storm. Christ, you are so good, so strong. You don't need any more of this ugliness tarnishing your life, and it fuckin' has." He was angry at himself. "If I wasn't such a selfish bastard I would let you go, let you run a mile away from this life."

My mind panicked at the thought of losing him, but the rational part of me considered the possibility of running from the danger that the club and Cade represented.

Cade watched me closely as if he was trying to read my mind. "But I can't, Gwen. I can't let you go. The thought of not being with you, not being able to protect you, sleep beside you, sink into you at the end of the day, that thought scares me shitless. And the thought of another man ever touching you"—he literally shook from rage –"drives me crazy." He kissed me hard before pulling back. "I love you, Gwen, fuck I should've said it the moment you made my goddamned life saying those words to me. I love you more than anything, baby."

Holy crap.

Well, that's what I called an "I love you." My biker knew how to say it right.

"I love you too, Cade," I whispered before he devoured my mouth, yanking the blankets away, roughly hissing when he saw I was naked.

"You are fucking stunning, baby."

He kissed me again, roughly tweaking my nipple, I moaned into his mouth. His callused hands venture down my torso until they reached my drenched core. He thrust a finger inside me and I saw stars, my orgasm creeping up my spine already.

"Cade," I murmured as he sucked my nipple. "I need you inside me." I writhed as his finger moved faster.

"Not yet, Gwen, I want to watch you come around my finger, want to feel your little pussy pulse on my hand," he replied roughly, his words unraveling me. I cried out.

I was in a fog when Cade entered me, pleasure shooting through my already sensitive flesh. His eyes never left mine while he made slow love to me, the emotion and love behind his eyes nearly tearing me apart. All of a sudden, I was riding waves of pleasure, clenching around him again. I heard his grunt as I milked his release out of him.

He lay on top of me for a while, breathing heavily. "I love you, babe," he told me quietly.

I looked back up at him and everything else faded away, the club, the danger, my love for this man played the trump card. "I love you too."

Cade kissed my head and moved so he was still half on top of me, but not squashing me. "Sleep, Gwen," he ordered.

I wouldn't have thought I would be able to sleep with my beast of a boyfriend not only still on top of me, but inside me, but I did.

⊏⊐

I woke slowly, with pleasure shooting up my spine with Cade's mouth buried between my legs. I put my hand on his head, unable to speak as an orgasm rippled through my half asleep body. Cade crawled up as I recovered from the aftershocks. Without a word, he grabbed my hips and placed me so I straddled him. I let out a rough gasp as he impaled me, pleasure making my mind fog. My brain only thought of pleasure after that.

Afterwards, I collapsed atop of Cade, we were both breathing hard after our climaxes.

"That's a perfect way to start the morning," I whispered, nuzzling his neck.

Hands at my hips gave me a squeeze. "If only I could stay buried inside you all day," his voice vibrated in my ear.

"I don't think I would survive that," I giggled before slowly lifting myself off him and heading to the bathroom.

I peeked at my man over my shoulder, he looked sexy as sin lying naked on the bed, rippling muscles and covered in tats. I felt a flutter between my legs at the sight of him.

"I'm taking a shower," I informed him. "Want to scrub my back?" I asked with a cheeky smile.

His eyes darkened and he stalked from the bed, picking me up and taking us towards the shower.

⊏⊐

I frowned into Cade's small mirror. Yesterday I didn't have much time to pack anything half decent with Lucky standing at the door impatiently, but I thought I looked okay.

I was wearing high waisted white slacks, a white blouse, and super high tan wedges. Maybe white wasn't the best choice while staying at the club, but I wouldn't be here much longer as I had to get to the store. It was only me and Lily today, but I was sure Amy would refuse to stay here without me, so I guessed she would be coming too. I turned just as Cade emerged from the bathroom, towel around his waist looking good enough to eat.

"As much as you look sexy with your stubble, honey, I'm glad you shaved. I think my inner thighs have whisker rash," I joked, looking down at my phone at a text from Amy.

· · ·

Amy: Get me the fuck out of here now, bitch. I am about to murder some biker ass.

I laughed, thinking of the tantrum she had last night when she found out Brock had demanded she sleep in his room, with the prospects enforcing it. After many curse words, she had decided she would barricade herself in the room, locking Brock out. Guess he got in.

Me: But what a fine ass it is.

I knew my text back would get a reaction.

Be ready to leave in 5. I added, deciding we could get breakfast on the way.

"You're not going anywhere, Gwen," Cade growled from over my shoulder, obviously reading my text.

I jumped, not even hearing him approach. I regained my composure, whirling on him.

"You have to stop reading my texts over my shoulder. I hate it," I scolded, frowning at him, which was hard to do when he was only wearing a towel.

"Get used to it, babe, got to keep an eye on you somehow. Especially when you have crazy ass ideas like leaving the club. Your store is closed until we sort this shit." His tone was serious.

Anger bubbled up inside me and I was barely able to stop myself from slapping him. "Excuse me?" I asked quietly.

Cade crossed his arms, trying to intimidate me with his macho stance. "Your store is closed until we get these pricks out of the picture. It's an easy target, too vulnerable."

My temper flared to epic proportions. "You think you have the right to dictate whether *my* business opens or not? Are you fucking insane?" I shouted, going toe to toe with him, even if I only came up to his shoulders with heels on.

"You think for one second I'm taking a risk with your safety, Gwen? The store is closed, end of story." His voice was raised, he obviously wasn't used to people arguing with the great and powerful Cade.

"Fuck that!" I screeched. "There is no way in hell you're telling me how to run my business. I have staff that expect to get paid, orders to fill, it's my fucking livelihood. Those thugs aren't going to come back, they aren't that stupid. I am *not* letting this shit run my life, not again." I was breathing heavily, anger pulsing through me.

Cade's eyes flared and he turned away from me, his arm sweeping across his dresser, sending everything on top crashing to the ground. I jumped at his sudden outburst but refused to back down.

"How the fuck am I even going to think straight knowing you're vulnerable? Anything could happen to you and I won't fucking be there!" He whirled back around to face me, his hands clenched into fists at his sides.

"Well, you're just going to have to find a way to deal with it. You're not stopping me from living my life. I refuse to let this shit stop me from doing anything, and I am not dealing with your macho man shit today!" I yelled back, breathing heavily, anger like a fire ripping through me.

Cade's face turned into a mask of pure anger. He prowled up to me, pushing me against the wall. My heart threatened to beat out of my chest as he wrapped his hand around my neck, applying enough pressure that I felt the strength he had, but not enough to hurt me.

"Why can't you just do as I fucking say? No arguments," he hissed, eyes dark.

I didn't recognize his face with this much anger directed at me. "Get your hands off me," I managed to wheeze out as I tried to push his iron chest.

Cade glanced down at his hand with disgust and immediately released me, taking two steps back. I rubbed my neck trying to get my breathing steady. I glanced up at him, unable to fathom what just happened.

Cade's face was marred with regret. I straightened and reached over and grabbed my bag and phone. Cade stayed frozen, looking down at his hands as if he was unable to believe what they had just done.

"I'm going, you can't keep me prisoner here. I have a life to live," I said quietly but firmly, looking at him with determination in my eyes.

He lifted his head, his face blank. "I'll put Skeet and Rosco on you. You are not to leave their sight." His voice was low, dead.

I nodded and walked quietly to the door, unable to be in the room any more. He didn't say a word as I exited.

"Come on, Amy, let's blow this popsicle stand," I called through Brock's door, surprised she wasn't sitting at the bottom of the stairs waiting for me to exit.

The door flew open and an angry looking Brock stormed past, giving me a stiff chin lift. Amy followed him out, flipping the bird to his back.

"Asshole," she muttered.

"Bitch," he yelled over his shoulder.

Despite my somber mood, I couldn't help but be a bit amused, even if I still didn't know what was going on with Amy and my brother.

"Whoa, what's going on there?" I teased.

Amy glared at me. "Don't. Even. Ask."

I guessed everyone's day was starting off like shit. We made it to the common room and saw Skeet and Rosco waiting for us.

"Ready to go, ladies?" Rosco asked politely.

I gave him a proper look, he wasn't bad looking, ripped of course, but that seemed to be a requirement for being in the club. He kind of reminded me of some of the sleazy Italian guys back in New York. Slicked back black hair shining with grease, a gold chain around his neck and dark pronounced features. Not my cup of tea, but nothing to sneeze at.

Skeet was a bit smaller, still built but leaner, with more of a runner's body. He wore slim black pants and a tight wife beater under his cut, making him look even slimmer. He had amazing curls, which contrasted with his harsh face, scarred in a permanent grimace with a line going from his eyebrow to mouth.

I wonder how he got that.

"What the fuck is this?" Amy hissed, gesturing to the men.

I gave her a look, telling her to reign it in. "Cade wouldn't let us leave without babysitters."

She opened her mouth to protest.

"No complaining, let's just get out of here." I nodded to the men and we walked out to my car.

Luckily I was allowed my car, the guys were going to follow behind. As we got in, I caught a glimpse of Cade sitting on his bike. His stare bore into me, I quickly got in the car, avoiding his gaze.

"Uh-oh, trouble in paradise?" Amy asked, catching the exchange.

I reversed, resisting the urge to hit his stupid motorbike, and sped off out the gate.

I glanced at Amy over my sunglasses. "I'll tell you mine if you tell me yours?"

She laughed. "Biker men are assholes, no way am I breathing Brock's air if I can help it. There's nothing to tell," she lied, inspecting her manicure.

"Bullshit. There is definitely something going on. Does that mean you and Ian are over?" I was hoping to finally get something out of her.

She sighed, looking out the window. "We were never even properly together. I don't know what to think. I finally start getting over him with someone that drives me crazy and is a polar opposite, then he comes back fucking my head up then dropping a bomb that he's quitting the Army. I can't deal, it's too much to handle. I told him we'd talk when he came home, if he really is leaving, but I don't know if I can do it, Gwennie."

I gave her a look filled with sympathy, she really was in a prick of a situation. I loved my brother and didn't want him getting hurt, but there was so much in play here, especially adding Brock in the mix, the waters were definitely muddy.

She gave me a sideways glance. "I feel weird talking to you about this, there's nothing going on so can we just drop it?" she pleaded.

I didn't believe her, but I nodded. "I'm always here if you need me though, Abrams."

She smiled. "I know. Are you going to tell me what's going on between you and your delicious man?"

"Not a chance in Hell. Let's just forget about men for the day, okay?" I asked as if it was even possible.

"Best suggestion I've heard in ages," Amy replied.

The day passed by quickly, there was no more creepy deliveries or car bombs or drive bys or anything dramatic. Although I was jumpy for most of the day, convinced a spider would crawl out of somewhere. We tried to keep the incident quiet, but this was a small town and the cat was out of the bag.

Or the spider was out of the box.

I thought it would keep people away, but it had the opposite effect. Everyone stopped by to see if I was okay and get their fill of the town's latest gossip. I expected more anger at the club for bringing this kind of thing into town, but everyone spoke reasonably highly of the club, talking about how they organized charity runs and helped fund the children's center down the street.

Rosco and Skeet hadn't left the store all day, they looked vigilant, always scanning the street. I bet it got boring, hanging out in a women's clothing shop all day, so I made an effort to buy them lunch and coffees to get them through the day. I also gave them magazines, but they had gone unopened. I guessed there was no time for leisurely reading when one was guarding against a possible gang attack.

I sighed, letting the last of the customers out before locking the door behind them. I had let Lily go early because she had a test to study for, and she had been about as jumpy as me, steeling worried glances at Rosco and Skeet all day.

I turned to Amy, who was counting the register, then glanced to Rosco and Skeet lounging on the couches.

"Who's keen for pizza?" I rubbed my hands together at the thought of the carby goodness.

Amy screwed her face up. "Cheese, grease, and about a thousand calories?" she replied, then a light sparked in her face. "Count me in, maybe if I gained a hundred pounds I wouldn't have to worry about the unwanted advances of some biker idiot. As long as we get ice cream too."

I laughed. "Awesome."

The men were smirking at Amy's latest comment. "Are we allowed to stop by the pizza place and grocery store without you two getting raked over the coals?" I asked sarcastically.

Neither said a word, they just stood still grinning. I guessed that was a yes.

⌐⌐

"Holy crap, I feel like I'm about to explode," Amy groaned as she tossed the empty ice cream carton into the direction of the trash can then flopped back down onto Cade's bed.

I lay down beside her, unbuttoning my pants. "Yes, I feel like I may just slip into a food coma."

We had just consumed a huge pizza and a carton of ice cream, which did nothing to quell the sick feeling in the pit of my stomach I had had since this morning. If ice cream didn't cure it, shit was serious.

After getting back to the club with our goodies, we had managed to slip through the women and children and escape to Cade's room, but not before Steg had approached me. We were almost to the stairs when he and one of the older men had emerged from "church." He spotted me and made a beeline.

"Shit," I muttered under my breath.

Amy followed my gaze. "Uh-oh, biker prez, twelve o'clock."

Steg had a surprisingly soft look on his harsh face when he approached. His hand cupped my chin and my eyes flared in surprise.

"Gwen, you okay?" he asked softly, and my stomach dropped.

Had Cade said something to him about this morning? Surely not, they barely got along. At a loss of what to do, I nodded awkwardly.

"You're strong," he stated, his tone sounding like he almost respected me. "Yesterday, you held it together. Other bitches would've reacted, possibly causing even more shit. You did good, did right by the club."

Whoa.

Had I just gained the approval of someone who I suspected may or may not be an evil man? My question was answered when he bent down to kiss my cheek, gave me a firm nod then disappeared. I was so shocked I was pretty sure my mouth was wide open.

"What the fuck?" Amy sounded just as confused as I was. I grabbed her hand and dragged her towards the stairs.

"I will not even be attempting to figure out what just happened, my head is too full."

We had spent the rest of the night hiding in Cade's room. I had learned that he and the boys were away doing something – I wouldn't like to think what – and were not expected back for a long while. I had mixed feelings about this, one part of me was relieved. I had spent the day avoiding all thoughts about this morning, and I needed time to get my mind straight.

I was scared, seeing Cade lose control that reminded me a little too much of the violence that had been unleashed on me a year earlier. I didn't want that to happen again. I was sure Cade wouldn't hurt me, the look of disgust at himself this morning showed how much he obviously hated himself for his moment of anger.

I loved him, a lot. I couldn't just write off this incident though, seeing him that angry had been scary, but I knew he had a temper and it had been from worrying about me. I didn't want to justify his behavior, but I knew how much he hated feeling powerless.

Crap.

"Earth to Gwen." Amy was staring at me looking slightly concerned.

"Sorry, Ames, was a million miles away," I replied, hoping to sound breezy. I didn't fool my BFF, though.

"What happened with you and Cade this morning? I know it must have been serious, you've been off all day."

I sighed, not wanting to lie to her. "We had a fight this morning, it got...intense," I told her vaguely.

Her eyes flared in anger and she pushed up onto her elbows.

"He didn't hurt you did he? My threat still stands, I will de-ball that man, even if it would be a crime not to let the world see how beautiful your babies would be."

My friend was protective, I knew she would want to get involved in this and I didn't have the energy. "No, he didn't hurt me, he's just protective. He didn't want me going anywhere. I disagreed, it got heated. You know me, I hate being told what to do. It'll be fine," I tried to reassure her and myself at the same time.

Amy left not long after our talk about Cade, receiving a text from Rosie saying they could bunk together. Obviously whatever had happened with Brock had been serious and he didn't want her in his room any more. I was infinitely curious about this, but Amy was locked tight and I didn't want to push her.

I found it hard to find sleep, not having Cade next to me and not wanting this to be permanent, and then I questioned myself for yearning for Cade. I finally drifted off into a restless slumber, waking up and reaching for Cade.

Sometime during the night I woke yet again, but this time I had firm arms wrapped around me and I was tucked into Cade's chest. I looked up at him, groggy, trying to decide whether I was dreaming or not. He must have sensed my gaze because his arms tightened.

"Sleep, baby," his voice was rough.

Still half asleep I burrowed back into him, trying to get as close as I could. "I love you, Cade," I whispered, feeling his body go tight around me, I drifted off before he could reply.

I woke to an empty bed. I looked around and deduced I was alone. Had I dreamt him? I sighed, trying to gather my thoughts and figure out the disaster that seemed to be my life. I felt sick about the way things were with Cade, he was out doing God knows what, obviously in danger and things were weird with us. I didn't want that, no matter how out of hand things got yesterday, I couldn't be without him. Period.

If that made me a stupid woman who was blinded by love, then I guessed I had better get used to those rose tinted glasses, I wasn't going to bolt and spend the rest of my life wondering what if. Yeah, a sensible man who wore a suit to work and had zero risk of coming home riddled with bullets was probably the best option. But that wasn't me, unfortunately I wasn't sensible. I did crazy shit, I needed a man that could handle that, handle me. And I needed Cade like I needed Chanel, so I would work something out.

On that thought, my phone rang I reached to the nightstand, glanced at the display and answered.

"Hey, Mum," I greeted, happy to hear from my mother.

"Hi there, sweetheart, not catching you at a bad time am I?"

I sat up in bed, leaning against the headboard. "No, I just woke up."

"Oh that's good dear, how are you? How's Amy? How is your brother? Gosh I miss him, we hardly ever hear from him. The day he retires from the Army will be the day I sleep sounder," she stated, sounding emotional after her quick-fire questions.

I sighed and set out to quell my mother's worry, if that was humanly possible.

After a long conversation and a quick talk with my father, who was a man of few words, I rang off feeling emotionally lighter. Talking with my family somehow made me feel better even if I hadn't told them what was going on.

⊂⊃

"I think I'm ready for a beer. Or five. And I need to sleep in my own bed, how long is this lockdown shit going to last? My patience is like, worn the fuck out," Amy complained, collapsing on the couch at the store. It had been another busy day, and we were exhausted.

I looked up from counting the till with sympathy. "I feel you, sister. There is only so much time a girl can spend in a biker clubhouse, especially with limited wardrobe options." I sighed, thinking of my walk in back home. "If we don't get this shit sorted by tonight I'm going to hunt down these fuckers and give them a beat down," I declared, feeling feisty.

This earned a snort from one of the prospects, who had pulled babysitting duty for the day. I glared at him, not for the first time. I didn't like him at all.

He leered at Amy all day as well as anything walking into the store wearing a skirt. He had a shaved head, beady eyes and a gross goatee that made him look like a sleaze bag, which by his actions today, was a right assumption. He had ignored my glare to take a phone call.

Amy met my eyes. "Before we beat down any rival gang-bangers, can we start with him?" she asked pointing her eyes in Taylor's direction, currently outside talking heatedly with someone.

"He is seriously sleazy, his beady little eyes have been creeping me out all day."

"You and me both," I replied, gathering up the cash I had counted. "I'll go put this in the safe then we will get to those beers," I called over my shoulder, walking out the back.

I started towards my office, then noticed the back door which led to the back alleyway was open. Something settled in my gut. I didn't leave that open, in fact, it had been locked. Shit. I turned to call to Amy and came face to face with the scariest looking guy I had ever seen.

Tattoos everywhere, even on his face and a distinct spider crawling up his neck. I had never seen someone with tattoos pretty much covering his entire face, they were meant to intimidate, and by the look on his face, this guy definitely meant me harm.

I dropped the cash, opening my mouth to scream as well as preparing to kick him in the nuts. None of this happened, the goon just smiled, holding something up to my neck, and then everything went black.

CHAPTER 14

I WOKE UP SLOWLY, feeling groggy and confused. It took me a moment to remember what happened and another second to realize I was tied up.

My hands were bound over my head and I was somehow hanging off the ceiling, my feet barely touching the ground. My dress had been taken off and I was clad only in my bra and underwear.

Panic began to set in, memories flooding back to the last time I had all my power taken away from me. It took all of my effort not to hyperventilate. My breathing was already laboured from being in this position.

I slowly lifted my head to survey my surroundings. I was in a garage by the looks of it, a tool bench was directly across from me, scary looking instruments were scattered atop it. I gulped, seeing what looked like dried blood covering them.

"I see the princess has awoken."

Scary man strolled into my vision and a couple of equally scary guys stood behind him, arms crossed, glaring at me.

Fuck, this situation was all too familiar, and I was terrified beyond belief. Fear a physical thing taking over my nervous system.

I took a breath. No, this time I had someone who would come for me. Cade would come for me.

Scary guy stood so close to me I could smell his rancid breath. He stroked my cheek and I flinched away, trying to stay balanced even though my wrists were burning and my legs were jelly.

"Don't know how Cade landed a high class piece like you, can't wait to find out what you taste like," he drawled.

My stomach lurched as he ran a hand down my torso. "Well, basic hygiene was a start, you seriously need a tic tac," I replied sarcastically, with false confidence.

He glared at me, pulling my torso flush towards his, so I could feel his erection. "You're not going to be so smart after I'm done with you, bitch. Although I do hope you have a little more fight than the last one, the fun was over far too quickly for our liking."

He leaned in and licked my cheek.

Bile rose up in my throat and I struggled not to throw up. Fire ran through my veins as I realized he was talking about Laurie. This is the man who killed that poor girl, the man that almost killed Bull and scarred the club. The fucker.

Fury replaced my terror, fury at this disgusting excuse for a human, someone who thought he had the right to hurt people, to ruin lives. I brought my knee up to connect with his crotch with as much force as possible. He doubled over, grunting in pain.

"Get your filthy hands off me, you piece of scum," I hissed, relishing in the fact I caused that sick man pain.

He straightened, and without me realizing it was happening, his fist connected with my face. My head cracked to the side and pain pulsed through my skull.

"You bitch!" he snarled, punching me again and I felt my lip split.

My eyes watered, but I'd had worse than this, I could handle this. I spat out blood that had flooded into my mouth.

"That the best you can do, you pussy? My grandmother hits harder than that." I smiled at him and watched as his tattooed face turned red.

I was prepared for the next punch that landed on my stomach, but the pain still surprised me. I hoped he hadn't cracked a rib, those took ages to heal. I was forced to stay upright, my binds making me unable to fall. My ribs were on fire, but I didn't let it show.

He smiled, the same smile he gave me back at the store, before turning his back to me. "You obviously have some problems learning when to shut the fuck up, don't worry, I'll teach you, and I'll enjoy it too." He turned, holding a very scary looking pair of pliers. "Maybe I'll start by ripping some teeth out, then you won't be so inclined to mouth off." His voice was ice.

I began to tremble. Shit, this is bad. This guy was obviously a psychopath and by the looks of those bloody pliers, he had done this before. Before he could take another step towards me, all hell broke loose.

The doors, which must've lead into a house, crashed open and the two goons who had been quietly watching pulled guns. The sound of gunfire rang in my ears and I saw the two men go down.

I watched in horror as Scary Guy pulled a gun and started shooting at the door where Bull, Brock, and Cade were standing, guns drawn. Scary Guy was standing in front of me, which I guessed was why none of them shot back, in fear of missing him and hitting me. Instead, Bull rushed forward, *in the path of bullets,* and tackled my would-be torturer to the ground. He wrestled the gun out of his hands and commenced in beating the shit out of him.

Cade appeared in front of me, taking my scantily clad body

and battered face in with a mask of fury and concern. Quick as anything, his face changed and he gazed at me with an expression so gentle I almost cried. Yes, *that* was what made me cry, not the man who had just punched me in the face and was about to pull out my teeth.

I was so weird.

"I'm going to get you down, okay, baby," he murmured in a voice so soft it was hard to believe he had possibly killed two men.

He reached up with a long knife and cut me free of the rope holding me to the ceiling. I collapsed into his arms, unable to hold my weight. His arms circled around me, holding me tight. Brock appeared in front of us, shrugging off his cut then his shirt, handing it to Cade who grunted thanks.

"Arms up, baby," Cade ordered quietly.

I obeyed silently and he pulled the shirt over my head covering me. He cupped my neck with his hands, his face like thunder as he examined my battered face.

He gathered me in his arms and glanced at Brock. "I'm getting Gwen out of here."

Brock just nodded.

"You two on cleanup, the boys are on their way," he barked before striding towards the door.

I regarded the bloody scene clinically, none of it sinking in.

Brock gave Cade a hard look, then directed a softer one at me.

That was all I saw before Cade took us through a dirty house and out onto the street. We were in a seriously dodgy neighborhood, nowhere that looked familiar, and I wondered where the hell these bastards had taken me. I didn't have much time to contemplate this as an SUV screeched in front of us at the curb. I jumped for a moment, thinking it was more of the Spiders.

"It's okay, baby, it's just Lucky," Cade told me quietly.

Lucky jumped out of the driver's seat and hissed when he saw me, his normally carefree face marred with fury.

"Those fuckers dead?" he barked at Cade, his voice feral.

"Yep," Cade clipped. "You take my bike, I'll take Gwen in the cage."

Lucky nodded tightly, starting toward the house. He stopped in front of me, stroking my cheek softly and wordlessly before continuing.

Cade opened the passenger door, depositing me carefully on the seat before buckling me up. Our eyes locked for a beat, something passing from him I didn't entirely understand, but something important. I didn't get long to scrutinize it as he closed my door and rounded the car.

He took off quickly, weaving through the streets at speed.

"Where are we?" I whispered, trying to find a familiar landmark.

"Barnett, next town over," he replied, eyes focused on the road.

That would make sense as to why I didn't recognize where we were. Silence descended as we left the town behind, the road looking all but abandoned. I felt overwhelmed, but numb at the same time, my brain not being able to handle all the crazy shit that had just happened.

My face was hurting like a motherfucker, not to mention my ribs, which were on fire. I gingerly touched my lip, wincing at the pain that erupted. Cade must've seen this because he slammed on his breaks and pulled off the road. He was out of the car and by my side at lightning speed before unbuckling me and turning my body to face him. He lightly touched my face, eyes hard.

"You hurt anywhere else?" he asked evenly, voice flat.

I gulped and glanced down at my torso, not being fooled by his flat tone. I knew he was barely restraining his fury, but he would see my ribs sooner or later. His eyes followed mine and he lifted the edge of Brock's tee up to expose my ribs. I heard his hiss of breath as his eyes encountered the purplish bruise already forming. His stare came level with mine, eyes glittering with caged fury.

"They touch you?" he managed to grind out.

I knew how much he feared the answer, he was barely holding on.

I clasped my hands around his neck, pulling him between my legs. "He didn't touch me, you got there in time. I knew you would," I spoke softy.

His eyes focused on my lip, the bruise that I knew was already forming on my cheekbone. His huge palm spanned my ribs, touch feather light.

"I didn't get there in time, the fucker put his hands on you. Had you hanging off the fucking ceiling in your underwear." His voice was almost a snarl. "He marked you. You're *hurt*."

"You don't get it, Cade, I knew you would come. I've been in that situation before, and I was paralyzed with fear last time..."

Cade's eyes became midnight at my words, body stiff.

I tightened my grip on his neck. "This time I wasn't paralyzed with fear, I didn't feel hopeless. Because I *knew* you would come for me." My voice was fierce.

Cade stared at me for a second as if he was mentally pulling himself together. He closed his eyes then plastered my body into his, my butt left the seat and I had no choice but to wrap my legs around his waist. He held me tight, face in my hair.

"Fuck, baby, when I got that call you'd been taken." He sucked in an audible breath. "I never want to relive that moment, for as long as I fuckin' live. You were gone for four hours, longest four hours of my life. Knew the boys were one step away from locking me down, but I couldn't have that. I knew how terrified you would've been, hating the way we left things. I walked through that door, not knowing what I was going to find, but if you hadn't been whole baby, I would be Bull, breathing, existing, but not *living*."

He pulled his head back, resting his forehead on mine. "Need you, Gwen, like I need air. This life is fucked, it ain't what you deserve, but I'm going to clean this shit up now. It will never touch you again."

His voice was firm, resolved and I believed him.

"I can't promise you I'm going to be a choirboy, that'll never be me. But I am getting the club away from any kind of business that could get you hurt, 'cause I am never putting you in danger again, for as long as I fuckin' live. And I intend that to be a good long while, so I can make my life with you, put a ring on your finger, my babies in your belly."

My breath left me in a whoosh, this was a shit ton of information to take in at one go. Babies? Marriage? I had never even considered this, my life having been focused on my career, my friends. Now I had this declaration on the side of the road after being kidnapped and beaten — this day was definitely crazy.

I gazed into Cade's eyes, not knowing how to reply but somehow knowing I wanted all of that with him. I didn't know what to say, so I kissed him. He complied for a moment before gently pulling away.

"Gwen, your lip, I'll hurt you." He sounded conflicted, I could see the desire in his eyes, the same need that I had to be close to him, to connect with him.

"I don't care," I whispered against his mouth, resuming the kiss.

His reservations forgotten, Cade attacked my mouth with a ferocity that I had never experienced. It was beyond a kiss, it was a promise, a claim. I ignored the pain in my lip, he pushed me back against the car, mouth never leaving mine. I felt his hardness pressing up against me and I moaned, wrapping myself against him even tighter.

Cade stopped the kiss, eyes on mine. "Jesus, Gwen, fuck." He shook his head slightly as if he was trying to get his thoughts straight. "As much as I would love to get inside you, I am not doing it on the side of a road, with you hurt. We need to get you to a hospital."

I gave a little mew of protest as he deposited me back in my seat. He smiled, it was tight and his eyes were stormy, but it was a smile.

Cade got back into the car, getting us back on the road home. I looked over at him, he had one hand on the wheel, the other lay on my bare thigh.

"Honey, I know the concern you have for me comes from a place of love, but can we maybe skip the hospital visit? It's just a couple of bruises, nothing that Ibuprofen and a bottle of wine can't fix."

I attempted to sound breezy, but my voice was shaky. I wasn't going to deny that I was hanging on by a thread, I had been kidnapped and beaten by murderers for crissake, which was kind of scary. But I also knew I wanted to steer clear of hospitals, not only due to the fact I fucking hated those places, but I was scared at the memories those sterile walls might uncover.

"A couple of bruises?" Cade replied quietly, his knuckles were white on the steering wheel. "Look in the fucking mirror, Gwen. Half of your face is swollen and bruised, your lip is busted. Best case scenario is your ribs are badly bruised, but they're more likely cracked so you're going to the hospital. And you're staying there until someone can assure me beyond a shadow of a fucking doubt you will make a full recovery, in addition to prescribing painkillers that numb everything down to a broken fuckin' fingernail." His tone brokered no argument.

"Okay, I get your need to protect me, and your alpha male blood is probably boiling right now, but I *hate* hospitals. Not just because they are full of germs and death or because the bed sheets are as scratchy as a fleabag motel's – don't even get me started on the gowns. I could get over all of that to give you peace of mind, but I just can't go into another hospital, not after spending weeks in one a year ago. I don't think I can stand being the victim again. Please, Cade." I knew my tone might have bordered on pathetic, but I would rather wear Crocs for a month than be back in a hospital bed.

Cade glanced at me, I knew he was battling internally, and my puppy dog eyes didn't help his struggle, but they helped mine.

"I'm getting a doctor to meet us at your place, he can check you over there, but if he even *thinks* you might need a hospital visit, you'll be going." He sighed as if he was dealing with a child who didn't want to have a nap.

"Thanks, Cade," I replied quietly, placing my hand atop his.

The hand at my thigh squeezed. "Sure, baby. We can't have my precious princess in scratchy sheets." A hint of teasing was in his voice.

Now that was settled, my mind wandered to some important points. "Okay, um, Cade?" I asked hesitantly.

"Yeah, babe?" he answered, eyes back on the road.

I fiddled my hands together, trying to ignore the throbbing in my face. "Some pretty heavy shit happened back there, I was kind of kidnapped and you and the boys killed those men." My voice was quiet, almost trembling.

Cade didn't say anything, his hand was still tight on my thigh, fury seemed to pulse through the cabin of the truck.

"Aren't we going to call the police?" I asked. "I mean, I don't think you guys will get in trouble for shooting those men, it was self defense and all," I added quickly.

I knew the chances of the club letting law enforcement know they had killed three rival gang members was slim to none. I didn't know how to get right with that, even though these men were evil. I was struggling because at the same time, a small part of me was glad they were dead after what they had done to Laurie, and most likely other women.

"Already called them," Cade replied and I blinked.

"Really?"

"Yeah, babe, really. Called Crawford the second I found out you were gone. Wanted every available man looking for you." He glanced at me. "You're the most precious thing in my world. I love the club, but there's no competition. Your safety is everything to me. After today, boys will be questioning the way we do business. We aren't losing another woman." His tone was determined.

I squeezed his hand. "You haven't lost me. I'm right here."

He brought our intertwined hands together and kissed mine.

"What do I tell the police, though?" I asked.

I was very conflicted about lying to the police. Those men were evil, there was no doubt about that, but I couldn't get right with the fact they were dead. Things were spiraling, I really hoped this wouldn't be my life, lying to the police, covering up murders. And I was a terrible liar, I could never tell a lie, my family would always see right through it. So would the police, for that matter.

When I was fifteen, I got caught by the cops drinking by the river. When they had asked my name and age I had replied, "Jane Miller, twenty years old." I had also managed to blather on about how I was here on holiday from Australia, all the time talking in a terrible accent. They didn't buy it, maybe because my accent sucked, or maybe because one of the cops was my dad's friend and had known me since I was five. I had been a little too tipsy to realize that. I bought myself a month's grounding with that lie. I feared the consequences could be much worse if I was to lie badly this time around.

"Fuck, baby. I would never ask this of you unless I had to, I hate dragging you into this shit. I promise I'll fix everything. This isn't going to be your life, I'll make sure of it." His eyes were blazing on mine, silently apologetic.

"Okay, just tell me what I need to say. I'll try my best not to put on an accent," I mumbled.

━━

"I was going out the back to put the money in the safe when I saw the back door was open. I knew something wasn't right so I started to yell, but he was there." I was recounting it like it happened to someone else. Like I'd been an observer to my own kidnapping. "He was bald, had a spider tattoo crawling up his neck and a scar underneath his eye. His whole face was tattooed actually. He touched me with something, a Taser I guess, then it all went black."

Cade was stiff beside me as I recounted what happened. My voice was unusually strong, it had something to do with the man who had refused to let me go since we had arrived home.

Luke was already waiting for us, Cade insisted on paramedics checking me out before I said a word. There was nothing seriously wrong with me apart from the fact I was going to have one hell of a shiner for the next couple of days. And I would have an uncomfortable mid-section for a couple of weeks until my ribs healed.

"I woke up tied to the ceiling, I don't remember getting there. All I remember is seeing that man and then everything goes black," I explained to Luke, who was sitting in my living room with a tight expression on his face, writing this down on a notepad.

The sheriff, whom I had only just met, was sitting beside him. He was an older man who looked tired and jaded. His grey hair was thinning, and he had a slight paunch hanging over his belt. His eyes were kind, though.

"When I woke up, he was there with two other men." I paused. "He said something about Laurie," I continued and I heard Cade's sharp intake of breath. Luke's face turned stormy. I told them what he said quickly, the energy in the room electric.

"That's when I kneed the bastard in the nuts." This earned a kiss on the head from Cade, a tender look from Luke and a smirk from the sheriff.

"He had some pliers and was going to pull my teeth out, I must've fainted then I guess. The next thing I remember is Cade pulling me down." I smiled up at him, his eyes intense on mine. "I knew you would come for me," I whispered and his face changed to a fiercely possessive expression, which made my body tingle, despite the circumstances.

He didn't say a word, just cupped my face in his hands. His lips lightly touched mine, carefully brushing over my split lip.

I turned my head back to Luke, who had a blank expression on his face.

"And how did you know where Gwen was?" he asked Cade, voice professional but tight.

I glanced back at Cade, realizing I hadn't even asked him this myself.

"Had a friend keeping an eye on neighborhoods where the Spiders frequented. Spotted them carrying Gwen into a house, got lucky." Cade's reply was terse.

Luke's face threatened to change from the blank expression he was wearing. "And why didn't you call us the second you found out where Gwen was?" His voice was definitely not professional now, there was no disguising the anger in his tone.

"I wasn't real keen on wasting time, considering I knew what these guys could be doing to Gwen." Cade's voice was hard, but he ran his hand down my cheek and lightly across my bruised skin.

"I obviously didn't get there fast enough. Got to the house, place was empty apart from the garage. That's where they had Gwen hanging from the ceiling in her underwear."

The energy in the room turned wired as I watched both of the policemen's expressions tighten, looking at me with concern and anger.

Luke seemed to check himself. "You with anyone?"

Cade nodded. "Brock was with me when I got the call."

I wondered why he left Bull out.

"And was anyone else there when you two arrived?" Luke asked.

"No, they must've heard us arrive. Bolted just as we got there," Cade lied smoothly.

Luke raised a disbelieving eyebrow. "And you didn't give chase? You just let the men who kidnapped your 'Old Lady' get away?"

Cade's body went tight. "I was more concerned that my woman was hanging from the ceiling beaten, half naked and unconscious," Cade bit out.

"You expect me to believe that you let the men who beat Gwen, who were most likely responsible for Laurie's murder just run off? Especially when we got reports of an explosion at the Spider's compound, with multiple fatalities." Luke's tone was accusing.

I straightened at his words. Multiple fatalities? Were the men that I had come to like and respect responsible for this? I was barely able to hide my tremble. This whole situation was snowballing into something I wasn't sure I could deal with.

"I don't give a shit what you believe, Deputy. It's the truth. As for the explosion, that's the first I'm hearing about it, I'm not going to say I'm sad about those rats being exterminated, though." He sounded convincing. I would've believed him, if I hadn't seen what I had seen today.

Luke wasn't at all convinced. "You think you're untouchable, you can go around this town like the law doesn't apply to you. I'm going to find proof that this was you, and I'm going to take you and your lowlife gang down," he spat, eyes full of hatred.

"Good luck finding proof that doesn't exist, Crawford." Cade was calm, expression hard.

Luke looked like he was going to say something else when the sheriff stood.

"That's enough, Deputy, we have their statements. Miss Alexandra here has been through enough and doesn't need this shit. She's back safe, thanks to Mr Fletcher. I have a feeling those bastards are long gone, so the chances of finding the kidnappers are slim. We will look into it, though." The sheriff gave Cade a meaningful glance before continuing. "As for the explosion, that is not our jurisdiction, but the sheriff over in Barnett is a buddy of mine. They have other suspects who are not Mr Fletcher or any of his associates, as they all have alibis. I suggest you shut your mouth on that matter."

Holy crap. This so sounded like the sheriff was on the Sons' payroll. Luke got to his feet, looking murderous.

"You've got to be shitting me, you know this was them. Jesus, are you seriously *protecting* these criminals?"

The sheriff's gaze turned dangerous, a quick change from the impassive look on his face moments before. "You watch what you're saying, son, and remember who you're talking to. Stand down before I lose my temper," the sheriff ordered quietly.

Luke was quietly seething, but he didn't say a word, just held himself stiffly for a moment before turning to Cade and me. He glared at Cade, but when he turned to me his fury had all but disappeared, a tender gaze looking more at home on his handsome face.

"I'm glad you are safe, Gwen, I was worried sick. We'll have lunch again this week if you're feeling up to it." He delivered that parting shot before turning and walking out the door.

Shit. I hadn't told Cade about the lunches I shared with Luke on a semi regular basis. I didn't tell him because I knew he wouldn't like it (huge understatement, he would lose his shit) and I liked Luke's company. He was a decent man and we got along well.

My feelings for him were purely platonic and I genuinely wanted us to be friends, which was hard considering his hatred towards Cade. But we never addressed that leather clad elephant in the room, always steering clear of subjects pertaining to the club. I knew Cade was angry because his body tightened even more. He gave me a look before standing and shaking the sheriff's hand.

"Thanks for everything, Bill, you have the club's gratitude." He sounded respectful, which surprised me.

Bill stared at him. "Don't need the gratitude, just need you to reassure me that no more shit is going to hit my town." His voice was hard.

"Trust me, Bill, club's looking to move in different directions. After today you have my word nothing else is hitting Amber." Cade's voice was resolute.

Bill looked at him a beat then nodded. He then focused his attention on me, face soft. "Glad you're okay, beautiful. By the sounds of it, this boy got lucky getting you. You take care of yourself."

I nodded, unable to think of a proper response. I was surprised at the sheriff's words and I wondered if Luke had been talking about me. Bill gave Cade another nod before seeing himself out.

Cade turned back to me, face unreadable. "Lunch?" he asked quietly.

Uh oh. How was I going to get out of this? My luck seemed to have turned for the day, because at that moment, the door flew open and a tear streaked Amy ran through it. Her gaze darted around the living room before settling on me, eyes narrowed on my face, she strode towards me. Brock entered the room behind her.

"Gwennie! Oh my god. Oh my god." She threw her arms around me.

I tried not to flinch when she squeezed my ribs.

She quickly pushed back and gaped at my face. "Those fuckers," she hissed.

"Amy, it's okay," I started softly, but she ignored me.

"Those fuckers!" she yelled, and I jumped. "How can this be happening to you *again*, Gwen? You've been through enough. Jesus, you've been through Hell. You almost died at the hands of crazy fucked up men, now after finally healing, some other bastards get their hands on you. *Um no*. This is not acceptable." Her voice was in danger of breaking and I watched as she tried to fight the tears that threatened at the corners of her eyes.

"Amy," I said softly, but she ignored me again. Her eyes found Cade, standing across from us, arms crossed, face still blank.

"What have *you* done about this? Are you going to make sure this isn't going to happen again? If you don't, I'm calling my father and he's going to send his jet to come and take us away to an island far away, where there are no men within miles. Actually, fuck that, I'm calling him now." She unearthed her phone and began furiously swiping at the screen.

Cade's face was no longer blank, he uncrossed his arms and opened his mouth.

"Babe, cool it. It's sorted. Put the fucking phone down and chill the fuck out," Brock ordered, cutting Cade off and coming closer.

This was a surprise, I didn't even expect him to arrive with Amy, much less be speaking to her. I didn't have much time to think on this, though.

Amy whirled on him. "Cool it?" she uttered dangerously, glaring at Brock.

"*Cool it?*" she repeated, voice shrill. "Are you fucking kidding me? Did you see Gwen lying in a hospital bed, hooked up to monitors, on *life support*? No. Did you listen to a doctor say she might never wake up? No. Did you sit by her bed for almost two weeks, waiting, thinking over and over how you could've stopped this, seen the signs, maybe saved her from the horror she endured? No you didn't! *I did.*"

Tears streamed down her face. I went to put my arms around her, soothe her. I had never seen Amy like this. Brock beat me to it. He gathered her up, putting his arms around her, stroking her hair and kissing her head. I expected her to fight him, push him away. But she didn't, she burrowed into his neck, hands clutching his tee.

I watched in fascination as Brock's usually hard glare softened into something so tender it made my heart melt, just a little. He lifted her up, and without a word carried her out of the room.

"Did you just see that?" I asked Cade, my voice a little breathy. "She didn't even try to fight him or call him a biker asshole or anything."

I was shocked and torn between happiness that Amy had someone that cared for her and disappointment that I might not be having her as a sister-in-law anymore. I frowned. I was really looking forward to being an aunt.

I glanced over at Cade who, hadn't said a word. His eyes were black and a muscle in his cheek was twitching. I fought the urge to roll my eyes, he was such a caveman.

"Seriously, Cade, you all but thump your chest and proclaim 'Gwen is mine' every time we see Luke. He gets the message. We've had lunch like three times, I enjoy his company, purely as a friend. You have to trust me and let me have friends that happen to have penises," I finished, quite proud of how firm I sounded. My hulk of a boyfriend was pretty scary when riled.

He continued to stare at me with that blank look on his face, arms crossed. "This isn't about fuckin' Crawford. Although I'm dis-fucking-pleased you kept your little lunches from me," he bit out.

I threw my hands up in the air. "He speaks! I was beginning to think I was destined to have a mute for a boyfriend. The plus side would be not having to deal with all your macho man comments," I joked, but Cade wasn't even cracking a grin.

I began to read the intensity in the air and got a bad feeling. I cautiously walked up to him and put my hands on his waist.

"What's wrong then?" My voice was soft and I craned to meet his stormy eyes.

His body was hard against mine, not responding to my touch.

"Amy's right," he growled, voice rough. "You've been through Hell and getting involved with me put you right back there. I got you *kidnapped*."

It pained me to hear the raw emotion in his voice. I put my hand to his cheek, opening my mouth to say something, soothe him, but he got there first.

"Men put their hands on you." His hand lightly trailed my face. "You should never have once known violence, not again. You are perfect, pure. And so fucking tiny, any man that would hurt you doesn't deserve to breathe. And I got you hurt again. Christ I put *my* hands on you because I was going crazy at the thought of anything happening to you."

"Cade..." I felt this was going in a terrible direction. I wanted to tell him I was okay.

"No, Gwen." He removed his hand from my face and stepped away from me, his face back to blank. "I thought I could protect you, protect you from the ugliness of this life, not let it taint you. I was wrong. Even if we get out of the gun business, I will always have enemies, enemies that would use you. I can't live with that. We have to end, this is over."

He delivered the verbal punch and I almost doubled over. His voice and face both were void of emotion, which I knew was a lie. He loved me, he was trying to protect me. Before I could argue, he stepped towards me, cupped my head and roughly kissed me. I didn't have time to process this, he released me and walked towards the door. He couldn't leave.

"I tried to commit suicide," I blurted and he froze. "Well, I didn't physically try, someone stopped me before it got that far, but I was going to. No one knows apart from Alex and Bull."

I talked to his back, he didn't turn, but he didn't leave either. He just stayed rooted to the spot, maybe it was good I didn't have to look into his eyes while I laid myself bare.

"It was six months after my attack, I went through Hell trying to heal physically, but I got better. Mentally, I was still in that warehouse. I barely ate, hardly ever slept, I saw their faces every time I closed my eyes." I paused, taking a deep breath before I continued. "I couldn't get clean. No matter how hard I tried, I felt dirty, tawdry, broken. I felt like I would never get better, that I would be sentenced to the nightmare of a life I was living. I had dedicated friends, a loving family. They all wanted to help, tried so hard, but they couldn't. They couldn't *fix* me. So I was going to take the coward's way out. The selfish, easy way out. I planned on swallowing a bunch of sleeping pills, convinced I wanted to die. I almost succeeded."

Cade's hissed breath echoed through the room, but he still didn't turn. I wanted to go to him, but I couldn't, I couldn't bear to see what might be disgust or rejection in his eyes. So I carried on, I had to make him understand.

"I was lucky. So incredibly lucky that I had a friend who saw the signs, he knew what I was going through, he suspected what I was going to do. He walked in on me with a handful of pills. He saved my life," I whispered. "I managed to get help, talk through my issues. But until I met you, I was still broken. I was resigned to the life I was going to live. I wasn't unhappy, but I would never have the appetite for life I used to have. Or so I thought."

The energy in the room turned electric, but Cade still didn't turn. I willed myself to finish what I had to say.

"I'm not trying to say that I would ever consider hurting myself again. I'm in a good place now, a healthier place, but *you* fixed me. You scared away my demons, made me fall in love with you. I don't care about the club, what you think might happen. I trust you, feel safe with you. I'm not letting you walk out of my life because you are trying to protect me. If you walk out that door you will hurt me more than any evil thug ever could." I finished on a whisper, my voice barely audible.

The silence in the room rang in my ears, I felt sick at Cade's lack of response. I didn't know what to do, I was about to run out of the room and go and curl into a ball of despair when he turned.

All of sudden he was right there, in my space, hand yanking my head to his and his lips meeting mine. The kiss was frenzied and tender at the same time. His mouth plundered mine with an intensity I could hardly fathom. This kiss mirrored the one we had on the side of the road, so full of emotion and passion I could hardly stay standing. Cade's hands moved to my butt and he lifted me, my legs instinctively going around his waist. He never broke contact, but I felt him walking, climbing the stairs.

The door to my room slammed behind us somewhere far away, I was in a fog, almost delirious. I ground myself against him, craving him, aching to get as close as possible. My hands went to my tee, pulling it off, having to break contact with Cade while I yanked it over my head was near painful. I ignored the twinge in my ribs. In a flurry of desperate activity, we were finally both naked, Cade gently laid me down on the bed, his body settling on top of me.

His eyes met mine, the look on his face so incredibly tender, my heart jumped. Then he was inside me. I moaned into his mouth, pleasure and relief flooding through me. He pulled his mouth back and slowly moved, eyes never leaving mine. One of his hands bit into my hip, the other roughly cupped my face. I could tell he was holding back, treating me like I was made of glass on account of my injuries.

"You are the strongest, bravest, most caring person I have ever met. You fucking amaze me. Every time I slide into you I thank God for making such a perfect creature." His voice was rough, he didn't stop moving, eyes locked on me.

I swear, my heart stopped, warmth spread through my body as Cade brought me to the most intense orgasm I've had, like, ever.

Everything else melted away.

***

It had been an indefinite amount of time, minutes or hours. I wasn't sure. Cade was still on top of me, still inside me. Neither of us had said a word. Cade slowly pulled out of me, his body leaving mine. I made a little whine of protest, digging my hands into his back. He smiled down at me and it was the most erotic and beautiful thing I had ever seen.

"Don't worry, baby, I'll be inside you again soon. I actually plan on being inside you for the rest of the night. As long as you aren't hurting." He glanced down at my ribs with concern. "But we have to talk first."

He rolled onto his back but brought me into his side carefully, pulling my leg so it was cocked over his and tucked me into his shoulder.

I still hadn't said a word, he stroked my hair.

"What you said before, Gwen, you were wrong. You're not

weak, nor are you a fucking coward. Don't want you ever saying that about yourself again." His voice was still tender but it had a bite. "You're human. What happened to you was fucking horrific, I know men who would've broken down under the weight."

"But I did break down," I whispered, voice ragged.

Cade lifted me up slightly so his eyes were on mine. "Like I said, babe, you're human. But you're also the kind of person who has friends who would lay down their lives for you. Friends who would do anything for you, like save your life."

My breath hitched a little at his words and he kept going.

"Says a lot about you, babe, that you would inspire people to be that devoted to you. It's 'cause you're special, so goddamned amazing that people gravitate to you. I owe Alex my fuckin' life, he saved you so you could be brought to me. You're strong, babe. Even after trying to hurt yourself, you fought back, became yourself. Not a lot of people would do that, most people would spiral and find themselves in a blackness they couldn't escape."

His rough hand stroked my face, reverence in his gaze.

"Because of who you are, Gwen, you not only pulled yourself out of that blackness, but pulled out one of my best friends. You are strong, baby, one of the strongest people I know. Never doubt that, even after today. I nearly fucking broke down, seeing you hanging from that fucking ceiling. You were the one that brought me back from the edge, your spirit, your faith in me."

Tears were now falling down my cheeks at Cade's words and the undisguised love in his gaze. I couldn't believe the heartbreaking tender things that were coming out of my gruff biker's mouth.

"I love you," I said quietly. "Promise you will never try to leave me again?"

Cade's gaze turned hard, possessive. "Nothing in this world is keeping me away from you, baby."

He then spent the rest of the night inside me.

CHAPTER 15

ONE MONTH LATER

"YEAH YOU GO, VINNIE!" I shouted at the television screen, almost spilling popcorn in my lap.

Amy snorted beside me, and I whipped my head towards her.

"The Rock is so much better than Vin, he's kicking his ass," she declared, eyes still on the TV.

I gasped. "How could you...? What makes you...? I can't even believe you just said that!"

Amy rolled her eyes. "He has like eighty pounds on him and about six inches, in height *and* width." She grinned wickedly.

I threw a piece of popcorn at her. "Take that back, Vin Diesel is like a thousand times more of a badass than *The Rock,*" I sneered at his name.

She threw an M&M at me. I caught it in my mouth and smirked.

"Vin Diesel is an *actor,* The Rock is a WWE world champion, he is the badass of all badasses," she proclaimed after giving me a high five for my catch.

"Um, have you not seen *XXX*? Vin kicks some serious ass in that movie. He's like a freaking super hero, not to mention all the *Fast* movies," I retorted.

"Gwen, you do know movies aren't real, right? He didn't actually battle Columbian drug lords and do all that shit with the cars." She was talking to me like I was a small child who was slightly slow.

"What do you think *WWE* is, Amy?" I asked in the same tone.

Amy was robbed of her smart retort when I heard a chuckle from the door. My eyes landed on Cade, who was leaning with his arms crossed, amusement dancing on his handsome face. Seriously, it should have been illegal for him to look that hot.

He was in head to toe black. Black jeans, tight black tee, black motorcycle boots, and his cut. He hadn't shaved, so his face was rough with stubble, his black hair looking professionally messed. He looked delicious and dangerous.

I sighed. "We are both wrong, I think the biggest bad ass of them all is standing in this room. My man could take both of them on and win," I said dreamily, shamelessly checking him out.

"You aren't wrong," Amy breathed, doing the same thing.

Cade ignored us and his gaze settled on the TV. "What are you watching?" he asked frowning.

"*Fast and the Furious*," I replied, eyes back on the movie.

He watched for a beat with an eyebrow raised.

"Well, it isn't technically any of the movies, it's just all the fight scenes with the hot guys from all six movies," I added, eyes on Paul Walker.

Cade didn't say a word, just strode over and picked me up off the couch, throwing me over his shoulder. I squealed as he smacked my ass.

"I'm going to fuck you so hard you'll feel me in your throat," he growled in my ear and I got instantly wet. "Then I'm going to burn that fuckin' DVD."

———

The month after my kidnapping had been one of the happiest of my life. Which was weird, you'd think after getting kidnapped and beaten again it would drag me back to battle with some old demons and maybe force me to reconsider my life with Cade.

It had done quite the opposite.

Cade had hardly let me out of his sight the entire time, his protective instinct even more intense than normal, if that was humanly possible. I couldn't say I didn't like it, because we had been having a lot of sex.

I mean, *a lot*.

In the store, my bed, his bed, the beach, his bike. The club. At first he was reluctant, treating me like I was made of glass, especially since the bruising on my face got worse before it got better. For the week it took to fade, I would catch Cade staring at my face with a pained expression, knowing he was blaming himself. No matter how hard I tried to tell him otherwise, he was convinced it was his fault. There was no more talk of him leaving me, he just got down to business.

One thing did come of my kidnapping. The club decided to get out of guns, immediately. Cade had left the morning after I was taken to take a vote at the club. He came back with a black eye, but the vote had passed. Turns out he and Steg had disagreed over the idea and it turned physical. Steg had been forced to pass the vote, as the majority of members wanted to get out.

Cade had told me the legit businesses were doing well enough, not to mention the garage itself. He had also mentioned they did some sort of security work but hadn't elaborated much, which made me infinitely more curious. Amy and I had started a stealth campaign to find out, although we had been foiled at every turn. Turned out they were good at the security thing.

Nevertheless, things with Steg and Cade were tense. Although the last time I had been at the club with fading bruises, Steg had silently kissed my black eye. At this, Cade was so pissed he looked like his jaw was about to shatter. I, on the other hand, felt differently. I was beginning to seriously doubt my first impressions of Steg, he was tender with Evie and the kids around the club. But he was also a hard ass and I couldn't shake the feeling there was something bad under the surface, but he seemed to love his family.

The club had overwhelmed me with their show of support the last month, the boys all stopping in on a regular basis. They came and had dinner, not disguising their fury at my injuries, nor their relief at the fact I was still breathing. The person I saw the most of was Bull. We seemed to have established some sort of connection.

Knowing he was able to save me from the same fate as Laurie healed him slightly. But he would always be broken. He wouldn't say much, just come and sit with me if I was alone in the store, come for dinner when Cade had to be away. I enjoyed his company, though and tried my hardest to make him laugh at my stupid jokes. He didn't, but I would keep trying.

I had also found out – to my immense relief – the club wasn't behind the explosion at the Spiders' clubhouse and therefore not responsible for the murder of a whole gang. Cade had told me they had more than a few enemies, which included the mob –the legit *Sopranos* type – who were responsible. I knew they were far from good men, but I was still firm on my belief that two wrongs didn't make a right. Which seemed to differ from the club's version of justice.

Another thing that happened was I finally told everyone in my life about Cade. A thing I had been putting off doing, partly because I wanted to make sure things were solid with us before declaring my love for him to all my friends and family, but mostly because I was a wuss. It didn't go exactly as I planned as I discovered when I rang my mother a few days ago.

I sat in my office working up my courage after I had been chatting to her about random things for about ten minutes.

"So did I tell you Nancy Goodwin, you know that girl Alice's mother?"

She didn't wait for me to reply, as usual.

"You know the girl you went to high school with? Quiet girl, nose always in a book, but a pretty wee thing?"

Again my mother didn't wait for me to confirm I knew who she was talking about.

"Well, it turns out she has been having an affair with a *thirty year old man and is now pregnant with twins.*" She whispered the last part, as if it was the code to a radioactive bomb.

"Mum, I've got a boyfriend," I announced, not reacting to her earlier statement. Although I was shocked, Alice was only a couple of years younger than me, her mother was no spring chicken.

"Oh, honey, I've been waiting for you to tell me for *weeks,* I'm so glad we can finally talk about him," she gushed, sounding excited.

"What do you mean 'you've been waiting for me to tell you'?" I asked quietly.

"Oh darn," my mother whispered quietly back and I knew something was afoot.

"Mum!" I demanded with one word.

"Oh, it's nothing, Amy just sent me a picture of you and your young man. He is smoking. I knew you might be hesitant to tell us, but I know what a man in love looks like and that boy is smitten. Not to mention Amy approves and I trust her judgment even though she did like that awful collection by Versace—"

"Mum!" I snapped, trying to erase hearing Mum calling Cade 'smoking' and plotting Amy's murder at the same time. "Let's go back to the part where Amy sent you a picture of me and Cade."

"Like I said, I approve, even if he is a bit rough around the edges, he is one fine male specimen."

I cringed at the thought of my mother checking out the 'specimen.'

"Are you happy, Gwen?" my Mum asked, seriously now, with a bit of emotion in her voice.

I sighed. "Yeah, Mum, I love him." I told her quietly. There was silence over the phone then a sob.

"Mum?"

"I'm fine, dear, just happy to hear you're happy. Oh no, the Stevenson's have just turned up. They're here an hour early, seriously, these people. I haven't even changed out of my gardening clothes! I hate to cut this short, Gwen, but I'll have to talk to you later. I'll call when your father is around. Love you, sweetie pie, I am so happy for you." Her voice broke slightly at the end.

"Love you too, Mum."

I rang off quietly seething at Amy, trying to think of ways to get away with her murder. I shelved that thought, deciding to cross someone else off the list.

"I am wearing fur underwear, I repeat, *fur underwear*. What the fuck do these stylists think they are doing? I will do almost anything in the name of fashion, but the matching booties are where I draw the line." Ryan answered the phone without a hello, launching into conversation, like always. I giggled.

"Well, hello to you too, my darling friend," I greeted sarcastically.

"Did you not hear me, Gwennie? *Fur underwear*. It's freaking a thousand degrees out here. I'm sweating my man parts off," he complained.

"With great modeling prowess comes great responsibility," I told him sagely.

I could almost see Ryan scowling down the phone.

"How's the little town anyway? Been to any hoedowns?" He quickly changed the subject, obviously over his tantrum.

"Ha ha, Ryan, you do realize it is in California, by the beach right? Whatever. I've got something to tell you."

"Oooh, you're finally getting a boob job?" he asked excitedly.

"No!" I exclaimed, looking down at my B cups self-consciously.

I actually had toyed with the idea of increasing my chest to a more substantial size, not Pamela Anderson, just more than a handful. But Cade had been showing me he more than appreciated my mere handful, I had been feeling good about them, until now.

"Dammit," he mumbled, "I was going to be your nursemaid, had the perfect outfit and everything."

I scrunched up my nose at my gay friend nursing my boobs back to health.

"Well sorry, Florence, ain't gonna happen."

"Oh well, I'll find another use for it," he replied, mind obviously wandering.

"Ryan. Something to tell you, kind of important?" I probed.

"Oh, go ahead, girl, tell me the news," he said, sounding less interested.

"I have a boyfriend," I blurted, deciding to dive straight in, hoping Amy hadn't beat me to the punch on this one as well.

There was silence on the other end of the phone.

"Hello? Have I finally managed the mean feat of rendering Ryan Jackson speechless?" I asked sarcastically, hoping his response would be a happy one. I got my answer when I heard a squeal girlier than mine down the end of the phone. I held it away from my ear a second.

"Crap, Ryan, you promised you'd warn me when you do that, I don't want to go prematurely deaf," I whined, maybe understanding why people kept saying that to me.

"Oooo weee, girl, this is *fantastic.* You're finally back on the horse! You're back on the horse right? In the biblical sense? He better be hot, what am I saying, you're in the middle of nowhere. Please don't tell me his sister is also his cousin."

I rolled my eyes, Ryan was a snobby Manhattanite through and through with a flair for the dramatic.

"Seriously, Ryan, you need to stop with the comments, Amber is my home now. And I think you would eat your tongue if you saw the caliber of men down here," I lectured, but Ryan was already cutting me off.

"Okay, okay, whatever. Tell me more about him. How long have you been seeing him? Oooh what's his name? I'll stalk him on Facebook."

I chuckled. "He's not really the kind of man that has Facebook, Ry, and I've pretty much been seeing him since the first day I got here. Took him a week or so to crack me, though," I laughed again, thinking back to our first meetings.

There was silence on the phone again before a yell. "*What?*"

I held the phone out again, oh boy, Ryan sounded angry.

"You've been in Nowheresville for more than three fucking months! And you're telling me this *now?* This is bullshit, I can't believe you didn't tell me."

"Ry, there's been a lot going on and things have been complicated – " I started to explain, feeling guilty.

"Complicated? Well, you've certainly had enough time to call and tell me you finally got off the wait list for your Birkin, and you couldn't *wait* to call me and tell me Orlando and Miranda broke up," he spat.

"Hey!" My voice was raised now too. "I've been on that wait list for like *years*, that was a big deal." I stroked my Birkin lovingly. "And you were over the moon about Miranda and Orlando, he's on your celebrity bonk list."

"Enough," he snapped. "I cannot believe Amy didn't even tell me this shit."

"I swore Amy to secrecy, Ry, this isn't her fault," I argued.

"Oh puleeze. Amy couldn't keep a secret even if it meant she could have Chanel's entire fall line. She told me about Kyle Winters like, a second after she found out."

I gasped. "That bitch," I whispered, mentally thinking up more ways to torture my big mouthed best friend.

"I simply cannot have this conversation with you right now, Gwen, I am too mad. I will call you when I decide I am over it." His voice was uppity. I knew he was pissed and hurt.

"Ry, please..." I pleaded into the phone, but he had already hung up.

"Fuck!" I yelled and grabbed my beautiful purse, in search of Amy.

———

I screeched up to the clubhouse after hearing Amy was there picking up Rosie. I didn't even want to wonder why she was showing up there. Things between her and Brock had been tense, to say the least. I had already assembled my emergency kit for when WWIII went down between them. It was red wine, chocolates, and all the horror movies I could find of people in love getting murdered gruesomely.

I narrowed my eyes when I saw her walking towards me,

laughing with Rosie. Lucky and Cade were milling by their bikes nearby.

I got out of the car and slammed my door. "You!" I shouted, pointing at Amy and stomping towards her, hearing my heels click on the concrete.

"Oh shit," Lucky cursed from nearby.

Amy had the gall to look confused. "What, Gwen?"

"You sent my mother a picture of Cade and me? How freaking dare you, Abrams! That was not your place. And I can't *believe* you told Ryan about Kyle Winters, you swore you would take that to your grave." I was inches away from her face, yelling in it.

I ignored the fact that Cade and Lucky had approached and we seemed to have more than a few spectators. Rosie was watching, half shocked, half smirking.

Amy's expression turned from confusion into realization, and she leaned into me. "Well, *someone* had to tell your mother. At the rate you're going, she'd learn about it when she got your wedding invite," she joked and I saw red.

I let out a scream of frustration.

"Babe," Cade warned from behind me. I was sure he was having flashbacks of our front lawn wrestling match.

"Oh no, brother, I suggest you stay out of this one. The Old Lady is looking wild, you don't interrupt bitches with this shit." Lucky sounded serious, I whirled to see a grin on the bastard's face.

Cade had ignored him and was walking towards me. I held up a hand.

"Stay out of this. You have far too much testosterone to be involved in this conversation," I told him, whirling back to Amy.

"I was going to tell Mum, in my own time, it's only been three months. I don't see you running to tell your parents about you and Brock, or you and Ian, for that matter."

Amy scowled. "This is different, Gwen, and you know it. You guys are the real deal, and you are in Bad Ass land, three months is like *forever* to these guys."

I let out another little scream. "Are you fucking serious? I don't even know what to say to you. You are *looney tunes*." I made the universal crazy gesture. "And I am so pissed at you for telling Ryan about Kyle. I may never forgive you for that." I glared at her.

"Who the fuck is Kyle?" I heard Cade snap from behind me and ignored him.

Amy's glare turned into a smile, and she glanced at Cade. "Oh come on. How could I not tell Ryan? It was hilarious. Seriously, Gwen, he owned a comic book store."

"So? There's nothing wrong with that, he had a business," I argued.

"He still lived with his mother." She grinned.

"He was saving a deposit for an apartment," I retorted.

"He had *Star Wars* sheets."

I cringed.

"And tried to get you to dress up as Princess Leia," she finished.

I heard Lucky's choked laughter from behind me.

"You bitch," I whispered, unable to believe she just said that in front of my super-hot boyfriend and his equally hot friends. It wasn't my fault I was blinded by the nerdy cute thing he had going on. "I am so getting you back for that," I shot at her, feeling a blush creep up my cheeks.

"Sorry, Gwennie, never fucked any creepy nerds in my time," she snorted, inspecting her nails.

I sneered back at her. "Remember the time you had to cancel on me last minute for that dinner in that random place in Brooklyn after you had that bad facial?"

She scowled. "How can I forget, I couldn't go out for like three days after what that witch did."

"Well, I was already halfway there and decided to still go 'cause I heard their pasta was to die for," I continued and she looked bored. "Anyway, when I got there, I ran into a certain WWE star, and we talked for like *ten minutes.*"

I smirked as her face paled. "You're lying."

"Nope, didn't tell you 'cause I knew you'd be gutted. He even asked me to have a drink with him, gave me his number and everything."

Amy looked like I just shot her puppy. "No he didn't."

I rifled through my purse, grabbing my phone. "I'll prove it," I said, pressing some buttons.

I still had the number, because even though I was with The Prick at the time and blinded by stupidity, you're not *not* going to save a super-hot, super famous guy's number.

I just prayed he hadn't changed it. Shit he was a celebrity, he'd probably changed it like three times over. I realized this as the phone was ringing on speaker. This could be embarrassing.

There was silence as the phone clicked onto answering machine, I held my breath until I heard the distinct voice of Amy's all time celebrity crush. Her face fell as she heard it too. I hung up triumphantly.

"We are even now, though that doesn't even equal what you did to me with my mother. I am not speaking to you for the rest of the day. No, make that the rest of the century," I decided.

I started back towards my car before turning, "Oh and email me that picture of Cade and me, I don't know when you took it, if my mum approves it must be good."

That was Tuesday. It was now Friday and I had basically forgiven her, it helped that the photo of Cade and me was, like, awesome. We were at a club party and I was sitting on his knee, head turned talking to someone beside me. Cade had a hand to my neck, stroking it and looking at me with a look full of awe and tenderness, it made my heart melt just a little.

I had gotten it printed as soon as possible and put it beside my bed. Cade had seen it, gotten a copy and kept it in his wallet. He didn't say a word to me, I had found it yesterday when I was paying for pizza. I put it back without a word, but my heart had felt like it was going to explode with the amount of love I had in it.

"Babe?" Cade said, bringing me back to the present.

He had just fucked me as hard as promised, I was tucked into the crook of his arm, my whole body jelly.

"Umm I don't know if I will be able to regain coherent thought for at least an hour," I whispered dreamily. "I'm pretty sure you just fucked my brains out."

Cade's body rumbled underneath mine and his chuckle vibrated in my ear.

"Yes, well, I needed to erase the images of certain Hollywood actors my woman seems to be infatuated with," he replied, half joking.

I put my hand on his chest and stared up to him to see a slight hardness to his otherwise tender post sex stare. I couldn't help but giggle, just a little. This didn't help, Cade's arms tightened around me, and his stare threatened to turn into a full blown frown. I leaned down and kissed one of his (hard, tattooed, did I mention delicious?) pecs.

"You can't seriously be jealous of fictional characters, can you, Mr Big and Scary Biker Man?" I teased.

Cade's frown deepened and he moved me to lie on top of him fully. I struggled not to squirm as my *down there* area was more than a little sensitive.

"I am not jealous, seeing as I'm the one who just had his cock inside you and it's my cum currently leaking out of your sweet pussy," he growled and I felt said area tingle. "But I do want you to delete that number," he continued, sliding his hands down my spine gently.

"Seriously? You can't tell me to delete *his* number," I replied, smiling at him playfully.

Cade obviously was not amused. "Yes, I fucking can. I can tell you to delete any man's number that wants in here," he stated, putting his hands between us and sliding a finger through my wetness.

My eyes rolled into the back of my head and I couldn't find it in me to get angry about yet another possessive statement, especially when I would never actually call some actor who plays a hard ass on TV when I had my very own real life hard ass in bed with me.

"Hmmm," I moaned as Cade's finger found my magic and delightfully sensitive spot.

"My baby is ready for me again so soon?" he whispered roughly in my ear.

All I was able to let out was a low moan, and I moved myself against the rough muscled body of my man, communicating I was indeed ready. He flipped me over quickly, covering his body with mine before devouring me with a kiss.

"My baby is greedy for my cock," he murmured, mouth inches away from mine.

I nodded, wrapping my legs around him and he then proceeded to fuck the rest of my brains out.

___

A few days later, I was pouring Amy and myself a glass of wine when I heard a knock at the door.

"Gwen! Can you get that? I just painted my nails and I can't move from this spot for three more hours until my polish is sufficiently dried," Amy called from the direction of the pool.

I rolled my eyes, walking towards the door, wine in hand, hoping the visitor would be Cade. I hadn't seen or heard from him since yesterday afternoon when he disappeared on club business. I hated myself for admitting it, but I missed him already. I promised myself I would not turn into a crazed pathetic woman over him. Opening the door, I screamed.

Ryan stood in front of me, grinning. "Gwen, I'm excited to see you too, but let's not deafen me and my beloved shall we?" he remarked dryly.

I ignored him and squealed again, jumping into his arms.

"Gwen, please tell me you're getting kidnapped or the new Birkin has just been hand delivered to you, they are the only reasons I would not be totally pissed about my ruined manicure." Amy walked into the foyer frowning at her hands. Her expression brightened when she saw Ryan. "Oh my god! Ry!" she shrieked, nails forgotten.

I looked over Ryan's shoulder to see Alex grinning, walking up the pathway, arms laden with bags. I grinned back and ran towards him, throwing myself at him. He dropped the bags to pick me up, hugging me tight.

"Alex, sweetie, I know we're very excited to see Gwen, but could we *not* drop Louis Vuitton on the dirty ground?" Ryan called out from the door, only half joking.

We both ignored him, Alex pulled back to stare at my face, hands at my neck.

"You look great, G. Happy," he told me quietly, eyes full of pride.

I felt my own well up with tears. "I am, A, I'm doing so good, and I didn't think I could get much happier, but you guys just proved me wrong." I beamed at him, wrapping my arms around his muscled body once again.

"What the fuck?" a very pissed off male voice asked from behind me.

I released Alex to see Cade, Brock, and Bull staring at Alex and me with varying degrees of anger. Bull's face was blank as usual, but his eye seemed to be twitching. Brock's face was hard, but his gaze was on Amy who had walked down to join us, holding hands with Ryan, who, had obviously forgotten about his Vuitton because he was gawking at the three bikers before him. I didn't blame him, three fine male specimens encased in leather just meters away? It was a lot to take in.

"Jesus Christ, Abrams, get back inside the fucking house and put on some fucking clothes," Brock barked, ignoring Alex and Ryan, striding towards Amy.

She put a hand on her bare hip, eyes narrowing at the approaching biker. "Seriously? Do not order me around like some caveman, asshole. It's a bikini, and I'm pretty sure a little thing called Feminism happened about fifty years ago, giving women the right to wear whatever they want and not have to listen to arrogant pricks." She finished by yelling in his face when he got to her.

I bit back a laugh at how familiar this conversation was to the ones I regularly had with Cade.

He ignored her, wrapping his hand around her wrist and dragging her back into the house, while she fought him and cursed him.

Ryan watched with a raised eyebrow, a grin threatening the corner of his mouth, obviously amused. Alex hadn't been. I had to hold him back when Brock grabbed Amy, whispering in his ear to reassure him he didn't have to take on three big men to protect us. Which he would, in a heartbeat.

"I'm *so* going to like it here," Ryan declared, joining Alex and me, oblivious to the hostility radiating off my boyfriend.

"Ryan, Alex, I'd like you to meet my boyfriend Cade and his friend Bull," I said carefully. "And Cade and Bull these are my best friends Ryan and Alex."

I was trying to think of a subtle way to inform Cade they were my very *gay* best friends, as I knew he was getting jealous, but Ryan took care of that. He pushed forward, shaking both of their hands, looking like drool might drop out of the corner of his mouth.

"Seriously, Gwen told me about you guys, but I totally thought she was exaggerating. If I wasn't, like, madly in love with this one," he pointed with his thumb to Alex, "I would move here, like, tomorrow." Ryan grinned at them. "Now let's get this party started! I brought Dom, which I hope hasn't been broken by the careless throwing around of my luggage." He gave a pointed glance at Alex, turning on his heel to grab his bags.

Cade stayed put, face unreadable. I suddenly panicked at what his reaction would be to my two very gay best friends. He came from a small town, was in a motorcycle club and was a serious macho man to boot. I couldn't imagine him being ready to wave the rainbow flag. *Shit.* Surprisingly, he stepped forward, pulling me to his side and firmly shaking Alex's hand.

"Nice to meet you, bro, any friend of Gwen's is a friend of ours," he said sincerely. I let out a breath of relief when Bull followed suit.

"Good to meet you too, Gwen has told me a lot about you, I'm looking forward to getting to know you better," Alex replied carefully, sounding a lot like a protective older brother, and eying Cade's cut skeptically.

"Hello? Very expensive champagne that needs to be drunk here?" Ryan called out from the porch, shaking the bottle, saving me from passing out from testosterone overdose.

"We better get inside and open that wine before my little queen throws a tantrum," I joked, pulling Cade, and gesturing to Bull and Alex who walked in front of us, conversing about who knows what. This would be interesting.

"So, he owns a strip club?" Ryan exclaimed loudly, the results of our drinking session causing his voice to increase multiple decibels.

"Ry, inside voice please. I would rather you didn't inform the entire bar," I scolded.

Ryan waved his hand. "Puleeze, honey, this is a small town, I bet you were the last to know. We *have* to go there." He decided, getting up on unsteady feet.

We were in Laura Maye's bar again, having a girls' night. Ryan obviously counted as a girl, and Alex was watching some game with Cade and the boys. Football maybe, hockey, or baseball? I honestly didn't know, my ears glazed over at the talk of sports. But I was happy they were all getting along so well and that everyone had taken the gay thing without comment.

Rosie and the girls were meant to be meeting up with us later, but Amy and I had wanted time alone with Ryan first. I had decided to abstain from telling both him and Alex about the me getting kidnapped thing. Considering everything that was going on, I didn't need that little gem of information in the mix.

"I second that," Amy chimed in, finishing her drink and grabbing her Prada. "Let's go and check out these girls that Cade has to 'check in on.'" She finger quoted the last bit.

"Let's skip past the fact that you are both insane, and just land at the fact we are meant to be meeting Rosie and the girls any minute and none of us are sober enough to drive." I stayed seated, toying with the olive in my martini.

Amy pulled out her phone, fingers moving at lightning speed. I was impressed, I'd lost the ability to text after my third cocktail.

"Two birds, one stone. Rosie is picking us up and taking us to the strip club," she declared, clearly pleased with herself.

I groaned as the two of them pulled me out of the chair.

"This is a terrible idea you guys. There's nothing to gain by going out there, and we always get into trouble whenever you both agree on a plan after martinis."

"Oh, come on, you know you're curious about this place, we need to do the recon. Don't tell me it hasn't been driving you insane." Amy crossed her arms, daring me to argue.

I felt deflated. It had been gnawing at me knowing Cade was involved in a place where beautiful women took their clothes off in front of him.

"And name one time that we got into trouble with martinis," Ryan challenged, arms crossed.

"You almost got me arrested for stealing that cop's hat."

Ryan rolled his eyes "*Almost.* But didn't."

"Plus you ended up dating him for like a month and we got to bypass traffic whenever we were with him," Amy chimed in.

Fuck. Bad example. The traffic thing had been handy.

"You got us banned from the Ivy for a *year,* Amy's dad had to pull strings to get us back in," I gave them another one.

Ryan rolled his eyes. "Totally not our fault. How were we meant to know that guy was married? And that his wife would be a biter?"

"Come on, Gwennie, you know you want to," Amy interrupted.

I blew out an exasperated breath. "Fine, but we're just looking then leaving."

"That's my girl!" Amy clapped her hands. "And we have to have at least one drink." She ushered me out of the bar before I could argue.

⊏===⊐

"So, this is it."

Rosie pulled up in front of a nondescript building that looked well maintained, and not at all like a strip club. It had a red sign reading "Diamond Lounge" in elegant script and a bouncer at the door.

"I have to say this is an excellent idea, I've been wondering what this place was like for ages," Lucy put in from the back, where she was squeezed between Amy and Ryan. She and Ryan were well on their way to becoming besties, the way they had been cackling in the backseat the entire ride.

Rosie grinned at me. "I gotta agree, Gwen, ever since the boys opened it I've wanted a peek, but Cade was always foiling our attempts, he would not be happy about this *at all*." She gave me the impression she didn't mind this one bit. She opened her door and everyone else followed suit.

I looked to the ceiling of the car. "Please don't let me get arrested tonight," I pleaded before jumping out.

The bouncer gave us all a questioning look, but opened the door for us. We all walked in, Ryan and Lucy whispering to each other linking arms, Amy and Rosie laughing. Once I got a good look at the interior I was surprised. It was almost *tasteful*. Apart from the women dancing naked on the poles, of course.

The lighting was dim, a soft glow radiated from candles on the tables. Black cushioned chairs were clustered around round silver tables and they looked comfortable. One must be comfortable for a lap dance, I guessed. A long runway split the bar in two, jutting off a stage. It had a pole at the end of it, which a blonde with huge boobs was currently hanging off. Other girls danced on circular mini stages that were peppered around the room. Some were cozying up to various men, of which there were many. The place was packed.

"Okay, now we've looked, and I feel sufficiently persuaded to get breast implants and lose ten pounds, time to go," I instructed my friends.

Ryan cocked his head at me. "Um, no way, we're staying and discussing what size you should go to, we have a lot to refer to here. And look! We've got us a table." He pointed to Amy, who was sitting at an empty table giving us the thumbs up.

I groaned as Rosie and Lucy grinned at me, walking to join Amy.

Ryan linked his arm with mine. "Come on, Gwen, it's just a bit of fun, what trouble could we possibly get into?" he asked innocently.

After two surprisingly good cocktails, I hated to admit I was having a great time. This place actually felt like I was in a trendy bar, well one with an almost exclusive male clientele that had naked women dancing in front of me. The service was good, the cocktails were great, the company was pretty awesome as well.

I was surprised we hadn't gotten any sleazy advances from guys. I wasn't being full of myself, it was just we were pretty much the only women in a bar full of guys, and my companions were nothing to sneeze at. Amy looked like she should be modeling for Victoria's Secret, Lucy looked like a sexy Snow White with her milky skin and black hair, and Rosie looked like a biker goddess.

My thoughts were interrupted when I felt conversation stop. My head crooked to where all of my friends where glaring, apart from Ryan, he just looked puzzled.

"Well, isn't this pathetic, Cade's latest piece resorting to staking out his bar. He dumped you already, sweetheart?" a nasally, spiteful voice asked me.

Great, just what I needed. Ginger stood at the edge of our table, flanked by two equally skanky friends. She had gotten her roots done since the last time I saw her, but it wasn't much of an improvement on the "Whore Chic" look. She had cheap looking extensions in, which only made her stringy hair look worse. The faux leather dress she was wearing with a zip running down the whole front should have been burned, along with the thigh high heeled boots she was wearing.

"You coming in for a job interview, sweetheart?" I asked, looking her up and down. "I don't think even a strip club would lower themselves to hire something like you. Maybe Burger King?" I suggested sweetly.

A gaggle of laughter erupted from behind me, and Amy gave me a fist pump.

Ginger's face reddened and she narrowed her kohl-rimmed eyes at me in a death stare. "Bitch, you are just the flavor of the month, Cade will come back to me, he can't get enough of my pussy," she snarled, stepping closer to me.

"Well, aren't you classy," Ryan put in, giving her a cold gaze.

She glanced at him, taking in his printed shirt and tan slacks. "Shut up, fag, no one asked your opinion."

Oh no she didn't.

Amy clenched her glass and directed a withering glare at the bitch. I knew she was seconds away from throwing said glass at her.

"I suggest you shut your crude mouth and walk away before I catch an STD. Or lose my temper," I informed Ginger through gritted teeth.

Ginger rolled her eyes, smirking. "Like I'm scared of some townie, I'll wipe the floor with you, bitch."

I tried to get up, but a hand on my arm stopped me.

"She's not worth it, my darling, what if you rip your Chanel?" Ryan asked me conversationally, glancing at my dress. I was inclined to agree with him until Ginger ran her poorly made up mouth yet again.

"You see, this world has a way of getting rid of the women who don't belong here. Just ask Laurie. Oh no wait, you can't."

"She *did not* just say that," Lucy declared icily.

Amy and I stood up at the same time, both advancing on the gaggle of skanks. I was closer, so I got to Ginger first, not before she reared her fist back trying to punch me. I caught it in my hand and laughed in her face.

"Didn't your dad ever teach you? You *never* rear back when trying to hit someone." I shook my head. "Stupid whore."

I raised my other hand in a lightening quick move and clocked her in the nose. She went down like a sack of potatoes. Amy and Rosie were taking care of the other two while I knelt down, grabbing Ginger by the hair, avoiding the blood coming out of her nose. I seriously didn't want that anywhere near my dress.

"Don't you ever talk about my friends in a derogatory way ever again. Actually, don't ever come close enough that we have to choke on your cheap perfume. And if you so much as *think* that girl's name one more time, you'll be sorry," I told her evenly.

She glared at me, trying to struggle out of my grasp. "Fuck you." Her voice was slightly garbled, due to her bloody nose.

I gripped her hair and pulled, making her cry out. "Now, that wasn't the apology I was looking for. How about we try that again."

I pointed her head to Ryan, who was calmly sipping his cock-tail, looking amused.

Ginger kept struggling, and for once kept her mouth firmly shut.

I shook my head. "I'm not letting go until you say the words, or until your cheap extensions give out."

She gazed at me like she wanted to scratch my eyes out, then she turned to her friends for support. One had run off, and the other had her hands behind her back and Amy hanging onto her, smirking.

She stubbornly stayed silent a moment more before whining. "Fine. I'm sorry." She glared at Ryan, looking like the words caused her pain.

I smiled. "That wasn't so hard now, was it? Run along now, I'm sure you have a penicillin shot to take." I let her go, pushing myself up and dusting my hands on my dress.

Ginger scrambled to her feet, holding her nose, looking like she wanted to lunge at me, but her obviously more intelligent friend dragged her away.

"That was like, the highlight of my week, Gwen! You rock. I didn't know you had it in you," Lucy exclaimed, eyes wide, smiling from ear to ear.

"Neither did I," a deep voice agreed from behind me.

Oh please, don't let that be who I thought it was.

I turned slowly to find my fears confirmed. Cade stood a couple of feet away, arms crossed and a blank expression on his handsome face. Alex, who was beside him and used to this kind of thing with Ryan, Amy and I, only shook his head with a grin. Lucky, who had also seen the performance was wearing a shit-eating grin.

"Holy fuck, Gwen, that was fucking awesome, and like off the charts hot. Props to you Ames and Rosie."

He nodded at the girls beside me, who freaking *curtseyed.*

Drunken idiots. Brock only had eyes for Amy, giving her a smile, which made *me* blush.

"Um. Hi, honey, how was the game? Did the...team win?" I asked conversationally, like I wasn't standing in my boyfriend's strip club where I had just punched his ex-girlfriend while he and his friends watched.

"I wouldn't know. Since my security team called me,

informing me my woman, sister, and their friends had arrived at my club. I decided to miss the end of the game to come down and see what you were doing at a strip club." His voice was even, not betraying any emotion, apart from a slightly raised brow. "Turns out that was a good choice, considering that was more entertaining than any football game."

I blushed, looking around expecting to see other people in the bar staring at our impromptu slut smack down. Surprisingly, only a few men gave us sideways glances, everyone else had eyes on the dancers. Maybe this kind of thing happened all the time.

"Football! I told you," Amy whispered triumphantly from beside me.

I rolled my eyes. "Not really an important point right now, Abrams." I was more worried about what hid behind Cade's emotionless façade than my ignorance when it came to American sports.

"Oh, come on, Cade, lighten up, so we disobeyed your orders and came to the strip club that *you own*. Big whoop. You are not the master of the universe and we are adults who are entitled to do whatever we want. And tonight we just so happened to want to do some boob job research and teach some sluts a lesson. Get over it and have a drink," Rosie piped in from behind me, her words slightly slurred but still scolding her older brother.

"Well, I could sure use a beer, and a private dance after that performance," Lucky smirked and walked off in the direction of the bar.

Alex shook his head again at Amy and me before joining Ryan and the girls at the table. That left Cade, Brock, Amy, and I all staring at each other. I could feel the burn of Cade's gaze on me. I opened my mouth to say something, I'm wasn't sure what, but I figured alcohol would help me out when a horny biker beat me to it.

"Abrams, back of my bike. Now," Brock commanded gruffly.

Amy narrowed her eyes. "Oh, I'm sorry, I think I may have just landed in a parallel universe where you have the right to order me around like a dog. No wait. In no universe do you have that right." She glared at Brock.

His gaze turned glacial. "Get your skinny ass out the door now, Amy."

She stood her ground. I was impressed. "Make me," she challenged with a smug smile.

They both stared at each other, neither one backing down until Brock threw up his muscled arms.

"Fuck this. I don't need to put up with your shit, there are plenty of women around here that are a fuck of a lot less trouble than you."

He stormed off, tagging a barely clothed waitress around the hips and dragging her into a back room. To be fair, she looked more than willing. Amy's smile dimmed, her eyes on the door before she shook herself out of it, turning to the table.

"We need shots!" she announced shakily.

I had been too busy watching all of that unfold to notice Cade's attention had not left me. I glanced back to see his intense gaze burning into me.

"We're leaving," he announced hoarsely, eyes hooded.

"Okeydoke," I replied immediately.

I wasn't feeling like asserting my feminine independence like Amy. In fact, I was feeling desire pooling at the bottom of my stomach at the way Cade was looking at me.

I turned to my friends, who were laughing over cocktails.

"My favorite part was when Gwen said, 'Didn't your dad ever teach you? *Never* rear back when punching someone.' Fucking classic," Lucy exclaimed, while everyone else cackled with laughter.

"Okay guys, as much as I would love to hear you keep talking about what a bad ass I am, I'm leaving," I announced to the little group.

I ignored the groans of protest and blew them all kisses before Cade, who had ran out of patience, grabbed my arm and nearly dragged me out of there.

⸺

We arrived at Cade's, and I was already soaked with desire. The entire ride I had plastered my body to his, feeling his muscles taut and hard, knowing he was hanging on by a thread. This thought was confirmed when he slammed me against the wall as soon as we got through the door.

"Jesus Christ, baby, you're full of fucking surprises. Even when I think I couldn't get more turned on by you and your hot little body and your smart fuckin' mouth, you do something else to prove me wrong," he grunted out between his plundering kisses.

He yanked off my dress roughly, my worry for my couture vanished and was replaced with sheer animalistic passion. I moaned as Cade sucked my nipple through the lace of my bra, his hand delving into my panties.

"Knowing you can handle yourself like that, stand up for your friends like that, and still be sweet and wear the fucking ladylike shit you wear. Drives me crazy," he snarled biting my neck and pushing a finger inside me.

I struggled to remain coherent, feeling the orgasm build up inside me.

"You're my bad little bitch hiding underneath all those fancy clothes, aren't you?" he asked roughly, tweaking my nipple.

I moaned, the pleasure and his words too much, I was unable to string any semblance of a sentence together.

"You want me to fuck you hard? I know you do, my little spitfire."

I screamed with an orgasm as he plunged into me, pounding me against the wall.

I wrapped my arms around his neck, clinging to his shirt, reveling in the frantic intensity of our joining. Cade was relentless, holding my neck with a firm grip, eyes burning into mine, searing into my soul. His fingertips bit into my ass as he continued to fuck me against the wall. I could feel myself building again, the friction against my clit almost too much.

"Cade..." I moaned breathlessly.

"Come again, baby," he commanded, gruffly, eyes never leaving mine.

A second later I did, I soared through my release, and through the haze I felt Cade's body tighten at his own. Unable to hold myself up, I was thankful for his strong arms.

He pressed his forehead against mine breathing heavily.

"That was...amazing," I told him dreamily.

His hand circled my neck and he pressed his mouth to mine for a tender kiss.

"Yeah, Gwen, it was." Gray eyes searched mine. "And that better not have been you even considering doing anything with these beautiful babies." He cupped my breasts. "I forbid you to change anything about your body," he growled.

⊏⎯⊐

A couple of days later, Cade and I lay in bed.

"Happy, baby?" Cade asked me drowsily after he had finished ravaging me.

I was curled up in his arm's feeling sated. "Mmhmm."

Cade kissed my head. "I'm glad you've got such loyal friends," he murmured.

"Yeah, I'm pretty lucky. I just wish they didn't have to leave," I replied, thinking back to the tearful goodbye earlier today.

"I'm sure we'll be seeing a lot of them, babe. Maybe we could take a trip to New York sometime soon?" Cade suggested.

My heart leapt at this. Going to New York with Cade? Despite some of the more recent terrible memories that city contained, it also contained some of the happiest of my life. I would love to create new ones with the man I loved. Not to mention, I couldn't wait to see the leather clad Cade in some of my glossy old haunts. I giggled at the thought.

"I'd like that," I whispered softly before drifting off.

CHAPTER 16

I WOKE to Cade's hands running down my body and his mouth at my neck, which was not unusual. What was unusual was the sharp pain in my stomach followed by an overwhelming wave of nausea.

I shoved Cade off me, which only worked because he wasn't expecting it. I didn't have time to take in his confused and angry "What the fuck?" I just pulled the covers back and ran to the bathroom.

I barely made it to the toilet before I emptied the contents of my stomach. Not nice. Especially when halfway through, Cade pulled my hair back and rubbed my back soothingly.

This was so embarrassing.

My super-hot and bad ass boyfriend was witnessing me throwing up. I grabbed a piece of toilet paper to wipe my mouth before trying to push him away with my hand.

"Go away, I don't want you to see this," I whined. I had no chance to hear his answer because my body had decided my humiliation was not complete and I heaved into the toilet again.

Cade's hands left my back and neck and I breathed a sigh of

relief, which was short lived as he returned quickly. I felt a cold flannel and the back of my neck. I sighed, the coolness soothing my burning hot skin. I decided I was not going to vomit again and therefore flushed the toilet and tried to snatch the flannel from Cade's grasp.

"Please, I'll be fine in a second, just leave," I whispered, my voice hoarse.

Cade didn't answer, he gathered me up in his arms and I gingerly peeked at his concerned face through my hair.

"You don't have to carry me, Cade, I think I can walk," I muttered, focusing on settling my uneasy stomach.

He deposited me on the bed carefully, not pulling the blankets over me, which I was thankful for. I felt his hand at my forehead, then the bliss of the cold compress replacing it.

"You're burning up, baby." Cade's voice was full with worry and he frowned down at me. "What did you eat last night?" He stroked my face, speaking softly.

"Um, just pasta, then junk food with Amy. Nothing that will make me sick, just make my ass fatter," I joked, feeling slightly better.

Cade continued frowning. "Your ass is not fat, it's perfect," he clipped, I tried to resist an eye roll. "I'm gonna call the doctors, make sure I can get you in as soon as possible."

I grasped his hand as it reached for his phone on the bedside table.

"Cade, I don't know if it's necessary to call the doctor just yet, it's probably just a stomach bug. I'm sure I'll get over it in no time." I tried to sound optimistic, but I still had a slight churning in my stomach.

Cade's eyes softened slightly and he leaned back towards me. "I don't like my baby being sick," he declared.

"Well, it was bound to happen since the human race is susceptible to becoming under the weather sometimes." I glanced at Cade, in all his naked glory finding it hard to imagine his head down a toilet. "Well, maybe not super bad ass bikers like you, who would be too tough to let anything as common as the cold get you down," I joked, smiling at him.

My smile didn't last for long as I felt another lurch in my stomach, which caused me to bolt to the bathroom. Cade was right behind me yet again, holding my hair and stroking my back tenderly. It was super sweet, but I would rather not have my probably invincible boyfriend witnessing me emptying the contents of my stomach into a toilet bowl. After I decided I was finished for the time being, Cade scooped me up in his arms yet again and directed us back into the bedroom.

"Wait," I commanded, trying to get down.

"Stop it, Gwen, let's get you into bed," he replied softly but firmly, pushing my damp hair out of my face.

"Can I at least brush my teeth?" I requested quietly but my voice had a bit of a bite.

Cade set me carefully down and handed me my toothbrush and toothpaste before landing a kiss on my forehead.

"I'm going downstairs to get you some water and dry toast, baby, will you be okay here for a couple of minutes?" His arms were at my shoulders like he was afraid I would collapse.

The concern in his face and his actions made me warm up a little inside and I smiled at him. "I'll be fine, honey, thank you. I'm starting to feel a bit better," I told him truthfully.

He raised an eyebrow like he didn't believe me but squeezed my arms. "I'll be right back," he promised.

I watched him a second, wondering how he could be the fiercest man I knew when it came to dealing with kidnappers and such, then also be heartbreakingly tender when it came to me.

After getting me toast and water and fussing over me for about an hour, Cade was hesitant to leave me alone.

"Cade, I promise the chances of me dying of the stomach flu in the short time you are away are slim to none," I said, my joking words deepening his scowl. I sat up slightly in bed to meet his stare, he was standing beside the bed with his arms crossed.

"I'll be fine," I tried to convince him. I was feeling much better than I had an hour ago. Cade obviously didn't believe me.

"It doesn't sit right with me. Leaving my woman sick in bed, I wouldn't be going unless I had to. But this is a pressing security job, I'll try and be as quick as I can," he said looking more than a little conflicted.

I took his hand, pulling him down to sit on my bed.

"I'm *fine*," I repeated. "It's a bug, and I'm already starting to feel better, and unfortunately it is beyond all your manly powers to heal me anyway. So instead of sitting here, watching me get over this when there is nothing you can do, go and provide some security for someone who I'm sure you can help much more than me at this moment," I told him softly.

He paused for a beat then responded. "My manly powers?" His expression had changed and the corner of his mouth turned into a slight smirk.

I smiled back. "Yes, your manly powers, which include, but are not limited to, saving me from kidnappers, chasing away my demons, and giving me the best orgasms of my life," I declared, watching Cade's face grow soft.

"Well, you better rest up and get better so I can give you some more of those orgasms when I get back," he ordered in a tone I couldn't decipher. He leaned down and kissed me tenderly on my forehead. Before walking towards the door, he turned back to me. "I talked to Amy and she said she's coming home at lunch to check on you, and I want you to call me if you feel any worse, then no arguments, I will be taking you to the doctors."

"Yes, sir," I replied with a smile. "Now go and put those muscles to good use."

The corner of Cade's lip twitched slightly. "Love you, Gwen."

My tummy dipped in a good way when I heard those words, which I would never tire of hearing. "Love you, Cade."

He watched me for a second, then left.

Pretty much as soon as Cade left I felt heaps better, so I got up and showered, dressed and had a small breakfast. I was still feeling slightly queasy, so I quelled the idea of going into the store and passing along my germs to customers. Well, that and the fact that I knew Cade would be pissed if he knew I wasn't resting.

I had gotten used to his over protective ways and sometimes even liked it, knowing it came from a good place. But there were still other times when it pissed me the hell off. I was lying on our couch in the sun, typing orders on my laptop when Amy arrived home.

"Hey, Gwennie, just come to make sure you haven't carked it," she called from the door, entering the room with a bottle of lemonade and a brown bag. "I also have brought supplies known to settle a stomach bug," she declared, sitting on the couch beside me and pulling a sandwich out of the bag.

"I'm actually feeling much better now," I told her, sitting up and placing my laptop beside the food. Which I immediately ripped into.

"That's weird, considering Cade told me you were super sick this morning," she mused while I took a bite. "You're not preggers are you?" she joked, retrieving a salad out of the bag.

I froze mid chew, frantically thinking of dates in my mind while struggling to swallow. Amy noticed my reaction and turned towards me, salad forgotten, her expression disbelieving.

"You're on the pill. You couldn't seriously be pregnant, could you?" she questioned.

I remained frozen, and shrugged, silently freaking out.

"Okay, when was your last period?" she asked rationally.

"I don't know," I replied, trying to think back.

Amy sat back and narrowed her eyes. "You don't know when your last period was? Seriously you're not the woman who doesn't know she's pregnant until she pops the baby out on the floor of a Walmart, are you?"

I scowled at her. "I've been skipping my period since I've been here," I muttered, silently cursing myself for wanting uninterrupted sex with Cade. Which he had, by the way noticed, and that conversion was only slightly awkward. My stomach began to drop as I realized this was an actual possibility. The pill wasn't a hundred percent effective and we hadn't been using anything else.

"Holy shit, I can't be pregnant," I said, more to myself than Amy. I shook my head, "No, I'm not, just because I was sick one morning does not automatically mean I'm up the duff. I probably just ate something weird yesterday," I said firmly, convincing myself.

Amy, unfortunately, was not convinced.

"How about you take a test just in case, you really want to be sure about these things." She stood. "I've got a pregnancy test in the bathroom. I always keep one, you know, just in case." She tugged me up off the couch, depositing my forgotten sandwich on the coffee table.

"I really don't think I need a test," I argued as she pushed me into the bathroom.

"I disagree, and it's better to be safe than sorry, right?" She turned and handed me a test.

I took it, convincing myself I didn't need it. I moved my attention to see Amy standing in front of me expectantly.

"Oh, fine, just to get you off my back," I declared, moving towards the toilet.

Amy settled down on a chair, not caring that I was going to pee right in front of her. I didn't care either, we were best friends, and due to long lines in nightclubs and lack of bathroom space, we had peed in front of each other many a time.

I awkwardly took the test and laid it on the counter before I started pacing.

"I won't be pregnant, I can't be, right? I take the pill religiously. I have never missed a day. Nope I'm not," I ranted to Amy while pacing, certain that I was right.

⸺

"It's official, you're knocked up," Amy stated, looking at the pregnancy tests that were scattered around me on the floor of our living room, where I was currently sitting. Freaking the fuck out. I had made Amy run out and get five more tests, convinced the first one I took was wrong. It wasn't, considering the second, third, fourth, and fifth were all positive.

"Holy shit, this so isn't happening," I muttered, while going through all the possible reactions Cade could have to this information, then thinking I was going to be a mother.

A mother.

I hadn't really thought too much about kids. Yeah, I thought they were cute and all, but I didn't have that yearning in my loins like a lot of my other girlfriends. I thought one day in the future I could be open to the idea, and lately I had been more than open to the idea after how things were going with Cade and I. But I was thinking in the *future*. Not now, when Cade and I had barely been together four months, when I had just opened a new business. I was twenty freaking five. I still had at least four more years of child free party life ahead of me.

"Oh my god, Ames," I groaned looking up at her. "I've been drunk. Like, a lot. I don't know how pregnant I am. Holy crap what if I have, like, totally fucked up my child just because I can't pass up a good cocktail? I am a terrible mother and I haven't even given birth yet," I whined, sounding near hysterical.

Amy bent down and gave me a firm slap on the cheek. "Snap out of it," she ordered.

I held my cheek in shock. "You just hit a pregnant woman," I gasped, even though it didn't actually hurt that much, it was the principle of the matter.

"No, I slapped some sense into my best friend to stop her freaking the fuck out. You are not a terrible mother, especially when you just found out you were pregnant twenty minutes ago and have not chugged down a tequila shot in that time," she explained, kneeling beside me.

"No, I haven't, but I could seriously use one," I groaned thinking about the fact I would have to say goodbye to tequila for months, nine of them.

I stared at Amy seriously.

"What if I have actually hurt my baby?" I asked voice small, feeling fear for the little being growing inside of me. And feeling already attached to it.

Amy looked at me softly. "I'll call the clinic now, get you in. But I seriously doubt a little bit of booze will harm Cade's child, his super sperm beat birth control, it can probably handle anything," she joked, pushing up and giving me her hand to pull me off the floor. "And my friend Trina didn't know she was pregnant until like four months, and those four months just happened to be when we were on a bender in the South of France. Seriously, she partied *hard.* Kid's fine, even a little too smart if you ask me, little fucker is better at math than me," she told me, smirking.

I smiled weakly back at her, unable to muster much more with all the thoughts swirling in my head. What if Cade thought I did this on purpose? What if he didn't want our child?

My heart plummeted and I placed my hands protectively

over my still flat belly. *No*, I argued with myself, *Cade would want it.* On the side of the road not one month ago he declared he wanted me pregnant. Granted, he was reeling from my kidnapping and probably meant a little further on than this.

I started pacing, scattering the pregnancy tests across the floor, all the while trying to prevent a mental breakdown. Okay, I was pregnant, it's not like this didn't happen all the time. I should be happy that this wasn't the result of a night of too many tequila shots and too little inhibition. This baby was conceived out of *love.*

I just hoped Cade was ready to be a father. I didn't know how ready I was to be a mother. I had passed out sunbathing a week ago and the burns were only just starting to fade. How could I keep a tiny human alive when I couldn't even properly apply sunscreen?

I was still pacing when Amy walked back in, my gaze darted up to her.

"You get me in?" I demanded, maybe a little sharply. But I was worried about the health of my child.

"Got us an appointment in an hour." She looked pleased with herself.

"Okay great, thank you, thank you!" I didn't stop pacing.

Amy leaned on the door jamb, looking more calm and collected than I could ever be.

"How can you be so calm?" I all but shrieked. "I am knocked up and it is so not planned. I haven't even been with the father a year. I don't even know if Barney's carries a proper maternity line! I'm going to get fat, and my feet will swell. Holy fuck, I won't be able to wear heels and if I do I'll look like Kim Kardashian."

I panicked and glared at Amy who didn't look at all concerned about the very real possibly I could be facing elephant feet. And *flats.*

She strode over and gripped my arms, eyes twinkling. "Chill, Gwennie. This is freaking awesome news."

My eyes bugged out at her statement, and I opened my mouth to repeat everything I had just said, maybe a decibel louder, so she could get it.

"I grant you, maybe not the best timing," she said quickly before I could get started. "But you have a man that friggin' adores you and will be over the fucking moon about you having his bun in your oven. Not to mention, I will make sure we get you the most kick ass maternity wardrobe. I'll research options today," she said thoughtfully, and seriously.

I took a deep breath, trying to calm myself, but failing. "Okay, just tell me something to take my mind off my freak out," I ordered, needing to be distracted.

She thought for a minute, then her face got serious. "Well, I've finally made up my mind about what's happening with Ian and Brock."

"*What?*" I all but screeched, my mind well and truly off the bun in my oven.

Amy flinched at my yell, but I ignored it. "When did you decide this? Oh my god, did you choose Ian? Are we finally going to be sisters?" I asked, almost jumping up and down. She opened her mouth but I interrupted. "But then again, I really do like Brock. He's super dreamy and bad ass. And he's one of Cade's best friends, so I'll finally have someone who can relate to all the bad ass biker shit." Oh crap, I actually found myself conflicted about her decision, even with my brother and potential nieces and nephews on the line. "Well?" I demanded impatiently.

I didn't get to hear her answer because the front door opened and Bull strode in. No one knocked anymore. He did a chin lift to Amy then focused on me.

"Gwen girl, Cade wanted me to tell you he got held up. Also he wanted to make sure you were okay. What are you doing out of bed?" he clipped, glaring at Amy and me standing in the middle of the living room.

His gaze moved down to his motorcycle boot, which was inches away from one of my pregnancy tests. I watched in horror as he picked it up, looked at the result and grinned.

I stomped over to him and snatched the test out of his hands. This was the first time I had seen Bull smile, like, *ever*. I hadn't needed all my lame jokes after all. An illegitimate pregnancy made the fucker happy.

"Eww, Bull, don't touch that, it has my pee on it! How embarrassing," I muttered, hiding the pee stick behind my back and glaring up at the dangerously handsome biker who was now wearing a shit-eating grin.

"You pregnant, babe?" he asked softly, happiness saturating his tone.

"Um, looks to be the case, big man," I uttered quietly, nervous for his reaction.

Even though it seemed he was pretty fucking pleased. This was confirmed when he pulled me into a big bear hug and squeezed me tight against his hard body. I was shocked for a second, Bull had never physically embraced anyone since I had met him. I cautiously put my arms around him, not reaching very far because he was big.

Bull gently released me and kissed my hair. "Fucking great news, Gwen," he whispered, eyes shining with emotion I didn't know he was capable of.

I smiled shyly back. "You think so? This wasn't exactly planned, Cade might not—"

"Cade will be fucking thrilled," Bull cut me off, sounding firm.

"Okay," I said quietly, feeling better with how sure he sounded. He was his best friend, he was sure to know, right?

"I hate to interrupt," Amy cut in from behind me. "But,

Gwen, how about you go and get changed and we'll hit the pharmacy before we go to the docs, get you loaded up on all that prenatal shit."

I turned to her. "Yeah, that's probably a good idea, Abrams, this kid's going to need all the vitamins it can get," I replied stroking my stomach, still worried about the possible affect my love of alcohol could have had on my child's development.

"You going to the doctors? What for?" Bull interrupted, sounding concerned.

Amy waved her hand. "Oh, it's nothing, we just need to make sure my little alcoholic over here hasn't made her unborn child partial to cosmos inside the womb," she said casually.

I glared at her.

"It was a *joke*." She rolled her eyes. "Like I said, Cade's kid probably has a badass super sperm force field around it or something."

I popped my eyes out at her. "I am not even going to deign that comment with a response." She was cuckoo.

"I'm coming," Bull declared.

"Seriously, honey, you don't have to, it's just a precaution," I told him, thinking of Bull being present while a doctor put that ultra sound thingy up my lady parts.

"I'm coming," he repeated firmly. "Cade can't be contacted for the rest of the day, and I ain't asking."

"Okay, but you are staying in the waiting room."

⸻

So that's how I arrived at the doctor's office, trailed by my insane best friend and a member of my boyfriend's motorcycle club. Amy checked me in while Bull directed me to the little seated area, which consisted of out of date magazines, uncomfortable chairs, and pamphlets on everything from STDs to asthma.

I snatched up every single one the contained the word preg-nancy or had a baby on the cover and sat down next to a ten-year-old boy and his mother. Bull decided to stay standing, then main-tained the universal bad ass stance, crossing his arms and spreading his feet slightly. He looked like he should have one of those ear pieces in and be guarding the president.

The boy beside me glanced at Bull, then at his cut, and gazed up at him in awe. His mother smiled warmly at him. Bull directed a scowl their way before his face turned away. I saw his tenderness had been short lived. I decided not to pay much atten-tion to this as I had pamphlets to read and got started on the one on top of my pile. I had only just read the first sentence when it was snatched out of my hand.

"Hey!" I snapped at Amy as she sat down beside me, throwing my pamphlets in the trash can beside her.

"You don't need to read them, Gwen, it just tells you the hundred thousand things that have like a point one percent chance of happening. It will only freak you out more, then convince you your child will be a hermaphrodite," she declared, picking up an outdated copy of *People*.

I snatched the magazine out of her hands. "Yeah, well maybe I need to know about that stuff. I had two glasses of wine at dinner last night. *Two*. Not to mention the three beers I had on Monday or the mimosa I had on Sunday. Oh my god, my child is going to be a hermaphrodite." I panicked putting my head in my hands. "I'm a terrible person."

"Now, now, Gwennie," Amy cooed rubbing my back. "I'm sure the baby will be fine. You are not a terrible person. There are mothers who shoot crack in their arms nine months pregnant, *they* are terrible people."

I took a breath, feeling slightly better. She was right.

"And if your baby is a hermaphrodite, at least you get to choose whether it's a girl or a boy, I'd go for girl, personally. Then you can put it in little dresses and stuff," she added thoughtfully earning another moan from me.

———

"Well, there it is," the doctor declared, pointing at the freakily real image on the ultrasound machine.

The image of *my baby, our baby*. And it was cute, you could see its little head and everything, this technology was the shit. I was so worried I was going to be like Rachel off *Friends* and not be able to see my child on the screen. But I saw it. A tear rolled down my cheek, emotion I couldn't even fathom welled up inside me, love for this little being threatened to explode my already full up heart.

"Is it...okay?" I asked, my voice choked up. "Like healthy?"

The doctor smiled at me. "Yes, your baby is perfect, Ms Alexandra, looking to be at just over two months along."

"Two months?" I whispered disbelievingly. That meant I had been pregnant when I was kidnapped. Oh my god, I could have lost my baby. The beautiful little baby on the screen in front of me could have been lost. Anger and protectiveness I didn't know I had welled up in me. Then I realized two and a bit months is a long time to be pregnant without knowing. I was such an idiot.

"Um, shouldn't I have been getting other signs of being this far along?"

"Yeah, shouldn't she at least have gotten some kind of baby bump? And bigger boobs?" Amy piped in from beside me, eyes looking suspiciously red.

The doctor laughed a little. "Some women don't show at all until three or four months. You could even wake up one day with a slight bump, due to the baby moving. And every woman's body changes differently when she's pregnant," she added, eyes twinkling.

My doctor was nice, and pretty. Okay, more like a bombshell. She looked a hell of a lot like Marilyn Monroe, white blonde, curly shoulder-length hair. She had flawless pale skin and curves I would kill for. What's more, she had a great bedside manner and made me feel super comfortable, despite the fact she had a prime view of my hoo ha. She was definitely going to be my baby doctor. Or midwife. Oh my god, I didn't even know what to call a baby doctor.

"Wow, Gwen, you lucky bitch, you might not even get fat at all. Maybe your Kim Kardashian worries are over," Amy said, eyes on my flat stomach.

I ignored this. "So you are sure there's nothing wrong, no signs of trouble?" I asked again. "I didn't know I was pregnant, especially this far along, until today. I haven't exactly been consuming the most healthy foods for a baby."

Amy snorted from beside me and I glared at her.

"Yes, your baby is fine and looks to be strong as well."

Amy groaned. "Man, the curiosity kills, I wish we could tell if it was a girl or a boy."

I turned my head to her. "I'm sure you will find other things to occupy your time, rather than ponder if I'm carrying a boy or a girl."

"Well, that makes buying baby clothes and decorating that much harder. How am I going to get unisex baby clothes? I *despise* yellow," she whined.

"I'm sure you'll find a way to survive," I informed her dryly. "I wish Cade was here for this."

"I can give you a picture to show him if you want?" Sarah, the doctor, said, pressing some buttons on the monitor.

"That would be awesome," I replied, my eyes fixed on the screen.

My little moment with my unborn child was interrupted.

"Hi, is this the Barney's children's department? This is Amy

Abrams, I need to have the latest baby collections sent to me. Unisex please. But no yellow."

———

I left the examination room clutching the little roll of pictures tightly, Amy chattering excitedly beside me.

"See, I told you! That baby is strong as an ox! Nothing's going to get that little super baby down. And did you hear the doc? Two months. You had that bun in your oven when you were kidnapped, and it still stayed strong. You're going to have your hands full with this kid." Her eyes were glued to her phone, online shopping no doubt.

She was not wrong. I felt like I was floating on cloud nine, my baby was healthy. Our baby would be perfect. We approached Bull and he stepped forward, looking slightly anxious. I beamed at him and thrust the pictures in his face.

"Look! This is our baby, you can actually see it. Like eyes, nose, everything. Isn't it cute?" I waved the pictures in his face, which obviously wasn't working for him because he grabbed my wrist to carefully take them out of my hand and study them closely.

The depth of emotion on this tough, usually staunch man was staggering. I watched as his eyes turned tortured, I could see he was thinking of a moment, if the past had been different. A moment where it would be his baby he was looking at had Laurie not been murdered. Tears welled up in my eyes and I reached for Bull's arm, but was interrupted by a loud and familiar voice.

"Bull! Gwen! Yo!" Lucky strode towards us with his usual grin.

Oh shit. I didn't need another one of Cade's brothers finding out about our little bundle of joy before he did. What was he doing at the doctor's anyway? Wasn't he some bad ass that refused to acknowledge he wasn't indestructible? Maybe all those dalliances with various women were catching up with him. I tried to snatch the photo out of Bull's hand but it was too late.

"What are you guys all doing here? I heard Gwen was sick, shit is it serious?" Lucky approached and his grin turned to concern, he then glanced at what Bull had in his hand. He snatched it.

"What do we have here that you're looking at so intently. I hope it's not any naked photos..." he stopped short when he got a look at the little piece of paper. I watched as his mouth opened in shock. "Seriously, you guys are into some sick shit..." he began, then a grin spread across his face. "Holy shit, Princess, you're pregnant?" he all but yelled.

I winced as people started to look our way. "Try not to announce it to the whole town, Lucky, Cade doesn't even know yet," I scolded quietly.

Lucky ignored me and pulled me into his arms. "This is fucking great! You guys having a kid, I mean, fuck! This calls for celebration, we're having a party. Tonight!" he decided, putting me down.

"Um, no party tonight," I argued, ignoring the slight falter in Lucky's smile. "I want to tell Cade first. *Alone.*"

Lucky smirked. "Fair enough, Princess. I can imagine his reaction might not be suitable for a whole party full of people."

I poked my tongue out at him, forgetting for a moment that I was a mother now and shouldn't be doing such immature things. He slung an arm around my shoulder and patted my belly softly.

"Real mature, Princess, think you might have to find better comebacks, since you're going to be a mom and all," he laughed as our crew walked out the door.

"I'm going to be a *mum*," I corrected him. "My child is growing up half kiwi, you know."

"Yeah, he's also growing up half Templar." He winked. I just rolled my eyes and ignored the 'he' in that sentence. Why were men always convinced women were having boys?

━━━

The aroma of garlic and chicken wafting around my nostrils made my stomach roll slightly, but I ignored it. I was too excited about the fact that Cade would be home any minute and I would get to tell him about the baby. I was still nervous, like really nervous, about his reaction, but the boys had quelled my nerves slightly.

I had decided to make him a delicious dinner at his house, partly because we hadn't been here in a while and partly because I wanted us completely alone to hopefully celebrate. I had stuck the ultrasound photo on the fridge, hoping he would notice it when he went to get his beer. Which was pretty much the first thing he did when he got home, after making out with me, that was.

I got the chicken out of the oven, turning my head away from the smell. Morning sickness my ass. I had thrown up twice this afternoon, which didn't bode well for the rest of my pregnancy. Figures, Cade's child would be a handful, even in the womb.

My stomach dropped for a different kind of reason, hearing the telltale sound of Harley pipes coming down the driveway. My nerves were interrupted by my cellphone ringing. I picked it up, intending to ignore the call until I saw who it was.

"Matt! How the heck are you stranger?" I greeted warmly.

"Hey, sweetheart," Matt returned, tone unusual.

Matt was the officer who found me after my attack. He had taken me to the hospital and stayed with me until Amy had arrived. He also visited me the day I woke up. He was sweet and caring and helped me get through my therapy. We had become great friends, although I hadn't heard from him since I'd moved.

"I am so sorry to do this, I've missed talking to you and all, but this isn't the best time. Can I call you back?" I asked him, hearing Cade's bike stop.

"Not really, Gwen, I've got some news." This pulled my attention away from the door, which I knew Cade would be walking through any second.

"What is it, Matt? Finally popped the question to Misty?" I joked, still unable to read his strange tone. It wasn't urgent, but he sounded like it was something important.

"No love, it's about O'Fallen," he told me quietly.

I braced myself against the counter, my knees threatening to buckle.

Oh no, please tell me this fucker wasn't messing with my life again. Not again, not with me and my child.

"He hasn't escaped has he?" I whispered into the phone, praying for the answer to be good.

"No, Gwen. He's dead. He was found in his cell early this morning, stabbed."

My breath left me in a whoosh at this news. I barely registered Cade walking through the door, concerned eyes already reading my distress.

"Dead?" I repeated.

Cade heard this, strode towards me and yanked me into his arms, eyes locked on mine.

"Yeah, honey. Usually I'm not the kind of man that relishes delivering this type of information. Shit, I never thought I'd be glad at the news of someone being murdered. But I am, after what he did to you and countless others. I can sleep easy knowing the world is rid of that maggot," he declared fiercely.

I listened to his words, but barely heard them. Cade was staring down at me, worry clear in his expression. I could tell he wanted to yank the phone out of my grasp, but I had a death grip on it.

"Gwen? It's over, honey, he can never hurt you again," Matt told me softly.

"Um, thanks for telling me, Matty," I said quietly. "I'm glad I heard it from you. Can I call you back? Kind of a lot to deal with." And I had the small problem of Cade, who was squeezing me so hard my baby was in danger of popping out seriously early.

"Yeah, of course, Gwen. Call me if you need anything. I'm always here."

"Thanks, Matty, give my love to Misty."

"Will do, Gwen, bye."

I took the phone from my ear and stared down at it blankly.

"Baby," Cade called, lifting my chin to look at him gently.

"Jimmy is dead," I told him, my voice flat.

Cade looked at me carefully and stroked my face, gathering me deeper into his arms. I relaxed into them, letting his strong body and manly scent comfort me.

"I don't feel anything," I said, turning my gaze up. "Nothing. Not sad, not happy, just detachment. It just feels like *news*." Maybe it was the fact I was going to be a mother and had a child to think about, or the fact that my life was amazing. Nothing could taint it.

Cade was rubbing my shoulders, his eyes burning into mine, searching for the truth in my words, no doubt worrying for me. I seriously loved this man.

"That's good, baby," he said evenly, calmly.

I was surprised. I expected him to have more of a reaction. One thing about my man was that he didn't hide his emotions, well, anger at least. All of a sudden, a thought turned my blood to ice.

"You don't seem surprised," I whispered, trying to step out of his arms. They tightened around me. He was silent for a beat, face blank.

"No, Gwen, I'm not." His voice was flat.

"You knew about this?" I stepped back fully, Cade let me. "Please tell me it's because you have some kind of Google alert on his name or friends at the prison."

Cade pulled at his neck, muscles bulging as he did so. "Yeah, baby, I've got friends at the prison," he replied softly, his meaning clear.

"You had something to do with this?" I asked, wishing him to tell me otherwise.

He continued watching me, stepping towards me, freezing as I flinched away.

"I couldn't let him go on breathing after what he did to you, Gwen. He needed to be taken care of. I didn't want any more chances of him hurting you again." His voice was devoid of emotion. As a matter of fact, it was like we were discussing what to have for dinner, not him ordering a hit on someone.

"He couldn't hurt me again!" I yelled at him. "He was locked up *for life*. He was paying for his crimes, for every single person he hurt."

Cade stiffened, his fists clenched. "That wasn't enough for me, Gwen. I couldn't sleep at night knowing someone who hurt the most precious thing in my life was still in this world."

"And how do you think I'm going to sleep at night knowing the man I love *ordered a hit on someone?*" I all but screeched. "It isn't up to you to play judge, jury, and executioner! How am I going to keep on living like this? Am I going to have to worry whether you're going to off someone for stealing my parking spot, or getting the last pair of shoes I wanted?" My voice was still loud, maybe bordering on hysterical.

"Jesus, Gwen. This is different and you know it. I'm not a fucking monster. I'm not like him!" Cade exploded, temper flaring.

My temper was threatening to match his, which may or may not have been due to pregnancy hormones.

"Maybe not yet, Cade! But when human life means so little to you, when it's so easy to end it with just a phone call, who knows where that will take you. I'm not living like that my..." I cut myself off from saying '*my child will not live like that.*'

The look of rage and hurt on Cade's face cut through me like a knife.

"Fuck this!" he roared. "Fine, Gwen, if you don't want to live with a monster, then I'm gone, I won't be a part of tainting your life any more." He pushed past me, slamming the front door. I heard the roar of Harley pipes as he hurtled down the driveway.

"Shit," I muttered to myself.

I sank to the floor, tears streaming down my face, my hand lightly cradling my stomach.

CHAPTER 17

I WOKE up early the next morning to a rolling stomach. I quickly pulled back the covers to Cade's bed and made it to the bathroom in time. After divesting my stomach of last night's chicken, I placed my head against the cold porcelain, dread washing over me remembering the disaster of last night.

After I had a little breakdown on the floor, I finished making dinner, made Cade a plate and put it in the fridge. I went to bed early, hoping to wake up to Cade, so we could sort things out.

It was morning and the bed was empty. He hadn't come home. I didn't know what to think about the fact that he was the one who was responsible for Jimmy's death. I did know I really hurt him, basically calling him a monster. There was no way I could agree with ending someone's life, even if he was a scumbag of epic proportions. But I couldn't say I was sorry that Jimmy was dead.

It was like a weight gone from my shoulders. That also scared me. I was telling the truth when I said those things to Cade last night, if you have someone who loves you enough to kill for you, where did they draw the line? What justifies ending someone's life in the name of someone else?

I shook my head, this was all too much to handle on top of an unplanned pregnancy. I knew I had to talk to Cade. He would be at the clubhouse, and I could only hope the big mouths over there hadn't uttered a word about my little bun. They were worse than women.

My phone started ringing, I jumped, hoping it would be Cade, but looking down at the display it was my mother. I frowned and let it ring. I couldn't deal with talking to her just now, I needed to sort things out with my man first before informing her she would be a grandmother.

___

I pulled up to the clubhouse feeling nervous and nauseous. The words from our fight last night rang in my ears, Cade's parting shots still causing me pain. I knew it was just because he was hurting, we could fix it. I walked through the door and my heel crunched on an empty beer can.

"Whoa," I whispered.

They had definitely had a party last night. People were passed out on every available surface, booze bottles littered the floor and the room stank. I didn't want to look at anything too closely, even though I had become a bit more hardened to these kinds of things since becoming an Old Lady. I made it to the hallway to see Bull emerging from his room, a look of panic crossed over his face before he quickly masked it.

"Hey, big man," I chirped, trying to sound cheerful. "Looks like a big night, how's the head? Cade sleeping it off?" I smiled at him, putting one foot on the stairs.

The look crossed his face again and he ran a hand through his hair. "Sweetheart, Cade's not here, he left out on a run early this morning. I'll have him call you as soon as he gets back, okay?" His voice was strange and he kept glancing up at Cade's closed door.

I frowned at him, something was wrong. Oh god. He was up there with someone. I tasted bile. No. Cade wouldn't do that.

"That's okay, I'll just wait in his room," I told him firmly, needing to make sure.

Bull grabbed my arm lightly. "You don't want to do that, Gwen," he said softly.

That sick feeling came back. The one that had nothing to do with morning sickness. I struggled not to throw up on his shoes. I yanked my arm from his and raced up the stairs.

"Gwen!" he yelled after me, but I was already pulling the door open, preparing for my heart to shatter.

Cade sat up in bed slightly, rubbing his eyes sleepily.

"Gwen?" he asked, voice husky.

I breathed a sigh of relief. He was alone, in his stupid messy bed. I moved to sit gingerly on the bed.

"I came to say I'm sorry, I shouldn't have said those things last night."

Cade opened his mouth, but I held up my hand to silence him.

"Let me talk. We've still got a lot to discuss, but I overreacted and said some nasty things I didn't mean. The reason I blew up so much is because of hormones. You know those nasty ones you get when you're pregnant? The freaking things magnify every emotion I'm feeling and may or may not turn me into a psychotic mess. And also make me crave Oreo sandwiches." My stomach rumbled at the thought of it. "So as long as you keep us in constant supply of Oreos for the next seven months or so, I may be able to stop you from having me committed."

I took a deep breath from my babbling and peeked through my lashes at my man, sitting statue still, with an unreadable expression on his face.

"I'm having your baby, Cade," I told him quietly.

He gazed at me in shock and for a split-second, I was worried. That was until he grinned so wide I thought his mouth might split open. I had never seen a look like the one of pure joy he was wearing at that moment. He reached for me but froze when the door to his bathroom opened. My head turned and my stomach dropped, Ginger leaned against the door jamb, wearing Cade's tee and a nasty grin on her face.

"Well, this is awkward," she spat out of her vile mouth, smirking.

I looked between her and Cade, horrified and heartbroken. I ran to the door, hoping I didn't vomit on the way out.

"Gwen!" Cade roared.

I was already halfway down the stairs, tears rolling down my face. I stumbled at the last few and almost fell, but Bull was there to catch me.

"Whoa, Gwennie, it's okay," he told me, with pity and fury in his eyes.

I yanked myself away from him, stumbling, surprised I was even still upright. I turned away from Bull and ran towards the exit, focusing on getting away from this place before Cade caught me, before I had to look at him.

The father of my baby.

The love of my life.

The man who fucked someone else on the same night he told me he killed Jimmy.

The pain of betrayal and my heart breaking was sharp and almost caused me to double over. I heard Cade crashing down the stairs and struggling with Bull. The ringtone of my phone pierced my emotional fog, I retrieved it from my purse. It was Mum, again. She had tried to call me about three times since this morning.

I picked it up. "Mum, I can't talk right now, I'm trying not to commit double homicide," I gritted out, deciding anger might work best for me as I stumbled into the parking lot.

I heard Cade yelling behind me. I intended to run for my car until my mother's choked voice on the other end phone, saturated in grief, brought me to a standstill.

"Gwen, it's Ian. Ian's dead," she cried.

She might have continued speaking, but I couldn't hear through the roar in my ears.

"No," I whispered.

This couldn't be happening, this wasn't real. There is no way Ian could be *dead*. That was impossible. The sobs at the end of the phone told me different.

"No!" I screamed, jerking the phone from my ear and hurling it at the wall in front of me. I didn't react as it smashed against the brick. Pain, like nothing I'd ever felt before slashed through every fiber of my being.

I thought I knew about pain, having been as close to death as I had. But I knew nothing. Nothing.

Jimmy breaking my ribs with his steel cap boots? A feather touch.

My skull being broken when it hit concrete floor?

A gentle kiss. My cheek opening when a ring tore through the skin?

A cool breeze.

They were nothing compared to the agony I was going through at this moment. I heard people calling my name around me, but I couldn't see through the pain, I couldn't breathe through the pain. I collapsed just as strong arms caught me. Nothing registered.

"No, no, no, no," I chanted. *This isn't happening, this isn't real, someone made some sort of mistake.*

I clung to the delusion, the desperate hope that this wasn't real. But the pain was real. The agony of my soul being ripped apart, of my heart shattering into a million different pieces, that was real. Suddenly real pain, physical, in my stomach caused me to double over.

"Gwen!" Someone screamed my name in desperation.

I felt wetness between my legs. *My baby* was all I thought before I blacked out.

—————

CADE

Cade heaved back the covers, yelling Gwen's name as she ran out the door. He put on some jeans, glaring at the whore walking towards him. Any other bitch with half a brain would catch the look on his face and run a mile. Not this cunt.

"Let her go, baby, she needs to understand—"

He cut the bitch short with his hand on her neck and pushed her roughly against the wall. He relished the sound of her choking.

"Shut your fucking mouth, bitch. I didn't go fucking near you last night. Didn't touch your disease ridden body. I went to sleep alone. Now, whatever the fuck you thought when you skulked in here is something you will regret for the rest of your life." He slammed her against the wall then roughly dropped her, following Gwen.

When he reached the bottom of the stairs, Bull seized him by the shoulders, slamming him against the wall, a lot rougher than he had Ginger.

"What the fuck, brother? You have a woman like Gwen, a woman *pregnant with your child* and you fuck around on her with that skank? You are one sick fucker," he snarled, his voice vibrating with fury.

Cade shoved him back just as roughly. "I didn't fuck around

on her! Let me the fuck go so I can tell her that!" he bellowed, ready to kill his brother if he stopped him getting to Gwen.

Bull looked at him a beat then stepped aside.

Cade ran through the carnage of the night before, ignoring the groans as he trampled on the people passed out on the floor.

"Gwen!" he roared again, seeing her stumble out the door and into the parking lot, phone to her ear.

He got to the door, not slowing his pace, but relieved when he realized he would reach her as she stopped dead. He tried to bury the fury at what that slut Ginger had done. It was hard, the flames of anger were burning at his throat, but they were quelled at the thought of Gwen pregnant with his child.

Gwen growing his baby inside her, creating their family. He couldn't help but smile on the inside, despite the fact he had a fuck ton of explaining to do. Gwen would believe him. She had to. She knew he would never do that to her.

His thoughts froze as a tortured "No!" filled the air. There was so much pain in that one word he broke into a sprint, watching Gwen throw her phone then double over in pain. He made it to her just in time to catch her in his arms.

"Gwen baby, talk to me, what is it?" He stroked her head struggling to keep the panic out of his voice. His concern for her, for the baby almost crippled him.

"Gwen!" he asked again, frantic, running his hands over her, searching for an injury, a cause for the horrible sounds coming out of her. Tears streamed down her face, a grimace of such raw pain covered it, he flinched.

"No, no, no, no," she whispered over and over, her voice anguished.

"Baby tell me—" Cade was almost over the edge when her cry of pain interrupted him, she clutched her stomach and fear ran ice cold through his veins. At that moment, Lucky and Steg came sprinting over, faces grim.

"What is it, Cade, what's wrong with Gwen?" Lucky bit out eyes frantic.

"Call a fucking ambulance. Now!" Cade screamed and he watched in horror as blood trickled down her legs.

———

GWEN

I woke to that beeping again. That all too familiar hospital beeping.

Great.

I cracked one of my eyes open, expecting to see Ian curled up in the corner. Then the horror of it all washed over me. The phone call, Mum's tortured voice, Ian. He was dead.

My brother was dead.

I vaguely noticed the beeping beside me getting louder as the pain ripped through me once more. How could this be real? This couldn't be real. Ian wasn't dead. No, someone else was, they just thought it was Ian. It's just a big mistake. Yes, it had to be a mistake.

I struggled to contain my breathing as Sarah, my baby doctor, rushed in looking worried. A fresh wave of horror settled over me. The pain. The feeling of my baby leaving me, dying.

No, no, no.

Tears streamed down my face as Sarah approached the bed.

"Gwen, sweetheart, I know it's hard but I need you to take a deep breath and calm down. You hear that beeping? That's your heart and it's hammering away pretty hard. We need to try and slow it down a bit," she explained calmly.

"My baby?" I asked her, my voice dead.

She took my hand and I prepared for the blow. She squeezed

it and smiled weakly. "The baby is okay, Gwen. Everything is fine."

I blinked, barely allowing myself to believe it. "But the pain, and I was bleeding—"

"You had a nasty shock and your baby wasn't prepared for what your body was going through. Especially given the fact your blood pressure was already a little high. I know it's scary, but thirty percent of women experience cramps and bleeding in the first trimester and considering the news you received, it's not surprising."

She gave my hand another squeeze.

"Now, I have your fiancé outside, he was not happy to be left there. In fact, it took three of his friends to convince him to stay in the waiting room. You think it would be okay to let him in? You know, before he ruins anymore furniture?" She grinned, writing something in my chart.

"Fiancé?" I croaked, confused.

Then thoughts of Cade came back. Cade and Ginger. My life was falling apart lying in this hospital bed. Cade didn't deserve to see me. To see our baby. But Sarah didn't deserve to have her office trashed by the asshole either. I opened my mouth to agree when a commotion outside stopped me.

"Fuck this, I've been waiting out here for almost a fucking hour. I don't give a shit what procedure is, I'm seeing my fucking woman!" a familiar angry voice shouted as the doors crashed open.

A frantic looking Cade stormed in, followed by two very pissed off looking orderlies. His eyes fell on me and instantly softened to a look of love and relief it almost pierced the feeling of emptiness and despair that surrounded me.

Almost.

"It's okay, guys, we've just got one concerned dad on our hands. You can go," Sarah told the orderly's and they looked relieved at not having to try and drag Cade out. They turned and shut the door behind them.

"Gwen. Baby. Jesus Christ." Cade rushed over, kneeling over me, pulling his face to mine so our foreheads touched. He closed his eyes, leaving us like that for a second before he opened them, eyes falling on mine. He straightened and turned to Sarah, clutching my hand.

"Is she okay? Is the baby...?" he choked, looking like he couldn't physically finish the sentence.

"She's fine. Mr Fletcher. The baby is fine too," Sarah reassured him.

I watched the relief wash over Cade, his eyes closed for a second and his shoulders sagged as if a weight had been lifted.

"Thank God."

He pulled my hand to his mouth, gently pressing his lips against my knuckles. I watched him woodenly. My hand moved to my stomach, my love and happiness for my little bun the only thing keeping me going. Cade followed my hand, his covering my own, weakly smiling at me.

"Thank God," he repeated, holding my gaze again.

His hand didn't leave mine as he focused his attention on Sarah.

"But why did this happen? She was in pain, bleeding. Are you sure everything is okay?" he fired at her with an edge to his voice.

Sarah stood at the end of the bed looking at us both, addressing Cade. "As I was just telling Gwen, babies respond to their mother's distress. And I understand, Gwen had just gotten some bad news." She pointed a sympathetic glance at me and Cade's hand squeezed mine.

"But let's give Dad a look so you can feel better." She wheeled an ultrasound machine over from the corner and gestured for us to remove our hands.

She exposed my stomach. Cade's eyes were glued to my belly in a look so intense I forced myself to glance away before it could affect me. After putting the cold jelly on, she moved the wand and we both watched the screen. I looked at what I had seen the day before, reassured to hear the little heartbeat.

Cade's grip was iron on my hand. I had never seen a look on his face like the one he was currently wearing. His eyes glistened, he gazed down at me with pure joy on his face.

"That's our baby," he murmured roughly, stroking my cheek.

"As you can see and hear, we have a little fighter on our hands," Sarah informed us.

I registered the screen, the baby, the father's joy, but I couldn't bring myself to find any response. A numbness settled over me. I was relieved beyond belief that my baby was okay, but that's all I could feel, all I let myself feel. Sarah put the machine away and she stood at the end of my bed again.

"When Gwen's body went into shock, so did the baby. And as the baby isn't equipped to deal with stress, it gave us signs of distress. Now Gwen's blood pressure is also quite high, which is slightly worrying. I would advise you to stay rested for the next couple of days, try to avoid stress. I know that's not something that can be controlled at this time. But we can monitor you, just in case." She smiled sadly, pity in her eyes.

Pity for me. The girl whose brother just died. The grief cut through me like glass.

"I can't stay anywhere rested. I have to get a flight. I have to get to New Zealand as soon as possible," I informed her flatly.

"Gwen, sweetheart, the baby, I don't know if that—" Cade began, voice tender but firm.

I ignored him, keeping my eyes on Sarah. "Will the baby be okay? Hell, I'll even hire a doctor to fly with me," I told her, unable to fathom the thought of being unable to see my parents.

"Honestly, Gwen, the bed rest is just a precaution, a flight is obviously not ideal at the moment, but I am reasonably sure the baby will be fine. The biggest worry on a flight is a blot clot, but as long as we can get your pressure down the risk lowers significantly. We'll keep you here for observation for a couple more hours, just to make sure your blood pressure comes down, then I'll be able to clear you for flying. I'll come back and check on you in a bit." She turned to leave the room, but Cade stopped her.

"Reasonably sure?" he bit out. "I want you to be one hundred percent sure that my baby and future wife are going to be safe before putting them on a twelve-hour flight. I am not letting Gwen anywhere near a plane for 'reasonably sure,'" he declared hotly.

I felt my temper flare from somewhere, but Sarah spoke before I could.

"Mr Fletcher, I would never put my patient on a plane if I thought there would be any risk to her or the baby's health. That's why I'm monitoring her. The baby's heartbeat is strong, her blood pressure is coming down, she's healthy and young. Now of course, even in a healthy pregnancy there will never be a hundred percent certainty that everything will run smoothly. But I can assure you, she will not be getting on that plane unless I am sure she and the baby will not be at any unusual risk." She maintained eye contact with Cade, not backing down.

I would've been impressed, had I been able to focus on anything but my sorrow.

Cade continued to glare at her a beat, then nodded stiffly, returning his concerned gaze to me.

"I'll leave you to it. You will be discharged as soon as your blood pressure gets back to normal and stays there. Should be a few hours," Sarah cut in, before moving to the other side of my bed not occupied by a big biker. She squeezed my hand. "I'm so sorry about your brother, Gwen," she told me sincerely before walking out.

I followed her with my eyes, wishing for glorious oblivion to stop me from getting crushed under the weight of my sorrow.

"Baby?" Cade muttered softly, his hand stroking my face so tenderly you'd think I was made of glass.

I felt like it. I felt like I would shatter at any moment. But I couldn't. I had a little baby inside me, who needed its mother to be strong.

"Gwen. I need to explain about before, with—"

I held my hand up, halting him. "Cade, my brother is dead. Do you think I *care* you fucked some whore?" I said, my voice flat.

Cade flinched, I regarded his stricken face, feeling detached. He stood, towering over me in my bed, his hand going down to cradle my stomach above the blanket.

"Gwen, you need to know—"

"I don't need to know anything!" I all but screamed, my voice ragged. I took a deep breath. "I don't need to know anything but the fact my brother is dead. I will never see him again. My baby will never get to know his or her uncle. All I need right now is to get out of here so I can go home." My voice was back to the flat, emotionless tone I thought I might come to adopt.

Cade sat on my bed carefully, stroking my face again. I didn't push him away, didn't respond to his touch. I just stared at him blankly.

"Gwen, the idea of you flying that far, with the complications with the baby...I can't have either of you in any kind of danger." He was trying to treat me with care, but it didn't stop what his true meaning was to fire up a spark inside me.

"I would *never* put my baby in danger," I hissed.

"I know you wouldn't, Gwen, but you won't be able to control what happens when you get on that plane." His voice brokered no argument, but hell if I wasn't giving him one.

"You're right. I don't have any control," I agreed acidly. "I don't have control over the fact my brother is dead, that my parents are beyond devastated, that my heart is broken. And I can't control the fate of my baby, as much as I wish I could shield it from everything in this world, I can't. We could die in a car crash on the way to the airport. I can't control that. But I would never let anything in my control hurt my child, or even give anything the possibility of hurting *my child*. There is no way you have any say in my staying here once I get the all clear from the doctor. I need to go home and help my parents bury their son. I need to bury my brother."

I didn't allow the expressions on Cade's face permeate. I didn't allow him to speak.

"I need you to leave," I told him flatly, eyes on the ceiling.

"I'm not fucking going anywhere." Cade's voice was concrete.

The fire that had so quickly sparked inside of me withered, the strength to fight him just wasn't in me. I was too busy using it to try to fight the grief that was crushing my chest. Too busy trying to fight off the reality that my brother was actually gone. So I just ignored him, stared past him, to the monitors that showed my baby's heartbeat. I focused on that, clinging to that little sound like it was my lifeline. Cade was talking, stroking my face, kissing my head. I ignored him.

"Gwen."

He softly grabbed my face, pulling it close to his, forcing my gaze away from the monitor. He opened his mouth, but before he could speak, the door opened and Amy burst in. She stood at the door, her face red and splotchy, eyes rimmed red, pain etched into every inch of her body. We just looked at each other a beat. A single tear ran down my best friend's cheek.

"Gwennie," she choked before rushing to the bed. She didn't even acknowledge Cade, who stood to let her crawl in next to me. She sobbed quietly, her body shaking next to mine, I held onto my best friend for dear life.

Amy clutched my hand as the plane touched down. I looked over at her makeup free face and attempted a weak smile.

"Well, we made it home and this little one has behaved." I put my hand over my stomach, letting the relief wash over me.

She squeezed my hand and looked down at my stomach.

"I expected nothing less from our super baby." She attempted a jaunty wink, but couldn't hide the raw pain that lurked beneath her eyes. Yet again, she was trying her best to take care of me, help take on my grief when her own threatened to drown her.

I sighed, gazing out to the tarmac and into the windows of the airport that held my parents. I yearned for the comfort of my mother's arms, the strength from my father's embrace. I was also dreading the moment I saw them. The moment I saw the loss in their faces, the point where this would all become real. The moment when my blissful numbness would crack away to reveal the agony that threatened to destroy me.

The last few days were a blur. I had stumbled through them like a zombie, unable, unwilling to feel anything. I was detached, my emotions unplugged.

I had ended up having to stay overnight at the hospital and Cade never left my side, sleeping in the chair beside my bed, while Amy lay beside me. I paid him little notice, clutching Amy's hand, lying wide awake with my eyes glued to the ceiling.

I knew he watched me most of the night, I could feel his gaze on me. When I was discharged, I discovered the entire club camped in the waiting room.

Even Steg.

I guessed that would've surprised me had I not been blissfully detached. I would've also been touched by the concerned faces, the loving and thoughtful words coming from the staunch bikers, but I woodenly stared past them all, clinging to my little world of unfeeling.

Amy had arranged her father's jet to be ready as soon as I was discharged, having my essentials packed and ready to go when she picked me up from the hospital. We were meant to be leaving straight from there, and Cade all but exploded when he learned this.

He was pushing me in my chair to the curb when Amy pulled up. She jumped out of the car and directed a glare at him — someone obviously filled her in. She wiped the scorching look off her face and smiled down at me weakly.

"I've got everything we need for our trip, Gwennie. Daddy's jet is waiting for us at a small airstrip outside of town and it'll take us to LAX where we've got the next plane to Auckland. Daddy also insisted we take his doctor with him on the flight. Just in case."

She looked at my stomach and leaned down to help me up, pointedly ignoring Cade , until he stopped her with a hand on her wrist.

"What the fuck do you think you're doing, Amy? You can't just take the mother of my child halfway across the world. Wherever she goes I go," he growled, fury saturating his tone.

Amy raised an eyebrow and glared down at the tattooed arm covering hers, her look glacial. "You can take your hand off me right now," she hissed and continued to help me up when Cade complied.

He gripped my shoulder.

"I can and I will take Gwen back to her *family* and her *home*, to the people that love her. In case you've forgotten, she's going to attend the fucking funeral of her only brother," she snarled and a blade went through my soul.

"It just happens to be convenient that her home is as far away from you as humanly possible, and a silver lining in this fucking nightmare is the fact that you are a criminal with a record, which means you aren't going *anywhere*."

Without waiting for a response, she gently helped me stand from the chair directing me away from Cade and the men who had stopped behind him. The men I considered family.

"Jesus, Gwen, wait," Cade pleaded. The grief and anger in his voice made me turn.

I put my hand on Amy's arm. "It's okay, Amy." My voice was still cold, flat.

She glared at Cade then took her hands off me. As soon as that happened, Brock surged forward, pulling her away and hissing frantically in her ear.

I didn't move an inch, Cade was on me in one stride, framing my face with his hands. His eyes locked with mine, face hard and soft at the same time.

"Baby, Gwen. Just give me some time to sort this shit out. I'm coming with you. You are not facing this without me. I won't let you go through this without me." His words were firm, his tone a promise. "I love you to the depths of my soul. The baby too. I won't let you go through a second of this without me by your side," he finished softly, hand caressing my belly.

I stared back at him, the love, concern, anguish in his eyes failing to affect me. My emotions were locked up deep inside me. I couldn't let them out. I couldn't have the loss coursing through my veins like a poison. I was afraid I wouldn't survive.

"You need to let me go," I responded flatly.

His arms tightened on my neck. "Baby, *please*." His voice almost broke and his stare burned into mine.

"Let me go now, I have a plane to catch." I watched him flinch at my tone. What he didn't do was let me go.

"Gwen—"

"Let me go!" I screamed in his face, my voice cracking.

Someone grabbed his shoulder, pulling him away. I took my

chance and hopped into the door that Amy was holding open for me, she had obviously managed to pull herself away from her own angry biker.

I watched as Cade fought off Bull, yelling, throwing punches, never taking his eyes off me. Lucky and Brock joined in, struggling to hold him back. Unable to watch anymore, I turned my head as Amy drove away.

That was about twenty-one hours ago. I had barely slept, my mind going over everything and nothing at all. Thoughts, memories tugging at the corners of my mind, refusing to let me welcome oblivion.

Amy and I disembarked, walking along the tarmac of the small airport. The mountains of home surrounded me like a warm blanket, even with the bitter winter wind biting at my skin. We emerged at arrivals and I zeroed my parents out immediately.

My usually immaculate mother was wearing faded jeans and a sweatshirt, her face free of makeup, eyes rimmed red — she looked gaunt and grief had settled over every inch of her small frame. My father was staunch, strong, as usual, his arms around my mother. His eyes were the only things that betrayed him. They were full of sorrow and devastation. I was engulfed in my mother's arms the second we reached them.

"Oh, Gwennie, my baby," she sobbed, clutching me to her.

My father's strong arms circled around us both. I looked up at him to see his eyes glistening as he kissed my head. I clung to what remained of my family.

CHAPTER 18

TWO MONTHS LATER

"YOU KNOW WHAT, Mum? I think this gardening thing is actually growing on me," I informed her, my hands digging through the soil. I held them up, inspecting my nails, which were caked with dirt. "Even if it destroys my manicure."

My mother smiled. "Well, it's only taken twenty-five years," she replied dryly. "And you're supposed to wear gloves." She waved her bright pink flowered ones in my direction.

I turned my attention back down at the soil and sighed. "I like the feel of it between my fingertips, it's...soothing."

My mother's smile turned sad, I could tell her thoughts were turning to worry. And grief.

"Gwennie. Sweetheart, you know you need to talk, you can't keep this bottled up. You haven't even cried since the funeral." Her voice was wobbly.

She was right. I hadn't shed a tear since they had put my brother in the ground. Hadn't spoken a word of him, if I could avoid it. I couldn't. I couldn't open that dam, because I was afraid if I did I would never plug it back up. I couldn't let myself let go of the carefully put together pieces of my soul. I would shatter.

I stood up abruptly, dusting my hands off on my already dirty dress. "Mum, I don't need to talk okay? Just let me be. Please stop pressuring me when I don't have anything to say."

She stood too, eyes glistening. "Gwen..." she looked as if she was going to push it.

"Okay, my two best green thumbs, time to go, I've got us booked in for three." Amy stood on the porch, her heels not permitting her from venturing onto the grass.

I would have laughed if I had had the ability. My Manhattanite best friend may have settled into life in the country all right, but she was yet to adopt the gumboots that were second nature around here.

"What are you smirking at, Martha Stewart? I know for a fact you're in desperate need of a manicure," she shot at me.

Amy was trying as hard as she could to hide her grief. But it leaked out every now and then. I would watch her face grow dark and tears well in her eyes when something she said or did reminded her of...him.

I was trying to ignore my own suffering as best I could, so I focused on hers. She had lost him too. The man she loved. We were both as broken as each other, trying to hide our wounds as best we could. The breeze rustled my dress and my thoughts ventured downward, to the round bulge of my stomach.

"I'm coming, just give the pregnant woman some slack, I'll be waddling soon." I made my way through our garden, Mum at my side.

"Soon?" Amy raised a brow. "I think I detect a slight waddle now."

I gasped, grabbing my mother's hand, turning to her in horror.

"Did you hear that, Mum? She said I *waddled*. I'm not waddling. Am I?" I asked desperately.

My mother smiled through the pain that was in her eyes and touched my stomach lightly. "Well, I wasn't going to say anything..." she joked, sneaking a glance at my so called best friend.

"Oh you two are pieces of work, making fun of the pregnant lady. You do get how delicate my hormones are right now? And that I'm holding gardening scissors?" I glared at them both, shaking my weapon threateningly.

My mother rolled her eyes lovingly. "*Shears,* my doll, they are called shears."

"Whatever."

I tossed the *shears* on our outdoor table just as my father emerged from the direction of the shed.

"What are my girls bickering about now?" he asked, looking at the three of us, pretending to glower.

I rushed up to him clutching his arms dramatically. "Daddy, *please* tell these evil women that I do not waddle. I'm barely pregnant!" I exclaimed.

Dad hauled me into his arms and put his chin on my head.

"You, my beautiful girl, do not waddle," he reassured me.

I sighed into his embrace.

"You galumph and it's adorable," his voice was amused.

I extracted myself from his arms and glared. "You are all bullies. My own family! I know if Ian was here he would..." I stopped abruptly, hands over my mouth as the dark shadow of my words settled over us all. The smiles and jokes were gone, replaced by sadness and grief, I struggled under the weight of it. I hadn't said his name since...No.

"Mouse," Dad said softly, his voice raw.

I took a deep breath and pulled myself together. "Excuse me, everyone, I'm covered in garden scum, I must change before we head to the spa. I would frighten the public like this." My voice was saturated with forced cheerfulness and I ignored the worried faces of my loved ones.

Without waiting for a response, I quickly dashed back into the house. When I reached my room, I slammed the door behind me, collapsing against it, closing my eyes.

I mustn't let myself think, about it, I mustn't remember.

I went to my closet, eyes avoiding every picture I knew would destroy me. I had memorized where they were, I knew where I couldn't look. I could have taken them down. But that would mean touching them, God forbid I got a glance at the photo inside the frame. It was worse in the rest of the house. My mother decorated in memories.

I distracted myself with what I was going to wear. And that was a good distraction, my growing belly had a huge effect on my fashion choices. I had pretty much had to overhaul my entire wardrobe, not that that was a chore. Plus, I would've had to do it anyway considering most of my stuff was in the States.

Tut tut, Gwen. Mustn't let my mind wander that way either.

My stomach went from flat to baby bumpin' almost overnight. The doctor was right. At least I had bypassed the awkward "is she fat or pregnant" stage. I was definitely pregnant. At four months, I had kept my small frame, which made my baby bump all the more prominent. I was all belly and boobs. I was more than a little pleased my lady lumps had grown a bit bigger.

I chose a mocha colored maxi dress that was tight and gently hugged my belly. I slung a braided belt just underneath the swell of my stomach and wrapped a scarf around my neck. I put on some boots and a denim jacket to ward off the chill, it was autumn at home now, it was still warm, but the air had a bite. I inspected myself in the mirror.

My hair had grown a bit longer and thanks to the same hormones I mostly cursed, it was full and shiny. That was the only thing I had of the so-called pregnancy glow. Due to constant morning sickness, which had barely let up, my face looked sallow. The makeup which usually covered the dark circles under my eyes was absent, so my lack of sleep was obvious. The worst thing was my eyes. They were empty. I tried as hard as I could to plaster on a fake smile, to seem like I was healing, hell, sometimes happy. But I couldn't hide the dead that was staring back at me, the life that was gone from my eyes. It took all of my effort just to get out of bed every morning, to act like every breath I took wasn't agony.

I could try and tell myself it was all from losing...him. But I would be lying. The person that held some of my light, the person that maybe had a shot of putting it back in my eyes, was on the other side of the world. I hadn't spoken to him since that day outside the hospital. Not for his lack of trying, he called daily. Multiple times, never mind the time difference.

I wondered if he ever slept. I didn't answer the phone anymore. I was a coward and let Amy or my parents do it. I couldn't hear his voice. I knew he was upset. Upset was maybe too light of a word. I had heard him screaming through the phone at Amy one day, demanding to speak to me.

"You calm down right now, biker boy, or I'm disconnecting this number and making sure no one will speak to your cheating ass. The only reason we don't all hang up on you is because Lacey has us all convinced you have a right to know about your kid. But you keep talking to me like that and I'll face Lacey's wrath and never let you speak to anyone here again. Comprende?"

I let that conversation bounce off me, not letting it sink in. Like I did with most things that threatened my mental shield. The only reason why he wasn't here right now was because of something to do with his record and New Zealand's policy with people with convictions. Someone kept delaying the legal proceedings that he needed to go through to get into the country, which I was grateful for. Or told myself I was grateful for. I couldn't admit to myself that I was yearning for him, craving him like a drug.

He must've felt the same because after a phone call with him, my dad had hung up and said, "I wouldn't be surprised if that boy sprouted wings and flew himself down here." I pretended not to hear the grudging respect that crept into his tone.

So here I was, the Queen of Denial, my hold on the title was shaky, but I refused to let it go. I heard a soft knock on my door before it opened slightly.

"Can I come in, Mouse?" Dad asked.

"Yeah, Dad," I replied, sighing and walking out of my closet.

He stood in the middle of my room, staring at one of the pictures I was forbidden to look at. The look in his eyes couldn't be described as merely sad. More like anguished, ruined, destroyed. It quickly flickered away and his strong Dad mask settled back in, he looked me up and down, smiling.

"Didn't think you'd ever get prettier, darling, but with my grandbaby inside you, you are magnificent."

My eyes prickled. "Thanks, Daddy."

"Now I know you won't talk to me about before—"

"Please, Dad," I begged, not wanting someone else trying to force me to talk. Dad had let me be so far.

"No, I won't say anything, you'll talk when you're ready, sweet girl. But sit with me a sec." He sat himself down on my sleigh bed, patting the flowered duvet beside him. I paused for a moment before I sat down next to him.

"You know how happy I am to become a grandpa," he started carefully and I tensed.

"Don't get defensive yet, Gwen. I can't wait to meet that little baby. I know that he or she is going to have so much love surrounding it, it's going to be a lucky kid." He paused and I waited for it. "But that kid also needs its father. Nothing can replace a father's love, I'm telling you that from experience." His eyes twinkled. "I know there are some problems with you and this Cade fella. I ain't going to try and give an opinion on your private relationship, that's between the two of you. Problem is, it's not just the two of you anymore."

He gazed pointedly at my stomach before continuing.

"Now, when that boy isn't yelling down the phone, I get the impression he cares a great deal about you and that baby. Hell, I think you are what tethers him to this earth. I say this 'cause I know how that feels. 'Cause I feel that bout your mother, you," his voice cracked, "and your brother. I can't say I'm too happy about the fact that the reason he's not here is due to problems with the law. I can't judge the man based purely off that, though. I know little about the man, but what I do know is he loves my baby girl and is desperate to see you, hear your voice. I also know that your brother approved of him. The last time I spoke to him, I was not feelin' the love towards your new man, was so worried I thought about hopping on a plane. Your brother stopped me, I trusted his judgment." He cleared his throat, "So maybe consider picking up the phone, I know you might need to talk to him just about as much as he needs you."

I opened my mouth to argue, but I knew my argument was weak, so I closed it again.

"I support you in anything you do, honey. I've said my piece. What I want more than anything is my baby girl happy. Which I know you ain't now," he finished softly.

"I don't know if I can ever be happy again, Daddy," I declared my biggest fear brokenly.

Dad stroked my face then put his hand on my belly. "Oh my little mouse, I know you can. You just gotta let yourself." He kissed my head then left me sitting there, his words hanging in the air.

I lay in bed later that night, full as I could be with food my mum had cooked. Full with the love for the company I shared my table with tonight, full with my child. But somehow, I still had a gaping hole, right there in my soul. I was afraid it might never be mended, I might always be broken, empty. Only half enjoying company, only half tasting the food that I ate, feeling guilty every time I smiled.

There was no guarantee that Cade could repair my hole, fill me back up, but I knew he would die trying. I looked at my phone display, the name staring back at me. Two months was a long time to think, the more I thought about that awful day the more things didn't add up. When I had walked into Cade's room, he hadn't seem panicked, glancing at the bathroom door like any half intelligent man would. He had been happy, ecstatic when he learned of the baby, I remembered the unhidden joy on his face. It was not the face of a man who knew he had a whore in the bathroom, no matter the words that had been said the night before, I knew he wouldn't cheat.

Maybe I was kidding myself, the scene had been damning, maybe I was grasping at emotional straws. But maybe I was right. Maybe Dad was right. I already loved my baby with as much of my broken heart as I could. Who was I to deny it the love of its father? I took a deep breath, and put my thumb to the name on the screen.

"Well, Gwen, I have to say I'm glad you have your appetite back." My mother informed me with a smile.

I let out an unladylike snort as I shoveled my second plate of eggs into my mouth. She was right, suddenly I was eating like a pubescent boy. I made my father drive half an hour to the closest dairy last night to get me a banana milkshake. And pickles.

It was two days after our little chat. I had called Cade. Only to have it go straight to voicemail, I chickened out on leaving a message, deciding on picking up the phone the next time he rang. But after being stuck on the phone multiple times with every single person in my family and all of my mother's nosy friends, I hadn't heard from him. I was worried. But I was too scared to call him again. So I ate.

"I am too, my sunshine," Dad chipped in putting his arms around my mother and kissing her head.

"But I will say, I don't know if the chickens will lay quickly enough to keep her in eggs, we may need to buy some more." He grinned at me, I swallowed my mouthful, poking my tongue out at him.

"Well, you may as well buy a milkshake machine too, Daddy," I said sweetly, giving him a wink.

Amy sauntered into the room looking a million bucks like usual. Her hair was swept up in a ponytail, she wore white jeans and a camel-colored cashmere sweater. Not exactly country appropriate, but at least the heels on her boots were thick.

She had lost some serious weight, I couldn't help worry. Her curves were disappearing and her cheekbones sallow. I wasn't one to talk, but I hoped my eating habits might inspire hers. My hope flared when she scooped some eggs onto her plate followed by a healthy dose of bacon.

"Morning, family," Amy declared, smiling at my parents, then bending down to pat my stomach. "Morning, Supe."

She smirked as I rolled my eyes at the nickname for my bun. She barely had two bites when her phone rang, she glanced down at it before standing. "Excuse me, gotta take this, it's Rosie, about the store." She quickly walked out of the room before answering.

Guilt blossomed in my stomach. I felt terrible for leaving the girls' in the lurch with my store. I hadn't really talked to anyone. I was too afraid Cade would hijack the call. So Amy had taken care of what needed to be taken care of. Rosie was a star, dealing with everything from the orders to the payroll. I owed her big time.

Not to mention I had dragged Amy halfway across the world and not mentioned a return date. She could have gone home with Ry and Alex, who flew over for the funeral and stayed for a week after. I could tell she was reluctant to leave, to face the reality of getting on with life, but I did know I had to figure it out and soon. I didn't have long before I wouldn't be able to make the twelve-hour flight until after the baby was born. And even after, I didn't want to be *that* mother with the screaming baby on the plane.

A small part of me wanted to stay here, at my home in the country, my quiet retreat where I felt safe and comfortable. But it was also where memories of my brother lurked around every corner, and Cade did not. I contemplated this all over my plate of eggs before I sighed and cleaned up. I took my jacket and boots from beside the door, turning to my parents.

"I'm going for a walk, I need some fresh air."

"Okay well, take Gunner with you. That fat dog needs some exercise."

I looked at my father. "As if he would let me go anywhere without him." My point was proven when an excited but over-weight Lab bounded through the door I had just opened. "See you in a bit."

I strolled around my childhood home, admiring it as I moved further away. It was big, but not obscene. Two storied, with a porch wrapping around the entire back and steps leading down into a huge garden. Huge pillars held up the balcony, which jutted off the upstairs living room, the backdrop of the Southern mountain ranges our backyard.

I left it behind and let my feet take me to my place, *our* place.

Gunner was puffing beside me but happily smiling up at me. Ian used to argue that dogs couldn't smile, but I disagreed, we had a perpetually happy Lab.

I marveled at the amber and orange hues that decorated the trees, and the leaves that crunched under my feet. I loved my home in autumn, it felt like a new beginning. I made it up the gentle slope, not liking to admit my panting sounded dangerously close to Gunner's.

I patted my stomach.

"This is your fault, Bun, I used to be in great shape. I swear, if you make my ankles swell I'm giving you a baby mullet."

I reached the top, ambling over to a swing hanging from a huge old oak tree, its leaves shimmering gold. I sat down on the swing, moving back and forward, casting my eyes upon the rolling hills of home. This was our place. Mine and Ian's. He built this swing when I was eight for me to play on, and then it became a place for me to escape in my teenage years. Cry away heartbreak, run from my parents after yet another grounding, or to dream about starting my life in New York. Ian would promise me nothing bad could happen up here. A single solitary tear escaped my eye. I sat in silence for a long while.

"You lied, Ian. Bad things can happen here. They did happen. You're gone. You left me. I'm so *angry* with you. How could you leave us? How can I handle all of this without my big brother? You're never going to meet my baby. Never going to make any of your own, I'm never going to see you again. It hurts so much, I feel like I'm going to be like this forever. Am I ever going to be happy again?" I pleaded against the wind, the breeze carrying my words.

I laid my head against the swing, wishing for the millionth time that I could travel back in time.

"I can promise you that you are going to be happy again, Gwen, no matter what it takes."

I froze, standing to turn towards the source of the deep voice, I couldn't believe it. I must be hallucinating. Cade was standing in front of me, eyes glued to mine. His hands were in his pockets and I let my gaze roam over every inch of him. His hair had grown longer, kissing his shoulders roughly. Half of his face was covered by a substantial beard, much more than the couple of day's growth I had been used to.

His eyes were glittering with emotion, locked on me, drinking me in. He looked ... wild. He was wearing all black, not surprisingly. A black thermal, his black leather jacket, which I was surprised to see was not his cut. Black jeans on his legs and his motorcycle boots. He was bigger than I remembered, two months and he had more muscle, if that was possible. He also looked ... ravaged.

I barely suppressed a flinch, seeing my strong man looking unraveled like that pained me. I gaped at him in silence, frozen, unable to move, to speak. I didn't know what to say, to do. I was too scared that he might not be real. His eyes moved down from my eyes to my stomach, the dress I was wearing was pre baby. It was a light pink knit and long sleeved, made from a tight jersey material, straining over my bump.

His face changed, softening, even under his harsh features, I didn't have much time to contemplate this, as he advanced on me in a few quick strides. He surprised me by kneeling in front of me, his hands spanned my belly, and he rested his head against it for a moment, then softly kissed me on top of the fabric. He stayed like that for a while then stood, pulling my forehead to touch his, grey eyes searing into mine.

"Gwen. You, round with my baby, it's the most beautiful thing I have ever seen. *You* are the most beautiful thing I have ever seen." His voice was rough, full of emotion.

I gazed into the eyes of the man I loved, unable to form words. The words to tell him how much I missed him, how it had felt like a physical pain to try and struggle through every day without him, how I wished he had been here to watch our baby grow.

"I'm so sorry I took so long to get here, baby. I've been thinking of you every day, every second. It's been killing me not seeing you, hearing your voice. Knowing you were in pain, knowing every day you were changing, our baby growing inside you. You don't know the amount of times I considered chartering a fucking jet to get to you." His eyes searched my face. "It nearly shattered me, talking to your family, not being able to hear your voice, not being able to touch you, not being able to see your beautiful face." His hand moved to cradle my belly. "Not being able to experience every second of our child growing inside you, that has been pure torture. I spent hours staring at that fucking picture you left on my refrigerator, staring at my baby."

His face was tortured and soft at the same time, his gaze was so full of emotion I couldn't process it all.

"Say something please, Gwen," he pleaded.

I couldn't. There was nothing I could say without letting myself shatter. So I pressed my mouth to his, needing to feel our physical connection. He took over the second my mouth touched his, probing my mouth, sliding his tongue along the seam.

I yielded to him, letting him inside clinging to him for dear life. The kiss went wild, savage. I ran my hands through his long hair, needing to touch more of him. His hands left a trail of fire over my belly, up to my breasts, squeezing them tightly. I cried out, surprised at how sensitive they were. He stopped instantly.

"Did I hurt you?" He loosened his hold on me a fraction, his eyes searching mine, full of concern.

I shook my head. "The opposite. You're the only person that can heal me," I whispered.

And that was it. My shield shattered into a thousand pieces and I collapsed against him. All the pain that had been coiled so tightly stretched to every part of me, and I sobbed into his jacket, barely noticing his arms wrap around me, hands stroking my hair.

I don't know how long we stayed like that. I clung to him for dear life, reveling in the strength he represented. I sniffled against him as he wiped the last of my tears from my face and kissed my head.

"Everything is going to be okay, Gwen." His voice was so strong, so sure, I actually believed him.

━━

I stood in front of the mirror in my bra and panties, rubbing the cream on my stomach that promised to reduce stretch marks. It'd bloody better. I had had the stuff flown over from France, I *really* didn't want stretch marks.

After Cade had found me and I had cried every tear in my body, we had slowly walked back to the house. He never let me go even for a second, as though he thought I would float away. When we got to the house, I was surprised to find I had more tears to shed with my family.

It was exhausting, painful beyond belief, but it helped. Not a lot, but a little. I still felt like I was bleeding from the inside out, but the pain lessened a bit, or maybe I became stronger. Either way, we gave Cade the tour, avoiding Ian's old room like the plague. I was surprised to find that his bags had been deposited in my room without a word from my father. He had always been strict and unbendable about that certain rule. Later on in the night after a beer or two, he had proclaimed, "The jig's up, Mouse, you're pregnant, can't see him staying in your room's gonna change that much."

My face flamed, and Amy had snorted with laughter. I froze and watched her, it was the first time she had laughed since it happened. My mother and father must've noticed as well, but they were better at hiding their reactions.

Even with the undercurrent of sorrow that seemed ever present at the table these days, it had been nice. Cade and my father got on like a house on fire, although I suspect Cade may have had words with my father before searching for me. My mother, of course, adored him from the get go.

I was worried he might've been overwhelmed, but he seemed completely comfortable, although his hand was still clutching mine, even though he could only eat with one hand. This was the case for me too, but I could barely nibble, so much was going through my brain. He noticed this and immediately let me go.

"Eat please, babe. I know our baby is getting big and strong, but you need more meat on your bones," he told me softly.

I nodded, he clasped my hand again and brought it to his mouth, kissing it softly before setting it down on the table, allowing me to pick up a knife and fork.

I put a couple bites in my mouth before I realized the table was silent. My mouth full I looked up to find everyone staring at Cade and me. My Mum's eyes were full with tears, my father's were on Cade, full of respect. Amy's were full of happiness and something else.

"What?" I demanded through my food.

My mother's eyes instantly narrowed. "Gwen, don't talk with your mouth full, Cade will think we're savages," she scolded.

I almost choked on my food at this ridiculous remark, managing to swallow without needing the Heimlich. Cade smirked at me out of the corner of his mouth.

I noticed movement out of the corner of my eye, Cade leaned against the door, his eyes glowing. I didn't move my eyes from his, but I felt shy under his gaze. I grabbed my robe to cover up.

"Don't," he commanded, his voice barely above a growl.

He slowly walked towards me, eyes devouring me. I shivered as he approached. He stood in front of me and slowly rubbed his hand against my belly, spreading the cream across its considerable expanse.

His eyes glued to my stomach, his voice was rough and soft at the same time. "What's this for?"

I swallowed, his hands sending tingles down to my toes. "It's for, um, stretch marks. So I don't look like a tiger when Bun comes out," I joked.

His eyes snapped to mine. "Any evidence you've carried my child is welcome to me." His voice was full of possession.

"Bun?" he asked after a beat, eyes locked on mine.

"Well, um, when I found out about the baby, Amy and I joked about a bun in my oven. Guess the name stuck with me." I was surprised that my voice was shaking, there seemed to be electricity crackling between us.

Cade got that unreadable look on his face again, gazing down at my stomach in awe. "Bun," he repeated softly.

"Amy calls her Supe because she thinks you have super sperm," I blurted.

Cade looked at me, face blank, then barked with laughter, then he stopped abruptly. "Her?" He continued his one syllable conversation.

I fiddled with my fingers, until he grasped them, I felt his gaze burning into mine and I lifted my eyes to meet his.

"Well, I don't know for sure, I never let the doctors tell me. It just didn't feel right, you know, without you," I stuttered over my words, feeling ridiculous for being so nervous, this was the father of my child for crissakes.

"I just have a feeling, it might be a she," I told him quietly.

His hands moved from mine, down to my hips, toying with the sides of my underwear. He growled slightly, then I was up. My legs automatically circled his waist as he carried me out of the bathroom to my bed, not showing any struggle at carrying my extra weight. He placed me down gently, slowly peeling off my underwear, kissing my legs on the way down. Butterflies fluttered in my stomach as his touch set me on fire.

He slowly worked his way back up, stopping at the crease in my thighs, inhaling like it was his first breath in months then continued up. My breath came in pants as he kissed every inch of my stomach, worshiping me. He made it to my breasts, fingers making short work on the front clasp, when I was exposed to him, he let out a hiss.

"Sooo pregnancy makes your boobs grow, who knew?" I told him breathlessly.

His gaze ignited me, hands cupping my newly sensitive breasts. I moaned as his lips closed over my nipple, the sensation nearly unbearable. I was teetering on the edge, barely able to breathe as he pushed me over when his hand moved down to my clit.

I let out a soundless scream as my orgasm washed over me. It seemed like hours later that I came down. Cade's eyes were glued to my face, his own dark with desire.

"You are the most magnificent creature I have ever seen," he declared roughly, his tone riddled with desire, his eyes almost black.

I slowly regained coherent thought and realized he was still dressed, I sat up slowly. "You. Naked. Now," I commanded, breathing heavily.

Cade smiled wickedly and stood, divesting himself of his clothes in record time. He knelt before me, pulling me gently to the edge of the bed, spreading my legs. "I need to taste you so badly, baby." His face disappeared between my legs and I suppressed a scream as he devoured me like a starving man. Riding my second orgasm, I vaguely noticed Cade's body on top of mine.

"I need you inside me more than I need to breathe," I whispered to him.

His hands framed my face, kissing me tenderly as he pushed inside me, he let out a grunt of pleasure as he filled me to the hilt. I opened my eyes.

"I love you."

His eyes were fierce. "I love you too, my soul, baby."

I woke suddenly, terrified it was all a dream, that I was still alone and broken. Cade's arms tightened around me, his face close to mine in an instant.

"What is it, Gwen? Are you okay? The baby?" His hands moved to my stomach.

I let out a breath of relief, kissing him lightly. "She's fine. I just had the most terrible feeling I dreamed you. That you weren't really here, it scared me."

Cade leaned over and switched on the light. I squinted for a second, my eye's adjusting.

"Can't have this conversation in the dark, Gwen," he explained softly.

I nodded against his chest. I heard him take a deep breath, preparing for something.

"The day. That morning, what you saw before you found out about Ian," he began.

I felt nausea at the pit of my stomach. I hadn't forgotten about what had happened since he'd arrived, just buried it. He sensed my tension and grabbed my chin, eyes blazing.

"I didn't touch her, Gwen. You need to know that. I hate to bring her filth into our bed, but this needs to be said, I don't want its poison to sit in your mind."

He paused and kissed my nose tenderly before watching me. He must have been content with what he saw, so he continued.

"After our fight I was pissed. Pissed with you, pissed with myself. I was angry with you because you were right. I don't regret that he's dead, especially when we're going to have a little girl, I don't want her walking the same earth as him."

His eyes blazed with protection for our unborn daughter. Something warm settled in my gut.

"But I know how you feel, what you meant. I want our child to be proud of me. I will protect you both with my last breath, won't let anything hurt you. But I won't let the taint of what I have done enter our house. Our family. I promise you that." His eyes were faraway for a moment. "Anyway, I got drunk. The club was having a party, but I stayed away and chose a bottle of Jack for company. I sat for hours, thinking of everything, wanting to go back to you, but I was too fucking proud. Baby, it has haunted my dreams for sixty-three days that I didn't go back to you, I'll never forgive myself. I dragged my sorry and drunk ass to bed. I did that alone, Gwen. I swear to you."

His face was right in front of mine, eyes not wavering. I believed him, with every inch of me, I believed him. I opened my mouth to tell him that, but he put his hand to my lips.

"Let me finish, baby. The next thing I know I was waking up to my beautiful girl telling me the best news I've ever heard and making me the happiest son of a bitch on earth. Then the whore skulked out from the bathroom. The look on your face, Gwen, I swear to God I'll never forget it. You broke. Right there in front of me. Later on, I found out the fuckin' slut walked in not long before you arrived. Bull told me. Saw her sneak in, drew the wrong conclusions. But she must've picked my tee off the floor, used the bathroom then stayed in there, chose her moment when you got there."

His words were laced with fury and I could tell even now, two months later his anger with still blazing.

"Never wanted to lay a hand on a woman so much in my entire life. I wanted to fucking kill the bitch," he spat.

"But you didn't." It wasn't a question. I knew he wouldn't.

"No. As much as I wanted to, I handed her over to Rosie and Evie instead." He smiled without humor.

I raised a brow but said nothing, I would so be ringing Rosie tomorrow.

Cade tightened his arms around me then kept going. "Then I saw you, baby, you collapsing in my arms, hearing you fall apart, thinking I was watching you lose our child." He shuddered. "Thought I had died and gone to Hell. Got a respite when I heard our baby's heartbeat for the first time. That was until I saw nothing on your face. Heard the lack of emotion in your voice. You are the most vibrant person I know and that just disappeared. *You* disappeared. You were a shell, Gwen. Scared the shit out of me. You leaving me outside that hospital damned near ruined me. Wanted to kill my brothers, myself. Anyone that was responsible for me not being by your fucking side when you put your brother in the ground." His words bit through me and the pain was so sharp it surprised me. I couldn't have this.

"Cade," I whispered softly, brokenly.

"No, baby. I will never forgive myself for the fact you had to do this without me, I couldn't be there to shield you, to protect you best I could. Watch you grow with my baby in you. It's all on me. And the decisions and the club that led me here."

"Stop," I commanded firmly. "Stop doing that, blaming yourself. The club. They're your family. And just like any family they have their downfalls, but no matter what, they love you. Things are going in a different direction now, right?"

Cade said nothing, just nodded stiffly.

"We can't change the past," I said quietly. "I would give *anything* to have that ability. But I can't. We just have to live every day in the present. I love you. I don't blame you for anything. You're the reason I'm not falling into a thousand little pieces right now, you're holding me together."

"You're the one doing that, babe. I'm in fuckin' awe of you." Cade's mouth covered mine and he was inside me the next moment. We didn't say another word for the rest of the night.

CHAPTER 19

I WAS HUMMING CONTENTEDLY the next morning, pouring pancake batter into the pan, sneaking glances at Cade, who was sipping coffee and reading the paper. It was such a domestic situation, one that I never saw myself in, but one that felt completely natural.

Gray eyes met mine. "Concentrate on the pancakes, Gwen. I don't want you burning yourself. Or my breakfast," he teased.

"Stop distracting me then," I snapped.

"I'm readin' the paper, how is that distracting?"

"You're just being all sexy and irresistible and it's distracting, okay?" I declared, my hormones telling me to jump him on my parent's kitchen table.

His eyes darkened as he read the desire in mine.

"Pregnant and barefoot in the kitchen, Gwen? I'd never thought I'd see the day." Amy walked into the kitchen, poured herself a cup of coffee, smirking between Cade and I.

"You watch your mouth if you want pancakes, Abrams." I pointed my spatula at her warningly as she walked over to me, putting a cup of the sweet, sweet nectar into my free hand. I brought it up to my face and Cade's angry voice stopped me.

"You're not allowed coffee, Gwen!" he growled, looking as if he was going to waltz up and snatch my precious away from me.

I cradled it protectively to my chest. "I know." I glared at him until I was sure he was staying put. "I just like to smell it."

I took a huge inhale and let the scent dance into my nostrils before Amy snatched the cup away from me and sat at the table.

"Seriously, Mouse, I don't know why you torture yourself with that every morning. You can be a weird kid sometimes. Just drink decaf if you're that addicted to the stuff." Dad entered the room smiling, kissing me on the forehead.

"I'll drink decaf when you drink non-alcoholic beer," I told him, turning back to my pancakes.

"The day I drink that horseshit is the day Hell freezes over," my father proclaimed with ferocity, before pouring his own coffee, as if to taunt me.

"Decaf," I muttered to the pan in disgust.

I flipped a pancake onto a plate and was preparing to pour another one when I felt it. I grabbed my stomach, the glass jug slipped from my hands and shattered on the floor. Cade was by my side in a second, Dad was on his feet, phone in hand. I was impressed with their reflexes.

"What's wrong, Gwen?" Cade looked terrified with his eyes glued to my stomach.

"I'm calling the doctor," Dad declared.

I smiled, catching them both off guard. "I'm fine, both of you calm down. Dad, hang up the phone." I grasped Cade's hand and put it over my belly. His eyes widened. "She just caught me by surprise that's all," I said softly, relishing the feeling of my baby kicking at Cade's hand.

Cade seemed hypnotized for a second, then he shook his

head, he didn't move his hand from my belly, but he put the other under my legs and carried me to the table.

"I don't want you cutting yourself," he explained, a twinkle in his eye. I knew he was remembering back to a time not so different than this, apart from the fact I was carrying his spawn now.

Our moment was broken when Dad and Amy rushed over.

"Supe's kicking, let me feel!" Amy demanded placing her hand beside Cade's.

"Gotta know if my grandkid's gonna be an All Black." Dad put his hand there too.

Three heads looked up at me smirking before they released their hands, well actually, two did. One very masculine, tattooed hand stayed sprawled over my swollen belly. I covered it with my own, looking into the gray eyes of my man, his expression sending a warm feeling to my toes. We stayed like that, staring at each other silently, enforcing a bond that would keep us connected forever. The little person inside me that we both created out of love, the baby that would forever be ours and would be loved by countless people. Cade framed my face and pressed a firm but chaste kiss on my lips.

My father, bless him, broke the moment. "What are you two lovebirds up to today?" he asked, his tone light and happy.

Not that fake cheerfulness that he had been putting on for two months, protecting his girls from the depths of his grief, being strong for us. No, this was genuine, the warm feeling continued to sneak its way into my heart, then I did something I hadn't genuinely done for two months. I smiled.

"Well, father, I thought I could show Cade around town, then go for a drive up to Malcolm's Peak." I informed him, turning to Cade, I continued. "Let's see how you handle New Zealand life, my hunky American."

"Nice meeting you, Cade, you're not a bad bloke...for a Yank. You take care of this girl," Gray barked at Cade gruffly, giving him a firm handshake.

His eyes softened towards me and then to my belly.

"This baby comes home with an accent, we got problems." He roughly kissed my head then sauntered off to his table.

I giggled and looked over to Cade, who just shook his head and took a pull of his beer.

It had been an eventful day, showing Cade "around town" didn't take long, considering our town consisted of one main street, a handful of shops and three cafes. That didn't mean we weren't busy.

We stopped off for a coffee, and as was per usual in a small town such as ours, we bumped into a thousand people I knew. This normally didn't bother me too much, considering I didn't make it home often and I genuinely liked most of the people. But this was one of the first times I had been out and about since the funeral. I hated the sympathetic glances, the hand squeezing, the "how are you holding ups?" everyone meant well, but it was suffocating.

Thankfully, I had a hunky biker, who distracted most of the well-meaning locals away from their pity party and into a full-scale interrogation, with some overly friendly arm touches and eye fucking from the younger, female generation. I had narrowed my eyes at this and stuck my belly out, rubbing it in front of them, communicating that I was *pregnant with his child*.

Some people.

Thankfully, we escaped unscathed and spent the rest of the day driving around the countryside, even Cade's usual hard exterior cracked taking in the beauty of home. I could tell he liked "Malcolm's Peak", considering he stood taking in the view of our little valley silently for a good five minutes before jumping me and making love to me on the bonnet of my dad's truck. It was amazing. Apart from the fact I was slightly worried my fat pregnant ass would make a huge dint that would be hard to explain.

After those activities, I figured Cade would be thirsty, so I took him to our local pub. On arrival we were swamped down with greetings, hugs – for me – and firm handshakes and back slaps – for Cade. The reception was slightly different from that of the café, as the patrons here tended to be old, gruff farmers and laborers who didn't drool all over my drool worthy man and hand out condolences. Instead, they gave Cade wary looks, glancing at his attire and tattoos with speculation, and more than a little protectiveness.

A lot of these men knew and respected not only my father but also my...Ian. Which meant they took it upon themselves to be secondary protectors of my honor. Sweet, but also annoying. Especially when you're fifteen and hanging out at the only twenty-four hour fast food joint at three in the morning, more than a little tipsy, and one of the men happen upon you then take it upon themselves to drag you home.

But when I was twenty-five, knocked up and devastated from loss, I found it comforting. I was worried for a split second that they would take him outside and try and rough him up a little, considering they all knew he had been MIA for two months. But thankfully, they didn't.

Another thing that I was thankful for, was the fact they didn't treat me like some victim of loss that needed to be handled like glass. They shot the shit, some giving Cade withering looks, most giving him shit –that he took remarkably well – and then they raised a glass, "To the best brother, son, and rugby forward we knew." I choked up a bit on that one, but raised my lemonade and bit back the tears.

"Anyone else going to approach the table trying to kill me

with a scowl then try and crush my bones with a handshake?"
Cade asked evenly.

"Oh probably, it's not even happy hour yet," I told him
sweetly.

He smirked, rubbing his hand on my thigh. "I like this for
you, baby. That you got so many people who obviously care about
you, respect you, got your back. It's special, this whole damned
place is spectacular."

I scrutinized the pub with fake interest, taking in the dated
stools and tables, the slightly stained carpet and the faded yellow
paint.

"Well, spectacular isn't the word I'd use for this particular
establishment, I'm glad you like it all the same."

Cade grinned outright, and what a sight to behold that was.
"Fuck, I've missed your smart mouth." His hand moved from my
thigh to brush my belly lightly. "This town, this country. It's
freaking amazing, babe. I see how you love it so much." He
regarded me like there was something else moving in his mind.

I didn't have time to ask him what because hurricane Amy
strolled through the door. Conversation stopped and every head
turned to look at my best friend. Granted, in a small-town pub in
New Zealand, strangers stuck out like a sore thumb.

But this was something else, a drop dead gorgeous girl like
Amy strolling into this place was like a fish jumping out of water
and walking around on two legs. It also didn't help she was
dressed like she was about to head off to a five star dinner, not
indulge in some hearty, honest, pub food.

Her long red hair tumbled over her shoulders, a mass of curls.
She had on a gray, long sleeved knit dress that went down to her
ankles and had huge slits up both sides, it was skintight, not
leaving much to the imagination. She wore modest – for her –
heeled ankle boots and a camel-colored draped leather jacket.

Definitely not the jeans and thermals most other women in

here were wearing. Well, except for me. I was wearing leather leggings, a cashmere charcoal sweater, and knee-high boots. Everyone around here had accepted my inability to wear the local uniform years ago, but they hadn't seen the likes of Amy. She was joined by my parents, who spotted us and waved. My father went off to the bar, no doubt to get drinks, but was deep in back slaps and man hugs before getting anywhere near. Mum spotted a couple of friends and waved Amy on.

"Sup, skank, biker dude, Supe." Amy patted my tummy, sitting herself beside me.

"Hey, whore," I replied.

Cade did a chin lift, grinning.

"This your local watering hole before you started sipping cosmos in the land of velvet ropes?" Amy asked, taking in our surroundings, winking at some of the men still staring.

I snorted. "You could say that, though I could count the times I've gotten drunk here on one hand. I was usually out looking for trouble, not staying in the one place I couldn't find it. Not with all these guys around anyway." I smirked. "Although, there was one night I did beat them all in a skulling competition." I spoke a little louder, just so my neighbors could hear.

"You hustled us, girl, which means you didn't win anything, you forfeit on account of deceit," Bluey, one of the losers of that night exclaimed passionately.

"We agreed we do not speak of that night," Louie scowled at me before turning to contemplate his beer.

"I'll take you on right now, rematch, little girl." Seventy-five-year-old Elliot declared, standing from his stool raising his beer.

I pointed down to my stomach, "Not really in the position to chug beers, on account of the little human growing inside me."

"Humph excuses, excuses." Elliot rolled his eyes at me before rejoining the men, a couple glaring in my direction. I blew them all kisses, turning back to Cade and Amy.

"It's still a sensitive subject," I explained.

"How long ago did this happen?" Amy asked grinning.

"Oh about six years ago," I deadpanned and Amy burst out laughing.

Cade just gave me a look before he pulled me in for a kiss.

"Looks like you've been holding out on me and the boys, Gwen," Cade whispered, eyes twinkling.

"Oh, just you wait, biker boy, I'll whip all your asses once I get this little sucker out," I told him, deciding it was time to put some of those cocky assholes in their place.

I waited for Amy and Cade to laugh, or even smile. It was a joke, I thought I was pretty funny, but their faces turned serious and I was met with silence. I felt like Ben Stiller doing stand up.

Cade cleared his throat, an intense expression on his face. "You planning on coming home to Amber then, Gwen?" he asked softly.

Realization dawned. My offhand comment had given these guys a much-needed clue as to my plans for the future. Was I going back to Amber? This place, this town was my home, it always would be. It held a huge chunk of my heart, contained people who I loved, respected, grew up with. It had been an amazing place to grow up, somewhere where I had no worries, the horrors and reality of the world outside rarely touched me here.

I had always thought I would eventually come back here and raise a family. But in my mind that was always someday. It was way in the future, an undedicated date I had given little thought to. A twenty-something girl living a glamorous lifestyle in New York barely thinks of the future, apart from wondering about Louis Vuitton's next handbag collection.

But this was now. Not someday, vaguely in the future, and I had a lot of other people to consider in this decision, not just myself. As much as the idea of staying here, where nothing ever changed, or would change, appealed to me, I knew I couldn't. I couldn't stay in the place where every day I would have to drive down the road where Ian and I would have four-wheeler races, drink in the pub he bought me my first legal beer, take my child to the school where he and I had gone. It would shatter me.

"Yeah," I replied quietly. "I'm coming home."

I woke up for the second morning to be encased in Cade's arms, my back snug to his chest, his arm protectively cradling my belly.

I instantly felt it.

Different. For the first time in two months, I didn't feel like a thousand-pound weight was pressing down on my chest, making me almost physically unable to get out of bed, to face the day. I felt happy. Then I felt guilt. So strong it washed over me like nausea, settling in my stomach. A tear rolled down my cheek and I held my body taught trying to stop myself from shaking with silent sobs.

Cade's arms tightened around me. "Gwen? What is it? Are you okay?"

He flipped me on my back, hovering above me, worried eyes searching my face. I looked at him a beat then burst into tears. He sat back on the bed pulling me into his arms, I buried my face into his shoulder and tried to stop, but the tears kept coming. Cade rubbed my back.

"It's okay, baby."

I didn't say anything for a while, my emotions churned through me, rendering me speechless. How could I talk if I didn't even know what I was feeling?

Cade pulled me back slightly, to meet my no doubt tear stained eyes.

"Want to talk about it?" he asked softly.

I bit my lip. My silence, my denial had been the only thing keeping me together the past two months.

"I woke up, with you, after last night having such an amazing day with you, and a night with my friends and family. I woke up and I was happy." I hiccupped. "But how can I be happy? My brother's dead. His life is over. I'll never see him again, and now I feel so guilty for being happy because he's *gone*." My voice broke on the last word. "I've been trying so hard to be strong, for Mum, for Amy, for Dad, and for the baby." My breath caught, I tried to calm myself.

Cade yanked me up so I was straddling him, his hands framing my face.

"You don't need to be strong, baby. I've got you. I'm going to take care of you and our Bun." One of his hands moved to my stomach. "You're going to be happy and you aren't going to feel guilty about it, because one day you're going to realize all your brother wanted in this world was for you to be safe and happy, and he wouldn't want you stopping living your life because you were clinging onto his."

His gray eyes searched mine, he looked strong, determined, like he would do anything for me.

"I love you so much," I whispered.

"Love you too, baby." His hand pulled me down to his mouth and he slowly kissed me, hands running up to my breasts, caressing them.

I moaned, deepening our kiss, craving him, needing our connection. He roughly squeezed my nipple, sending a rush of heat between my legs. I rubbed myself against his growing erection, both of us already naked. His hand moved between us to my clit. I gripped his shoulders hard as his circled it with his thumb.

"Cade," I whimpered.

"Come for me, baby," he growled, eyes never leaving mine.

I cried out as my orgasm rushed over me. Cade didn't let it

stop as he thrust in from underneath me while I was riding the last wave. He grabbed my neck pulling our foreheads together. His mouth met mine for a frenzied kiss before he moved to my nipple, sucking it. The sensation shot through my sensitized breasts and I shuddered.

"You're going to come again, Gwen," Cade commanded roughly.

I didn't answer, but I felt myself building, Cade clutched my hips pounding into me hard and deep. I managed to stifle a scream as I came, feeling myself clenching around him milking his release. I collapsed on top of him, rather clumsily, with my belly between us.

Cade lifted me off him, tucking me into his side, pulling my leg over his body. I felt him dripping from between my legs. So could he, because he slipped his hand down there, I shuddered, still feeling sensitive.

"My cum dripping from your pussy, my baby in your belly, fucking perfect," he grunted, bringing his fingers to my lips.

I opened my mouth and sucked, tasting our combined fluids.

Cade claimed my mouth. "Still the hottest piece I've ever had. I'm the luckiest son of a bitch in the world."

I rested my chin on his shoulder. "You won't be saying that when I'm in my third trimester, when I'm fat with swollen feet and a screaming bitch because I can't fit into heels," I told him seriously.

"You won't be fat, you're fuckin' pregnant and beautiful. And I'll just have to find a way to keep your mind off your feet," he declared, rubbing my breasts thoughtfully.

"Well, right now my mind is on food. Bacon in particular, with banana and maple syrup."

He laughed and I laughed too. Not letting myself feel guilty. Letting myself live.

Half an hour and a shower later, I was happily munching on my plate of deliciousness, my breakdown a distant memory. Cade sitting beside me, chomping on some eggs, helped a lot.

"Sweetheart, are you sure you want to eat *that* for breakfast? That baby needs some nutrients," my mother asked me, entering the kitchen. She looked down at my plate with a raised eyebrow.

"Banana is full of potassium, Mum," I declared.

"And what is bacon and maple syrup full of?" she countered, setting a green tea beside me.

"Happiness," I said without missing a beat.

Cade chuckled beside me and Mum shook her head with a smile.

"Where are Dad and Amy?" I asked between mouthfuls.

It was after ten and Amy was usually down here inhaling her eighth cup of coffee by now. My father could be anywhere, considering he was up at six.

"Your father, believe it or not, is teaching Amy how to ride a quad bike."

My mouth dropped open, luckily I had swallowed my food already.

"No way?" I pushed my chair back, my breakfast forgotten. "I've gotta see this!"

"They're out at the back paddock, you want to take the truck?" Mum smiled. I was guessing she'd already seen the spectacle.

I grabbed my jacket, slipping on some gumboots, Pink Hunter boots, mind you.

"No, I'll just take a bike." I glanced at Cade, who, up until now, had been smirking into his breakfast, now he was glaring at me.

I gestured the universal "come on" at him. "Hurry up, don't you want to see this? We've got two more bikes in the shed."

I yanked up my second boot and straightened, opening the door. Moving at his usual macho speed of light, Cade was beside me, blocking my way, arms crossed. Now it was my turn to frown.

"What you doing, big man? Put your boots on or I'm leaving without you." I was already figuring out tactics to get around him.

"You're not going anywhere on a fuckin' bike," he declared.

I paused, mid tickling strategy. "What are you talking about? It's the quickest way to get up there."

"Jesus Christ, Gwen, you're almost five months pregnant you aren't getting on a four wheeler," Cade all but exploded.

"Yeah, I've noticed, considering my belly's grown a bit. Its not like I'm hopping on a dirt bike to go trail riding. It's a four wheeler and it's pretty much straight flat to get to the paddock," I told him impatiently.

"It's not safe," he bit out through gritted teeth.

"It's no less safe than driving in a car, I've been on four wheelers since I was a kid, Cade. I know what I'm doing." I glared at him. "Mum, a little help here, tell him," I whined, looking over to the woman that should have be sticking up for me, given she birthed me, but the kitchen was empty. "That witch, she got out of here as soon as this started. My own mother," I muttered, disgusted.

I tried to push at Cade's rock hard abs while trying not to run my hands under his t-shirt and forget about the whole thing. What was I angry about again?

"For fuck's sake, Gwen, you're arguing about our child's safety here, just take the fucking truck." His voice was a near yell.

Oh yeah that's why. "Our child is not in any danger. I'm not an idiot, I don't go more than thirty and stick to the even terrain. And Dad or Mum are usually always with me," I told him defensively.

"What?" His voice turned dangerously quiet.

Oh shit. Maybe I shouldn't have alluded to the fact I had already been doing this for months.

"You're not telling me you've been riding on one the entire time?"

I wouldn't have been surprised if steam came out his ears.

"Well, I don't have my magic carpet to safely fly me around, so it's my only means of transportation," I shot at him sarcastically.

"Don't get cute," he warned. "What if something had happened to you?"

"It didn't."

"What if it fucking did?" he bellowed. "Do you have any idea how I would cope if something happened to either of you?"

I didn't answer because I was guessing it was a rhetorical question.

"I'd be fucking ruined! The thought of you crashing." He visibly shuddered.

I started to feel a bit bad, reaching up to stroke his arm. "Nothing happened and nothing will. I'm not risking Bun. Dad even makes me wear a helmet." I scrunched my nose up.

"I'm serious, Gwen. Just take the truck, please." His voice was more even now, but still rough with worry and anger.

I let out an exaggerated sigh. "Fine. But hurry up. It doesn't take long to master the art of a four wheeler and I don't want to miss the swearing and tantrum throwing before she gets the hang of it." I tried to push past him but he grasped my hips.

"Thank you, baby." His voice was soft now, and any residual irritation I had been harboring for his over protectiveness melted away. "Oh and knowing you can handle a four wheeler? Hot as fuck." Cade's eyes roughly glazed over as he yanked me in for a rough kiss.

Turned out we did miss the swearing phase, because surprisingly, Amy was a natural. She rode around like a mad woman, skidding around corners with no fear, screaming with delight like a child, my dad laughing beside her. It sent a warm feeling through my bones to see them both happy again. But I couldn't help but pout like a child as I watched from beside Cade, unable to join in on the fun.

"I would be out there with her having fun if it wasn't for you," I whined.

Cade kissed my head. "I'm not apologizing, baby. Even if you weren't pregnant, I wouldn't want you out there with that crazy woman." He watched Amy with a frown.

I scowled at him. "I wasn't talking to you." I looked down at my stomach. "It's a good thing I love you, Bun, or else it would seriously be a baby mullet."

Apparently Bun had an opinion on my baby mullet plans because she chose that moment to kick furiously. I took Cade's hand and put it over the spot where she was playing soccer with my uterus. I watched as a soft look went over my hard biker's features, eyes wide in amazement.

"Second to being inside you, this is the best feeling in the world," he declared roughly.

I melted a little at that statement and rewarded Cade with a big smile. Something crossed over his features and his face turned serious. His hand went to his pocket, and to my amazement, he went down on one knee, revealing a box in his hand.

"Holy shit," I whispered. "Holy shit," I repeated this time nearly yelling when I saw the white gold, princess cut, huge diamond ring sitting in a telltale powder blue box.

"Didn't really plan on doing this at this exact moment, planned on doing this a lot earlier. The night before I found out you were pregnant, actually," Cade said hoarsely. "Honestly, knew you were mine from the moment I laid eyes on you. I am the happiest motherfucker on earth to have you, to have our baby. Just need to give you my name and I'll walk around beaming for the rest of our lives."

I felt tears slide out of my eyes, and I hoped I wasn't ugly crying in the middle of the most beautiful moment of my life.

"Marry me, baby," he whispered softly.

I just nodded my head through the tears so I wouldn't say something soppy like "a thousand times yes," which was what I felt like screaming.

Cade grinned, sliding the perfect diamond onto my finger before rising up to lay a scorcher on my lips. The bikes stopped beside us, and I remembered our audience.

"Holy shit, did you just propose?" Amy screamed at Cade.

She squealed and leapt off the bike to hug us both. As soon as we were released, she clutched my hand and inspected the ring. She let out a slow whistle.

"This is a seriously nice rock, custom Tiffany, three carats at least. The biker has taste." She looked at him, impressed.

I looked over her head at my father who was grinning from ear to ear.

He strode over, pulling me into his arms. "Happy, Mouse?" he asked into my hair.

"Yeah, Daddy," I whispered back.

ONE WEEK LATER

"I feel like I could sleep for a week," I declared, collapsing on my bed, my bed back in Amber.

It had been a seriously big few days. We flew out from home

a week after we got engaged. Mum insisted on throwing us a small engagement party with close friends and family.

Needless to say, my parents were over the moon for me, and I was surprised to learn that Cade had asked for my father's blessing before popping the question. I didn't think bad ass bikers asked permission for anything, including the hand of a girl who was already pregnant with his child. I said as much to Cade, and his face was unreadable when he answered me.

"I already asked your brother, babe. Back when he was at home, knew I was going to marry you. Also knew how much he meant to you, wanted him to be down with me having you for life, he only took a little convincing."

I was sucker punched by that answer. I stayed silent for about five minutes, then let a single tear out before letting my man know just how amazing he was.

Still, if my parents were at all nervous about the fact my fiancé and baby daddy was a huge, tattooed biker, they didn't act it. They treated him like family already, which was amazing. He had wanted to marry me right there and then, but I argued that I didn't want to have a shotgun wedding and also I couldn't fit into a Vera Wang.

He didn't care too much about Vera, no, scratch that, he didn't care about Vera at all, he certainly didn't give a crap about a shotgun wedding. I managed to convince him to wait until after the baby was born and I had enough time to squeeze my post-partum body into my dream wedding gown.

It was emotional goodbye for us, to say the least. Amy and I had let my home be the cushion for our grief and were reluctant to leave it. I was near heartbroken to leave my parents. But they promised they would be over before the baby was born. Mum would've hopped on the plane with me, but Dad convinced her Cade and I needed time alone.

After an exhausting goodbye and a long flight, we were

greeted by an army at the airport. The entire club, plus Rosie and the girls took up the entire arrivals gate. I was overwhelmed, but I managed to keep back the waterworks as I was pulled into countless rough hugs and forehead kisses. Not to mention the escort of motorbikes, which followed us home. Although they must've guessed we needed rest, since no one stopped.

Cade chuckled, joining me and gathered me in his arms back in the present. "Considering you slept the entire plane ride, I find that surprising."

I raised my head from where it had been resting comfortably on his beautiful sculpted chest. "Hey, pregnant women need their sleep!"

My gaze wavered back down to his torso, encased in his standard black tee, muscles bursting out.

"But maybe not right now, I'm feeling a burst of energy," I said, pushing up his tee.

CHAPTER 20

FIVE MONTHS LATER

"FUCK, COCKSUCKER, ASSHOLE!" I yelled, glaring down at the fork I had just dropped.

Stupid chubby pregnancy fingers.

"Now that's the kind of language I like to hear from a pregnant woman."

I directed my glare at the owner of the voice. Brock stood with his arms crossed, leaning against the door of the kitchen.

"Trust me, your vocabulary would be a hell of a lot more colorful if you were one week overdue, fat, frustrated and couldn't even *see* your toes let alone touch them," I hissed. "Stop staring at me with that stupid grin and pick up my fork for me." I pointed to the floor while continuing to glare.

Brock raised his eyebrows but didn't move, grinning like the cocky bastard he was.

I suppressed a growl. "I may have lost my fork, but I still have a knife," I threatened, waving it around with my free hand, the other was balancing my food.

Brock slowly pushed off his perch, sauntered over to me and handed me the fork. I snatched it off him, my manners gone along with my due date. I whirled around, chucking the fork in the sink, after being on the floor of the club's kitchen no way was I putting that in my mouth, I'd probably catch herpes. I got a clean one, leaned against the counter and attacked my meal with gusto.

"Nice bite, what are you, a wolf?" Lucky joked, pushing past Brock to lean beside me on the counter.

"Fuck you both," I snapped.

"I thought pregnant women were meant to be all lollipops and rainbows, full of joy," Lucky exclaimed sarcastically.

I stopped eating and stared at him, seriously considering murdering the perpetually happy little fucker. "Well, my pregnant joy is taking a break at the moment, Buddy. Might be because everyone automatically treats me like I'm handicapped once they see my stomach. Giving up their seats, letting me go in front of them in line, some people even talk slower to me. Like having a baby growing inside of me automatically makes me temporarily brain damaged." I took a bite of my food and chewed furiously. "Don't even get me started on the people that think it's okay to just walk up and touch my stomach. *Strangers,* fondling my stomach. Bet they wouldn't like it if I rubbed their non-pregnant bellies back. Actually, I *know* they wouldn't like it, considering I did it today and trust me, she did not like the taste of her own medicine."

Both men looked at me a beat then roared with laughter. I watched them with a death glare until they finally stopped. Lucky brushed a pretend tear from his eye.

"I like the pregnant, Gwen. She's feisty, we could patch you in at Sergeant at Arms."

"Yeah well, it's going to be the homicidal Gwen if these chilies don't work," I told him, forking another load in my mouth.

"What are chilies going to do, make you sweat out all your mean?" Brock teased.

I smiled fakely at him. "No, genius, they'll induce my labor," I declared, watching in satisfaction as both grins were wiped from their attractive faces and they took a synchronized step back.

They both stared at my stomach like I'd informed them it was full of explosives about to go off.

My smile got wider. "If I didn't know any better, you two bad ass bikers look *scared* at the prospect of imminent labor," I teased, my mood heightening significantly.

"You mean you could do that, *right now?*" Lucky asked, edging away from me, his face a mask of terror.

"If the universe had any compassion for me, these will make my water break right here on the kitchen floor," I told them with mock seriousness, enjoying the looks of horror on their faces.

"Fuck, shouldn't you be in, like, a hospital or something?" Brock asked, looking like he would piggyback me to one if it meant he didn't have to face the reality of childbirth.

"What the fuck, why does Gwen need to be in hospital?" a worried voice barked.

Cade pushed past the two idiots to put both hands on my belly. "Is it happening, baby?" His concerned eyes searched my face.

I laughed bitterly and put my plate of chilies down. "No, the universe hates me, this little girl is supremely comfortable curled up in my stomach, playing soccer with my bladder. Just teasing these two wusses." I sneered over my shoulder at the men.

"We are not wusses. We just don't like the prospect of you *leaking* all over the club floor," Lucky shot at me.

I attempted to step around Cade to get to Lucky, to do what, I wasn't sure, sit on him maybe, but Cade's arms stopped me.

"I can't wait until you knock someone up, asshole, to see how she responds to comments about leaking women," I snarled.

Lucky's face blanched and Brock whacked his shoulder.

"Let's get some beers, brother, leave Cade to deal with his little wildcat," he chuckled and then turned to Cade, face serious. "Good luck, man. Can I get your bike if she murders you with that fork?"

I growled throwing my fork at them, too late unfortunately, because it just bounced off the closing door. I almost stomped my foot in frustration. I directed my anger at someone else, the someone else standing right in front of me.

"This is all your fault. You're the one that put this baby inside me, you and your stupid super sperm. Now I'm fat and cranky and hormonal. You put her in, now you get her out!" I demanded, actually stamping my foot this time, glaring into my fiancé's gray eyes, which were dancing with amusement.

Cade pulled me into his arms kissing me firmly. "You are not fat. You are beautiful, you have never been more beautiful to me than you are right now."

I raised an eyebrow. I knew he was lying. Granted, my maternity wardrobe kicked ass. Today I was wearing a white gypsy style sundress with beautiful blue embroidery, wide sleeves and an empire waist that fell over my stomach. It showed a decent amount of leg, lucky for me, cankles were not something I had gained, but unluckily due to the "unable to see my toes" situation, I had to wear flat metallic flip flops.

"Seriously? I feel, and look, like Free Willy."

"How about I take you upstairs and show you just how sexy you are?" Cade whispered in my ear, trailing kisses down my neck, his hand sliding up my dress.

I leaned my head against his shoulder and let out a slight whimper.

"Well, sex is another thing on my list to get this little girl out," I told him slowly.

Cade growled and picked me up, directing us towards his room.

———

It had been a roller coaster few months. It was amazing to be back, surrounded by my dysfunctional biker family and back at my store for some normality. I was beyond happy with Cade, even if his normal crazy protectiveness had been ramped up due to the human growing in my stomach.

That protectiveness seemed to have extended to every member of the club as well, considering the fact there was almost always someone around. Rosie and the girls had been amazing, treating me exactly as before, handing me orange juice instead of margarita when we were poolside.

The whole town seemed to have rallied around me. I had constant visitors to the store, just coming in to chat to see how the pregnancy was coming along.

Luke was almost a daily visitor, bringing me a muffin every time he stopped by. My appetite being the way it was, I almost offered to have his child every time he handed me the ball of delight. I would have, except...you know.

Amy seemed to be back to her colorful self, or she was doing a real good job of hiding her grief. She didn't say a word about Brock to me, even though there were more than a few meaningful glances from both sides. I had watched him pull her away for more than a few heated conversations.

Whether she thought I would judge her or not, she remained silent on the subject and I didn't want to push it. Not that I did judge her, she deserved happiness, wherever she found it. And I also had realized she never told me who she was choosing before all the shit went down.

There was still a dark cloud that hovered over my happiness.

Sometimes I would be doing something normal, like cooking dinner and the loss of Ian would creep up on me, the pain slicing through me like a knife. Sometimes it would last for a moment, other times I struggled to get through the day.

I spoke to my parents regularly. They were keeping busy, always doing something, going somewhere, but they were struggling. I would hear it when my mother's voice started to crack on the phone or when my father spoke just a little too rough. I kept waiting for it to get easier, it didn't. I guessed I just had to get stronger and maybe remembering Ian wouldn't hurt quite so much.

The baby was something for me to focus on, to look forward to and alternately freak the fuck out about. After much debating, Cade and I had decided we would live out at his place. I felt like I was abandoning Amy, since we hadn't even lived in our house a year, but she convinced me she didn't mind.

"Seriously, Gwen, I love you and living with you is the best, but I like my beauty sleep so you're practically doing me a favor by taking you and your future child somewhere I don't have to hear it screaming at two a.m," she joked. "And it means we've got another redecorating job on our hands. Got to revamp Cade's bachelor pad so it's suitable for you and Supe."

I agreed with her on that one. Cade's house was nice, and more than big enough for the three of us, but its décor screamed 'single man'. I had expected some argument from Cade on that score, but he had just kissed me on the head and said "Do whatever you want to make it a home for you and Bun. Just don't do anything with the fucking TV."

I did get an argument about was who was paying. I had been more than happy to finance the renovation, considering I was the one insisting on it, but Cade got seriously defensive when I mentioned it.

"You are my woman, and this is my baby, I will take care of

you both, you aren't paying a fucking cent," he declared over the dinner table. I fought the urge to roll my eyes, I had expected nothing less from the macho man.

"Cade, it's not like I don't have the money, and I think you underestimate my freakish ability to spend. I can pay." I didn't even know why I tried to argue.

Cade's eyes narrowed. "I know all about your spending habits, Gwen. I've seen your fucking closet. I've also seen where you grew up, the car you drive and the house you bought. It's not lost on me you come from money. But the moment you became my woman, the moment I put that baby inside you and that ring on your finger, those moments meant I take care of you in every way. Including bankrolling whatever crazy shit you've got thought up for this house. I got money, babe, I'm more than able to keep you in the lifestyle in which you are accustomed."

I opened my mouth at this point to argue with his prehistoric ideas, but he stopped me.

"I know that doesn't make you happy, but how about you put your money towards our little girl's future, like her college fund and no doubt to fund an addiction to expensive clothing she will inherit from her mother."

I had stewed on that for a moment, deciding not to fight over something he obviously wasn't budging on. He was also right, my little girl was going to be clad in designer from birth.

So Amy and I had taken a trip to L.A. to hit this baby furniture boutique that we had found online and shopped up a storm with Cade's credit card. I decided to fit out the baby's room in neutral colors, no tacky pink screaming everywhere.

We put the nursery in the back room of Cade's house, it was big, had heaps of natural light and a view of the ocean. I had it painted all white, then got one wall painted with a tree of life design. It was a golden brown, simple, taking up the entire wall, its roots crawling from one edge of the room to another. No leaves, a symbol of eternal life, like the tattoo my brother had on his back.

I had Cade's hardwood floors polished and varnished and they looked amazing. I had a huge sheepskin rug shipped over from NZ so my feet could feel home and put it in the middle of the room. The crib was white and old fashioned, with white frilled bedding and a huge butterfly mobile hanging above it. I had a white wicker rocking chair sitting beside the crib, my mum used to always talk about rocking me to sleep so I wanted the same for my baby.

There was a big wicker sofa in the corner that had a light pink afghan thrown on top of it and hand printed butterfly cushions. There was a changing table underneath the window and a huge old free-standing wardrobe beside it. I loved the room and so did Cade.

"Was expecting a fucking explosion of pink and bows, babe, prepared to live with it too, but this is perfect," he said, after seeing the final product.

I was slightly affronted that he thought so little of my taste, but cut him some slack since I had turned his house into a war zone. And because he was putting up with my pregnant mood swings.

Cade loved me being pregnant. Every time he was near me his hand would rest protectively on my belly, and he would talk to it when we were in bed. He even insisted on putting my stretch mark cream on. Me turning into a beached whale hadn't dampened our sex life, if anything I was hornier, not that Cade complained. He couldn't get enough, even dragging me off into a dark corner at the clubhouse during a party. He had bent me over an old car and made me scream, luckily drowned out by AC/DC.

Club business had been quiet also. They were out of guns completely and so far hadn't had any backlash. Their security business was booming, according to Cade, but he refused to take any assignments that would mean leaving me for even a night.

"Missed out on two months of your pregnancy, Gwen, not missing a fucking second more if I can help it."

Things between him and Steg even improved. They had some kind of mutual understanding. They would never have that father and son bond back, but there was some form of respect. Steg was slowly proving me wrong about my first impressions, treating me with care ever since I had got home. He had been at the airport when we got back and had given me a warm embrace and sincere words about my brother. And every time I saw him, he kissed my head and asked the same question.

"How's my little Templar going in there?" Meaning Bun. Since Cade was the closest thing he had to a son, our baby was going to be treated as his grandkid. I didn't actually mind too much, especially since, to my shock, Evie had taken on the grandmother role with everything she had. Not that anyone would ever mistake her for a grandmother. But she was always coming to the store, bringing baby gifts – a pink "Sons of Templar" onesie was my favorite so far – and had helped me oversee all of the renovations to Cade's house. Not to mention she always brought whatever I was craving that week, even when for an entire week it was cottage cheese wraps with pumpkin seeds. Luckily Cade was just as patient, I had made him leave the house at 2:00am to go and get me grapefruit, near tears.

─────

So that led me back to now, after two amazing orgasms, but unfortunately no labor.

"Fuck," I muttered after coming down from my wave of pleasure.

"Not the response I'm used to getting, babe," Cade remarked

dryly from where he sat behind me. My back was resting against his chest and he was sitting up slightly against the headboard, his arms around my belly. It was the only comfortable and humanly possible cuddle position, thanks to the fact my belly that should have its own sun.

"You know full well *that* was great," I huffed. "But I thought in addition to an orgasm, I might also get a baby out of me."

Cade's chest vibrated as he laughed, hands caressing my stomach. "She'll come out when she's ready. I bet she's just stubborn, like her mother."

I rolled my eyes. Cade hadn't always been so breezy about our child's lack of eagerness to leave the womb. He had actually been worried out of his mind the day after the due date, dragging me to the doctors demanding to know if the baby was okay.

After some reassurance, he had calmed down. Although, I thought he might've attempted to bring an ultrasound machine with him if he could've hidden one under his cut.

Our post sex cuddling was cut short when Cade and the guys had to go check on some security thing, he did tell me what it was, but I was currently neck deep in self-pity, so I didn't listen.

It was too hot to be this pregnant!

Cade had commanded me to either stay at the clubhouse with the remainder of guys left behind or have someone drive me if I was going to go anywhere. Since I was bound to pop at any given moment, Cade wouldn't let me be alone. Considering the fact that my girth couldn't fit behind a wheel anyway, I didn't have much choice.

———

A couple of hours later, after making Bull take me to get five ice creams, I was happily sucking away at number three while watching my boxed set of the *Walking Dead* on the club's huge flat screen. I was hoping one of the frights I had been getting would shock the child out.

"That would never fucking happen, you can't get a head shot from that far away," Bull growled from beside me.

"You're seriously questioning the realism behind a program that is based on flesh eating zombies?" I asked with a raised eyebrow.

I could tell he was about to prepare a retort when his phone buzzed.

"Got it," he bit after answering. He stood, strapping on his on gun.

"Gotta go, sugar." He kissed my head then moved his eyes behind me.

"Steg, you good to stay here with Gwen until the boys get back?"

"Sure." Steg came into my line of sight, a warm smile looking weird on his harsh face. I hadn't even realized he was here. I had assumed as the club president he would be heading whatever security mission they were on.

"Gwen, try not to give birth while we're gone," Bull joked before heading for the door.

I flipped the bird to his retreating figure. But really I was just happy that this new Bull could even joke. Something had changed in him since I'd gotten back. He spoke more, spent more time with the guys instead of sitting alone with a bottle of Jack. He hadn't quite progressed to laughing, but I could handle the dry jokes and occasional smiles if it meant he was getting better.

The sound of his bike roaring off alerted me to the fact that it was just Steg and me left. That would've left me quaking in my Choo's normally, but since I was wearing flats and starting to feel differently about the gruff club president, I wasn't set to have a panic attack. Didn't mean I wasn't slightly intimidated.

"*Walking Dead,* huh? Darryl can sure shoot the shit out of a crossbow," he remarked to my surprise, sitting on the sofa next to me.

I stared at him in disbelief until he shrugged.

"Evie loves this shit."

I smiled and relaxed, turning my head back to the blood and gore.

⸻

I jerked awake to the sound of a door slamming. I sat up, disorientated. The TV was still going, so I mustn't have been out that long. I looked to the empty sofa beside me and guessed Steg had had enough of zombie shows. I stood slowly, stretching my uncomfortable body.

"Can't you please just decide to come on out, Bun? Mummy is dying to get you into a little Burberry dress." I tried bribery, guessing my daughter might just leave the womb for Burberry if she was anything like her mum.

"Wouldn't count on that baby or you wearing anything apart from a bullet, bitch," a voice snarled from behind me.

I jumped to see a man with a gun pointed at me standing in the doorway. I cradled my hands over my stomach protectively, fear like ice running through my veins.

"What do you want?" I asked him evenly, intent on getting myself and my baby out of this unharmed.

"Don't remember me, Gwen?" The man spat out my name.

I searched his face, something about him familiar, then it dawned on me.

"Taylor? You're—"

"I was *meant* to be a Templar, thanks to you I'm fucking no one," he snarled, taking another step toward me.

I took in his greasy hair, and steel blue eyes, remembering the sleaze ball that was "protecting me" the day I got kidnapped. I noticed a scar running from his temple to his chin, marring his features.

"You noticed my new look, did you?" he asked. "That's courtesy of your Old Man, my punishment for letting his bitch get pinched." His voice was full of spite.

My eyes darted around, where was Steg? I knew he would never be too far away. He wouldn't leave me, would he?

"You don't want to do this, Taylor." I tried to speak calmly, to reason with him. No matter what, I had to protect my child, and I was going to.

He bit out a bitter laugh. "Oh, but I do, Gwen. No other club would touch me after Templar's kicked me to the curb. Not even the fucking competition. They all think I'm useless." He was almost yelling now, spittle flying from his mouth. "I have a feeling once I deliver the body of the Old Lady and kid of the famous Fletcher, I'll be getting offers all over the fucking country."

Okay, so this guy is insane. I could hardly move, my body shaking from fear, watching him move closer with that gun pointed at me. I took a small step back, now he had rounded the couch, I wanted to put something between us.

His eyes flared, and he shook the gun at me. "Don't move, bitch!" he screamed.

Then it all happened in a blur. Steg jumped over the couch, tackling Taylor.

"Get the fuck out of here! Now, Gwen!" he roared, wrestling with the man.

I started for the door, wrestling my need to help, but knowing I had to look after my baby. I heard a grunt, then an unmistakable sound of a body hitting the floor. I turned, dreading to see the one getting up. To my relief, Steg pushed himself off the floor, he shoved Taylor's gun down his jeans then bolted to me in concern.

"Is he dead?" I asked, my voice calm.

"Nope, just knocked out, the boys and I will deal with that

motherfucker. I need you to go outside and call Cade. I'll tie this piece of shit up," Steg grunted.

"Um I think we might have to change our plans, Prez," I informed him calmly.

"Why?"

"Because my water just broke."

We both looked down at the puddle beneath my legs and I gingerly stepped out of it.

"Okay. Give me a sec, honey, I'll call Cade." Steg pulled out his phone, trying not to look freaked, but he didn't hide it that well.

Bikers were weird, they could wrestle men with guns but couldn't handle a woman about to give birth.

"Cade, we've got a situation, Gwen's—" Steg barked into the phone, but a gunshot cut him off. And so did the bullet that went through his chest.

I screamed as he collapsed onto me, giving me no choice but to go down to the floor with him.

"Didn't hit me hard enough old man," Taylor sneered standing above us, brandishing another weapon. "Didn't count on me having a second piece either, stupid fuck. Too busy worrying about this cunt. Everyone's so concerned about you, Gwen. What's so special bout you? Got a magic pussy? You let the whole club have a piece?" he asked grinning down at me.

Steg's blood was pouring out of his chest, his back leaning against my knees. I pressed my hands against the wound, trying to stop the bleeding, trying not to panic.

"You've just shot the club's President, Taylor. They'll come after you now. Won't stop until you're dead. You need to leave now before they get back, maybe we can get Steg some help. If he survives, maybe they won't kill you."

I desperately tried to reason with him, knowing if Steg was going to survive he needed a hospital now. Not to mention, so did

I. I couldn't let this freak know I was in labor. He seemed to consider it while pacing back and forward, gun trained on me.

"I think it's just a bonus I've got the Prez as well as the Princess," he said, eyes flaring. "Maybe I'll keep you around though, just until you push that kid out, then I'll put a bullet in you, sell the baby off to the highest bidder. I could get some serious cash for the VP's kid," he informed me calmly. The psychopath.

Bitter anger washed over me at the thought of this fucker harming my child. Not going to happen. I sucked in a labored breath as a vice tightened on my stomach, my first contraction whipping through me.

Luckily Taylor was focused on his phone and was furiously typing, so he didn't notice. I focused on breathing through the pain, on being strong enough to get myself through this. A couple of minutes passed and I got my bearings, thankful that Taylor was still glued to his phone, muttering to himself. I took a moment to look down at Steg.

"Can you hear me Steg? Don't die, please don't die," I whispered, pleading silently for him to open his eyes.

His breath rattled and his arm lifted weakly. "Gwen," he spluttered. "My pants." He coughed again, blood running down the side of his mouth.

Pants? The gun!

The one that he had shoved down the back of his pants. The way he was positioned meant I could slip one of my hands under him to reach it. That meant letting go of the wound in his chest that I was trying to stop bleeding. If I didn't, we'd both probably die anyway. And my little Bun would too. The roar of motorcycles gave me the distraction I needed as Taylor darted to the window.

"Fuck!" he roared turning the gun to me. "Fucking Fletcher! Get up now, bitch, you're my only chance to get out of this breathing." He strode towards me, just as my hand closed around the gun tucked into Steg's jeans. I didn't hesitate, I pointed it at his approaching form.

CADE

Cade flew into the compound, fear and rage curled at the pit of his stomach. His shaking hands could hardly grip his bike, he was that afraid.

Steg's call ending in a gunshot and Gwen's scream had put ice in his veins and fire in his belly. They had been five minutes away, stopped at some fucking bar. Cade had assured himself that Gwen was safe and his brothers had joked it was his last time to enjoy a cold one before the baby came along.

Not that he gave a fuck.

He couldn't wait for his kid to get here. He also planned on getting Gwen pregnant again the first chance he could. His woman was stunning, but swollen with his child, she was out of this world.

Now all he could hear was the shot and her scream. He couldn't see straight at the thought of a bullet anywhere fucking near Gwen. His fucking kid. He was as good as dead if anything happened to the two most precious things on this earth. Fury coursed through his body as he thought of what he would do to the motherfucker threatening his family.

He launched off his bike, not even noticing it crash onto the concrete. His gun was in his hand and he was sprinting towards the clubhouse when he heard it. Three gunshots. It felt as if three rounds had been drilled into him, but he didn't slow his pace. He was about to rip open the door when a strong hand gripped his shoulder.

"Let me the fuck go now, brother! Or I won't be responsible for my actions," Cade snarled.

"You can't go bursting through the door without backup, not knowing what's on the other side brother. Do this smart. So we can get Gwen out safe. Without her Old Man getting full of lead." Bull's face was an inch from his, his voice was flat, but his eyes glittered with fury.

Cade nodded stiffly, every fiber of his being was screaming at him to kick through that door, no matter what was on the other side. He'd happily face a thousand bullets if it meant Gwen and the baby were safe.

An agonizing thirty seconds later, everyone was in place and they burst through the door. His stomach roiled at what he saw. Gwen trembling, covered in blood, trying to stop a flow of blood that was streaming out of his President's chest. A body was face down in front of them, missing half a head. He didn't take any of it in, he just rushed to his woman.

GWEN

I shot him three times, just in case. I think his head was gone after the first, but I kept going anyway. Once I was sure he was dead I threw the gun beside me and plugged my fingers back in Steg's chest, trying to listen for his breath. I panicked when he was silent.

"Please breathe, please be alive," I chanted down at his ashen face.

My whole body tightened as I felt another contraction.

I barely noticed the door crash open and someone gently remove Steg from my lap. I panicked until I saw it was Cade kneeling in front of me, I met his eyes.

"I shot him. Three times. I'm pretty sure he's dead now. I had to though, he was going to hurt my baby," I babbled, not registering the paleness of Cade's face.

"You did good, baby, real good. I'm so proud of you," he reassured me, stroking my face, eyes darting over my body.

His presence made relief settle over me, this was short lived when a contraction made me scream. Cade's hands were running over my bloodstained clothes frantically searching for a wound. I was aware of him barking orders at men surrounding us.

"Baby coming...now," I choked out between breaths.

He froze and his eyes met mine before he lifted my dress to see blood running down my leg.

"Someone get a fucking truck. Now!" he roared gathering me in his arms.

I screamed again. Shit, this was happening too quickly. "No, no, put me down, the baby is coming *right now*," I bit out against the pain, feeling an overwhelming need to push.

Cade nodded, his face determined, calm. He placed me down on the couch, the *Walking Dead* still on the TV. He propped me on the arm, so I was sitting up slightly, spreading my legs and taking off my underwear.

I was in too much pain to be embarrassed or notice Bull, Brock and Lucky standing nearby, looking shit scared and helpless.

Lucky stepped forward uncertainly. "I'll go and boil some water and rip up sheets," he declared.

"What the fuck are you talking about?" Cade growled at him, not bothering to turn around.

"That's what they do in the movies when someone's giving birth, right? I don't know what to do with them, but everyone always gets boiling water and sheets." He wrung his hands like a fretting housewife and I bit out a laugh in between contractions.

Cade's eyes softened before turning to Lucky. "Get a fucking doctor here now, dipshit," he ordered.

Lucky looked relieved and ran from the room.

"It's going to be fine, baby," Cade soothed, kneeling between my legs, looking like he'd done this a thousand times before.

I could only smile weakly before a vice squeezed my stomach. I let out another scream and Cade flinched.

"You gotta push on the next one okay, Gwen? Hard as you can," he instructed me, eyes meeting mine.

"Hey, Bull, wanna come up by my head so you aren't scarred for life?" I ground out through the pain.

Bull jerked like someone shocked him and he knelt beside my head. I gripped his hand and squeezed as the pain ripped through me like a thousand knives.

"Fuck, asshole, bastard!" I yelled and pushed as hard as I could.

I must've blacked out because the next thing I was aware of was a strange emptiness in my belly, mingling with the pain.

I was exhausted when Cade placed a screaming baby covered in goo on my chest. I gazed up at him for a second and it was like time stopped. It was just the three of us there, the clubroom, the frantic bikers running around, they all faded away.

"You did real good, baby," he said quietly, eyes fixed on the beautiful, albeit slimy baby.

I looked at my daughter and a piece of my heart I didn't even know I had grew when her little finger gripped mine.

"Isabella," I whispered, before darkness claimed me.

—————

I woke up to an all too familiar smell.

Fuck. I'm in hospital. Again.

I opened my eyes slowly and glanced around at pink flowers and balloons covering every surface.

"Hey there, sleepyhead," a husky voice welcomed me.

I turned my head to see an exhausted but ecstatic looking

Cade sitting beside me, with a pink bundle in his arms, his free hand gripping mine.

"You try pushing out a baby in a clubhouse with no anesthetic, you'd need a catnap too," I joked.

Cade's grin faltered slightly before he stood carefully. "Want to meet our beautiful daughter?"

I nodded and awkwardly pushed myself up, trying to ignore my discomfort. Cade's free arm braced mine to help position me.

He then placed the whole world on my chest.

"This is Isabella, I think you already knew that, since you named her the moment you laid eyes on her," Cade told me softly.

I didn't take my eyes off her. "Steg?" I asked quietly.

Cade paused and my stomach dropped. "He's fighting, doctors say it's looking good."

I let out a deep breath. Cade gently shuffled me over so he could squeeze onto the bed and wrap us both in his arms.

"You okay, Momma?" he asked me tenderly.

"Considering this is the happiest moment of my life...yeah," I said, thinking about how my life nearly ended in a hospital. Now it was showing more promise than I ever thought possible.

FIRESTORM

Want to find out how Amy gets her HEA?

Amy Abrams doesn't do love. Nor does she do emotional attachments, unless you count the connection she has with designer handbags. She grew up in an Upper East Side penthouse, which had about as much affection within its tastefully decorated walls as Castle Dracula. Her family is the precise reason why she points her red-soled heels firmly in the opposite direction of that dreaded four-letter word.

Then it happens. Love. It comes right out of the blue and knocks her off her six-inch heels. She learns that love comes with pesky side effects such as heartbreak, which seriously messes with the complexion. Amy promises herself that she'll never open herself to that horrible feeling again. She doesn't count on an infuriating, albeit drool-worthy biker to roar into her life and ruin the plans she had of locking up her heart. She keeps her distance, wary of the sinfully sexy biker whose tattoos should read Warning - dangerous alpha male, will screw up your life.

Amy may be an Upper East Side princess but she wasn't looking for Prince Charming. She wouldn't mind the name of his hair stylist, though. Brock certainly isn't a knight in shining armor, but he consumes her, body and soul. Drama pulls them apart; danger will bring them back together. When Amy is threatened Brock is there ready to save her life. Her heart is another story.

ACKNOWLEDGMENTS

It is beyond surreal to call myself an author and to have someone reading this right now.

I had a little dream to write a big book and I have to pinch myself sometimes to make sure this is real.

I didn't do this on my own. No way could I have done that. I'm so lucky to have people in my life that supported me and weathered my crazy. Gwen and Amy didn't come from nowhere!

My mum. You're always going to be at the top of the list. I would never be here if it wasn't for you. You shared your love of reading with me and told me I could be anything I wanted to be.

Dad. You're not here to read this but I know you're watching over me. I wouldn't be the woman I am without you. I miss you everyday.

Emma and Polly. My crazy girlfriends. One of my mother's friends read this book and commented that it was like listening to the three of us. I took that as a huge compliment. I am lucky beyond belief to have such special friends. I don't know what's tighter, our jeans or our friendship.

And you, the reader. You don't know how much it means to be that you're sitting here, reading these words. Thank you. For reading my book. For every review, comment and message. I treasure every single one.

ALSO BY ANNE MALCOM

THE SONS OF TEMPLAR MC

Firestorm

Outside the Lines: A Sons of Templar Novella

Out of the Ashes

Beyond the Horizon

Dauntless

Battles of the Broken

Hollow Hearts

Deadline to Damnation

Scars of Yesterday

UNQUIET MIND

Echoes of Silence

Skeletons of Us

Broken Shelves

Mistake's Melody

Censored Soul

GREENSTONE SECURITY

Still Waters

Shield

The Problem with Peace

Chaos Remains

Resonance of Stars

THE VEIN CHRONICLES

Fatal Harmony

Deathless

Faults in Fate

Eternity's Awakening

Buried Destiny

RETIRED SINNERS

Splinters of You

STANDALONE DARK ROMANCE

Birds of Paradise

doyenne

THE KLUTCH DUET

Lies That Sinners Tell

Truths That Saints Believe

ABOUT THE AUTHOR

Anne Malcom has been an avid reader since before she can remember, her mother responsible for her book addiction. It started with magical journeys into the world of Hogwarts and Middle Earth, then as she grew up her reading tastes grew with her. Her obsession with books and romance novels in particular gave Anne the opportunity to find another passion, writing. Finding writing about alpha males and happily ever afters more fun than reading about them, Anne is not about to stop any time soon.

Raised in small town New Zealand, Anne had a truly special childhood, growing up in one of the most beautiful countries in the world. She has backpacked across Europe, ridden camels in the Sahara, eaten her way through Italy, and had all sorts of crazy adventures. For now, she's back at home in New Zealand and quite happy. But who knows when the travel bug will bite her again.

Want to chat more and meet some other awesome readers? Join Anne's reader group.

www.annemalcomauthor.com
annemalcomauthor@hotmail.com

Printed in Great Britain
by Amazon

18274318R00257